THE BATTLES OF BEN KINGDOM

ONE WILL COME TO LEAD THE FIGHT, TO DEFEAT THE

DARKNESS, BRING THE TRIUMPH OF THE LIGHT.

ONE WILL COME WITH FIRE AS HIS CROWN,

TO BRING THE LEGION TUMBLING DOWN.

ONE WILL COME WITH FIRE IN HIS EYES,

TO PIERCE THROUGH THE VEIL OF WICKED LIES.

ONE WILL COME WITH FIRE IN HIS HEART,

TO OVERCOME ALL ODDS AND PLAY HIS PART.

ONE WILL COME WITH FIRE IN HIS HAND,

TO PURGE THE EVIL FROM THIS LAND.

ONE WILL COME TO PAY THE COST;

IF HE FAILS ALL IS LOST.

ONE WILL COME IN SUFFERING AND PAIN,

TO KNOW BETRAYAL AND BE WOUNDED AGAIN.

ONE WILL COME TO CHOOSE THE WAY;

E

To Ben and Lucy (the <u>real</u> ones)
Being your dad is the best thing about being me.
This book is for you.

First published in the UK in 2014 by Usborne Publishing Ltd., Usborne House, 83-85 Saffron Hill, London EC1N 8RT, England. www.usborne.com

Text copyright © Andrew Beasley, 2014

Cover and inside illustrations by David Wyatt. Map by Ian McNee.

A CIP catalogue record for this book is available from the British Library.

ISBN 9781409570325 JFMAMJ ASOND/14 03193/1

Printed in Chatham, Kent, UK.

THE BATTLES OF BEN KINGDOM

THE CITY OF FEAR

ANDREW BEASLEY

USBORNE

Contents

 ## Day One: 27th April, 1892

Day Two: 28th April, 1892

Day Three: 29th April, 1892

Day Four: 30th April, 1892

Day Five: 1st May, 1892

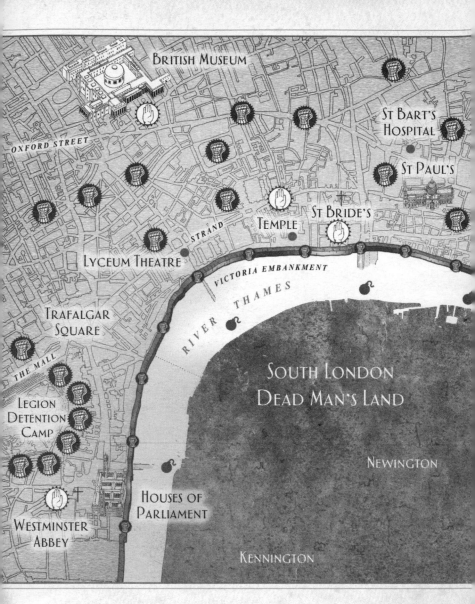

LONDON 1892

THE SMUTTS'S

ST PETER'S CHURCH

CHRIST CHURCH SPITALFIELDS

LIVERPOOL ST STATION

BANK OF ENGLAND

JOLLY TAR PUB

OLD GRAVEL LANE

TALLOW CHANDLERS' HALL

FENCHURCH ST STATION

TOWER OF LONDON

ST KATHARINE DOCKS

LONDON DOCKS

TOWER BRIDGE

OLD GRAVEL LANE

SOUTHWARK

BERMONDSEY

N
W — E
S

WATCHER RENDEZVOUS POINTS

LEGION TERRITORY

DEMOLISHED BRIDGES

LEGION WALL

DAY ONE
MR. SWEET'S LONDON
27TH APRIL, 1892

PROLOGUE

The Wall. Two short, hard words that had come to mean life or death for the people of London. It just depended which side you were on.

Captain Mickelwhite led his Legion brigade along the battlements, enjoying the slap of the sword against his leg. Overhead, thunderclouds were gathering and ravens croaked as they battled against the wind. The first drops of rain struck Mickelwhite as cold and heavy as stones, but he didn't care. He felt unstoppable.

The Legion had built the Wall in six weeks.

Six weeks of pain. And blood. And war on the city streets.

Mickelwhite smiled, a slash of red against his ghostly pale skin; he had never had so much fun.

Not many Londoners had known that conflict was coming. They had been too busy or too stupid to see the signs that a war had been waging around them for centuries; a secret, silent war. On one side were Ben Kingdom and the Watchers, spies and warriors living on the rooftops; and on the other was the Legion lurking in their maze of tunnels beneath the city. It was the oldest battle in the world, the eternal battle between light and dark. And the dark was winning.

Soon the Watchers would be no more.

"Quickly, boys," Mickelwhite urged his troop of boy-soldiers. "You know that it doesn't do to keep Mr. Sweet waiting."

The brigade had been together for a long time – first sharing a lowly barracks in the Under, the Legion's subterranean lair, then leading labour parties working on the Wall.

They were all young, Mickelwhite included, but they had grown up fast. There was John Bedlam, a short, stocky lad, born and raised in the Devil's Acre. Fighting came as naturally to him as breathing. Beside Bedlam was Jimmy Dips, a rat-faced pickpocket; then came Hans Schulman, a German lad with fists the size of ham hocks but a clumsy pair of feet. Finally, limping along in the rear was the hunchback, Munro, pulling his mangy three-legged bulldog, Buster, along behind him.

"Look," said Mickelwhite, surveying the bruised and broken city beneath them. The Wall surrounded it, as inescapable as a hangman's noose, marking the limits of Legion rule, the territory which Mr. Sweet had staked out for himself. "We did this."

"Makes you proud, don't it?" said Bedlam.

The Wall was not a thing of beauty. Houses had been torn apart to provide enough stone. Whole streets sacrificed for the great cause. Some buildings had become part of the Wall itself; their windows bricked up against the outside world, the rooms filled with rubble, their roofs fortified by coils of barbed wire. Jagged sheets of metal, spiked railings torn from front gardens, broken glass, wooden stakes with sharpened points; all crowned the Wall like a necklace of death. Anything and everything that could be used to repel an attack had found its way into the monstrous structure.

Rising in the west in Hammersmith, the Wall stretched as far Lime House Cut in the east. It snaked along the north bank of the Thames, where all the bridges stood broken, leaving the river like a moat. Only Tower Bridge had been kept whole, its drawbridge defiantly raised.

To the north, Legion rule stopped at Balls Pond Road. Beyond that, outside the Wall, London had been levelled to the ground for a distance of one hundred feet. All that remained was a swathe of debris and the skeletons of houses. This was the northern Dead Man's Land – littered with landmines and mantraps, it was a deterrent to both attackers from outside the Wall and would-be escapees from within.

And south of the river it was much worse.

That was where the resistance had been the strongest, stirred up by the Watchers. That was why the Legion had wiped South London off the map.

Mickelwhite felt a sudden wave of hatred towards Ben Kingdom and his rabble rousers. Bile rose in his throat and he spat out a curse. "Death to the Watchers!" he snarled.

"And death to Ben Kingdom!" said Bedlam.

About a quarter of stubborn Londoners had dared to resist Legion rule. They had fought back. But they had lost. And then they had been punished. It was these men, women and children who had built the Wall. With chains around their ankles, the work gangs had slaved day and night. Mickelwhite, Bedlam and a thousand other Legionnaires had cracked the whip until the work was done.

A short distance ahead, Mickelwhite could now see Mr. Sweet, standing alone on the windswept battlements. None of this would have been possible without him. Who else but Sweet would have had the courage and strength to achieve all this? Mickelwhite felt his breathing quicken as he drew near. It was an honour to be in his presence. Through cunning manipulation not only had Mr. Sweet made himself Prime Minister, but then, with treasonous audacity, he had kidnapped Queen Victoria and crowned himself as King in her place. And now, at Sweet's command, the Legion had bullied and beaten an entire city into submission. Truly, his deadly ambition knew no bounds.

Mickelwhite studied Mr. Sweet with admiration. The strong broad shoulders. The massive arms of a weightlifter. But…the scars…

It was forbidden to talk about Mr. Sweet's "accident", but it was no secret that he had suffered terrible burns during the Legion's battle against the Watchers at the Feast of Ravens. Mickelwhite couldn't forget the inferno that had swept through the Tower of London when the Watchers had attacked during Mr. Sweet's dark sacrificial ceremony of power. However, he could only guess at what remained of Mr. Sweet's once handsome face after the flames had caressed him from head to toe. That was probably why the great man had begun to dress so... *eccentrically*.

Mickelwhite could see the outline of the mask which encased the whole of Sweet's head; the hard lines of the eye sockets, the fierce point of the beak. The collar of the man's coat was wreathed in black feathers and on his head, encircling the shining dome of the mask, sat the crown of a king.

Not just any crown though. This was the Crown of Corruption – the great weapon of the Legion. It was set with the thirty Coins of Blood – the same silver coins that Judas, the great betrayer, had once held in his clammy palm – and it gave its wearer ultimate power to dominate the minds of weaker men. Sweet had made the crown his own, fixing shards of metal, daggers of broken glass, even long square nails around the iron band, until it resembled the Wall itself.

As they drew closer, Mickelwhite could sense the raw power radiating from Sweet. It was as if the man was a furnace and to draw near was to feel the blistering heat of the rage that boiled within him.

The young captain announced his presence with the Legion salute, slamming his left fist to his chest. "My Lord!" Mickelwhite declared.

The big man turned slowly and Mickelwhite felt

himself flinch as two eyes pierced him, as hard and unforgiving as metal skewers.

"So, it is finished," said Sweet. "*Finally*."

"Yes, My Lord," said Mickelwhite, nodding. "The Wall is now complete."

"Hmmm," Sweet growled. "Complete, you say?"

Mickelwhite could feel the sickly tide of fear rising inside the other boys; Sweet had that effect.

"Sector three is secure?" asked Sweet.

"Yes, My Lord," Bedlam snapped in reply. Sector three had been his to oversee.

"And the watchtowers?"

"Yes, My Lord," said Jimmy Dips.

"And the tunnels? Every conceivable exit blocked, including the outer limits of the Under?"

"Yes, My Lord," muttered Munro. He and Buster had only just caught up with the rest of the brigade, the dog whimpering at the boy's side.

"You were responsible for the work gangs who were collapsing the passages beneath Hackney Wick?" Sweet continued.

"Yes, My Lord," Munro mumbled, his eyes on his feet.

Sweet took a step forwards and plucked Buster up into his arms, stroking the dog's wet fur and scratching behind its ears. Mickelwhite couldn't help but notice the skin on

Sweet's hands, a patchwork of scabs and open sores; another souvenir of the flames.

"Didn't the Watchers lead an escape through one of those tunnels three days ago?" said Sweet, still fussing with Buster.

"Yes…but, my work party was one of the smallest and…" Munro's words dried in his mouth. "The tunnel is sealed now," he whispered. "It will never happen again."

"No," said Sweet, "I'm certain it won't."

Munro braced himself, waiting for the inevitable punishment for failure. He shut his eyes, but his master's blow never came.

"And so the real work begins," Sweet continued. "Every soul in London shall bow to me or face the consequences. The Watchers must be hunted down and eliminated, every last one of them. And Ben Kingdom must be made to suffer…" Sweet gestured towards his mask. "Just as I have suffered."

Sweet swung round towards Munro again, and offered the dog back to him with outstretched arms. Gratefully, Munro reached out to reclaim the only living creature that he could truly call his friend.

At the last instant, Sweet snatched the poor animal away and, in a single movement, flung Buster over the Wall.

They all heard the pathetic whimper as the dog fell. Followed by the awful crunch of its landing.

"You should be grateful," Sweet growled. "You find me in a merciful mood tonight!"

It was only then that it occurred to Mickelwhite that Mr. Sweet might be insane.

CHAPTER 1

THE WINGS OF DEATH

"Hold on tight," Ben Kingdom whispered.

Lucy Lambert gave him a wry look with her one good eye. A leather eyepatch hid the other empty socket. "I can see why you're our leader," she said. "I never would've thought of that."

Ben flashed her a grin. Both he and Lucy were Watchers. They lived and ran and fought on the rooftops of London – all they ever did was hold on tight. That night, however, they were hanging on for dear life.

For over an hour, Ben's squad had been hiding on the stone gallery above the ghostly white face of Big Ben. Rain had been falling steadily all evening and the sky had turned from grey to black to an angry purple. Up here, with the storm churning around them, Ben felt as if he was in the belly of the beast. The hair on the back of his neck stood to attention and his right hand trembled involuntarily, as if an electric current was passing through it. Then a fork of lightning blistered across the sky, followed by the deep booming rumble of thunder as the clouds around them began a battle of their own.

Water streamed down Ben's face beneath the rain's merciless assault. They were all cold to the marrow and afraid too, truth be told. That was why Ben made light of their situation. He was the leader of the Watchers, the one the prophecy called the Hand of Heaven. It was his duty to keep the spark of hope going. And since the Wall went up, hope was in short supply.

There were just five of them in the squad. Five Watchers against the army of the Legion. But Ben couldn't have chosen a better crew to stand by him. He looked along the line, saw the faith glinting in their eyes beneath the rain-streaked goggles, and his heart surged with pride.

Lucy Lambert was the bravest person Ben had ever met; fearless and loyal and true. Beautiful as well, Ben thought. He had known her for long enough now not to even see the scar that split her cheek in two. If he could choose only one Watcher to fight beside him, it would be her.

Next to Lucy was Valentine, a boy who had been an enemy in the Legion when Ben first met him. Valentine was a toff and he looked it, with his pointed nose and pinched lips, but Ben, like every good guttersnipe, knew better than to judge by appearances. Toff or not, Valentine was alright by him since he came over to the Watchers.

Then there was shaven-headed Ghost; so silent, so still. No one had ever heard the African boy speak a word, and yet they all trusted him – Ghost was a Watcher to the core. Ben met his gaze and gave him a nod. *We're gonna need your strength tonight.*

Last in the group was Nathaniel Kingdom, Ben's big brother. Anyone could see they were related; they had both inherited their father's strong features. But only Ben had their mother's flame-red hair. Ben had never had a chance to thank her for it though, because she had died giving birth to him. For a long time neither Ben nor Nathaniel nor their father had known how to handle the depth of their loss, but in the midst of the war with the Legion, they had grown closer than they had ever been. The risk of death made them all cling tighter to the things that really mattered.

For three months all they had known was war. Running. Fighting. Hiding. Knowing that the greatest battle – *the final battle* – was fast approaching. Every day they spread the word in the taverns, on street corners, in whispers, in private, out of the corner of their mouths. A simple secret message: *1st May, we take the city back. 1st May is Revolution Day!* That was when free Londoners were going to fight back against the Legion, and when Ben and the Watchers would destroy Sweet's grip on the city and restore the Queen to the throne.

Or die trying.

But before the final conflict could even begin, it was the Watchers' duty to get those not fit for battle out to safety: the youngest, the elderly, the invalids and the vulnerable. That was why Ben and his crew were clinging to the tower of Big Ben – watching over the latest in a long line of breakouts they had orchestrated.

On the ground, Ben's father, Jonas Kingdom, and Jago Moon, oldest, toughest and roughest of the Watchers, were preparing to help the new batch of escapees make their bid for freedom. They had to get them up and over the Wall to the boat that was waiting silently for them in the Thames. A boat filled with British soldiers.

For the last few weeks the Watchers had been working hand in hand with the army. Less than a mile away, on the far side of the death zone, the full might of Her Majesty's armed forces were waiting with loaded rifles and fixed bayonets. But that was all they had been able to do – *wait.*

For Queen Victoria was still Mr. Sweet's prisoner, and every Londoner had heard his threats pronounced from the battlements by loudhailer: *"Attack my city and you will be welcomed by your Queen's severed head on a spike."* No one doubted that Sweet would be true to his word.

And so the army was over a barrel and would remain that way, unless Ben and the Watchers could rescue the Queen. For now they played a deadly game of cat and mouse, with the Watchers sneaking out refugees and the army spiriting them away to safety. All in preparation for 1st May – Revolution Day.

From his viewpoint on the clock tower, Ben could see Watcher sharpshooters, poised and ready. They used weighted crossbow bolts instead of lethal pointed ones, but these were still enough to knock a Legionnaire unconscious. Life was precious to the Watchers – *all* life, including the lives of their enemies – but they still had to defend themselves. The sharpshooters gave ground cover. Ben's squad provided protection from above.

Because the sky was where the real danger lay.

The Legion was not simply an army of men – they were an ancient order, allied with the darkest forces of creation. Fallen angels fought for the Legion, beasts with the heads and wings of eagles, known as the Feathered Men. Every Londoner, even the staunchest Legion supporters, had come to fear the shadow of those wings of death. Very often it was the last thing a person saw, hanging over them, before beak and talons ripped them to shreds.

Just then, Big Ben tolled. This close to the huge bell, the vibrations rattled every fibre of Ben's body. Twelve melancholy chimes.

As well as the usual Watcher equipment – crossbow pistol, rope, extendable quarterstaff – Ben and his crew were wearing bulky backpacks. Ben could feel the weight cutting into his shoulders. He shifted uncomfortably, anxious to get going.

"Look!" hissed Lucy. "That's the signal!"

Ben followed the line of her pointing finger, trying to penetrate the darkness of the night and the sheeting rain. Nothing. He squinted, then he saw it at the foot of the Wall: the unmistakable flash of a lantern.

Ben felt his breathing quicken. It was time to act.

Lucy had drawn a brass telescope from a side pocket in her pack and lifted her single-lensed goggles to search the shadows, as one black shape after another broke away from the buildings below and set off towards the light of the lantern.

"Here they come," she said. The escapees were a sorry sight. Frail old women with unsteady legs, mothers with infants clutched tightly to their chests, young children with fear written on their faces. *Easy prey,* Lucy thought grimly, now scanning the clouds.

The Wall had grown more impenetrable by the day and it was getting harder and harder for Ben and the Watchers to find chinks in the Legion's armour. At the start, when the Wall was first being raised, hundreds had made a break for it. Ben had led escapes where the Wall was at its weakest, where there were blind spots between the watchtowers, or where the Wall was still low enough to be scaled. Under Watcher protection, people had fled across the bridges, even through the Legion's own tunnels, taking nothing with them but the clothes on their backs. But now the last of the tunnels had been sealed and the bridges had all been broken.

Far below, Ben could see the wreckage of Westminster Bridge and the gap where Lambeth Bridge used to stand. He closed his eyes briefly as he remembered the surge of people who had tried to make it to the other side of the river, and the terrible explosions that had halted them in their tracks. *There wasn't even much to escape to*, he thought bitterly. South of the River Thames, London had become a wasteland. Newington, Bermondsey, Southwark, Kennington. All gone. Reduced to dust and bricks and bones. The dead city.

A shot pierced the night air and Ben snapped back into the moment. He saw his father send a rope ladder rattling down from his exposed position on top of the Wall. Seconds later a stream of escapees began to scramble up like ants, up and over the Wall to the steam barges waiting on the other side. But a line of bobbing lanterns told him that the Legion patrols were approaching far too quickly.

A woman passed her baby up into Jonas's waiting hands. Another shot splintered the darkness. The woman was scrambling onto the Wall to join her child when the Legion bullet clipped her, spinning her off balance. She fell, only to be caught by Jago Moon at the foot of the ladder, but she screamed. And her baby screamed. Then the panic spread.

"I can't wait," said Nathaniel, climbing up on top of the balustrade and preparing to launch himself over the edge. "I can't just sit here and watch this."

"Not yet!" ordered Ben.

"Pa's down there!" Nathaniel was shouting now, as more shots rang out.

"I know!" Ben shouted back. "But we wait."

Ghost placed a firm hand on Nathaniel's shoulder and drew him back from the edge. The look in Ghost's eyes brooked no argument; he was with Ben.

Down on Horseferry Road, one of the Legion searchlights burst into life. A long finger of light raked the Wall, stopping once it had the escapees in its gaze.

"They're sitting ducks!" snarled Nathaniel.

Ben looked at Lucy and he could see that even her steely reserve was wavering.

"Ben..." she began.

"If we go too soon, then we lose our only advantage," said Ben.

It was then that three Feathered Men came screaming down out of the sky. The creatures flew in formation, whistling around Big Ben itself, so close that Ben could feel the downdraught of their wings as they swept by.

"Now we go," said Ben, climbing up onto the parapet and throwing himself into the air behind them.

Gravity grabbed Ben immediately and for an instant he was certain that he had made his last mistake. Heart in his mouth, Ben yanked hard on the cord on his backpack. Instantly the pack unfolded and two canvas wings snapped outwards, supported by spring-loaded metal arms.

And Ben wasn't falling any more.

As the wings took his weight, Ben enjoyed the rush of pure adrenaline. Behind him he glimpsed his crew, gliding into action in his wake.

While the Watchers on the ground fended off their attackers with crossbow fire, Ben's squadron would tackle the Feathered Men in the air.

The trick, Ben knew, was to take the Feathered Men by surprise. They considered themselves to be invulnerable, with their massive strength and ferocious anger. However, they would not be expecting an attack from above. The gliders could only carry the Watchers downwards, so the key would be to position themselves immediately over the Feathered Men, then strike hard and fast.

Ben used the guide pulleys and the movements of his own body to steer himself where he wanted to go. It wasn't as easy as he had hoped. Somehow Lucy drew level with him – she had the knack already, Ben noticed with a little envy.

On the ground, the last escapees were scattering, fleeing into any nook or cranny that would take them, like cockroaches on the kitchen floor. Ben couldn't see his father or Jago Moon or any of the other Watchers, but he knew that they would be the very last to head for safety. More than one Watcher had lain down his own life helping someone else to get over the Wall.

Ben could see a group of frightened children, separated from their parents in the confusion, and now at the mercy of the Legion. He knew that if the Feathered Men reached them, these kids wouldn't be rounded up and put into the detention camps with the other dissenters. They would be eaten.

It looked as if the lead Feathered Man had spotted the children too, as it angled its great body towards them. But before Ben could make a move to cut it off, he saw Valentine and Nathaniel make their descent towards it. The fallen angel gave an ear-splitting cry that was enough to make a grown man freeze in his tracks. Ben noticed a boy, hardly more than six years old, rooted to the spot at the foot of the rope ladder, unable to move as the horrible creature dived towards him.

Valentine and Nathaniel took careful aim with their crossbows. They would only get one shot. Two bolts sang out, finding a home in the foul creature's back. The Feathered Man continued in its arc towards the boy but, instead of snatching the child up in its talons, it ploughed into the rubble, twitching and flapping its broken wings. Valentine and Nathaniel hit the ground running. *That's my brother*, thought Ben, as Nathaniel seized the terrified child, flung him over his shoulder and then disappeared into the night.

Ghost, meanwhile, had actually landed on the back of the second Feathered Man. He silently dispatched it, then let it fall to the ground.

Ben urgently unfurled the weighted net that he had stowed in his own pack. He steered himself closer to Lucy, but the tips of their wings almost brushed in the process and he was forced to twist away. Heart hammering, he came in for a second attempt and this time managed to pass the other side of the net to Lucy. She gave him a smile of approval and together they positioned themselves above the remaining Feathered Man.

Although they were bestial in their hunger, the creatures were not stupid, and even as Ben and Lucy flew in to attack, the fallen angel spun round to face them, snarling and spitting as it came.

Lucy gave the nod and together they dropped the net. It spread out as it fell, wide enough to catch the evil being in its embrace. But anger kept the Feathered Man powering up towards them, beak reaching for their flesh through a hole in the net. Lucy was able to steer away, banking sharply to the left and bringing herself in to land on a flat roof.

Ben wasn't so quick.

The Feathered Man's wings were now tangled hopelessly in the net, but as it began to tumble out of the sky, it shot out one long-fingered hand and grabbed Ben by the ankle, taking him down too. The glider slowed Ben's descent for the first few seconds, then the metal armature of the wings sheared in two and Ben and the Feathered Man dropped together. In a struggling mess of limbs they landed hard on the cold, wet cobbles.

Ben blacked out for a second. He came to with his head spinning and the metallic taste of blood in his mouth. Stars swam in and out of his vision. Beside him, the Feathered Man was breathing heavily, a deep, rasping sound coming from its throat. Then its eyes snapped open and, still enmeshed in the net, it began to pull itself towards Ben.

Ben tried to get to his feet and promptly fell back to the ground again. He must have hit his head harder than he'd thought – his balance was all shot. Starting to feel the rise of fear, he looked around for a way to escape. The trouble was, London had changed since Mr. Sweet had begun his rule. Ben had always prided himself that he knew every street, every alley – but the Legion had set up roadblocks and checkpoints, making dead ends where none had existed before.

Ben began to shuffle backwards on hands and feet, while the world continued to blur like a bad dream. Lucy had seen him crash but more Feathered Men were already circling. The other Watchers were nowhere near and Ben was on his own in enemy territory. Sweet had spies on every street. Neighbours who followed their neighbours with beady eyes and tongues that were eager to wag. And the punishment for aiding Watchers was death.

Ben's vision cleared long enough for him to be able to see the Feathered Man gradually untangling itself. Its legs had apparently been broken by the fall, but its hatred burned as hot as ever. Slowly the creature hauled itself after Ben.

Ben looked into its cold avian eyes and knew that it would never give up.

Ben struggled to his feet. Nausea dragged him back down to the floor.

The clacking beak was getting nearer. Ben could see the thin yellow tongue and the pink gash of the waiting gullet.

In his last moment of consciousness, Ben imagined that he saw a figure charging through the rain. A tall man in a long leather coat. A man with a claw where his left hand should be.

Then Ben saw nothing at all.

CHAPTER 2

THE FORGOTTEN PRISONER

The Prisoner was alone in the darkness.

He had not seen any light since the Legion had captured him and thrown him into this dungeon. They were afraid of him, he knew that. Afraid of the blood on his hands and the sword which had slain so many Feathered Men. That was why they kept him in chains. The links seemed to glisten even in the gloom, but the Prisoner was not fooled by their beauty. The heavy metal shackles encircled his waist and then disappeared into the four corners of his cell, tethering him like some strange spider in the middle of a shining web. Tentatively his hands felt his bonds. He had done this hundreds of times before, always with the same result.

Pain.

Intense daggers of pain that left his fingers bleeding.

These were no ordinary chains. They had been forged from witch-silver and inscribed with foul oaths in an ancient and evil tongue. Worse than that, these bonds were empowered by the Crown of Corruption and the tyrant who wore it; while Mr. Sweet ruled, these chains could never be broken.

The Prisoner smiled to himself. But neither could the chains break *him*.

He had faith.

Even in this black hole. Even with his skin worn almost to the bone by the biting witch-silver. The Prisoner was certain that the Watchers would not leave him here to rot.

They would come.

Ben would come.

The red-headed street urchin was the only one who could destroy the Crown of Corruption and set him free.

Through the wall the Prisoner could hear muffled sounds of weeping. Thousands of men and women around the globe called the old lady in the cell next door their Queen, but to the Prisoner, she was just "Victoria".

The Prisoner sometimes wept too, when he thought of what the Legion was doing to London. Other times he sang. Long songs in a language which none of his captors understood. Songs about freedom and justice and truth.

His songs really upset the guards, he thought with a smile.

The crying and the singing helped to muffle the other sounds in the dungeon. The scratching of rats, the scurrying of beetles. The steady drip, drip, drip of water running down the walls.

From the far end of the corridor the Prisoner heard the sound of footsteps approaching and he cocked his head to listen more intently. He heard the click of a heel-spur striking the flagstones and the rattle of claws on elongated toes. The Prisoner knew what to expect even before the key turned in his cell door.

Although the light outside was faint, the mere flickering of a torch, it was harsh enough to sting his eyes and the Prisoner had to turn his face away as his jailer entered the room.

A huge Feathered Man strode in. Older, more powerful, more battle-scarred than the rest of his kin.

The Prisoner opened his eyes. "Abaddon," he said softly.

"I haven't gone by that name for centuries," said the Feathered Man with a scornful laugh as he placed the torch in a wall bracket. "Here they call me 'Grey Wing'."

"So then, Grey Wing, have you come to confess your wicked ways and beg for forgiveness?"

The Feathered Man laughed again and then lashed out, striking the Prisoner across the face and knocking his head sideways. "I need no forgiveness!" Grey Wing screamed. "I regret nothing."

"For now," said the Prisoner, his tongue testing for loosened teeth. "But one day you *will* regret the path you have chosen."

Grey Wing pushed his face close until the point of his beak was a hair's breadth away. The Prisoner could taste the raw-meat stench of the creature's breath.

"You are the one wearing the chains, and you would do well to remember that. You are waiting for a rescue that will never come. *Never.*"

"I believe in Ben Kingdom," said the Prisoner matter-of-factly. "I believe in the Hand of Heaven."

"Believe all you like, but these are the last days for the humans."

"Mr. Sweet is a child pretending to be a king. His reign was destined for disaster from the start."

"There I agree with you," said Grey Wing. "His days are numbered...by me."

"You? Why? Isn't there enough bloodshed and fear in the Legion's new London?"

"Nowhere near enough," hissed Grey Wing. "I didn't ally myself with the Legion so that my fellow Feathered Men and I could be guard dogs! I will only rest when *everything* is destroyed. When every city is ash and no human is left breathing." The huge Feathered Man paused, panting heavily with emotion. "I will use the Gehenna Key…"

The Prisoner understood the full weight of that awful threat, yet he let nothing show on his face.

"I will unleash the creatures of the pit…" Grey Wing continued with manic delight. "And they will devour this world."

The Prisoner clapped his hands together slowly. "What will you do for an *encore*?"

"You would do well not to mock me!" Grey Wing snarled.

"Another empty threat," said the Prisoner. "If you had the Gehenna Key, you would have used it already."

Grey Wing made a low snarl. "I *will* have it. *You* will tell me where it is."

The Prisoner said nothing.

"I will hurt you if you don't tell me," Grey Wing warned, hopping closer.

"I don't doubt it," said the Prisoner.

"I *know* that you will tell me," Grey Wing sneered. "You

might have a prettier face than me, but we are the same – beings not of this earth. That means I understand you better than these humans ever could." Grey Wing examined him with huge unblinking eyes. "It also means that I know exactly how best to hurt you."

In a blur of savage anger, Grey Wing launched himself at the Prisoner and pinned him to the ground with his great weight, the tips of his talons piercing exposed flesh. The Prisoner writhed in anguish, but braced himself for worse to come. The witch-silver robbed him of the strength to fight back and he was at the mercy of a creature who knew no pity.

Slowly and deliberately, Grey Wing reached out with a taloned hand…

The Prisoner knew what was coming and set his jaw against it, gritting his teeth so hard that he thought they might shatter in his mouth.

The pain, when it hit, was excruciating, as if his soul was being torn as well as his body.

The Prisoner hadn't realized that he had shut his eyes until he opened them again and saw what Grey Wing was clutching triumphantly in his hand. Long, white feathers. Dripping red where they had been torn out at the root.

"What is an angel without wings?" snarled Grey Wing. "I can keep going until you are just as pathetic as those humans you care so much for… Or you can tell me where the key is hidden."

"I cannot stop you…" the Prisoner gasped in agony. "I cannot stop you from destroying my physical form, but that is merely a shell. You can never crush my spirit. The key is hidden beyond your reach and I will do nothing to help you. Enjoy this fleeting moment of power, Grey Wing, because – trust me on this – Ben Kingdom and the Watchers shall defeat you!"

Mention of that name spurred Grey Wing on to greater violence, plucking another fistful of feathers from the Prisoner's wings. "Before the night is out you *will* tell me where to find the Gehenna Key," Grey Wing hissed. "You have been forgotten. Ben Kingdom is not coming to your rescue. You belong to me, Josiah!"

CHAPTER 3

NO HIDING PLACE

B en woke suddenly and urgently from a nightmare filled with feathers and claws. He sat bolt upright and his head flicked from left to right, searching for an enemy, even as his hand instinctively went for his quarterstaff.

"Easy, son," a familiar voice growled in his ear. "You're safe."

Ben blinked as his eyes adjusted to the dim light of a lantern. "How long have I been out?"

"Hours," said Jago Moon. "Sun's just coming up."

Ben searched the gloom, anxious to see who else had made it out alive. Pa, Nathaniel, Ghost, little Molly

Marbank, Valentine and Lucy. Ben recognized more than a dozen other senior cell leaders too, brave boys and girls who ensured that Ben's plans were followed by the other Watchers scattered across the city.

Then there was the man sitting to his left. The man that made some of them uncomfortable. The man with a dinosaur claw where his right hand used to be.

Claw Carter.

The same Claw Carter who had been Sweet's second-in-command.

"Where are we?" said Ben, wiping away the cold sheen of sweat as his heart rate began to return to normal.

"Safe house," said Lucy.

"Mr. Smutts's place," Jonas Kingdom explained.

Ben nodded. That made sense. Smutts had been Ben's employer, way back when Ben was an apprentice cooper. Ben had saved Mr. Smutts from a fire which had engulfed his workshop, and now the man was repaying the favour in spades. If the Legion discovered Watchers in his house, then the whole Smutts family would get a one-way ticket to the detention camp in St. James's Park.

"How many did we get over the Wall?" asked Ben apprehensively.

Jonas reeled off the list. "We counted at least ninety into the steamships, but the Legion was on us too quick."

He shook his head. "The army could have taken twice that number."

"Casualties?" said Ben, dreading the answer. One was too many.

"Mostly flesh wounds," said Jonas, his voice flat. "But we lost two Watchers from the Hoxton cell."

Ben sighed. Every day their numbers were being whittled away. "And how did I make it out?"

"Stumpy," said Moon.

"Thank you, Professor Carter," said Ben, ignoring Moon's jibe. "I thought I was done for back there."

"You know it's the least I could do," said Claw Carter.

"He was remarkable," chipped in Valentine in his educated tones. Moon made a noise halfway between a laugh and a spit. Valentine purred on regardless. "I wouldn't say that it was all strictly Marquis of Queensbury rules" – which Ben took to mean that Carter had fought hard and fought dirty – "but, by jingo," Valentine continued, "the professor here was like poetry in motion. He really cut that Feathered Man down to size."

Moon chose that moment to blow his nose loudly and vigorously.

Ben understood where the animosity came from. Until he switched sides, Carter had persecuted the Watchers without remorse; accepting him as an ally was a challenge that pushed the Watcher creed of forgiveness to the limit. Carter had hurt them all in ways too numerous to mention. Ben himself would always be able to recall the day when Carter had used his claw to slit Jonas Kingdom's throat. These were not memories that they could simply wish away.

But Carter was a changed man, Ben was convinced of it. Ever since Ben had used the Hand of Heaven to bring the professor back from the brink of madness at the Feast of Ravens, Carter had thrown himself unreservedly behind the Watchers' cause. And besides, Ben was relying on Carter's knowledge of Legion tactics and the man's ability to navigate the labyrinth of the Under to help them snatch Queen Victoria back from the enemy. In spite of everything that had gone before, Ben sensed that he could trust Carter.

Or was it more that he *needed* to trust him?

Ben ached. All of his injuries were catching up with him. Run and hide – that was all the Watchers ever seemed to do. Food was scarce, sleep was scarcer. Ben knew that they couldn't keep going like this for ever.

"Right," said Carter, cutting through the battle-weariness that was settling upon them. "Can you go over the plans for tonight, Ben? Please repeat it slowly so that our older members can keep up."

Moon muttered under his breath. Ben didn't catch it all but it sounded more like something a drunken sailor might say, rather than a warrior monk.

"Tonight is the last escape mission," said Ben, "and then we're counting down to 1st May, Revolution Day."

"I'm ready," said Moon, his gnarled hand patting his swordstick.

"For this final run we're going to use the Liberator to get as many people as we can to safety outside the Wall…" The Watchers looked excited at the prospect. The Liberator was their airship and it had proved decisive in the past. "Strictly women, children and elderly folk first—"

"I can help with your bags, Mr. Moon," cut in Carter.

"Thanks," said Moon. "I could do with a hand. But then again, so could you."

Ben laughed, he couldn't help it. The others joined in, including Carter himself, and the atmosphere lifted slightly.

"Our scouts have informed me that there's a weak point in the Wall just north of Camden town," Ben said with a nod to Nathaniel. "Apparently the patrols are less frequent there and the railway goods yard should provide plenty of cover for the escapees to gather. The Liberator is hidden in one of the disused sheds, fully repaired and good to go. Mr. Moon, are you ready with the diversions?"

Moon grinned. "Me an' Lucy've got a special surprise we've been saving for the occasion."

"The Legion curfew sounds at nine and we leave at eleven," said Ben. "Between now and then, use your contacts, use your networks, spread the word. This is the *last* run. Anyone left has already chosen sides."

Images flashed through Ben's mind. Mother Shepherd, the glorious old woman who had led the Watchers before him – her body broken after she fell to her death from the dome of St Paul's. Josiah – the Weeping Man – the angel who had fought for the Watcher cause, until he was snatched away from them by the claws of the Feathered Men. All the other men, women and children who had suffered loss and heartbreak as the Legion had torn London apart. Ben's right hand began to throb with the injustice of it all. It was as if his flesh was metal in a furnace, filling with the power of the flames, being forged into something greater than it was before.

"Yes, we've lost loved ones," said Ben. "Yes, this city is hurting. But Revolution Day is coming. In four days' time, when every free Londoner rises up against the Legion, we *will* rescue the Queen and take London back!" Ben paused as the weight of his words set in. The odds were against them, they all knew that. Yes, they had a plan. What they really needed was a *miracle*.

"I understand how the Legion works," said Carter, "I know how Mr. Sweet thinks…"

"Funny, that," murmured Moon.

"Sweet is arrogant…*I* was arrogant," Carter conceded, "and pride is a weakness." Carter's intelligent eyes gleamed. "Mr. Sweet has built himself a kingdom with a crown to wear and a throne to sit on. He hates the Watchers – you especially, Ben. But the Legion regard the Watchers as an irritation, just as the grey wolf might regard a tiny tapeworm, *echinococcus granulosus*, as an irritation…right up until the moment when it eats its way through the wolf's internal organs, hooks its barbs into its heart and kills it."

Molly Marbank pulled a face and snuggled in tighter to Jonas Kingdom. Ben gave her a wink.

"So you're saying I'm a worm, basically," Ben said to Carter. "Nice."

Carter, for his part, looked perplexed. It was a perfectly good illustration as far as he was concerned. He'd always admired parasitic nematodes.

"As you all know, I'd hoped that we'd already have freed the Queen by now," said Ben, continuing where he left off. "But we still haven't managed to find where Sweet is holding her."

"There are hundreds of dark places in the Under," said Carter. "But I am confident that young Mr. Valentine and I will sniff the old girl out. Between us, we know the Under better than almost anyone."

"But six weeks in, we're no closer to finding her," said Moon.

"On the contrary," said Carter. "We know more than a dozen dungeons where she *isn't* being held."

Ben intervened as tempers began to fray. "And we *still* have four more days, don't forget." He caught their attention and held it. "We also have *this*," he said, raising his right hand – the Hand of Heaven.

An awed hush fell upon them. Ben was the *one* that the Watcher prophecy had promised. The one who would bring them victory…if he survived.

Since Ben had joined the Watchers and accepted his incredible destiny, he had found that his right hand was capable of extraordinary things. But he knew that its immense power came from a higher source outside of his control. Ben was the channel, not the river. He began to recite the great prophecy. Other voices joined with his until the attic was filled with their song.

"One will come to lead the fight, to defeat the darkness, bring the triumph of the light.

One will come with fire as his crown"

– Ben subconsciously ran his hand through his fiery red hair –

"to bring the Legion tumbling down.
One will come with fire in his eyes,
to pierce through the veil of wicked lies.
One will come with fire in his heart,
to overcome all odds and play his part.
One will come with fire in his hand,
to purge the evil from this land!"

"On Revolution Day," said Ben, "with or without the army, every Londoner who won't bow to the Legion will rise up as one. The plan is simple – every Legionnaire, every Feathered Man, needs to be busy fighting the uprising so that I can get to Mr. Sweet and use the Hand to stop him once and for all." Ben flexed the fingers of his right hand.

"The Crown of Corruption is the source of Sweet's power and only the Hand can destroy it. Break the crown, and we'll break Sweet's hold," said Moon. He chuckled, cracking his own knuckles in anticipation.

"To clarify then," said Valentine. "The mass uprising is a distraction, a ballyhoo to keep the Legionnaires tied up on all fronts."

"So that I," said Carter, "can somehow get Ben into the presence of the most intensely guarded man in all of London."

"A power-mad, paranoid, insanely vindictive and

spiteful dictator," added Lucy. "Who is also in league with the forces of Hell."

"And together," said Jonas, "we buy you both enough time to steal and obliterate Sweet's most treasured possession."

Moon grinned. "Sounds like the sort of thing I do for fun."

Suddenly a gunshot sounded in the room below. Ben froze, mid-smile. The deafening bang was followed by heavy footfalls and the bruising sounds of violence.

"Nobody move," Ben mouthed. If the Legion found them now…

Voices rose up through the floorboards. The bullying threats of Legionnaires, protestations from Mr. Smutts.

"I tell you, there's no one here!"

The silence in the attic was suffocating.

Gradually, grudgingly, the voices retreated.

Ben let out a long breath of relief, shifting his weight slightly as he did so.

In the confines of the attic, the creak from the floorboards sounded as loud as a cannon.

"What was that noise?" Hans Schulman demanded, giving Mr. Smutts a shove on the shoulder. The German

Legionnaire was a stocky lad, and Smutts staggered backwards. Behind Schulman, the rest of his Legion brigade laughed. Spurred on, Schulman buffeted the man again, punctuating each question with another blow. "Are you trying to hide something from us, old man? Do you think we are idiots?"

They had all heard the groan from the rafters overhead; Schulman knew that decisive action was required.

"How do I get into the attic?" he shouted in Smutts's face.

The man said nothing, but the flicker of his eyes betrayed the ceiling hatch, hidden in the deep shadows of the corridor.

"Quick!" Schulman ordered. "Bedlam, let me stand on your shoulders—"

"I'm the captain," Mickelwhite reminded him. "*I* give the orders."

"Forgive me, *mein Kapitän*," said Schulman. "But I am so sick of the Watchers and their pathetic resistance. I am anxious to snuff them out."

"Go on then," said Mickelwhite, with a patronizing air. "Be my guest."

Schulman didn't need to be told twice. He scrabbled up onto Bedlam's square shoulders and put one hand to the attic hatch, the other holding a loaded crossbow pistol at the ready. Mickelwhite gave him the nod and Schulman flung it open, shoving his head into the musty loft space, bringing up his weapon in the same instant. Using one meaty hand to hold on for balance, Schulman scanned around him in the darkness. He could see them all; these Watchers were legendary. Jago Moon, "Scarface", "the Mute", and Ben Kingdom himself, all waiting to taste death from his pistol.

Schulman grinned.

"What've you found?" Bedlam grunted, swaying slightly as Schulman began to grow heavy.

The German Legionnaire paused, enjoying the moment.

"Nothing," he said, letting the attic hatch slam closed and jumping down beside Bedlam. "Just rats."

"I've put poison down," Smutts put in. "I can't seem to shift 'em."

Mickelwhite turned on Smutts again. "We'll be keeping our eyes on you," he threatened. "You know what we do to Watcher sympathizers."

Hans Schulman certainly knew. And he couldn't imagine how terrible the punishment would be for someone like him: a Watcher spy in the ranks of the Legion.

CHAPTER 4

ONCE A THIEF

Ruby Johnson had no choice. She was a thief and so she did what thieves do. She stole and gave what she had stolen to the Legion, after she had creamed the best of the pickings off the top for herself. In return they gave her security, of a sort, and the pretence of a family; companionship without love.

Although she was dressed in a hooded coat with fur trim, she looked and felt more like a drowned cat than a sophisticated young lady. The storm that had arrived last night had brought nothing but misery. The fat, swollen clouds that filled the sky reminded Ruby of bruises, purple-black and sickly yellow. But she was the one taking the beating. Her feet squelched inside her ankle boots as rivers of rain tumbled through the streets. Hunger chewed at her insides. Worry squirmed in her mind. Ruby was wretched and weary. This was not how she had planned her life to be.

Things had been easier when she'd worked for Claw Carter. He had been her protector for a while, but now he was gone. Some said that he was dead, but Ruby preferred the other rumour; that Carter had defected to the Watchers and that he and Ben Kingdom were plotting Sweet's downfall. Ruby liked that.

She smiled as she thought of Ben. There was a time, not so long ago, when she thought they might have run away together and left everything behind. The Legion, the Watchers, the squalid streets, and the grinding hardship that was all kids like her and Ben could look forward to. But that plan had fallen through too.

And it had been her fault, Ruby remembered with a stab of regret.

The memory was etched as hard as diamond on her mind. The moment when everything could have changed, when Ben had the opportunity to destroy the last of the Coins of Blood – and Ruby had ruined it, all because she couldn't resist the pull of the cursed silver. Within the hour that blasted coin had become the last component of

Mr. Sweet's weapon of mass domination, the Crown of Corruption.

Ruby had been weak, and now all of London was paying the price.

So perhaps it was fitting that her new benefactor was a monster.

She was out stealing for him now. She had thought that Legion rule would make this part of her life much easier, but the streets had become more dangerous than ever. Thieves and thugs were running the city, and all the decent, honest, law-abiding people had either been rounded up and hauled off to the detention camp or were hiding behind locked doors, barricaded in their own homes. Ruby didn't have to worry about the police catching her, but she did have to be on constant guard to make sure that she wasn't mugged herself.

Most of the shops that she passed had been boarded up. There had been widespread looting when the Legion took control, and the shops that remained were only allowed to serve Legion members. If you weren't wearing a Legion armband – a black, gauntleted fist on a white background – then it was a case of "Sorry, not today".

"Miss Johnson," a snooty voice called out. "What an unexpected pleasure."

Too late, Ruby spotted Mickelwhite and Bedlam coming

the other way. She made to turn on her heel, but was too slow. *Damn it.*

Ruby halted and Captain Mickelwhite swaggered over to her, unhurried by the rain. Ruby had never liked him. He seemed to have a permanent sneer on his lips. She liked his companion even less – John Bedlam was a thug.

"I can't stay, boys," Ruby purred, putting on the charm. "Places to go, things to steal."

She began to walk away, only to feel Bedlam's heavy hand on her shoulder.

"Stay and chat, Ruby. Or haven't you got time for your old mates?" There was no mistaking the hint of menace in his tone.

Ruby smiled and flashed her emerald eyes. It had always been her way of turning situations to her advantage. "I'd love to have a chinwag, but I really am in a hurry." *To get away from you.*

Bedlam's hand did not move. "Well, how about you give us something to remember you by," he said, his fingers moving from her shoulder to the bag she carried. "What have you got in there, Ruby?"

"Let's have a look, shall we, John?" said Mickelwhite, yanking Ruby's satchel to him and rummaging inside. He quickly found a wallet that Ruby had lifted earlier, as well as some cheese and cured meat that she had wrapped in a piece of muslin; the meal she'd been saving for later. "What's that, Ruby? 'Help yourselves, boys.' Don't mind if we do."

Mickelwhite pocketed the wallet and split the food with Bedlam, then he turned the satchel inside out to make sure he hadn't missed anything before he flung it to the ground.

"Remember whose side you're on," he told her in parting.

Ruby retrieved her bag, clenching her teeth together hard. A single tear escaped and was lost in the rivers of raindrops rolling down her face. She felt angry and humiliated, but worse than that, she felt utterly alone.

Mickelwhite's words had struck a nerve; Ruby didn't feel she belonged on anyone's side. Not the Legion or the Watchers. She just knew that she wanted to get away from London and start her life over again.

And so she had been building up a secret stash – her "escape fund", as she called it. Enough to set her up in a new life. In the meantime though, she had to keep her head down. Keep her nose clean, serve her new master.

Which meant finding the key. Ruby had been given a description. It wasn't the sort of treasure that made her own green eyes light up, but someone else was desperate to get their hands on it.

Or rather their talons.

Why Grey Wing wanted the Gehenna Key was no concern of hers. All she knew was that she had to find it for him…or else.

Grey Wing squatted beside the pit.

The key is hidden beyond your reach… Those had been Josiah's exact words. A mere slip from the Weeping Man's lips, but it was enough to seal the fate of the Watchers… Of London… Of the world.

The Feathered Man croaked a laugh which reverberated through the cavernous chamber. The sanctuary of the Under was the Legion's cathedral. It was here that they carried out their ancient rituals. It was a place steeped in history and stained with blood. And beneath the huge vaulted ceiling was the anti-spire. A hole of impossible depth, filled to the brim with blackness.

No one knew what lay at the bottom – no *humans* knew, anyway. Grey Wing hopped, birdlike, around the rim of the pit, gazing into the dark. His unforgiving eyes filled with delight. With his long talons he felt around the flagstones at the lip until he found one that lifted. The long, lean muscles of his arms strained until the stone was removed. Beneath it was a keyhole. Almost affectionately,

Grey Wing let his talon trace the shape. All that was missing was the key. The Gehenna Key.

And what did a key do, except unlock a door?

Josiah had not told him where it could be found, not even as his wings were hacked off. But he had given Grey Wing an inadvertent clue. The key was beyond the reach of the Feathered Men…somewhere that Grey Wing and his kind could never go. That could only mean that it was on consecrated ground.

It might take time. It might mean that every church in London had to be reduced to rubble. But the Gehenna Key *would* be his.

Grey Wing listened intently, bending his head towards the lip of the pit.

It was very faint, but it could definitely be heard. Echoing from the depths.

Chittering. Scratching. Slithering.

"Not long," Grey Wing whispered. "Not long."

CHAPTER 5

THE GREAT ESCAPE

With night came the fear.

Ben could feel the sheer weight of it as the Watchers sneaked through the abandoned streets. Like a blanket smothering the city. *A wet blanket at that*, Ben thought, as he tipped the rainwater from the brim of his billycock. The storm was worsening. The clouds were gathering, circling overhead like carrion birds above a carcass.

The Watchers had made slow progress and they were in danger of not reaching the rendezvous in time. If they could have used their rooftop paths they would have covered the distance in half the time, but they knew that the Feathered Men were up there somewhere in the storm-ridden sky. And so they were forced to take a zigzag route through the streets, turning away each time a patrol came near or a curtain twitched at a window.

London had always been Ben's home. Noisy, smelly, raucous London. Life had never been easy, not for him or for any of the other kids growing up on Old Gravel Lane. Always hungry, always cold, always poor. But he could almost laugh; looking back now, it had been a walk in the park compared to trying to survive in the London that Mr. Sweet had made.

Ben picked up his pace, but then froze in his tracks as a hideous howling resounded through the darkness. Part bark, part shriek. All evil.

"Three Feathered Men," hissed Moon, his exceptional hearing making out the details even above the drumming of the rain, "and five Legion handlers. Heading…" Moon paused. "West."

Ben released his breath slowly. The Legion had taken to using the fearsome fallen angels as attack dogs, keeping them hungry and then patrolling the streets, letting them sniff out curfew breakers, escapees, Watchers. But tonight the Watchers were lucky – they were heading in the opposite direction to the patrol, north and to the east.

They skirted St Pancras station, then broke through a fence and scrambled out onto the silent train tracks, running low to the ground. Ben suddenly felt exposed and doubt came in search of him. As always when he felt vulnerable, Ben saw the faces of Josiah and Mother Shepherd and his own mother. All dead because of him.

Ben slowed, blinded by the torrent of images. Then stopped altogether.

Lucy knew that they couldn't risk being caught out in the open. The rest of their group had already moved on ahead, not noticing Ben falter. She touched Ben's arm and looked deep into his eyes. She had been doing that a lot recently. Ben had found it disconcerting at first – he wasn't used to someone, especially a girl, fixing him with such an intense gaze. But now he was glad of it.

She let her hand move to his shoulder, not letting her eye drop. "What would Mother Shepherd say?" she asked softly.

Ben listened and heard that magnificent old girl inside his head. "Watchers aren't slaves to fear," he replied.

"Damn right," said Lucy. "Now, let's keep going."

Together they left the tracks, clambered over a slick mountain of coal and into the depot yard where the others were waiting. Composed again, Ben was ready to deploy his team. His forces were going to be spread very thin.

"Mr. Moon, Ghost, Lucy, are you ready with the 'diversions'?"

Jago Moon patted his bulky rucksack and gave a broad grin.

"Nathaniel, Valentine, Professor Carter, pick your positions carefully. We're going to need your covering fire."

Nathaniel gave a mock salute. "Aye aye."

"Pa, are you sure you can fly the Liberator in this storm?"

"We'll soon find out, son," said Jonas Kingdom.

"And you've got the flare gun?"

Jonas nodded.

"Molly," said Ben, stepping in close and giving the little girl a hug. "This is goodbye for a while. Pa's going to get you out with the others."

Molly looked sad and excited at the same time. "Will I see you again?" she asked.

"Course," said Ben reassuringly. "As soon as this is all over." *If I live to tell the tale...*

There were no more words to be said as the Watchers went their separate ways into the night. With one arm round Molly and one round his father, Ben quickly guided them towards the shed where the Liberator was waiting.

Ben's pulse always raced when he thought about the Liberator. It was such a magnificent airship. A long streamlined balloon, filled with gas stolen from the gasometer near the Oval before the Wall went up, hung above a gondola of wood and brass. Sleek wings emerged from each side, with long propellers powered by steam pumps, fed by a large copper furnace. Harpoon guns were mounted on each side, ready to fend off aerial attacks. It had been built for speed and could carry about eighty passengers at a push. Without it, their war against the Legion would have ended at the Feast of Ravens. Since then the Watchers had been repairing her in secret, ready for this night.

Ben opened the huge shed door a fraction and all three of them slipped inside out of the rain. As they saw what waited for them, Ben and his pa exchanged glances. There must have been more than two hundred figures huddled together in the darkness. Ben looked around at the frightened faces. One woman had five children, all under the age of seven, clinging to her skirts. A mother cradled an infant in her arms, rocking her gently while she tried to stifle her own tears. An old man, bent double with age, stood side-by-side with his wife, their gnarled fingers interlocked, their knuckles white.

Ben did a quick calculation. The fathers and husbands in the crowd would all know that this flight was not for them, but plenty of the older lads would have to stay back too. He'd have to break it to them gently.

"You climb aboard, Pa," said Ben. "You too, Molly. Get the engines prepped and ready, I'll handle this."

Ben turned over a crate and stood on it to give himself a bit more height so that he could address the crowd. His quick mouth had got him in trouble most of his life and earned him more than one thick lip when he was running wild on Old Gravel Lane. But in the last few weeks his way with words had served him well. He smiled reassuringly at the anxious faces around him, pulled the lantern from his pack, unwound his matches from their waterproof canvas wrapping, lit the wick and let it shine.

"You all know me," said Ben. "I'm that ginger boy who's put the wind up Mr. Sweet's nightshirt."

"We know who you are," said one man gruffly. "You and your Watchers are the ones who brought all this down on our heads."

Ben hadn't been expecting that. "The Watchers risk their lives every day to keep London safe."

"And who asked you to, eh? Not me, not my family. We never asked you to bring your war to London."

"It's not like that."

"Isn't it? We were all getting on with our lives when – *bang!* – suddenly it's the Legion calling the shots and your lot stirring 'em up."

Back in the day Ben would have got into a scrap over

less, but Mother Shepherd had taught him that soft words could turn away anger. Some of the time, anyhow.

"It must feel like that," said Ben, changing tack. "But this war isn't something that we started or ever wanted."

There were murmurs of agreement.

"You must know that the Watchers are on your side, otherwise you wouldn't have risked coming here tonight."

More nods.

"Listen," said Ben, "the Watchers didn't start this war, but we *will* end it."

"1st of May," said a big man near the back of the shed, holding his wife and daughter. "That's the day, ain't it?"

"Revolution Day…" said Ben. He had given this speech over and over, in back rooms, in cellars, behind locked doors, telling the story of the Watchers, the ancient guardians of the city. *One last time…*

"When Big Ben sounds two in the morning, the Legion patrols will be at their lowest ebb and I'll need people like you to make the first step towards taking back our city."

"Do we look like soldiers?" said another worried man.

"Do I?" Ben challenged. "I'm only a lad but I'm not going to let that stand in my way."

The man was abashed. "Go on."

"I'm calling on every free Londoner to do whatever they can to keep the Legion busy."

"What sort of plan is that?" another man interrupted, before his friends shushed him.

"There are Watchers, like us, scattered all over the city," Ben explained. "By now those Watchers will have spread the word on the streets under their protection, just as I'm telling you..." Ben chose not to mention how many Watchers were imprisoned or missing, how many gaps there might be in the uprising. "On May 1st on the chime of two, all those who are prepared to be part of the rebellion, to stand up and fight to get this city back, will identify themselves by flashing a lamp from their window three times. With a Watcher to guide them, these units can then be deployed strategically. If a Legion patrol comes down the street, then it *must* be stopped, decisively and effectively—"

"Killed, you mean?"

"No," said Ben emphatically. "The Legion are the killers, not us. We'll have to use force, but remember, once we free Queen Victoria, then the army can come in and do any serious business."

"Supposing we join, what else might we have to do?"

"It's a long list," said Ben. "Every guard post, every watchtower on the Wall has to be disabled and put out of action, and the fence around the detention camp has got to come down. Then there will be Feathered Men to look out for…"

"Sounds dangerous."

"It is," said Ben, "but it's got to be better than hiding in a shed for the rest of your days."

"Hear, hear," said Jonas from the deck of the Liberator.

Someone at the rear of the shed began to applaud in agreement. The clapping was taken up, but Ben raised his hands to silence it.

"Thanks an' all that," he said, "but we don't want to draw attention to ourselves."

Almost on cue, the Liberator's engines began their low thrum as the steam from the boiler surged through the pipework. The balloon started to glow from within as the gas jets flared. There was no way that the Liberator was going to get over the Wall without *someone* spotting it.

"Right," said Ben. "We can start boarding now, but you can all see that the Liberator was only made to carry eighty. We'll do our best to get all the most vulnerable on board somehow…but some of you are gonna have to stay behind."

Ben braced himself for a barrage of abuse.

"I want to stay," piped up a lad, only a little older than Ben. "I want to say that I was part of Revolution Day."

There were murmurs of agreement all round and Ben

breathed again. "Well done, all," he said with relief. "Now let's get going."

A young mother was first up the rope ladder, followed by two boys only five years old by the look of them. "You can be stokers," Ben told them. "My pa is the captain, he'll tell you what to do."

An old man with a wooden leg approached. "I was a sailor all my life," he told Ben, "reckon I can handle one of them harpoons."

"It's all yours, grandpa," said Ben.

Quickly the deck began to fill. "Move down as far as you can," Jonas urged, as those at the back of the queue saw their chance of escaping dwindling. "We'll take as many as we dare, I promise."

One little girl started to cry as her father lifted her on board the Liberator.

"Goodbye, ducks," he said, his own eyes misting up. "Be a brave girl for yer mum."

Ben realized that this might be the last time he saw his pa, too. Ben looked deep into his father's eyes and then tipped his finger to the brim of his billycock hat in salute. They both understood the love that passed silently between them.

Before emotion got the better of Ben, he jumped down off his crate, pulled out his telescope and went over to the shed doors. It was time to make sure that everything was in place. How much longer could their luck last? Ben wondered. He scanned the yard, searching for his friends. And for the Legion.

He rubbed his hand over the end of his telescope, trying to clear the lens. He searched the abandoned yard again, looking for some sign of movement. Still nothing. Then he spotted Ghost, Lucy and Moon at the far side of the yard, surreptitiously planting packages around a row of huge oil tanks. The parcels were connected by a reel of wire, which Lucy was winding out behind them as they went. *That's my girl.*

Ghost flashed his lantern twice. The diversion was ready. It was time.

Nathaniel, Valentine and Carter were out there somewhere, in position to provide covering fire. Ben couldn't find them with his spyglass and that had to be a good thing. It meant that the Legion wouldn't be able to pick them off.

This is it, thought Ben. He raised his own bullseye lantern. It was the sort of light favoured by burglars, with shuttered doors which could be opened and closed to release a narrow beam of light. He signalled to his team. The last escape from London could begin.

This one's for you, Mother S.

The rain was playing ragged percussion notes on the corrugated iron roofs in the goods yard but it was not enough to completely drown the noise from the Liberator's engines. The airship was roaring into action.

"Stand clear!" Jonas ordered, making sure that no one was near the great propellers as he engaged the gears that brought them to life. The blades of wood spun slowly at first but soon they became a blur and the shed echoed with their steady throb.

The Liberator was dangerously overloaded. The entire deck was packed shoulder-to-shoulder. They had managed to get everyone on board. The question now was whether they could still fly.

There was only one way to find out.

Ben pushed open the shed doors and released the stow lines that held the airship down. Slowly the Liberator began to nose out of its hiding place and into the yard. The flames from the gas canisters illuminated the balloon. It was strangely beautiful. And perilously visible.

The Liberator was soon completely out in the open, but it didn't rise into the air as Ben had expected it to. For the plan to work, the Liberator had to get as high as possible as quickly as possible. However, to Ben's horror, it seemed to be bumping along the ground. It was too heavy for lift-off.

Ben was so fixed on the Liberator that he almost didn't hear the rush of feet behind him, heavy boots crunching on gravel. But at the last instant he spun and found himself face-to-face with a huge bruiser of a man, wearing a Legion armband. Ben ducked instinctively as a meaty fist swung through the air, missing his head by inches. Then he brought himself in close to the man's fat belly and jabbed upwards with a one-two-three flurry of rabbit punches.

The big man laughed. "Is that all you got, sonny?"

Ben had seen some ugly faces in his days, but this giant took the biscuit. His nose had been flattened against his broad face, presumably by better punches than the ones Ben had just thrown. His shaven head was criss-crossed with scars, and his jaw showed the signs of more than one knife fight. Ben took a step back, reaching for his quarterstaff even as he dared a glance over his shoulder.

He could see his pa ordering more gas to be released in a desperate attempt to get the Liberator off the ground. Some of the men from the shed had run out into the yard and were putting their shoulders to the gondola, trying to use their bodyweight to help the heavily laden airship to launch. *Come on,* Ben pleaded, willing the Liberator into the air. *Come on!* He breathed again as the airship bumped off the ground and began to rise, *at last*.

Taking advantage of the distraction, the Legionnaire lunged for Ben again. Ben whipped his head away from the blow and flicked his quarterstaff out to its full fighting length. The Legionnaire was strong, Ben could see, but how sharp were his reflexes?

Ben spun the staff in a blurring circle and then lashed out: a slash to the head; an uppercut to the body; a swipe to the legs. The Legionnaire swatted them away like flies.

Ben began to move backwards, using his staff to keep the thug at a safe distance.

"I'm gonna snap that stick," the brute said. "Then I'm gonna snap you."

What the Legionnaire didn't expect was for three of the men from the shed to sneak up behind him. Ben watched as they crept up – and then hit the Legionnaire with pickaxe handles. The big brute groaned as they hit him again and again, striking his shoulders, his arms, his legs. A normal man would have gone down instantly, but it took a concerted effort by all three until the giant wobbled and then fell face down in the mud.

One of the young men went to follow up with a blow to the Legionnaire's exposed head, but Ben stopped him.

"No," said Ben.

"They took my father to the camp, they whipped him,

humiliated him." All the pent-up anger came churning out. "Why shouldn't I pay one of them back?"

"Because we are better men than they are," said Ben.

The lad looked as if he was about to argue, but a noisemaker rattle cut him off. The time for talking was done.

Ben searched the Wall and spotted a solitary Legionnaire spinning the rattle furiously, like a football fan on the terraces, the loud clicking of the ratchet calling out to other Legion patrols. Ben saw a padded crossbow bolt take the Legionnaire clean between the eyes, knocking him out cold, but it was too late. Other rattles were sounding out, and whistles too. The Legion had been roused.

Ben signalled to Lucy to start her diversion as he began to sprint across the open ground of the yard. His pa was going to need all the help he could get.

Three more Legionnaires came running along the top of the Wall. They were all felled by Carter, Valentine and Nathaniel, firing padded bolts with the precision of expert snipers.

The Liberator was airborne but still flying low, barely ten feet from the ground. It needed to gain more height or it would never clear the Wall...

Then there was an almighty *whump!* and the ground

actually shook as Lucy pushed down on her first detonator. The explosives that Moon and Ghost had planted ripped through the oil tanks, sending a mushroom cloud of flames into the air. The heat was enough to wash over Ben, even through the rain, and he threw himself face down in the mud as shrapnel began to fall around him. Ben dared a glance at the Liberator and saw that the hot wind had actually worked in the airship's favour, helping to lift it higher into the air, although the gondola swayed alarmingly in the shock waves.

The Legionnaires were thrown into disarray, uncertain of what they were up against. Then Lucy pushed down on the second detonator and a row of explosives went off along the foot of the Wall itself, blowing out chunks of masonry. Ben stumbled back to his feet against the force of the blast. The Liberator was climbing steeply now, *thank God*, out of reach of the explosions. But the engines were making a high-pitched whine, straining with the effort. This was not the swift getaway that Ben had promised.

The confusion of the explosions had bought them precious time, but still Ben kept running towards the Liberator. They had badly underestimated how soon the Legion would arrive. Carter was a crack marksman, and Valentine and Nathaniel were both good enough shots, but it wouldn't be enough to hold back the tide.

So much for this being a weak spot, Ben thought, as an entire brigade of Legionnaires came running along the battlements of the Wall, Carter's crossbow bolts whistling around them.

The Liberator had reached the Wall but was still barely high enough to scrape over it. The first Legionnaires to arrive threw themselves at the airship, and scrambled on board like bloodthirsty pirates. The sound of the frightened children on the ship sent a tremor down Ben's spine. But the next noise to meet Ben's ears was equally chilling; it was the ferocity that only a mother protecting her children can possess. Ben saw the Legionnaires tossed back over the side and fall helplessly to the ground. Then there was a terrible rasping sound as the hull of the Liberator dragged itself over the ragged stonework of the Wall. Ben couldn't imagine how much of this punishment the airship could take.

He reached the foot of the Wall and drew a grappling hook from his pack. With an expert swing, he flung it up high and it landed with a clunk. Ben tugged on the rope to ensure that it was holding fast, and then shimmied up the Wall, putting all of his Watcher training to the test, grunting as he reached the top.

Somehow the Liberator had managed to get clear of the Wall and was heading out over Dead Man's Land –

Mr. Sweet's death zone. But it was moving far too slowly. And in spite of Carter's marksmanship there were still five Legionnaires standing on the Wall, with several who had been felled initially starting to come round. Looking along the length of the Wall, Ben could see Moon, Ghost and Lucy thundering towards him. Most of the family men had stayed to give their all so that their loved ones could escape, but for the moment, Ben was the only one near enough to make a difference.

"Oi, maggot pies!" Ben shouted. "Over 'ere!"

The Legionnaires took their eyes, and their crossbows, off the Liberator and turned to Ben.

"Don't you recognize your arch-enemy when you see him, then?"

Ben didn't give the Legionnaires so much as a second to react. Josiah the angel had taught him how to fight and Ben spun into action on the Wall battlements. He ran in close to the first stunned Legionnaire and elbowed him sharply across the chin, knocking him down in one. Then, taking advantage of the rain-slick stone, Ben threw himself into a low skid, feet-first, cannoning another Legionnaire onto his back. The others recognized that Ben was trouble and backed off, bringing their crossbows to bear, only for one to be knocked out by another shot from Carter.

Ben moved as if his body was no longer his own, all his training taking over. A sweep of his arm knocked a crossbow out of the way at the last instant, his other hand following through with a chop to the Legionnaire's neck which made the man crumple. This was fighting Watcher-style. No death, but some bloody good bruises. Extending his quarterstaff again, Ben spun it from hand to hand before jabbing it into one Legionnaire's stomach, bending him double, then lashed out in the opposite direction, whipping the crossbow from another Legionnaire's grip.

I'm winning!

It was Ben's last clear thought before the cosh struck him on the back of the head and sent him reeling. He turned to see the cruel leer of Captain Mickelwhite looming over him. Looking past Mickelwhite, Ben saw that Lucy, Ghost and Moon now had problems of their own. More Legionnaires had arrived, bringing with them a pack of Feathered Men. Even in his woozy condition, Ben could see that these Feathered Men had been worked up into a state of frenzy, drool dripping from their gaping beaks as they strained against their leashes, dragging their handlers along in their wake.

The Legionnaires let the foul creatures off their chains and Ben watched in horror as the Feathered Men pounced on his three friends. They disappeared from view, lost beneath a maelstrom of claws and talons.

As dazed as he was, Ben was aware that Mickelwhite was laughing. He took a swing at the Legionnaire captain, hoping to knock the smile off his face. But Mickelwhite dodged the blow, then planted his own punch in the pit of Ben's stomach, forcing the air from his lungs in a rush.

Twisting his head to look out over Dead Man's Land, Ben could see that the Liberator was not faring much better. Even though it was nearing the far reaches of the danger zone, it was under ferocious attack. The gunners on board were doing their best to stop Feathered Men from snatching the refugees out of the gondola, but they couldn't prevent them from slashing the balloon itself. Having managed to struggle up to a height of about thirty feet, the Liberator was dropping too quickly, nose first. The plan had been for the Liberator to make it over the houses and then land safely in Finsbury Park, but it was clear that it was never going to make it.

Still groggy from his beating and distracted by the Liberator's fate, Ben barely reacted as Bedlam grabbed him and forced him to his knees in front of Mickelwhite.

"Mr. Sweet is gonna make us princes for this," the thug said.

"It is finished, Kingdom," said Mickelwhite, drawing his sword. "Wave goodbye to your friends, then say goodbye to your head."

Through a haze of pain, Ben realized what he needed to do. He turned his back on Dead Man's Land and the Liberator and kneeled on the battlements, his head bowed, but his legs braced like a runner on the starting blocks. Triumphantly Mickelwhite raised his sword, ready to deliver a two-handed blow.

"Do it!" urged Bedlam.

"With pleasure," said Ben. Releasing all the energy coiled in his legs, he barrelled into Mickelwhite's solar plexus head first, folding the Legionnaire in two. Ben didn't stop when he came to the edge of the Wall and, before Bedlam or the others could react, Ben was diving through the open air and back into the depot yard. He hit the release toggle on his backpack and the glider wings snapped out, just in time to prevent him from doing himself serious injury.

Ben hit the ground running and kept going.

Above his head, he could see his friends' limp forms being carried away by the Feathered Men. Ghost and Moon were both motionless. Only Lucy showed signs of life, hammering at the Feathered Man holding her in an attempt to break its steel grip.

Then, from the other side of the Wall, there came the ear-shattering groan of splintering wood on stone – the sound of the Liberator crashing. There was a moment of silence, followed by the roar of an explosion. Ben felt his heart rip in two as flames from the Liberator rose high into the sky.

Day Two
28th April, 1892

CHAPTER 6

TICK, TICK, TICK

"We're going down!" Jonas yelled.

They had made it over Mr. Sweet's death zone but their luck had failed now. The line of gutted houses that marked the end of Dead Man's Land was looming up in front of the Liberator and Jonas knew that they were going to hit them, hard. Struggling with the wheel and lashed by the rain, Jonas felt as if he was the captain of a sailing ship about to run aground. Along the length of the deck, everyone grabbed hold and did what they could to protect themselves from the inevitable impact. Some of the women and children were screaming, but not Molly, Jonas noticed. She looked on him with absolute trust in her young eyes.

Hope I don't let you down, sweetheart.

They had lost far too much height, and one of the Feathered Men must have been lucky and slashed one of the steering cables. No matter how hard Jonas swung on the wheel, the Liberator was hardly responding, while the engines continued to power them forwards – straight towards the line of roofs.

The nose of the balloon missed the knife-edge of the tiles, but the wooden gondola underneath was too low. Jonas threw all of his weight at the controls, trying to give the Liberator some uplift.

It wasn't enough.

The gondola struck the roof with a bone-jarring jolt which threw everyone staggering forwards. Then the Liberator ploughed on, sheering up waves of roof tiles on either side, crashing through chimney stacks and sending them tumbling. The gondola itself began to splinter as it smashed against the wooden beams of the roof, threatening to tear the entire house apart beneath them. And still the Liberator would not stop.

"Brakes!" Jonas yelled, and two lads at the aft of the gondola responded as they had been taught, throwing out the anchors. The anchors did even more damage to the row of roofs, smashing down through the tiles before catching on beams. The chains rattled and then pulled taut.

The Liberator finally screeched to a stop with a jerk that knocked the passengers to their knees.

Jonas let out a long breath. "Is everyone alright?"

But then the Liberator jerked again. Its nose was suspended in mid-air, hanging out into empty space. Only the back half of the airship was settled on what remained of Holloway Road, held up by the anchors.

The Liberator lurched and began to tip forwards. From the rear, Jonas could hear the anchors straining against the beams that were all that kept it from falling. There was also an ominous hissing that could only mean one thing.

"Everybody off!" shouted Jonas. "Before the gas catches! Go! Go! Go!"

Rope ladders rattled down to the safety of the street. The Watchers and the more able-bodied passengers made human chains. Children and infants were passed hand to hand; the older, frailer escapees were lowered over the side in slings. They had to get down to the ground and out of the blast radius. If this much gas caught fire, the explosion would be devastating.

Soldiers in the street below, awaiting their chance against the Legion, were quick to react. They bundled the escapees away from the danger, passing small children down the line to safety.

Last to leave the gondola, Jonas slung Molly over his

shoulder and headed for the side of the airship. Out of the corner of his eye, he saw the propeller still spinning uselessly, its blades striking against the brickwork with each revolution. The world slowed around Jonas. He could see the propeller clearly, saw it chip against the stone, saw the spark as it flew up into the gas cloud...

Jonas turned his back to the ship, pulling Molly in close to him as he threw himself into a dive, even as the balloon exploded.

"God help us," he muttered as a wave of orange flame rolled over them.

Cradling Molly like an infant, Jonas found himself crashing through a hole in the roof, then tumbling through a second hole in the lath and plaster ceiling. The explosion raged overhead, a molten ball of fire. But its brilliant life was short, dying the moment the gas was all burned up.

Jonas blinked, surprised that he was still able to. He was white with plaster dust, and his nostrils itched with an acrid smell which could only be his own charred hair. Molly was beneath him. And beneath Molly was a musty old mattress. It had saved their lives.

"Gosh," said Molly.

"Quite," said Jonas.

They staggered down the stairs of the abandoned house and out into a hive of activity.

The army had been encamped all around the city for weeks, coming as close as they dared while Sweet still held the threat of the axe over Queen Victoria's neck. Now Jonas saw tears of relief from the escapees as the soldiers gathered them up, covering their shoulders with blankets, handing them mugs of steaming tea. It was a bittersweet victory; so many families had been separated when the Wall went up. So many loved ones were still trapped on the wrong side.

Jonas slipped a cartridge into the broad brass muzzle of his flare gun to let his own family know that he was fine. Then he aimed it into the sky, pulling the trigger. The charge sizzled away and then the night blistered red as the signal flare ignited. It was a message to the Watchers: *mission accomplished.*

Against the odds, the Liberator had brought them to the *real* London, beyond Mr. Sweet's reach. Through a gaping hole in the wreckage of Holloway Road, Jonas looked back across the wasteland of the death zone. It was painful to see the acres of rubble where people's homes had been demolished to ensure that Legion guards had a clear line of fire.

As if on cue, first one, then a barrage of bullets zinged through the air. Jonas shielded Molly with his body as the sky whistled with death. The Legion was using snipers to pick off anyone who strayed into their line of fire.

"Look out," he said, pulling Molly down behind a mound of broken bricks for cover. Daring a peek over the top, Jonas could see figures on the Wall, outlined by the oil fires still burning behind them. A row of guns flashed and seconds later the bang reached them, along with the deadly cargo.

Jonas held Molly's head in his hands, covering her ears. *Poor kid*, he thought. She had seen so much hardship already in her young life. No mother. A father who died, leaving her alone. Then a new start with the Watchers, beginning as a game of happy families, but ending up as a war. She was frozen cold too, soaked to the skin. He looked at her, seeing the trust in her big blue eyes, and was filled with a flash of longing for his own two boys, Ben and Nathaniel, both still inside the Wall.

"Ready, aim, FIRE!" barked an officer, and the soldiers unleashed their own volley in retaliation from within their makeshift barricade of half-demolished buildings.

Jonas knew that he had to find a more protected hiding place for both their sakes. Still shielding Molly with his body, they crawled back into the shell of the house they had fallen into and huddled together in the corner behind a mound of broken stone and fallen beams. Jonas was very aware of a ragged hole in the wall, where rain and bullets could reach in and get them. It wasn't the best defence in the world, but it would have to do.

They both shut their eyes while gunshots exploded all around them.

Jonas only opened his eyes when he heard another sound. Scrabbling. Scratching. Nearby, in the wreckage of the house itself. Jonas went rigid. It was the noise of claws against stone. He held Molly tight. Had a Feathered Man survived the destruction of the Liberator?

Whatever it was, it was getting closer.

Trying not to alarm Molly, Jonas reached out and clasped a broken brick. He wouldn't let Molly be taken easily.

Now there was a second sound. Low. Animal.

Laboured breathing, punctuated by yelps of pain.

Come on, show yourself. Let's get this over with.

A shape struggled over the debris and Jonas found himself staring into an ugly face. The eyes bulged. The mouth was wet with drool. The breath was repulsive.

Molly's face lit up. "Can I keep him?" she asked, scooping the bulldog up. It yelped and then broke wind contentedly as it settled in her arms.

While the bullets flew outside, the bulldog snuggled into Molly, responding to her petting with enthusiastic licks of her face. The poor creature had only three legs, although the stump had long since healed. How it came to be out in the death zone was anybody's guess.

"What will you call him?" Jonas asked.

"Clover," she answered with a smile. "Because he's so lucky."

He looked into Molly's wide doe-eyes. How could he say no?

Outside, the fighting was intensifying. The whole house was shaking around them as bullet after bullet struck. Then a voice boomed out over the battlefield.

Jonas felt his marrow turn to ice. It was the voice of Mr. Sweet, addressing them through a speaking trumpet.

"Have you forgotten my promise...? Attack my city and your queen shall die."

There was a collective intake of breath from the soldiers at the mention of Her Majesty.

"Throw down your guns *immediately* or I shall give the order to my executioner. One, two, three..."

Reluctant orders rang out down the line. "Ceasefire!"

Jeers went up from the Legionnaires on the Wall, filled with cruel obscenities.

Jonas made to cover Molly's ears but the girl was gone.

"Molly!" he called. "Where are you?"

"I'm out here," Molly replied. "Clover ran off and I went to get him."

She had crawled out through the hole in the wall, Jonas realized. The girl had wandered into the death zone.

"Stay there," said Jonas firmly. "I'm coming to get you."

Conscious that the Legion might shoot them any time they chose, Jonas got down on his hands and knees and climbed out after Molly. His heart was racing. Sweet's men had littered the death zone with traps; they were both risking their lives for the sake of a dog.

"I've found him!" Molly called. She looked delighted in spite of the fact that she was drenched to the skin again.

Jonas made his way across the rubble towards her. She was a full twenty feet away, standing absolutely exposed on the ruins of another house.

Suddenly, the expression on Molly's face went from joy to terror.

"I think I've done something wrong," she said softly.

"It's alright, Molly," Jonas reassured her. "You're not in trouble."

"I am," said Molly. "I stood on something and now it's going *tick, tick, tick...*"

CHAPTER 7

NIGHT-TIME AT THE WAX MUSEUM

Ben fell. The naked blast of exploding fuel drums washed over him, a hot wave that sent him sprawling. Moon and Lucy's distraction had worked all too well – the fire from the initial oil tank explosions had spread across the yard, igniting everything it touched. Ben threw his hands out to save himself, but he wasn't quick enough to stop his forehead from slamming into the ground. Dazed, Ben climbed back onto his feet. He was distantly aware that his hands must be bleeding but he didn't feel the pain. He stumbled another ten yards, then another fuel drum went up and Ben fell again, the heat of the explosion washing over his body even through the cold rain. His ears were ringing, a single piercing note which blocked out all the chaos of the night. Ben stood up one more time and felt the depot yard spin drunkenly around him. His vision started to blur...

The Liberator. Pa. Molly. Going up in flames...

Images kept hitting Ben's mind, like a boxer hammering at a punchbag, leaving him numb.

Ghost. Moon. Lucy. Captured by the Feathered Men...

Ben shook his head vigorously, sending droplets of water flying, as he tried to regain his senses.

"Over here, Ben!" A voice cut through the clamour. At first Ben couldn't locate where it was coming from, then he spotted a figure with a claw for a hand, beckoning him with urgency. Carter was waiting for him in the shadows with Nathaniel and Valentine. Ben lurched towards them, his feet skidding on the gravel. With every step he heard the hungry howling of the Feathered Men in the distance, getting closer all the time. He was about to fall again when a hand clutched his arm hard enough to make him wince.

"Come on, boy. We need to run!" hissed Carter. "You're the Hand. If you fall, we *all* fall."

It was the truth and Ben knew it.

At that instant the scarlet eye of a signal flare winked open in the sky. It was the sign that Ben had been praying for. *Pa made it!*

With that rush of relief, Ben found new reserves of energy. The hole in the fence where they broke into the yard was just ahead and he burst into a sprint towards it. They needed to get through the wire and away from the Feathered Men that were already bounding across the yard and would soon be snapping at their heels.

Ben pushed Valentine and Nathaniel through the hole first, then burrowed after them, the barbs of the wire snagging at him. Carter brought up the rear.

"I've brought a little something to throw our feathered followers off the scent," said the professor, pulling hunks of raw meat from his pack and tossing them to the ground. "It's poisoned, of course," he grinned. "There's enough sedative there to knock out a bull elephant mid-charge."

Over his shoulder, Ben caught a glimpse of the Feathered Men tearing into the slabs of flesh.

That could have been me, Ben thought.

The four Watchers ran for their lives.

Beyond exhaustion, beyond pain, by twists and turns, bedraggled and bedevilled, the Watchers somehow managed to put some distance between themselves and the Legionnaires, who were still struggling to drag the Feathered Men away from their tainted feast.

"Lucy…" Ben gasped in between ragged breaths.

"Ghost... Moon... Did you see where the Feathered Men took them?"

"They flew in the direction of St. James's Park," said Carter.

"Oh no." Nathaniel's words came out as a low moan. "That means..."

"The detention camp," said Ben. A place of misery and pain. "We have to rescue them!" He almost shouted the words.

"Naturally," said Valentine, "but can we see about getting ourselves out of this scrape first?"

"Which way?" asked Nathaniel as they reached a crossroads. Every second that they spent out in the open was perilous. All it would take was one pair of beady eyes... "Any ideas?"

"This way," said Ben, leading them west down Marylebone Road. "I know a place. There's a loose window round the back. We can shelter there."

"Are we going where I think we're going?" said Valentine.

With a certain amount of pride Ben took them round the back of a forbidding building and presented the window. He flexed his fingers with a flourish, put them to the wooden frame and pushed. Nothing happened. Embarrassment flushed his face. He tried again, applying more force this time.

"I think it must have been mended," he said eventually. "It opened alright last time."

"Let me," said Carter, stepping forward. From one of the pockets of his long leather coat he withdrew an oddly shaped piece of rubber, which he then proceeded to lick. "Watch and learn," said Carter, pushing the suction cup against the pane until it stuck fast. He held the rubber with his good hand and then, using the tip of his claw, traced a circle on the glass. Carter pulled and, with a rasping sound, the glass came free. Then he reached in, flicked the clasp and drew the window wide. "Let's get inside," he said. "We've lost them for now, but they'll keep looking for us."

"How can you be sure?" asked Ben.

"If I were still in the Legion, I wouldn't stop until you were dead," Carter replied.

There wasn't much that Ben could add to that.

"We'll have to go carefully," he said when they had all clambered inside. "There's probably a nightwatchman doing his rounds."

"If there is, I bet he's asleep," said Nathaniel. "I don't have much good to say about the Legion, but the curfew pretty much guarantees that even the criminals stay off the streets at night, at least if they know what's good for them."

"We'll have a quick look-see anyway, make sure there's no one around," said Ben. "Then we can make our plans. We have to break the others out of the detention camp, they're vital to Revolution Day." *And to me.*

Ben lit the stump of candle he always had hidden in his pack. They had only turned one corner when the light fell on a figure standing sentry.

Treading carefully so that his wet boots didn't squeak on the tiled floor, Ben approached, moving closer until his candle was level with the man's unmoving face.

"Blimey," said Ben. "Ugly geezer, ain't he?"

"Steady on," warned Valentine. "Keep your voice down."

"He can't hear us," said Ben, rapping his knuckles on the man's forehead. "He's made of wax."

"I know," said Valentine through gritted teeth. "We're in Madame Tussaud's, *everything* is made of wax, but... let's go quietly anyway. Discretion is the better part of valour, and all that."

Silently they trooped down the hallway. It was an unnerving experience to be surrounded on all sides by lifelike figures, frozen in time. As they passed, the light from Ben's candle reflected in a dozen glass eyes and he couldn't shift the feeling that there was dark intelligence lurking behind their unmoving features.

He had felt so pleased with himself when he brought his friends here, but it was starting to feel like a mistake. Like so much that had been pleasurable in London before Sweet rose to power, all the joy, all the beauty, had been stripped away. When Ben had sneaked in before he had been delighted to see the statues of the great and the good. There had been waxworks of noble men like George Washington and Benjamin Disraeli. Ben remembered standing in front of Napoleon and giving the Frenchman a two-fingered salute. He had stared at Queen Victoria for a full five minutes, imagining himself knighted by Her Majesty for services to the realm. He had smiled himself silly at the likenesses of the actress Ellen Tree and the singer Jenny Lind, the so-called "Swedish Nightingale".

There had been one room that made the ladies shriek: the Chamber of Horrors. Bloodthirsty stuff it had been too. Victims of the French Revolution. Heads in baskets. Executioners with axes. Ben had played the big man, but he hadn't lingered. The waxworks really were uncannily realistic.

But the museum they were now touring in the dark seemed like one big Chamber of Horrors. In line with Mr. Sweet's terrifying new reign, Madame Tussaud's had been entirely devoted to London's new fashion for the grotesque. Here the monstrous was celebrated and murderers idolized. Ben felt himself go cold as they walked the gauntlet of inanimate killers. Then they turned a corner and he saw that the worst horror had been saved until last.

"I shouldn't have brought us here," said Ben, unable to drag himself away from the appalling diorama.

He felt an arm around his shoulder. "Come on," said Nathaniel, with a sudden tenderness. "It doesn't mean anything."

Each statue in the museum, each scene, had a small plaque so that the visitor knew what they were looking at. The sign beneath these figures read simply: *The End of the Watchers.*

Ben would have recognized these characters even without it. One of them was him. The face wasn't right, but the ginger hair was spot on. Beside him was a girl, with an eyepatch and honey-coloured hair. Next in line was an old man with a fierce expression and white marbles for eyes.

There was no mistaking those heads.

Ben couldn't comment on the bodies, because these heads were on sticks.

And standing over them was a huge Feathered Man.

"We need to get out of here, and get out now," said Carter.

"I'm alright," said Ben.

"You're not the reason," said Carter.

The Feathered Man blinked.

Ben reacted too slowly, his own gaze still fixed on Lucy's wax head.

The Feathered Man lunged forward with a shriek, its beak wide. Fortunately, Nathaniel still had his wits about him. He grabbed the back of Ben's collar and yanked his brother out of the path of those deadly jaws. Ben and Nathaniel both went sprawling and the Feathered Man's beak closed on empty air with a bone-snapping *clack!*

Carter dived forwards, putting himself between the foul creature and the young Watchers. The two circled each other warily, the fallen angel hissing. The Feathered Man spread its huge wings in a display of savage authority, sending the wax statues tumbling in the process, the heads rolling across the floor. Then it opened its mouth and gave a scream full of fury and hate.

An ordinary man would have turned and run in the face of such pure anger and vicious intent. Claw Carter, however, chose that instant to jump closer to the creature. Before the Feathered Man could react, Carter had it in a neck-lock and wrestled it to the ground, as if he was a cowboy taming a wild bull. The Feathered Man struggled, fighting back with all of its sinuous strength. But Carter's grip only tightened, starving the creature of air and sending a tremulous vibration through its great wings. Carter was unrelenting. Without loosening his vice-like hold, Carter reached out with his good hand and managed to pinch the gaping beak shut. Ben saw the shuddering that had started in the wing tips spread to the fallen angel's arms and legs, and still Carter squeezed. The Feathered Man's eyes appeared to bulge as its body cried out for oxygen and then, with a final pathetic flapping of its wings, it lost consciousness and collapsed.

Carter raised his claw to finish the job—

"No," said Ben, stopping Carter's arm in mid-air. "You've done enough. We're Watchers. We have to be different to the Legion, otherwise what's the point?"

Carter obeyed, although his face was lost in shadows and Ben could learn nothing from his flat tone. "Whatever you say, Ben."

They moved on without another word.

There were no human guards in the museum and eventually they found a back room away from the gaze of the unseeing eyes. Carter tore down some curtains to act as blankets and they each tried to find a comfortable place on the floor. Without warning, fatigue overwhelmed Ben. It was a tiredness stronger and heavier than even his concern for the captive Watchers, pushing him down into a sleep he was unable to resist.

What felt like minutes later, Ben woke with a gasp, his forehead clammy with sickly sweat. The feeble light at the window told him that dawn was breaking.

"Lucy!" Ben blurted, the word escaping from his dream and into the waking world. Nathaniel and Valentine were beginning to stir, disturbed by his outburst. Claw Carter was already awake. Ben wondered whether the professor ever slept at all.

"A tunnel," said Ben.

"What?" said Nathaniel, scrubbing his eyes with the heels of his hands.

"We're going to dig a tunnel."

Nathaniel still looked blank.

"Valentine," said Ben. "You know the Under better than anyone – could you get us beneath St. James's Park?"

"Where the Legion take their prisoners," said Carter, catching on.

"Precisely," said Ben. "We've got three days till May 1st, and we're gonna need Lucy, Ghost and Mr. Moon there with us."

Carter stroked his long chin. "We go under the park

and dig straight upwards into the compound." He sounded quite excited by the prospect. "I haven't been on an archaeological excavation for years. I have one question though…"

"Go on."

"Do we *really* have to rescue Moon?"

CHAPTER 8

SCOUNDRELS, LOWLIFES AND ROGUES

"We need to talk, Ben," said Nathaniel Kingdom.

For the last hour or so, Claw Carter had been guiding their small party. A secret trapdoor in the basement of Madame Tussaud's opened onto a stretch of cobwebbed tunnel, which in turn had connected them to the main hub of the abandoned Under. By the swaying light of his lantern, the professor's face was intermittently flung into stark relief. They could both see the broad smile on the man's long, lean face, the occasional flash of teeth in the darkness. Somewhat disconcertingly, Carter appeared to be thoroughly enjoying himself.

"I don't trust him," whispered Nathaniel, when Carter

and Valentine seemed far enough away. "He's even humming to himself! What sort of man hums when he's trying to break into a heavily armed detention camp?"

Ben paused and heard Carter's tune for the first time. It did sound very jolly, all things considered. "We need him," said Ben. "How else could we navigate through the Under?"

Nathaniel shook his head. "Stop being so naive, will you? We have no idea where he is taking us. He could be leading us into a trap for all we know."

"I trust him," said Ben flatly.

"You've always thought the sun shines out of his backside, Ben," said Nathaniel angrily. "When we were just nobodies, back on Old Gravel Lane, you were always running off to see your precious professor. It made Pa and I feel like we weren't anything to you—"

"Don't bring Pa into this," snapped Ben.

Nathaniel had jabbed a deep wound and Ben felt the urge to hurt his brother back. What Ben wanted to say was that Nathaniel had always had the lion's share of their father's affections. That Ben had felt lonely in their family of three, always the odd one out. Was it any wonder that he had enjoyed speaking to Carter? At least the professor had treated him as if he was worth listening to. Instead Ben clenched his teeth and kept the words inside;

if Mother Shepherd had taught him anything it was to think before he spoke. *Life and death is in the tongue, Ben. Every man speaks his own destiny, for good or for ill.*

"Carter is my friend," said Ben; it was the only explanation that he could give.

"Exactly," retorted Nathaniel. "The man who tried to kill *our* father is *your* friend. Think about it." Nathaniel drew his finger across his neck, and Ben chilled at the memory of Carter's claw making that same journey across Jonas Kingdom's throat. "You're some sort of chosen one now," Nathaniel continued, "the one the Watchers have been waiting for—"

"You're a Watcher, too," said Ben.

"Yes," said Nathaniel, "for about four months, the same as you. That hardly makes us experts, does it? Anyway, as I was trying to say, I can go along with the idea of you being a hero – you're my brother, after all..." Ben was relieved to see the spark of warmth returning. "I can even cope with Carter being forgiven, which is sort of what the Watchers are all about – everyone deserves a second chance an' all that. But what I'm struggling with, what we're *all* struggling with, is how you can make the sworn enemy of the Watchers your right-hand man."

Ben could see that Nathaniel was trembling slightly. It was clear that he had been bottling these feelings up for some time. Although he was younger than Nathaniel, Ben knew that it was up to him to be the bigger man – that was part of what being the Hand was about. He put his arms around Nathaniel, and although his brother resisted at first, they soon melted into a hug.

"Pa's somewhere outside the Wall," said Nathaniel softly. "Josiah's dead, Mother Shepherd's dead, Lucy's a prisoner, Mr. Moon's a prisoner, Ghost's a prisoner and who are we left with? Carter and Valentine, both sworn members of the Legion until recently. Truth is, Ben, I'm frightened. Claw Carter frightens me."

"I know," said Ben. "I've been flung into the role of leader and I can tell you I spend half my time feeling scared. But if being a Watcher means anything, I think it means that we have to be brave, to take a chance…a leap of faith. And sometimes the biggest leap is to believe that each of us can be more than anyone else imagines. Look at me, Nathaniel. Six months ago I was nothing, just another mudlark, up to his neck in muck and trouble, with no future to look forward to except working too hard and probably dying young. And now I'm the Hand of Heaven, so they say."

Nathaniel listened.

"The Watchers didn't see a street rat when they looked at me," said Ben, "they saw something more. That's what the Watchers do, Nathaniel – they look for the best in people's hearts...and they find it."

"Well, it was buried pretty bloomin' deep in Carter," said Nathaniel.

"You're not wrong," Ben laughed.

"DON'T MOVE, MOLLY!"

Jonas Kingdom hadn't meant to shout but Molly had to understand the danger she was in.

He approached the girl carefully, picking a path towards her through the rubble. His eyes flicked between the girl and the ground before his feet. They had all seen the explosions when escapees had blundered onto a landmine in Mr. Sweet's death zone. One wrong foot...

Molly was quaking now. She looked so vulnerable to Jonas; a frightened little waif, standing on a bomb in the rain. She had the blasted dog cradled in her arms, but Jonas was grateful for it – the three-legged mutt gave the girl some comfort, breathing against her face in short, hot bursts and licking her affectionately.

Jonas reached Molly's side. "You're going to be alright," he said. "I promise you that, but you have to promise me something too."

Molly nodded, her eyes wide with fear.

"You have to promise to stand as still as a statue."

Molly nodded again.

"Good girl," said Jonas and he crouched down to inspect the situation. In truth Jonas had never seen a landmine before and he had no idea how to disarm one, although he did have a rough knowledge of how the monstrous things worked. You stood on one and that set the primer, took your foot off again and *BOOM*.

"You there!" A voice called out to them from behind the army barricades. "Get in, man, you're making yourselves open targets!"

Jonas turned and saw a British officer beckoning to them urgently.

"We can't, sir," Jonas explained, gesturing to Molly's predicament with a sideways tip of his head.

"Oh, I see," said the officer calmly. "Stay where you are, the pair of you, I'm coming over."

The soldier walked briskly over and joined Jonas in an examination of the landmine. "Beastly things," he muttered. "A coward's weapon."

The soldier kneeled and drew a screwdriver from his pocket, keeping up a running commentary of his actions. "I've dealt with a few of the blighters before," he said, smoothing his hand over the metal surface of the device until he found a raised panel fixed with four screws.

He set to work quickly and efficiently, removing the plate so that he could get to the deadly workings inside. "These are an especially nasty sort. Sweet's thugs have added a clockwork timer..." The man squinted into the dim interior and fished in his pocket for a pair of wire-cutters. "The trick is..." he said, gingerly reaching inside, "to remember the right order when cutting the wires..."

Jonas was frozen to the spot. He had been in some tight corners himself but he had to admire this man's steely calm. Probably only a few years older than Jonas, the officer looked like a military man from a long line of military men; clear eyes, strong mouth, neatly brushed moustache. The British Empire had been built on men like him.

"Red before yellow kills a fellow," said the soldier with conviction. "So, yellow it is." With that, the soldier confidently cut the first wire in two, although Jonas noticed a flicker of relief cross his face when they weren't all blown to kingdom come. Satisfied that they were in the clear, the soldier even gave a little whistle as he cut the red wire.

In a gentlemanly fashion, the officer rose to his feet and extended his hand for Molly to take. "This way, if you please," he said, like a prince from a fairy tale.

"This is Clover," said Molly, holding up the toad-faced

bulldog and waving him in front of the soldier. "He wants to be your friend."

"And what's your name, young lady?" asked the officer.

"I'm Molly," she said, beaming.

Regardless of the downpour, the soldier unbuttoned his greatcoat and swept it round Molly's shoulders. She almost disappeared from sight within its folds.

"Right," he said briskly, "let's get out of this rain." He indicated a green canvas tent a little way back from the front line of ruined houses. "Temporary HQ. Not much to look at but there's a paraffin stove inside and I can promise you both a mug of tea."

"Will there be biscuits?" asked Molly.

"For you, young lady, there just might be," said the soldier with a smile.

Gratefully they walked over and stepped inside, welcomed by a wave of warm air. Molly put Clover down and ran straight for the stove, extending her hands towards it.

The officer put his own hand out for Jonas to shake. "I saw you piloting that airship. Very brave thing that, saved a lot of people."

"There's thousands more on the other side of that Wall," said Jonas. "They all need saving."

"We know," the soldier sighed. "Sweet's got us trussed up like turkeys at Christmas, damn his eyes. We daren't risk Her Majesty's life. But give me half a chance…" He slammed his fist into his palm and rubbed his knuckles. "At least the Prime Minister made it out, although he's a shadow of his former self. Seems that he was the victim of some sort of terrible mental torture."

The soldier looked weary. "Sorry," he said, "where are my manners? I'm Carnehan," he said smartly. "Brigadier Daniel Carnehan, commanding officer 1st Battalion Coldstream Guards."

"Jonas Kingdom, at your service."

Carnehan's face lit up. "Not related to *Ben* Kingdom, by any chance?"

"My boy," said Jonas.

"Very pleased to meet you, sir," said Carnehan. "All we ever hear from the escapees are extravagant tales about this Ben Kingdom and the 'Watchers'. You appear to have a very remarkable son."

Jonas nodded. "That's one way of putting it."

"And is our plucky young lady your girl?"

"I'm more of her guardian, actually," Jonas explained. "I knew her father…it's a sad story."

"Aren't they all?" said the brigadier thoughtfully. "A child should have a family. My wife and I always wanted children but…" Carnehan's eyes became distant for a moment before he returned to the matter in hand. He pulled two chairs closer to the stove.

"I have to ask you," said Carnehan, beckoning Jonas to sit. "Is everything set for Revolution Day?"

For the next half an hour, the Kingdom brothers followed Valentine and Claw Carter deeper into the Under. It was very different to the first time that Ben had descended into the Legion's secret world beneath the London streets. When the Legion had been in hiding, the Under had been a bustling community; albeit a community of scoundrels, lowlifes and rogues. Now, walking behind Carter, Ben had the feeling that he was actually on one of the professor's archaeological expeditions, visiting the decaying remnants of a lost society.

The Legion had no more need to skulk in the shadows. When Sweet swept into power, there was a mass exodus from the Under, as its denizens snatched whatever property on the surface took their fancy. Well-to-do families in Mayfair found themselves slung out to live in the gutter, like the beggars they used to despise. Rumour had it that the Savoy had become home to the most notorious murderers.

The abandoned Under was a ghostly place, Ben thought, full of shadows and dark memories. Cups still sat on tables, half-eaten food rotted on plates, chairs were overturned where their occupiers had stood in a hurry and never returned. And yet Ben had the eerie sensation that they were not alone.

They only had their lamps to guide them and Ben couldn't shake the feeling that when their feeble light passed by, the shadows were moving behind them. More than once they all stopped, listening for footsteps that were not their own. They weren't helped by the *drip-drip-drip* of falling water, echoing through the tunnels. There was almost as much rain down here as there was up top, thought Ben. It was leaking through the brickwork, finding every weakness in the mortar. In some places it was running freely down the walls, so that they were walking through icy puddles. Ben was glad that they didn't have to venture into the lower levels; all this water had to be going somewhere.

The other noise that surrounded them was the shrill squeaking of the rats. Thousands of them, Ben reckoned, all happily making the Under into their own kingdom. Everywhere Ben's eyes fell, he spotted their bloated bodies and naked pink tails. Scrabbling up bedsheets. Scurrying across tables. Scampering over furniture.

Chewing everything, defecating everywhere; their huge black eyes always searching for more.

In one of the deserted dormitories Ben saw a mattress which appeared to be undulating. It took a moment for him to realize that it was one solid mass of rodents. He pulled the door shut and walked swiftly by.

"This is it," Valentine declared, swinging his lantern up towards the ceiling. "We're directly beneath St. James's Park."

Ben was glad of Valentine's remarkable knowledge of the labyrinthine Under. And he liked the irony that the boy's distant ancestor, Sir Alasdair Valentine, was the original architect of the Legion's home back in the days of Henry VIII and now the Watchers were using that knowledge against them. Yes, despite Valentine's background, Ben trusted him. When Ben had met him, the boy had been at death's door, riddled with consumption, before the power of the Hand had restored him to health. The first thing Valentine did with his new strength was get as far away from the Legion as he could; that was good enough for Ben.

Carter tapped on the ceiling with the tip of his quarterstaff.

"Your friends are about fifteen feet that way," he said.

Your friends, Ben noted. Not *ours*.

"We need to start gathering as much wood as we can find. We'll have to shore up the sides of the tunnel as we dig," said Carter. "I suggest we split up, we'll cover more ground that way. Nathaniel, Valentine, you're on wood duty. Straight flat lengths are what we're after. Ben, I want you to come with me."

"Why?" said Ben, feeling the control of this rescue mission slipping from his hands.

"Two reasons, actually. Firstly, because I need you to help me collect some excavating equipment. There's a tool locker on this level. We can hardly dig with our bare hands, can we? And secondly" – he grinned that grin again – "I don't think some of the other members of your little gang want to be left alone with me." This with a pointed look at Nathaniel. "I don't blame them," said Carter, sounding very reasonable about it. "If the positions were reversed, I wouldn't trust me either."

Ben fell into step beside Carter and they set off together, his brother and Valentine heading in the opposite direction.

"Work on the tunnels never really stopped," Carter explained. "If I'm right, and I normally am, we should find a store with some picks, shovels and other basic equipment just round this corner."

Carter brought them to a wooden door and promptly

chopped the lock out with his claw. "Open sesame," he said.

As Ben stepped inside, the crunch of a footstep behind them alerted him to another presence skulking in the darkness. Then, before he could react, Carter shoved Ben forward savagely. Ben staggered blindly into the dark confines of the tool store, falling to his knees as he tripped. He was back on his feet in an instant, but it was too late.

Carter slammed the door shut, holding it closed with his full body weight.

Ben hammered on the wood. "Let me out!"

There was no reply.

Desperately, Ben pounded on the wood again.

"Professor!"

The only answer was silence.

All of Nathaniel's warnings about Carter screamed in Ben's mind.

How can I have been so wrong?

CHAPTER 9

SWEET DREAMS

Munro looked down at the dagger in his hand. He had never been on any of the skirmishes with the other Legionnaires. They said that his lame leg held them back, that his crooked back made him a liability. They were wrong. Just as so many people were wrong about Munro all the time; judging him only by what they saw on the outside.

None of them really knew him. Knew what he was capable of.

Munro played with the knife, testing its tip with the fat of his thumb. It came away bloody. Munro smiled grimly.

He was waiting for someone.

Munro had joined the Legion because no one else would have him. His father had been a loveless man who looked on his son and saw an opportunity for profit. That was how Munro had come to spend his early years touring in a freak show, standing on a stage so that other children could point and laugh and stare. And when Munro dared to disobey his father, his father punished him. Sometimes with a stick, sometimes with his belt, but always with anger.

So Munro ran away. He begged on the streets. He stole to live. Everyone turned their faces away from him. Except the Legion. They could always find a place for one more outcast.

In the Under, Munro was warm, he had food more often than not, and people to speak to. Mickelwhite, Bedlam, Valentine and Jimmy Dips were the first boys that Munro could call "friends", although they were often cruel to him too. He cooked for them, cleaned for them, acted as their slave. His reward was to be tolerated.

Hans Schulman showed him occasional glimpses of kindness, but these soon vanished when the other boys returned to the barracks. And there was a time when Munro had thought that Ruby Johnson was his true friend. But then she had run away hand in hand with Ben Kingdom without even pausing to say goodbye.

Munro had love in his heart; he could feel it there. But there was no one for him to pour out his love upon, and no one who loved him in return. Only Buster had helped to ease the loneliness. Dear old Buster. How Munro missed the feel of the dog's rasping tongue on his face, and the warmth of his body beside him as he slept. Munro had been prepared to serve Mr. Sweet, to give him lifelong devotion. But that changed that night on the Wall when Sweet had taken Buster from him.

That was why Munro was hiding behind the curtain in Sweet's private chamber in the Tower of London. That was why he had brought the knife.

It had been easy to get into Sweet's chambers. He was Munro the crookback. Munro the laughing stock. Munro the whipping boy. He'd told the guards that Mr. Sweet had appointed him to be his jester and not one of them had paused to consider that it might be a lie. No doubt they all thought it would be amusing to see the funny-shaped boy hopping around in a clown's multicoloured motley, hitting himself with an inflated bladder on a stick.

He'd show them.

The door opened and Sweet marched in. He was wearing a red cloak today, with a huge collar of white feathers which matched the ivory of his raven-skull helmet. Sweet closed the door and then slumped against it. He seemed very tired, Munro thought as he studied him through a gap in the curtains, keeping his own breathing as quiet and shallow as he could.

Sweet slipped out of his magnificent cloak and, with trembling fingers, attempted to hang it on its hook. He failed twice and threw it down on the floor in contempt. Then Sweet lifted the crown from his head reverently and placed it on a velvet cushion, while he removed his ivory mask. There was a slight sucking sound as the mask came away from the raw red flesh of Sweet's scalp, and Munro flinched.

Sweet was appallingly disfigured. The fire at the Feast of Ravens had stolen all of Sweet's hair and left his flesh puckered and blistered. No wonder he wanted to keep his face hidden. Children had poked fun at Munro, but they would run crying from this man.

Sweet returned his mask to its home on a plinth. It sat in line with a dozen other masks, all in the shape of carrion birds with sharp beaks. Then Sweet's hand reached out for the crown and placed it back on his head.

"I know you're there," snarled Sweet.

Munro started to shake. He looked at the dagger and wondered what he could have been thinking. There was no way that he could hurt anyone deliberately; he had been on the receiving end too often. He wanted to throw the awful weapon away but he didn't dare move.

Sweet spun round, as if trying to catch someone by surprise, but he was facing towards the fireplace, not the curtains. Munro was confused.

"Oh," said Sweet. "It's like that, is it? You want to play games?"

Sweet snatched up a poker from the fireplace and brandished it in front of him.

"I can see you," Sweet sang, like a schoolboy in the playground. "One, two, three, ready or not." Then he lashed out furiously, using the poker to sword fight with invisible enemies. He smashed the candlesticks from the mantelpiece and then swung round again, hacking and slashing until all of his masks were scattered and he was panting for breath.

"You can't have it, it's mine!" Sweet sounded like a petulant child, refusing to share. He dropped the poker with a rattle and then clung to the crown with both hands, backing into a corner and dropping down heavily on his backside.

"Why don't you just leave me alone? I can see you in the shadows... Stop laughing... Please..."

Through the slit in the curtains, Munro observed the man who had made himself a king. Sweet was twitching, his head moving jerkily as if he was trying to follow some will-o'-the-wisp, always flitting at the edge of his vision.

The clock ticked remorselessly. The logs in the hearth crackled. Gradually Sweet succumbed to a fitful sleep. Periodically he would jolt upright and wave his hands in front of his face. "The flames," Sweet groaned. "The flames."

Scarred on the outside, scared on the inside.

Munro didn't need to take revenge. This man was hurting enough already.

He left Sweet to his demons and slipped away.

Ben's confusion was replaced with anger.

Ben snatched up a sledgehammer and swinging it as best he could within the confines of the tool storeroom, he brought it down against the door with a splintering *crash!*

The door gave and Ben kicked it wide with his booted foot, the sledgehammer still raised and ready. He burst into the tunnel, ready to confront Carter for his betrayal.

The scene that met him in the corridor did not match the picture in Ben's mind. It took him a couple of seconds to understand what he was seeing.

Instead of looking ashamed, as any traitor should, Claw Carter was standing there as bold as brass, with one foot on the chest of a prone figure, looking like a hunter posing proudly over his latest kill.

Ben suddenly felt rather self-conscious and lowered his sledgehammer to the ground as nonchalantly as he could manage. "So," he blustered, "what did you shove me in there for?"

"Because, Ben Kingdom," said Carter with absolute sincerity, "not so long ago you saved my life. And if you hadn't already spotted, I have been trying to protect *yours* ever since."

"So," said Ben, squinting through the darkness at the figure struggling beneath Carter's boot, like a beetle pinned to velvet. "Who have we got here then?"

Carter shone his lamp on the situation.

"Jimmy Dips!" Ben declared, recognizing one of Mickelwhite's brigade. "Still sticking your long beak where it's not wanted, I see."

Jimmy seemed offended by that remark and his weasel face twitched.

"How long have you been following us?" said Ben. "What have you seen?"

"I wasn't following you," Jimmy protested. "I was hiding."

"Why?" Ben demanded. "You're one of the bad guys, and if you haven't noticed, the bad guys are winning."

"I wasn't looking for you, honest," Jimmy stuttered. "I'm hiding from Mr. Sweet."

At that name, Carter removed his foot. "Tell me more."

Jimmy took a deep breath, and massaged his throat where Carter's boot had left a mark. "He's a monster," said Jimmy finally. "None of us dare tell him anything that he doesn't want to hear. Everyone is afraid of him, *everyone*. He hates the Watchers, especially you two – no offence – but he's just as spiteful to Legionnaires who upset him. He locks himself away and spends his days screaming and shouting to himself. The things he's done..." Jimmy broke off and for a moment Ben thought the boy was going to cry.

"I always knew that Sweet wasn't man enough to wear the crown," said Carter with a broad smile. Ben wondered whether Carter was considering trying the crown on for size himself. It was not a comforting thought and Ben chose not to dwell on it.

"So," he said instead. "What shall we do with Dips?"

"He's seen us, so we can't let him go." Carter stroked his claw for emphasis. "But we can't take him with us either, there are already too many rats in this place."

"Are you thinking what I'm thinking?" said Ben.

"Probably not," Carter replied.

"Let's tie him up."

"But I'll never survive down here on my own," Jimmy protested.

"I'll leave you my lamp," said Ben. "You'll have light, and you'll be able to burn through your bonds... eventually."

"And in the meantime, we'll be long gone," finished Carter.

Jimmy seemed relieved. "Why would you even give me a chance?"

"That's what Watchers do," said Ben.

"Apparently," Carter added under his breath.

CHAPTER 10

DOWN AMONG THE DEAD MEN

"Looking for the freak show, are you, mate?"

Munro ignored the insult. Freaks weren't bad company anyway. In his experience, they were far better than the louts who leered and shouted their pathetic jibes.

Munro remembered all of the other unfortunates that he once shared his life with. Rufus the wolf boy, every inch of his body covered in shaggy hair; Pinhead Morgan, with his tiny head resting on normal-sized shoulders. Tim and Tom, the conjoined twins. Nice lads all of them. The owner of the show – *not* a nice man – christened Munro "Quasimodo" and made him bang his head against a large bell for the amusement of the crowd. Munro remembered the rotten fruit that pelted him. The spiteful words that were spat at him.

Something soft hit Munro square in the back, striking him between the shoulder blades with a filthy wet sound. Munro turned and saw a couple of yobs wearing Legion armbands and laughing as if it was the funniest thing in the world. Munro still had the dagger on his belt and his hand went to it, but he knew that he wouldn't use it. He wouldn't lower himself to their level. Instead Munro ignored it, as he ignored the million offences that had gone before, and he scurried on through the city.

The further away from Sweet and the Tower of London he got, the better Munro felt. But he knew this was only the beginning of his journey. He had no real plan. When he thought about it, he supposed that he might become a beggar somewhere. He'd rather be an apprentice, but no one took on a hunchback when they had a choice. His name was Scottish, someone had once told him, and he wondered if he could get as far as Edinburgh or Glasgow? Maybe he'd just keep walking, get as far away from London as he could. Find an island where he could be left alone.

A patrol turned the corner then and Munro did his best not to draw their attention. He was still in the Legion, so far as they knew, so there was no reason why they should pay him any heed. Wasn't he just another Legionnaire going about his business?

Then he felt their eyes on him. The familiar mixture of fascination and disgust.

"Look at that," said the first. "Bet he broke his mother's heart."

They all laughed and it stung Munro, even after all these years. He picked up his pace, dragging his lame leg behind him.

He could hear their laughter long after they were out of sight.

He missed Ruby. He missed Buster.

But he wouldn't miss the Legion.

Ruby Johnson was being carried through the air by Grey Wing. Like second-class baggage, she thought. Or a dead rabbit in a kestrel's claws. Sharp talons dug into her shoulders, bruising her through her jacket. They were flying at terrible speed, the wind and rain scouring her face. With each twist and jolt, Ruby could feel her stomach churning. She was going to be sick any moment – she wondered whether her vomit would land on some poor pedestrian's head.

The Feathered Man wheeled again, and began to dive

133

swiftly towards the ground. Ruby was so relieved when they touched down that she actually dropped to her knees on the soaking cobblestones. The wave of nausea passed and she rose unsteadily to her feet. She had no doubt that her face had turned as green as her eyes.

Grey Wing had acquired some information about the Gehenna Key. It seemed that the Watchers had hidden it on consecrated ground, presumably so the Feathered Men couldn't get their filthy talons on it. So here she was, dizzy and drenched, on Lupus Street in Pimlico, gazing up at the spire of St Saviour's church, ready to do their dirty work.

Ruby didn't know what the Gehenna Key was for. Presumably it would unlock a vault containing some fabulous treasure; she couldn't imagine what else would be worth so much fuss. What she did know was that she had to search every church in London until she found it. This could turn out to be a very long day.

The Feathered Man hissed at her, then shoved her rudely in the direction of the gate.

"That's no way to treat a lady," Ruby scolded, trying to maintain her veneer of calm.

As Ruby crossed through the gateway and approached the grand arched doors, she had a sudden troubling thought. In her time, she had known more than one vicar who helped himself to the Sunday collection or drank most of the communion wine. She had also brushed up against some brazen villains who proudly went to church on Sunday and happily broke your legs on a Monday, and none of them had ever been struck by lightning. If the Feathered Men couldn't even put their toe on holy ground, then they had to be truly evil indeed.

Ruby glanced over her shoulder and the creature leered at her, watching her every move. She tried the handle of the door, but it was locked; a sign of the times. Fishing in her satchel, she pulled out her lock picks and was inside in under a minute. As the door closed behind her, Ruby rested her back against the solid wood and exhaled.

She had never been one for churches, mainly on account of her being a professional thief, and yet she couldn't deny that she felt a strange sense of peace in here. Or maybe it was just the fact that she would be spending a few minutes without the threat of being eaten alive by a fallen angel that felt pleasant.

Ruby stared down the long aisle, stately pews arranged on either side. Above her head, the vaulted roof was supported by graceful arches and pillars. It was all very imposing, but her eyes were drawn irresistibly to the altar.

All that silver! How had the looters missed that?

Ruby found that she was almost running by the time she reached it.

She had no idea how long she could keep being useful to Grey Wing. She knew that she had to find this key thing soon, but she also couldn't help wondering whether that would be the end of their not-very-comfortable arrangement. So in the meantime she had to get as much loot for herself – even in Sweet's new order, money still had a way of opening doors. And when she had enough, it would be "Goodbye, Legion", "Goodbye, London", "Hello, new beginning".

Ruby lifted the huge cross in the middle of the altar, but it was too big and bulky to fit easily in her sack. Instead she gathered up the candlesticks – nice pair, good craftsmanship – and a sort of silver dish with a lid, which she thought they kept the communion wafers in or something. They clanged together in her bag and it was only then that Ruby heard another sound, so near that she almost dropped her swag completely.

The never-ending rain made the sky black outside and the church was filled with shadows. The sound had stopped now, but Ruby knew that she had not been mistaken. She drew out one of the candlesticks. It was hefty enough to use as a weapon if push came to shove.

"I know you're there!" she called out.

Nothing.

Then the sound again. The soft scuffing of shoe leather on tiles; heavy breathing. Muffled tears.

"Who's there?"

Ruby braced herself for fight or flight, checking for the nearest way out, searching for movement in the church. It didn't feel peaceful any more, that was for sure.

Then she spotted a small head, peering out from behind one of the pews. It was just a kid – a frightened child with a dirty face and deep, tired lines around his eyes. As Ruby watched, two more heads popped up; a brother and a sister, she guessed – they had the same noses. Then, finally, a woman appeared, whose long hair was once probably very beautiful but was now matted and dirty. She spread her arms protectively around the children's shoulders and drew them closer.

"Don't hurt us," she said. Then, with a pained look at the doors and the brutal world outside, she added, "Please don't tell anyone, I'm begging you."

Ruby looked at the candlestick in her hand. It was one thing to be a thief when no one was looking, but it was quite another to be caught in the act. She didn't feel guilty exactly, but she wasn't proud of herself.

"It's for starving orphans," she said, by way of explanation. *Well, starving* orphan, *anyway.*

The family continued to stare at her.

"Is this your church?" Ruby asked. She might still be able to turn this to her advantage. Some local knowledge might prove very useful.

The youngest nodded.

"I bet you know all about it, don't you?" said Ruby.

The girl nodded again, enjoying the attention, although her mother still seemed wary.

"I'm looking for something very special," Ruby continued.

"Is it pirate treasure?" piped up the middle boy.

"Sort of," said Ruby, "but it is hidden."

"Definitely treasure then. Did the pirates leave any clues?"

It was a good question, and one that Ruby herself had put a lot of thought into. If the Watchers had hidden the key, then maybe she needed to think like a Watcher to find it. She had made a mental list of what she knew about the Watchers. They thought they were something special, she knew that much. They lived on the rooftops; should she be searching amongst the rafters? Out on the roof itself? They were non-violent, in a hit-you-with-a-stick rather than a stick-you-with-a-knife sort of way. Their symbol was an open hand, which always made Ruby think of surrender. What else? Ben Kingdom was a Watcher. So was that aggressive one-eyed girl, Lucy something. And Jago Moon; the blind bully, as the Legion liked to think of him.

"The pirates sometimes mark their spot like this," said Ruby, playing along with the boy's fantasy. She lifted her right hand and made the Watcher symbol. "Have you seen that secret sign before?"

The boy screwed up his face in concentration and scratched his head, sending lice scurrying. He looked as if he was on the verge of a great announcement.

"Yes?" said Ruby hopefully.

"No," said the boy.

"I have," said the girl, to her brother's obvious annoyance. And before her mother could pull her back, she scampered away down the aisle.

"Look, look," said the girl, pointing to a grave slab embedded in the church floor.

Brushing away the dust, Ruby read the inscription:

18TH NOVEMBER 1755 – 1ST JANUARY 1803
HERE LIES THE BODY OF
OBADIAH MOON
"RESIST THE DEVIL AND HE SHALL FLEE."

Obadiah Moon. *You've got to be kidding me… So they've been Watchers for generations.*

The epitaph went on and on and got really boring *really* quickly, but right at the end Ruby found what she was looking for. Hidden amid the curlicues was the Watcher symbol. Her heart beating heavily, Ruby placed her thumb on the symbol and applied pressure. Then came the *click* as a hidden panel came loose.

Curiosity seemed to have overcome the whole family and they gathered to stare over Ruby's shoulder as she carefully lifted the lid. Tentatively Ruby explored the dark hole with her fingers, dreading finding bones. When she found only dirt and grit, she grew bolder, pushing her hand into the corners and recesses of the concealed safe-box. There was nothing that felt like a key and Ruby's lip began to curl into a snarl of disappointment. *But wait, what was this?* Tucked in the furthest corner was a small square of folded parchment. *It might be a clue!* Ruby retrieved it carefully, blew away a layer of dust and then unfolded the delicate paper...

In a very elegant hand, it read: *You'll get no secrets from me, Legion SCUM!*

In anger, Ruby screwed it into a ball. Outside Grey Wing was screaming manically. Thunder rumbled like the gates of hell opening and the children pushed themselves against their mother for safety.

"I have to go," said Ruby quietly, "but I won't let on about you, I promise."

For some reason she thought of Ben Kingdom then, and wondered what he would do.

Just as she was about to leave, her conscience nagged at her and she dug into her bag, pulling out a hunk of bread and cheese that she had been saving. "This is your fault, Ben," she muttered under her breath. She gave the food to the little girl with some resentment, but the gratitude in the child's eyes caught her off-guard; it was almost overwhelming.

"Thank you, thank you, thank you," the children chorused.

"God bless you, miss," said the mother.

"It's not much," said Ruby, awkward with embarrassment.

She headed for the doors and the storm beyond. Outside the rain hit her. It was cold on her face and it should have brought clarity, but her feelings were confused. She'd needed that food for herself, and yet wished that she had more she could give.

Ruby walked slowly down the path to where Grey Wing was lingering, trapped on the unholy side of the gate. Her bag bulged with stolen silver, but she had failed to find the key... She said nothing as the foul creature plucked her into the sky again, heading for the next church to desecrate. The ground spun away, the buildings shrinking to tiny doll's houses as they flew up and up. Ruby shut her eyes and tried not to think about falling. The talons were like daggers, and Ruby had no doubt that the Feathered Man was hurting her for the pleasure of it. She opened one eye and regretted it, feeling sick immediately.

And yet in spite of everything, a small smile warmed Ruby's lips.

Those kids, their mother, were safe.

It felt like a triumph.

Chapter 11

The Coming Storm

Ben's shoulders screamed as he hacked away with his shovel. Sweat stung his eyes. The palms of his hands were raw with blisters, but he refused to give up, refused to slow down. Lucy was up there, in the detention camp. So was Ghost; so was Mr. Moon. He had to save them.

Ben, Carter, Nathaniel and Valentine worked relentlessly in five-minute shifts, pitting themselves against the dripping ceiling of clay. They had been working on the tunnel for so long that time had lost all meaning. None of them spoke, they only grunted with effort, but words were no longer necessary between them anyway. They were a machine with four parts working as one.

The digger was the first job, and this was the role that Ben attacked most eagerly. He hacked at the clay above him with a fury, inching his way towards Lucy. Holding the shovel over his head, Ben used it more like a pickaxe, chipping away at the layers of compacted soil. He kept his Watcher goggles on when he was the digger, shielding his eyes from the rain of falling debris. When they'd begun work on the shaft – what felt like a lifetime ago already – Ben had been forced to balance precariously on a makeshift ladder; but now he was able to brace himself against the sides of the shaft, supporting himself with his outstretched legs until his thighs burned and his calves trembled uncontrollably.

The propman was next. His role was to support the sides of the shaft to stop the wet clay from slipping in, using planks of wood salvaged from the Under. Carter had to teach all of them how to shore up a vertical shaft. Ben had worked with wood before, making barrels as an apprentice to Mr. Smutts, but this task was made all the harder by the sodden clay they were trying to hold back. Periodically one of the lengths of timber would slip, forced out of place by the weight of oozing earth. The first time it happened it caught Ben off guard. All of a sudden a plank burst out of position with splintering strength. The jagged length struck Ben hard on the temple, filling his vision with stars. He ignored the pain, letting the blood roll down his cheek to mingle with the sweat and dirt, but even as he got back to work he listened for the telltale creak, the three-second warning that the wood was on the move again.

The wood was provided by the scavenger, third man in the crew. It was a simple enough job – find wood and find it quick. For the first couple of hours Ben was able to ransack nearby chambers in the Under, grabbing bedboards, breaking tables into planks, chairs into props. After that, though, he had to travel further and further afield. Ben ran until his lungs burned and his side ached with a stitch that stabbed deeply enough to bend him double. Still he ran.

Fourth man was the clearer, whose job was to shovel away the debris from the shaft, stop the ladder from falling and pass up the wooden props. Clearing was unremitting, the mound of soil never seeming to diminish. Plus, as Ben discovered to his cost, it also ran the risk of injury when rocks, broken props and, on one occasion, a hefty hammer which slipped from a wet palm, could come crashing down on your head at any moment.

Rainwater continued to soak through the soil, forever undoing the work they had just done. Ben was dead on his feet. And yet he couldn't help but smile, knowing that the escape tunnel was being made possible by two ex-Legionnaires. It was Valentine who had led them to this point in the Under, directly beneath the prison camp. And it was Carter's knowledge, gleaned from a hundred archaeological digs, which enabled them to prop the shaft they were digging and prevent the whole thing from collapsing down on top of them. Carter, Knight Commander of the Legion, the scourge of the Watchers, and now the instrument of their salvation.

Get ready, Lucy. Get ready, Ghost. Get ready, Mr. Moon.

The Watchers are coming.

In the depths of the Under, the water was rising.

"Let. Me. Go!" shouted Queen Victoria. "I demand that I am released *immediately*!"

There was authority in those words, a streak of iron in the old woman's voice, but Josiah knew that she was calling in vain.

"Victoria," he said, speaking to his neighbour through the wall that separated them. For all her fire, Victoria was a grandmother and a widow, yet here she was, locked in the dark, with rats and bones for companions and with the water level rising by the hour. "You must save your energy," Josiah urged.

"I cannot rest," Victoria protested. "My people need me."

Here was a woman worthy of being Queen, Josiah thought. There was not one trace of self-pity in her words, only spirit and strength.

"Sweet has betrayed me," she continued. "I blame myself for not recognizing a villain with my own eyes. Just to think, that contemptible man has even dined at the palace."

"Evil often wears a pleasing mask," said Josiah.

"Yes, yes, I know that," said Victoria, prickling with irritation. "But it isn't often so bold as to take over one's government and then plant its ignoble backside on *one's throne*. What will become of my subjects with that lunatic as their ruler?" Her voice rose. "And how could such a repellent man as Oliver Sweet get even one true Englishman to follow him?"

"I told you about the Crown of Corruption and its fiendish power," said Josiah. "The weak-willed cannot stop themselves from obeying him... Although it is true that others have made the choice to follow evil without any such compulsion."

"One understands that," said Victoria, still bristling. "But does that mean that we will be left to rot here?" She was in full flow now. "Is that what you are saying?"

"No," said Josiah firmly. "Ben Kingdom has a plan, I sense it." His words carried with them the golden glow of faith. *"The Watchers are coming."*

High up on the Wall the rain was beating down as yet more clouds gathered to bring misery to London.

Mr. Sweet walked alone on the battlements. Alone except for damned voices inside his head and the ghosts that haunted him day and night. The Others were so loud, Sweet couldn't believe that no one else could hear them.

When he took the Crown of Corruption he had expected to hear just one voice – *his voice* – the loudest and most powerful in the land. But since the moment the crown touched his brow, Sweet had been bombarded by the Others and their ceaseless whispering. If he looked into a mirror, he saw a dozen faces staring back. The Others never left him. If Sweet walked into a room, they would be waiting for him; they lurked in the corners, under his bed, behind the door.

Sweet didn't know who the ghosts were, but he recognized something in them. They were the same as him; greedy for power, hungry for more. Insatiable. Ungovernable. These were the spirits of the men and women who had held the Coins before he did. Even in death, they couldn't let go of the Judas silver.

In his moments of clarity, when the voices were quietest, Sweet wondered whether it would have been different if his coronation had been completed in accordance with the prophecies of the Dark Library. The day had been right for him to take the crown – the Feast of Ravens, the night when the powers of evil were at their height. But there had been no sacrifice, no ceremony; Ben Kingdom had denied him that.

Sweet found his lip twisting into a snarl. He could feel the tugging of his flesh where the fire had wrinkled his skin like an apple left to rot. He would have his vengeance on that boy.

The guttersnipe was being hailed as the Hand of Heaven, the one who would defeat the Legion.

Sweet feared and hated the boy in equal parts.

"Ben Kingdom has a plan," the Others taunted. *"The Watchers are coming."*

DAY THREE
29TH APRIL, 1892

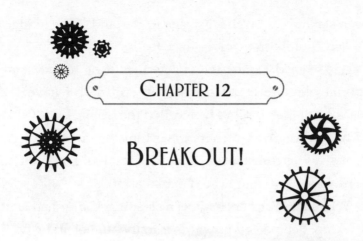

CHAPTER 12

BREAKOUT!

Ben didn't know when he had fallen asleep. He remembered that he had kept digging until all his strength had been spent, and only his willpower had kept his arms moving mechanically. Every muscle was complaining as he forced himself back up onto his feet and rolled up his sleeves. Valentine and Nathaniel were sleeping too, sprawled over a mound of wet clay from their excavations. His brother looked filthier than a mudlark, Ben thought and smiled as he remembered those simpler days.

"Good morning, my boy," Carter said cheerily as he hopped down from the vertical shaft that they had all been slaving on. "Welcome back to the land of the living."

Ben couldn't remember ever feeling so weary and yet Carter seemed almost rejuvenated, as if he found some special pleasure in adversity. Ben still didn't have the measure of the man, but he recalled the feelings of joy that *he* had when the Watchers gave him the chance to rise above his circumstances, and he was too dog-tired to think of a more complicated explanation.

While the Watchers had been sleeping, Carter had kept working. Ben peered upwards into the tunnel and gave a low whistle – Carter had cut another three feet through the mud on his own.

"I'm impressed," said Ben.

"Good," said Carter, "I hate to be unappreciated."

Then Ben's nose twitched; he hardly dared to believe what he was smelling. "And now I'm really impressed."

As well as scavenging oil lamps to light their work, Carter had also managed to find a hunk of ham, which was sizzling in a frying pan over a small paraffin stove.

"How?" said Ben, his stomach growling in anticipation.

"I've led expeditions across the glaciated plains of the Karakoram mountains, south of the great Tibetan plateau; I've crossed the endless dunes of the Kalahari desert; and I've never let my party go hungry. Although we did have to eat one of the native Sherpas once." Carter saw the expression of horror rising on Ben's face. "Sorry, Ben, just my sense of humour."

Cannibalism, thought Ben. *Ha bloody ha.*

Still, the bacon did smell wonderful and the other boys were being lured back into wakefulness by its siren call.

"Dig in, lads," said Carter, cutting off a thick slice for each of them.

Nathaniel grinned and juggled a hot piece of meat in his fingers before tearing off a chunk with his teeth. "Handsome," he said appreciatively.

"A most welcome repast," said Valentine, wrapping his own bacon in a handkerchief before gnawing at the corner.

The greasy bacon was such a treat that Ben found himself smiling even while his tongue was burning. "Ain't life grand," he said when he was finished, cuffing the fat off his lips appreciatively. "How much further do you reckon then, Professor?"

"By my calculations, we should break surface at daybreak, when with any luck the prisoners will be in the yard and the guards will be groggy," said Carter. "There's less than three feet to go."

"So what are we waiting for?" said Ben, sprinting to the foot of the shaft and monkeying up inside. "We've got Watchers to rescue."

* * *

With a crack like thunder, the whip lashed out. Lucy flinched as she felt its sting across her back but she didn't make a sound – she refused to give her guard the satisfaction. Instead, Lucy kept the agony bottled up inside, sealed with a promise. *Two days until the revolution,* she thought as she regarded the Legionnaire with the whip. *Just you wait until 1st May...*

Lucy had been roused from sleep before sunrise. Along with Ghost and Mr. Moon and all the others who had incurred Mr. Sweet's displeasure, she had been billeted in one of the wooden dormitories that had been erected in the detention camp. There were no beds to sleep on, no blankets to sleep beneath, just bare boards and the promise of death for anyone attempting to escape.

As a Watcher, escape had been on Lucy's mind from the second that the Feathered Men had brought her and her friends to St. James's Park. The detention camp was a desolate place. Like everything else that Mr. Sweet put his hand to, what once had been a place of beauty and joy was now home to misery and despair. A tall chain-link fence penned in the prisoners like cattle. Coils of barbed wire ran along both the top and foot of the fence. Anyone trying to get out that way would be cut to ribbons. As if that wasn't enough, every sixty feet or so, manned watchtowers loomed over them. Lucy had been studying the movement of the guards, searching for a weakness, but she hadn't found one. There were never less than six Legionnaires to each tower, ceaselessly scanning the camp with binoculars. There were rifles pointed in all directions, ready to halt any rescue attempt from the outside and quash any troublemakers inside.

"Eyes down!" the guard snarled again. "Keep walking."

Grudgingly, Lucy obeyed and fell into step with the other prisoners.

Ghost was in front of her. Moon was behind her. All day long they were forced to march up and down in the rain, in ranks ten wide by ten long, like an old Roman Legion. The difference was that the Roman soldiers had been training to reach the peak of physical fitness, whereas the prisoners were being walked to death. There was no let-up, no allowance for tiredness or thirst or aching hunger. You marched through the rain or you tasted the lash of the whip.

Lucy marched.

Movement over by the main gate caught her attention. She squinted through the rain. "New arrivals?" she whispered.

"No," said Moon, his two ears trumping her one eye. "You can hear from the sound of the suspension that the wagon is empty. This is something different; our old friend Mickelwhite has come calling with some of his brigade."

"You're sure?"

"Bedlam is wearing that boot with a squeak," said Moon. "He rolls his shoulders as he walks to try and make himself look big and he always favours his left leg. As for Mickelwhite, well..." Moon allowed himself a chuckle. "Even in all this mud he still walks like he's the lord of the manor and we're all dirt beneath his feet. His buttocks are so clenched I'm surprised everyone can't hear them squeaking too."

The wagon was a Black Maria, the sort of reinforced wagon that the police used to round up suspects, with four black horses harnessed to the carriage. The prison gates closed behind it and were locked again. As Lucy watched, Mickelwhite and Bedlam joined the guards, the rain dripping from their hoods and for a minute they joked coarsely while they warmed their hands around a blazing brazier. Two Feathered Men were chained beside them, like the largest, most ferocious guard dogs she could imagine; vicious and slathering. Mickelwhite laughed again and then pointed a long finger in the direction of the prisoners.

"Can you make out what he's saying?" whispered Lucy.

"Not all of it," said Moon. "Something to do with a circus. Whatever it is, it sounds nasty. Mickelwhite has come here to round up some participants."

The joking stopped and Mickelwhite marched over, shouting orders to the camp guards. "Line this miserable lot up!"

Instantly the guards began to bully the prisoners until they were standing in front of Mickelwhite, like troops awaiting inspection. Lucy, Ghost and Moon were three rows from the front. It wouldn't be long before Mickelwhite spotted them.

Ghost took one look at Lucy's flowing honey-gold hair and quickly whipped off his own scarf, wrapping it around her head. Lucy tied it tight and tucked the last few strands out of sight. Both their faces were brown with mud. It wouldn't stand up to close inspection, but it might be enough...

Mickelwhite began to pace up and down in front of them, strutting like a cockerel.

You," he addressed the prisoners, "have dared to defy our lord and master, King Oliver the Merciless! You have forfeited your right to citizenship in New London. But, His Majesty is prepared to offer you a chance at freedom."

A murmur went up. This had to be some sort of trick; it couldn't be true.

"I'm looking for volunteers for a...sporting event."

"I don't like this," said Moon darkly.

"If any man or woman here can stand five rounds in the ring with Mr. Sweet's champions, then they will receive his royal pardon and a second opportunity to take the Mark and start your life again."

Lucy spat on the ground; she couldn't stop herself. The Mark was the sign of allegiance to the Legion, a burning brand on the left palm which labelled you for ever as a servant of evil. That was not freedom as she understood it.

Even so, a young man standing in the row in front of Lucy cautiously raised his hand. "I'm in," he called.

Lucy ground her teeth as she felt Mickelwhite's arrogant gaze sweeping in her direction. She allowed her head to drop and hoped that it would be disguise enough. However, even as she lowered her chin to her chest, a movement behind Mickelwhite roused her interest.

The ground was moving.

A small spot, perhaps a dozen feet behind Mickelwhite, was writhing. Was it a mole?

Lucy couldn't drag her eye away. The soil continued to stir and then a single lump of bedraggled turf rose ever-so-slightly into the air. Lucy blinked. Surely it couldn't be...?

Ben!

She almost shouted out and her hand went to her mouth involuntarily. Ben had dug a tunnel. Lucy nudged Ghost and signalled with her eye but Ghost, ever vigilant, had already seen it.

Unfortunately so had some of the other prisoners.

A frisson ran through the ranks. One woman actually pointed in Ben's direction. "That's him, it's got to be," she said, so loudly she may as well be shouting.

"Shut it," said Lucy through gritted teeth. "You'll give the whole game away."

Moon had picked up enough from the whispers all around him. "Ben's come for us," he said. "Good lad."

A man in the front row stepped forwards, edging himself towards the hole. Then a second followed and a third.

Mickelwhite clapped his hands together in malicious glee, assuming that they were volunteers for his circus. But when more and more began to shuffle in his direction, his expression changed.

"Halt! I command you!"

"We go *now*," said Moon, his voice full of steel. "If we don't, it'll be too late."

With that, he put his hand in the small of Lucy's back and propelled her towards the tunnel, while he lowered his own head and barrelled towards Mickelwhite.

"Oi!" shouted Moon. "You, with the silver spoon in yer gob. Yes, you! Mickelwhite! You flap-mouthed whey-face! I'm talkin' to you!"

The Old Watcher shouldered through the crowd and threw himself at Mickelwhite before the Legionnaire could react.

"Ben Kingdom sends his love," said Moon, grabbing the captain by the shoulders and then butting him in the face.

"You've broken my nose, you old codpiece," Mickelwhite cursèd as he dropped to the ground. The guards in the watchtowers noticed the commotion and immediately shots began to ring out.

Lucy ran towards the tunnel for all she was worth, but others made it there before her, diving for the hole and half-falling, half-climbing out of sight.

It was a stampede.

Lucy had once seen a bull break loose in Smithfield market. Before the beast could be brought under control, seven people had been hospitalized and two were dead. But the animal hadn't caught anyone on his horns; the victims had all been crushed to death by other people. Lucy remembered the wave of terror that had spread through the market, the screams as people ran in every direction, falling over themselves in their panic to get away, trampling friends and family underfoot. That was what was happening in the camp.

Lucy saw men and women slipping in the mud as they dashed towards their only chance of freedom. The two Feathered Men had been let off their chains and one snatched up an escapee, shaking the man vigorously until the snapping of bones ended his escape attempt. Moon was surrounded by Legionnaires, lashing at him with their whips. Ghost was nowhere to be seen at all.

A stray bullet zinged past Lucy's ear. From the tower, Legionnaires were alternately firing rounds into the air and peppering the mud with shots in an attempt to force the prisoners back. Other guards ran across the yard, knocking prisoners down with their rifle butts, pushing them away from the tunnel and back towards their huts. Lucy caught more horrific glimpses of the Feathered Men's ferocity, driving the detainees back against the wire fence. Red splashes in the rain.

From one of the watchtowers, the dreadful wail of a siren cut through the air, summoning more of the fallen angels from their roosts, more Legionnaires to quash the escape. Another bullet hit the mud just in front of Lucy's feet. It was now or never.

She poured every last reserve of strength into a final push. Legionnaires were advancing from every direction and a hail of bullets and crossbow bolts sliced across her path. Incredibly she came through unscathed and threw herself into a dive, sliding across the mud on her belly until she was peering down the shaft.

Mud-slick bodies were scrambling down ahead of her but there was no mistaking the figure at the foot of the shaft, helping them on their way.

"Ben!"

She lowered herself over the edge. She was so relieved to see Ben that she didn't notice the Feathered Man swooping down until its beak was snapping at her face.

Lucy gasped in shock – then gasped again as a crossbow bolt pierced the creature's neck. Hurriedly she continued her descent, her feet scrabbling for purchase in spite of her Watcher skyboots. Just as her head dropped below the surface she caught sight of Ghost running after her, his stolen crossbow still raised.

It was a tight squeeze in the shaft. Lucy braced herself with her hands and feet, but the supporting props were slick with rain and she flinched as first her foot slipped off the wall, then a plank came away in her hand with a squelching sound.

Her heart was racing by the time she reached the bottom and almost fell into Ben's arms.

"I thought for a moment you were going to stand me up," said Ben.

Lucy smiled. "I'm washing my hair tonight," she said.

Claw Carter was waiting at the end of the passageway with Nathaniel, their hands outstretched to the fleeing prisoners who slithered and stumbled towards them. Ben knew that Valentine had bravely gone on ahead to lead the escapees to safety – hopefully they'd all meet up again at today's rendezvous. Ben was thrilled that so many had got out of the camp, but he knew that time was running out and he searched every face for Ghost and Mr. Moon.

Looking up through the shaft, Ben caught a fleeting glimpse of Ghost's shaven head peering down. Ben's hopes soared – only to be dashed again as a Legionnaire grabbed Ghost by the shoulders and yanked him away. Ben made to climb up after him but he halted as a rumble filled the underground corridor. The whole tunnel began to judder and a fine rain of dirt began to fall...

"Run!" shouted Carter. "Ben. Lucy. RUN!"

Lucy's ears rang as the props began to snap away from the sides of the shaft with the explosive bangs of Chinese firecrackers. Ben grabbed her hand and began to wrench her away from the danger but the roaring darkness was just too quick. With a hideous, hungry slurp the mudslide filled the shaft, winking out the light. Tons of slick soil collapsed in on top of them. Lucy clung to Ben's hand for dear life, but her fingers were not strong enough and as the falling earth smashed her to the ground she lost grip.

Mud filled Lucy's mouth. Her ears. Her nostrils.

Help! thought Lucy.

And then the mud stopped her thinking anything at all.

CHAPTER 13

THE SLEEP OF THE GRAVE

All that Ben could taste was mud.

He was disorientated, unsure of which way was up, or where he had fallen. The tunnel had disintegrated completely, burying him and Lucy, and goodness knew how many others, in a wall of clay and timber and debris. The darkness was absolute. Ben's goggles had prevented his eyes from being caked in liquid mud, but there was nothing to see. He felt like a fly trapped in treacle; the more he tried to move his limbs, the deeper the mud drew him in.

Mercifully, Ben had fallen with one hand near his face and he was able to scoop the soil out from between his lips. He snorted through his nostrils at the same time and, coughing and choking, he found that he was able to breathe a little more easily. Feeling with his free hand, he determined that there was a small air pocket around his face, although how long the air would last was anybody's guess. *Small breaths*, Ben told himself.

He realized then that he might die here like this. If the others had been crushed beneath the falling rubble and sea of suffocating mud, then this would be the end. Of him. Of the uprising. Of London.

Stuff that, thought Ben. It was his right hand that was free. The Hand of Heaven. And he used it to dig.

More than anything, Ben wanted to make sure that Lucy was safe and that added strength to his movements. His fingers touched something and he recognized it as a shoe. He ran his fingertips across it; more particularly it was a Watcher skyboot, he could tell by the gripped sole. *Lucy!*

He grabbed it firmly and gave a little tug. The foot inside did not respond at all.

Suddenly, in the small space he'd cleared around himself, a scattering of soil pattered down from above. Although his ears were full of dirt, he sensed vibrations through the debris. He wasn't alone, someone was digging him out! With that revelation, Ben felt the Hand of Heaven crackle with energy; a prickling sensation which grew into a heavy pulse of raw power. Ben recognized the feeling and welcomed it.

As the soil continued to shift around him, Ben freed his other arm and then put his heart and soul into unearthing Lucy.

He enjoyed a thrill of optimism as he found Lucy's hand. He squeezed it for reassurance.

"I'm here, girl. Hang on."

Lucy's fingers were cold and limp.

A hole appeared and through that hole came a beam of lamplight and Claw Carter's broad hand.

Ben clasped it firmly around the wrist and allowed himself to be dragged from the mudslide. His brother, Nathaniel, was there to greet him too. "I thought we'd lost you," he said softly.

"Lucy," Ben said, his breathing ragged as he gasped in mouthfuls of air. "Help me."

The three of them dug for all they were worth, throwing the waterlogged soil behind them in a frenzy of movement, until they had gradually revealed their friend's motionless form. Ben had a terrible sense that they were grave robbers, and once the idea had lodged itself in his mind it proved impossible to shift. When Lucy's body was finally free they fell into a stunned silence. Her lips were blue. Her eyelids were not moving.

Her chest was still.

Ben dropped to his knees and pushed his fingers between Lucy's lips, scooping out a handful of mud. No response.

Watcher training had taught Ben far more than just how to do battle. He pressed his lips to hers, shocked at the coldness of their touch. Then he breathed his own air into her lungs, expecting her to cough and come back fighting, just as she always had before.

Nothing.

Ben felt the terrible coldness begin to seep into *his* flesh too.

Not Lucy.

He tried again.

Nothing.

From somewhere in the tunnels of the Under came the sound of footfalls and the shrieks of Feathered Men fast approaching.

"Lucy!" Ben shouted. "Come back to us! Come back to me!"

Still nothing.

"Ben," said Carter, picking up his lamp. "We've got to go."

"I'm not leaving her."

Carter glowered. "Only *you* can defeat Sweet," he said.

"If the Legion take you, then we may as well all throw in the towel."

Nathaniel hesitated, reaching for a pickaxe to defend himself with. The footsteps were getting nearer, it wouldn't be much longer. "Ben…"

Ben was frozen.

He couldn't believe that Lucy was gone. Not Lucy.

The words of the Watcher prophecy came to mind, cutting through his thoughts like broken glass.

One will come to pay the cost, if he fails all is lost.

One will come in suffering and pain, to know betrayal and be wounded again.

Ruby Johnson had betrayed him when he put his trust in her. Was Lucy's death the wound that he had to bear? To lose Mother Shepherd. To lose Josiah. To lose Lucy too. It was too much.

The sounds of approaching Legionnaires and the howling of the Feathered Men was getting uncomfortably close. Ben was aware that Nathaniel was tugging at his arm. "We won't leave her," Nathaniel said. "We'll carry Lucy between us, but we've got to run! Now, Ben!"

But Ben couldn't run.

He dropped his face onto Lucy's shoulder, his entire body wracked with emotion. "You were the best of us, girl," he said, trying not to cry. Very gently he reached out with his right hand. His fingers were trembling uncontrollably. *Hold yourself together, Benny Boy.* He bit his lower lip in an attempt to rein in his emotions, but even so he could feel hot tears beginning to well. The scarf Lucy had used to disguise herself had fallen away, and a strand of golden hair was plastered to her face. Ben moved to brush it away. His warm fingertip touched her cold skin and—

Suddenly Lucy convulsed in his arms and sat bolt upright. Ben shot backwards as if he had been electrocuted, his right hand surging with power.

"Lucy!"

"Chuff me," exclaimed Nathaniel.

"Quite," said Carter.

They all stared at Lucy in astonishment, which turned to concern as she coughed up a torrent of thick brown sludge. When she had finished, Ben whipped off his scarf and used it to wipe the rank muck off her lips and face.

"I thought it was my turn to rescue you," he said gently, as she gazed back at him. Alive.

"Yes, yes, all very touching, but can we please start running now? Chop-chop!" said Carter impatiently. "You know, escape, defeat Sweet, that sort of thing."

The baying of the Feathered Men was on top of them now. They had perhaps seconds before they were discovered.

Ben lugged Lucy to her feet and grinned in spite of everything. "Let's get out of here."

The only exit open to them was the tunnel which Valentine had used to lead the other escapees to safety. Ben didn't have fond memories of it; it descended sharply into the flooded corridors below. However, all the while they had been digging through the mudslide to get to Lucy it seemed that the Feathered Men had been digging from the *other* side trying to get to *them*. Even as the Watchers turned to leave, a taloned hand broke through the mountain of debris, followed swiftly by the rasping beak of a Feathered Man.

Lucy gasped. At first Ben thought it was just shock but then Lucy half-collapsed into his arms, weak from her brush with death.

With a soul-shattering screech, the Feathered Man continued to claw frantically at the barrier that kept it from its meal. The Watchers *had* to get away.

Nathaniel and Ben supported Lucy between them and hobbled as quickly as they could towards the exit and the flooded tunnels beyond. Over his shoulder Ben could see that the Feathered Man had pushed its whole head through. It was the most repulsive one that Ben had ever seen. This fallen angel was gaunt, almost skeletal, with its entire bone structure visible through the tissue of its skin.

The head appeared to be diseased, with huge bald patches where its feathers had dropped out, revealing glimpses of the skull beneath. It might be sick, Ben thought, or it might be especially ancient. But either way it was angry about something.

The Feathered Man burst out in a shower of debris, long rivers of saliva dripping from its beak. Mercifully the tunnel was too tight for the fallen angel to be able to unfurl its wings, but instead it bounded in huge leaps. Another Feathered Man came clambering through the hole after it and behind *that* was a squad of Legionnaires...

"If we can get far enough ahead we can still lose them," said Carter, pulling the young Watchers after him. "We can use the water in the lower levels to our advantage. The Feathered Men won't have a scent to follow and we can lie low, perhaps find a way to detour around them."

"And if we *can't* get far enough ahead?" said Ben.

"Then it's been nice knowing you."

With Carter leading them, they splashed on, the water dragging at their legs as it grew deeper. Carter's skill kept them ahead of their pursuers but, with only one torch between them and with Lucy still struggling, Ben found it hard to believe that they were going to get away this time. He shuddered as the howls of the fallen angels resounded through the tunnel. They sounded as if they could chase for ever.

"I'm going to try something," said Carter, panting heavily. "We can't go on much longer like this."

"What have you got?" said Ben.

"It's risky," said Carter.

"Isn't it always?"

"This way," said Carter, leading them down an especially unappealing side tunnel. There were no offshoots from this corridor as far as Ben could see. Worse than that, it was a dead end.

"This doesn't seem like your best plan, Professor," said Ben as the wizened Feathered Man turned the corner, hissing triumphantly.

The young Watchers backed themselves up against the wall, getting ready to defend themselves.

"Do you trust me?" said Carter, stepping towards the advancing creature.

"Thousands wouldn't," said Ben.

"I know," said Carter. "But do you?"

"You can count on it."

"Good lad," said the professor, taking another pace forwards. "Then trust me now."

Both Feathered Men were in the tunnel and the Legionnaires couldn't be far behind. The diseased

Feathered Man blocked the corridor completely; there would be no escape without getting past it. The creature knew that it had won and was savouring the sensation, sniffing the air and barking. Perhaps it could smell human fear? Perhaps, for a fallen angel, the scent of trapped Watchers was like the dizzying smell of gin for a drunkard?

Nathaniel readied his pickaxe handle. Ben positioned himself in front of Lucy; his quarterstaff wouldn't be much use in such a confined space but he wouldn't go without a fight. Lucy promptly came out from behind him. She found a piece of timber floating nearby and took it in both hands like a club. "Side by side," she said. "Always."

Carter had nothing but his claw. He hugged the wall of the tunnel and crept towards the slavering beast.

"Stupid, aren't you?" Carter taunted.

The Feathered Man's neck stretched and it gave a shrieking roar. It took another pace forward.

"Is that all you've got?" the professor said dismissively. His claw hand casually reached up for a torch in its bracket on the wall.

"What's he going to do with that?" whispered Nathaniel. "It isn't even lit. Is he going to throw it and shout 'fetch'?"

"Wait," said Ben, his own mind racing as their options continued to dwindle. "Carter knows what he's doing. He doesn't want to die down here any more than we do."

Ben knew Carter must have been well aware that this was a dead end when he'd led them down here, so there had to be something about this tunnel that they could use to their advantage. But what? He examined Carter's movements. The professor's claw was still hovering by the torch bracket – was there something special about that?

Ben's eyes strained against the dark. Was that a row of black recesses across the ceiling? Ben suddenly understood and joined Carter in taunting the Feathered Man.

"Come on then!" Ben yelled. "You want to eat me, here I am!"

The Feathered Man shrieked again and took another step forwards. It was almost directly beneath the line of holes now. *Just a little closer...*

Then the fallen angel hesitated. Its head swayed from side to side. It sniffed again, clacked its beak...and took a step back.

Ben knew that they wouldn't get another shot at this. He dashed towards the Feathered Man and flung his hands around its neck, then heaved the creature forwards with all his might, bringing it under those ominous holes in the roof of the passage.

"Now!"

Carter pulled down the secret lever and a metal portcullis dropped from the ceiling. Ben threw himself backwards out of the way as a row of metal spikes pierced the fallen angel across the neck and shoulders, pinning it to the floor and pushing its head beneath the water. The limbs twitched and splashed spasmodically and then fell limp.

The second Feathered Man stepped forward, Legionnaires filling the tunnel behind it. Carter went for the lever again, this time pushing it to the left. With a rasp a whole section of the wall began to swing open.

"A secret door," said Lucy with admiration.

They hurried through and closed it behind them. The last thing that Ben glimpsed as Carter jammed the lock was the other Feathered Man beginning to feast on his fallen brother.

CHAPTER 14

THE CIRCUS IS COMING

Munro had spent the night under some canvas sacking in a side street in Islington. Two patrols had walked passed him and missed him. Munro was good at hiding. His father had been the sort of man you needed to hide from.

Munro had come up with a plan, of sorts. His work party had been responsible for ensuring that the tunnels in the Under which led out of Sweet's city were sealed. This Munro had done. However, he knew there was one tunnel which was still passable. It wouldn't be easy, especially because his shape wasn't designed for crawling through tight passages, and his legs weren't the strongest for pushing. But he would make it. By God, he would make it. The tunnel would take him under the death zone, with all its spiteful traps, and bring him up again somewhere near Highbury Fields, a posh part of London where Munro hoped they would ignore him rather than ridicule him.

First he had to get to an entrance to the Under. He hobbled through the rain, but halted when he heard unkind laughter up ahead. He didn't want to draw attention to himself if he could avoid it. He tucked himself into a doorway and watched as two Legionnaires hammered a poster to the wall. It didn't take long and they were soon on their way again, carrying a satchel that bulged with more posters to be put up.

When they were out of sight, Munro shuffled over to take a closer look. Ruby had taught him to read on the long nights they had shared in the barracks.

What he read now sent shivers down his crooked spine.

COME AND WITNESS
MR. SWEET'S
CIRCUS OF DEATH!
LAUGH
AT NATURE'S ODDITIES!

WONDER
AT THE SAVAGERY OF THE BEASTS!
THRILL
AT THE TORTURE OF OUR ENEMIES!
DELIGHT
IN THE FIGHTS TO THE DEATH!
30TH APRIL
LYCEUM THEATRE
DOORS OPEN AT 1 FOR 1.30 START
FREE ADMISSION
PERSONS OF A FRAIL OR NERVOUS DISPOSITION
ARE ADVISED NOT TO ATTEND

Munro ripped the paper off the wall. Furiously he screwed the poster up and shoved it into his pack where no one else could read it.

He paused to look at the Legion Mark branded into his left palm, the symbol that said he was the property of Mr. Sweet. The shame that Munro felt burned hotter than the branding iron ever did.

Ruby had visited seven more churches in search of the Gehenna Key. Seven times she had failed. She felt drained, emotionally and physically. Part of her dreaded finding the key, but she knew that Grey Wing would not allow her to string him along. She was the puppet here.

Grey Wing would keep her searching all day, and all night too if necessary. Ruby knew that she needed to solve the riddle of the key if she stood a chance of uncovering its resting place. And so, with some resentment, the Feathered Man had set Ruby down outside the Punch and Judy public house. After a few words, the landlord threw the fallen angel a hunk of meat and let Ruby in through the side door. Ruby knew the landlord well and had a long-standing arrangement with him. She paid him rent for a corner of his cellar and in return he looked the other way. Grey Wing would be preoccupied with feeding for a while; enough time to give Ruby a little breathing space and a chance to think.

She caught sight of her reflection in the mirror behind the bar as she headed for the cellar steps. The emerald eyes that looked back at her had lost all of their sparkle. *You're in over your head this time.* She inhaled deeply through her nostrils and straightened her shoulders; she had been in tight corners before and she would get out of this situation the way she had always done in the past – on her own.

Once upon a time she could at least count Munro as her friend, but he had betrayed her when she'd tried to leave the Legion. That was back when she thought she might have a future with Ben Kingdom. She and Ben were going to run away together; at least, that had been Ruby's plan. *A lifetime ago*, she thought with a sigh.

Down in the beer cellar, Ruby shifted one of the barrels, prised up the floorboards underneath it and pulled out a bulging hessian sack. It always lifted her spirits when she looked inside. The precious metal glinted back at her, shiny with the promise of her new future. She ran her hands over her secret hoard of loot, then emptied her backpack and added some more church valuables to the pile. Perhaps one or two more runs and then she would be ready.

The problem was that she couldn't *spend* stolen candlesticks and crucifixes. They were worth a lot but she would have to find a fence, a criminal who would buy them from her. And she knew from past experience that those deals had a habit of turning sour. If she was lucky she might get ten per cent of their real value. Ruby made a mental calculation – she didn't have what she needed. Yet. In truth there would never be enough, but three more jobs, she decided, and that was it. After that she would be upping sticks regardless. She didn't have the stomach for this any more.

Ruby just needed to find the key so that Grey Wing

would fix his beady eyes on some other poor soul. And when he was looking in the opposite direction, she would grab her loot and run.

She returned her treasures to their hiding place, pushed down the boards and slid the barrel back on top. Then she allowed herself a small glass of the landlord's watery ale and sat down to think.

Obadiah Moon had obviously known about the key, so it wasn't too big a leap to assume that Jago Moon might know about it too. Had the Moons been the guardians of the key down the generations? And if so, how many other Moons had there been, and where were they all buried?

There also remained the question of what the key was for. Ruby had started to have a sick feeling in the depths of her stomach when she wondered about that.

She could feel the cogs turning in her mind. *Gehenna*. What did that mean? She had heard the word once but couldn't place it.

Then it came to her. Claw Carter had spoken of it after one of his visits to the Dark Library, where the Legion kept its books of forbidden knowledge.

Gehenna – the place where the fires never cease burning.

Gehenna – where the screaming never stops.

Gehenna – Hell on earth.

The trapdoor to the cellar was wrenched open and Grey Wing thrust his head inside. "No more rest," he hissed, his yellow tongue struggling with the language of mortals. "Find the key. *Now!*"

CHAPTER 15

GOD SAVE THE QUEEN

"I am so sorry," said Hans Schulman. "I am very clumsy, *ja*?"

There was beer everywhere. It was all over the table in the guardroom, and all over the Jail Master General's trousers. Hans had come in on some errand, and managed to knock the man's pint mug over in the process.

"Imbecile," the Jail Master shouted, his enormous jowls wobbling in irritation as he began to wipe himself down.

"Let me help you," said Hans, grabbing up a cloth and furiously mopping the table, sending a candlestick crashing.

"Just leave it, will you?" said the Jail Master. "You're making it worse."

"Please forgive me," said Hans, his eyes dropping to the man's sodden trousers. "I'm sure that no one will think you have – what are the words? – wet yourself?"

"You're on a charge, chummy," snarled the Jail Master. "You're gonna get twenty lashes for that."

Hans had known that a punishment would be coming but it was a small price to pay. The Jail Master shuffled away to find some dry clothes...and left the keys in the guardroom unattended.

The rumours said that the key Hans was looking for was marked with crossed bones. No one locked in that cell had ever been released alive. Hans took it from its hook on the wall, slipped it into his pocket and walked away as quickly as he dared. There would be no coming back from this moment. He was a Watcher spy inside the Legion and he had just committed a crime punishable by death. When the key was discovered to be missing – and that *would* happen – then the Jail Master would be in no doubt as to who the culprit was.

Hans was a dead man walking.

And yet if this key did what he believed it might, then the risk was worth it. If Hans was able to release this prisoner, then the war against the Legion was closer to being won.

The city was slipping over the edge into chaos. The

Legion were drunk with power. Mr. Sweet himself was growing more dangerous by the hour. Earlier that day, Hans had witnessed five red-headed lads being dragged before him. None of them bore the slightest resemblance to Ben, save their hair colour, but Sweet's paranoia was so extreme that he executed them regardless.

Revolution Day was less than forty-eight hours away. It couldn't come too soon.

Hans had been undercover in the Legion for a long time and it had become second nature for him to eavesdrop on the villains that he lived alongside. Even so, he had almost gasped out loud when he'd overheard Sweet give away the one piece of information the Watchers needed.

Now, if Hans could get the Queen to safety, that would surely be the turning point of this war.

Using a lantern, Hans navigated his way through the Under. Water was running down the walls and the air was full of the scent of decay. Huge green and black patches of mould spread through the corridors like a disease. Here and there, clumps of sickly white mushrooms had sprouted up, eager to release their spores. And the deeper Hans descended, the worse it got. He covered his mouth and nose with his neck-scarf, but the rotting smell still made him gag.

Alone in the flooded chambers, Hans began to feel his mind playing tricks. He was not afraid of the rats that seemed to have been breeding in their hundreds, but he was troubled by the dark. He felt a stirring in the shadows, a sense that he was being followed, hunted even. Of course, when he turned round there was nothing – it was only his imagination – and yet his skin crawled with fear.

Eventually Hans reached a spiral staircase, water cascading down the steps around his feet. He moved down to the deepest depths of the Under, the lowest level, where the secrets and the horrors were kept. At the bottom of the stairs, Hans paused. The water level was almost at his waist here. He flashed his lantern down the corridor and found the dungeon doors. What could he hope to find on the other side of those bars?

Holding his lamp high, Hans waded cautiously along. He arrived at the first door and peered through the barred window. A skeleton grinned back at him, still manacled to the wall, waiting for help that never came. The next two cells were empty and Hans felt his hopes trickling away. Twice, he spun round, sensing another presence in the darkness. Twice his lantern found nothing.

"Help!" called a small, frail voice. "Is somebody there? Will you help me, please?"

It sounded like an old woman. Hans pushed his way through the water, hoping against hope that it was her. He saw a small, pink hand reaching out through the next set of bars.

"My Queen," breathed Hans.

Victoria no longer looked like a queen though. Her thin hair was plastered to her scalp, her skin was taut on her cheeks, her dress was in rags. But her eyes still glinted with strength.

Hans inserted the long key into the lock. It was stiff and he had to put both hands to it. He strained, but the key still refused to turn.

"Hurry," Victoria urged. "You must free my friend too."

Hans paused and put his face to the barred window of the neighbouring cell. He couldn't be sure at first, but he thought that he could make out a figure standing silently in the middle of the dungeon, fixed to the spot by lengths of chain. A tall figure with a strong, elegant face; dignified even though there were raw stumps on his shoulders where mighty wings had once grown.

"You!" Hans declared.

Queen Victoria gave a shrill scream and Hans was confused. Then a heavy hand landed on his shoulder from behind and he understood all too well.

Hans turned and his lamp illuminated a silver raven-skull mask beneath a crown of coins.

"Yes," said Mr. Sweet. "It's me."

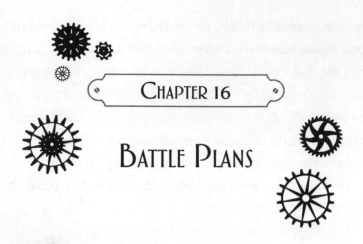

CHAPTER 16

BATTLE PLANS

Munro never made it as far as Highbury Fields.

The tunnel came up on the edge of the death zone. The rain soaked him as soon as he emerged and he sat for a while in an empty house, shivering and trying to get warm. His journey had left him exhausted and the idea of making it as far as Scotland seemed ridiculous. Munro's belly growled with hunger and his head throbbed so badly that his vision had begun to blur. Parched, he bent down and drank from a puddle, but the water was murky and left him feeling more disorientated than before.

Dazed, Munro wandered out into the ruined street. There he struggled across the seemingly endless mounds of rubble, as tall to him as mountains. He slipped and fell, grazing his hands and knees. But he hauled himself back upright again, or as upright as he was able, and kept going. Ten minutes later he fell again, harder and heavier, striking his head on a jagged chunk of masonry. This time he could feel the warmth of blood as it rolled across his eye.

In his imagination he could hear a dog barking.

He closed his eyes and knew that he didn't have the strength to stand up again.

The barking grew louder. It reminded him of…

Buster!

A rasping tongue lapped at Munro's cheek, bringing with it the familiar hot waft of old bones and bad teeth. Munro opened his eyes and saw his three-legged friend standing on a broken wall right in front of him.

"Who's a good dog?" said Munro, nuzzling his face against Buster's and receiving canine kisses.

"Clover!" called a girl's voice. "Where are you, boy?"

The girl came skipping over. "There you are," she said, rubbing the dog's head and making a fuss of his ears.

Munro shrank down, trying to hide his hump and the unfortunate lines of his face.

"Hello!" said the girl brightly, as if noticing him for the first time. "I'm Molly and this is Clover. He's the best dog in the world, aren't you, Clover?"

Munro was at a loss as to what to say. The girl wasn't shrinking back in revulsion, which was good; wonderful even. But the dog *wasn't* Clover, it was Buster.

Munro was about to tell the girl as much, but he could see how happy the three-legged bulldog made her.

"Molly!" called a man's voice. "What are you doing? I've told you not to wander off like that. It's not safe out here."

A soldier approached and Molly ran to him. "Look," she said. "Look what Clover has found."

"Good Lord," said the soldier.

Munro brought up his arms to cover his face. "I'm sorry," he mumbled.

"Here," said Daniel Carnehan, bending down to help Munro up. "You're hurt, sonny, let's get you seen to."

Munro said nothing as the brigadier and the little girl began to help him back to the army encampment. He didn't say anything when they cleaned his wound and wrapped it in a clean bandage. He didn't say anything when they brought him soup and a bread roll, then more soup and more bread, until he was fuller than he had ever been. But he felt a warmth inside. Then Buster scrambled up on his lap and Munro thought that his happiness was complete.

Munro fell asleep in that blissful state, breaking wind

as silently as he was able. He only woke when he heard voices talking about him.

"He's a Legionnaire," said Jonas Kingdom. "Ben described all the boys who were in Mickelwhite's brigade and he's definitely one of them."

"We can settle this easily enough," said Carnehan.

Munro trembled as the two men approached. Without protestation, he opened his left hand and showed them the Mark. "It's true, I was in the Legion," he told them, cringing in expectation of his punishment. "But not in my heart, never in my heart. Why else would I be running away?"

"It's alright, sonny," said Carnehan. "We're not going to hurt you."

"Please. I promise you can trust me," Munro gabbled. "I can help you, I've got information you can use against the Legion."

"Steady, lad," Jonas reassured him. "Tell us what you've got."

"Mr. Sweet has gone mad."

Carnehan paused. "How do you mean?"

As best as he could, Munro told of how he was going to assassinate Sweet but couldn't bring himself to do it. And of the demons that only Mr. Sweet could see

"I've also got this," said Munro, dragging the crumpled

poster from his pack and spreading it out before them.

The brigadier winced. He was horrified by what he read. The *torture* of prisoners. Fights to the *death*. This was the final straw. He screwed up the poster with a snarl. "I cannot allow this brutality. We aren't up against an ordinary enemy here. *Real* soldiers only fight against other soldiers, not civilians, not prisoners, not women and children. Sweet is a…" Carnehan paused, aware that there were younger ears present. "Sweet is a bully and a coward to boot." His face grew severe, adding years to him. "Sweet thinks that our hands are tied while he holds our dear Queen, but I have had the honour of meeting Her Majesty and I know that she would not want the British army to delay while her beloved subjects were being made to suffer in such a way. She is *one* woman and there are *thirty thousand* souls inside that blasted Wall." Carnehan drew in a long breath, as if stiffening himself for the decision he was about to make.

"First of all I need you to show me this tunnel of yours. If you used it to get *out*, then my men can use it to get *in*. Secondly," his moustache twitched ever so slightly, "I need you to return to the city and get a message to the Watchers."

Munro went pale at the prospect. "I'll do it for you," he said.

"Good lad," said the brigadier. "As commanding officer of the Coldstream Guards, I am issuing a new order to my battalion. Queen or no Queen, my boys in red shall fight alongside the Watchers on Revolution Day."

CHAPTER 17

THE LUCK OF
THE DEVIL

Carter took the Watchers down, down, down, until they reached the lowest level of the Under. They said nothing for a long time, afraid that their voices might carry and give them away. All the while, Ben listened for sounds of pursuit and the chilling calls of the Feathered Men, but they never came. They had given the Legionnaires the slip.

"I hope Valentine was lucky too," said Ben.

"We weren't lucky," Carter contradicted him. "It was my knowledge of the Under that enabled us to outfox our dull-witted trackers." He sniffed. "I'm certain Valentine's equally superior understanding of the complexity of these tunnels will have allowed him to keep the escapees out of harm's way. No doubt they are already tucked up in a Watcher safe house."

"I wish we could say the same for Mr. Moon and Ghost," said Ben. He couldn't shift the image of the shaven-headed Watcher being snatched away from the escape tunnel before he got a chance to descend. Maybe that was a good thing, considering what happened to the shaft a second later, but even so the knowledge that their friends were *still* prisoners of the Legion weighed heavily on him.

Experience had taught Ben that things never quite turned out how you planned. As if to prove his point, the ceiling above their heads suddenly groaned, releasing a shower of mortar and fragments of brick. They could all see it; the rainwater that had saturated the soil and collapsed the escape tunnel was wreaking havoc on the fabric of the Under.

"I never thought I would see the Under like this," said Carter, as they waded along another dark corridor. He sounded almost melancholy. "One of the unseen architectural wonders of the world, as important as the pyramids at Giza or the lighthouse at Alexandria."

"A rat's nest is a rat's nest, whatever you call it," said Lucy.

"Can art only be made by good men then, Miss Lambert?"

Lucy shrugged. "I don't know about that, but I know that dungeons and torture chambers aren't on my list of great achievements."

They fell into silence again. With every weary step the flood water dragged at their legs and sucked the warmth from their blood. And they still had such a long journey to make.

They had decided to return to Mr. Smutts's. Since the Legion had already searched there and found no sign of the Watchers – thanks to Hans – it made sense that the Legion wouldn't think of looking there again. That meant that they had to trek from one side of London to the other, all the way back to Old Gravel Lane. It was miles.

They trudged onwards, each lost in their own thoughts.

"You know that the Legion will have doubled the guards on the detention camp now," said Nathaniel. "I don't see us being able to break in a second time."

"We might not have to," said Lucy. "Just as your tunnel broke the surface, Mickelwhite was gathering victims to take part in a 'circus', whatever that means. Mr. Moon broke the captain's nose and Ghost was caught trying to escape – you can bet your life that Mickelwhite will want to punish them for that."

"A circus?" said Ben. "What's that all about?"

"History holds all the answers, Ben," said Carter. "Do you know how the Roman Emperors held on to their power?"

Ben shook his head.

"With bread and circuses."

"I don't understand," said Nathaniel.

"Free bread and free beer," Carter explained, "so the masses had something in their bellies, combined with gruesome spectacles to keep them entertained."

"Gladiators versus lions?" Ben gasped.

"Something like that."

"Wherever they are, we need them and we're going to find them," said Ben.

Carter drew in a breath as if to say something and then thought better of it. Instead they all kept their thoughts to themselves and concentrated on putting one foot in front of the other.

A day, *a lifetime*, later, Carter brought them to a halt beneath a manhole cover. The professor climbed up the iron ladder and cautiously lifted the heavy lid. The storm-laden sky was dark and Old Gravel Lane was eerily quiet. The curfew bell had rung and the street was deserted. Motioning for the others to follow, Carter hauled himself out onto the cobbles, his eyes constantly searching for danger.

Ben knew that they had to get under cover before they could breathe again, but as he lifted his face to the rain he found an unexpected grin forming on his lips. He nudged his brother in the ribs affectionately.

"We're home," Ben whispered. There was the Jolly Tar, the pub where he used to go and buy books from Jago Moon before it all began. There was the spire of St Peter's, stretching up into the stormbound sky...

There were faces looking at them from behind filthy windows.

"Quick!" said Ben, the smile gone. "The Smutts's place is just up here."

Hugging the shadows, the Watchers followed Ben. *Just a little further...*

Ben's hopes came crashing down. They had arrived at Mr. Smutts's house but there was no refuge to be had here. The windows were all broken. The door had been smashed off its hinges. A message had been scrawled along the wall in blood-red paint – *Watchers beware!*

Ben staggered to a halt, uncertain of which way to turn. His heart ached in his chest; after all the kindness that family had shown him...

An image of them flashed through Ben's mind – filthy and miserable inside the detention camp. With difficulty, he shook the thought from his head. They had to keep moving; make it to safety; make it to Revolution Day.

"What shall we do, Ben?" Lucy hissed.

"I don't know," said Ben. "But we can't stand here—"

"Psst!" called a voice from the gloom. There was something familiar in its bronchial wheeze that gave Ben hope. He turned. Standing in a doorway, beckoning with a tobacco-stained hand, was a shabby, unshaven man.

"This way, hurry," said the man in a rich Polish accent. He smiled, displaying an uneven row of brown stumps.

"Mr. Wachowski!" Ben exclaimed, greeting the old man who had lived in the basement back in the day when the Kingdom family had rented Mrs. McLennon's freezing attic room on this very street.

The man bustled them in through the doorway, which, like his teeth, had presumably once been white and shiny. "I have new lodgings, yes," Mr. Wachowski exclaimed. "Mrs. McLennon turned me out on the street."

"I know the feeling," said Ben, standing shivering in the man's corridor.

"I never knew why," Mr. Wachowski continued, then paused to dredge phlegm up from his rattling chest and spit it roughly in the direction of a rusting spittoon.

"A complete mystery," muttered Carter, following them inside and closing the door behind him.

Mr. Wachowski drew the bolts across the door and then led them into his room. It was tiny, filthy and cold. A meagre fire struggled in the grate. A single chair that clearly doubled as a bed sat in the corner, its horsehair stuffing spilling from a dozen tears. Mr. Wachowski drew the flimsy rags that counted as curtains across the window, and pushed his chamber pot out of sight under a stained table. The contents slopped alarmingly.

"Make yourself at home," said Mr. Wachowski. "So, you're famous now, Ben Kingdom. Lucky I found you, eh?" He paused to hawk up another mouthful of mucus. "Everyone in London knows your name and, to think, I knew you when you were this high." The old man's eyes glowed warmly. "Sit," he said. "Rest, please."

Ben didn't need to be asked twice.

The floor suddenly seemed to be as comfortable as a feather bed, and as he flopped down, Ben felt the arms of sleep wrapping around him. In the moment before his eyes shut, he saw Lucy and Nathaniel were already asleep, and even Carter was nodding. The incredible exertions of the day had caught up with them. They couldn't have stayed awake at that moment even if they'd wanted to.

Home sweet home, thought Ben, as St Peter's chimed eleven o'clock.

Mr. Wachowski looked down on Ben affectionately as he slept.

The old man shuffled around the room, quietly checking on his sleeping guests. He found a moth-eaten blanket and laid it carefully over Ben and Lucy, who were leaning against each other.

"You have a nice long rest, Ben Kingdom," Mr. Wachowski muttered. Then he left the room as quietly as he was able, pausing only to lock the door behind him. Regardless of the rain that was rattling down from the sky, regardless of the curfew, Mr. Wachowski walked along the corridor to the front door and stepped out into the night.

"This is my lucky day," he chuckled.

DAY FOUR
30TH APRIL, 1892

CHAPTER 18

DADDY'S GIRL

Ben and Lucy were in a universe of their own.

At some point, someone – Mr. Wachowski, Ben guessed – had covered them both with a blanket. The room, like almost every room Ben had ever slept in, was cold and damp and so Ben had drawn the blanket right up until it was covering their heads. Inside that tent, their breath made the air feel warm, almost cosy. Although he was more tired than ever, Ben woke after a short while and lay there happily, comforted by the sound of Lucy breathing and the knowledge that Carter and Nathaniel were both near.

"Are you awake, Lucy?" Ben whispered.

Lucy gave a low groan.

"I was scared back there in the tunnel, Lucy, when... you know... Anyway, I just wanted to say that...I'm glad you made it. That doesn't sound right. I mean, obviously I'm glad you're alive and not... What I mean is, I don't think that I could do this without you, Lucy... I... Are you hearing any of this?"

Lucy moaned again, louder this time, and started to toss her head from side to side.

"Lucy," said Ben, putting his hand to her forehead and finding it clammy with perspiration. Her eye was fluttering madly beneath its closed lid, and another tragic note escaped her lips. "Hey," said Ben, stroking her hair. "You're alright, Lucy, it's just a bad dream."

Lucy woke then, her expression full of panic as she looked around wildly, only relaxing when she saw Ben.

"It's always the same," she said softly, trying to get her breathing back under control. "My nightmare never changes."

"Do you want to tell me about it?"

Lucy looked uncertain, as if this was too much to ask.

"I'm here if you need me, Lucy. You've shown me what it means to be a Watcher. I'm only the Hand because you believed in me."

"And Mother Shepherd, and Mr. Moon and Josiah."

"Yes, and them, but mostly *you*. I think we're sort of the same, you and me."

Lucy gave a dismissive snort through her nose. It was a sad sound, Ben thought.

"Have I upset you, Lucy?"

"No, it's not that. It's just everybody says what a good Watcher I am—"

"Because you are."

"I know, Ben. I know. And for years being a Watcher has been everything to me. But it wasn't how I saw my life turning out, that's all." She broke off. "I never wanted to be a fighter, Ben."

Ben understood exactly how she felt. War was not a game that anyone would choose to play.

"You probably wouldn't believe it to look at me now, but I loved pretty dresses when I was a little girl. My mother always curled my hair and put ribbons in it. My big brother always teased me and tried to pull them out, but I didn't care… I was happy just to put my dolly in a pram and push her around the park on Primrose Hill." Lucy laughed at the memory, but Ben could tell that her happy story was about to change.

"And then my mother died," said Lucy flatly. "Tuberculosis… And one month later my father's regiment was posted to India. I think perhaps my father thought that the change would be good for me and my brother, take us out of ourselves again. India is a whole new world, Ben. It's so beautiful and different; the sights, the sounds, the colours, the animals – it's hard for me to explain... It *was* wonderful in many ways. My father tried so hard to make it work, Ben, to build a new life for the three of us..."

"So what happened?" Ben hardly dared to ask.

"The Legion happened, Ben."

Ben drew in his breath.

Lucy's voice wavered. "We fought them... I did my best, Ben, I really tried. But we lost." She couldn't hold back her tears. "I lost my eye. My brother. My father... We lost our family honour, too..."

There was so much more to this story, but Ben knew that this was not the time.

"And so I hid on a tramp steamer," Lucy continued, "and made the long voyage back to London alone. Mother Shepherd found me and the Watchers took me in and... well, here we are."

Ben didn't know how to respond. He heard the disappointment in Lucy's voice. "What would you like to have been then?" asked Ben. "In another life, if you could be anything."

"I wanted to be a dancer," said Lucy.

Ben took her hand. "You *will* dance, Lucy. One day, girl, I promise you."

"Ben...don't..."

"All we have to do first is overthrow Sweet, destroy the Crown of Corruption, defeat the army of the Legion, rid London of the Feathered Men and Bob's your uncle."

Lucy laughed, as Ben had hoped she would.

He was going to try to make her laugh again when he heard a sound that set his nerves jangling.

"Did you hear footsteps?"

Lucy shook her head, but they both sat up and freed themselves from the blanket, all their senses alert. Mr. Wachowski's room was silent, except for the breathing of the other Watchers. The fire in the grate had burned down to embers, but it gave enough light for Ben to see that one body was missing.

"Where's Wachowski?"

A shadow crossed the window and they both knew what that meant.

"We've been betrayed – *Watchers, to arms!*" shouted Lucy, her words cutting through sleep. Nathaniel and Carter responded within seconds, Nathaniel poised with his quarterstaff, Carter with his claw raised.

They all heard the key turning in the front door. Then the cough, gargle and spit that announced Mr. Wachowski's return. And the sound of boots which told them he had not come alone.

"Quick," said Carter, grabbing the chair and flinging it up against the door. "We've got to buy ourselves some time."

Mr. Wachowski and the Legionnaires were outside the room. Ben listened to the sound of a key slipping into the lock, followed by cursing as the Polish man tried his door but found it blocked.

"I thought he was our friend," said Nathaniel. "We used to live under the same roof. How could he do this to us?"

"The oldest reason in the book," said Ben. "Money. The Legion always reward their informers."

The chair shuddered as someone put their shoulder to the door.

"Come out, Ben Kingdom!" snarled the Legionnaire.

"Come out, Ben," said Mr. Wachowski, trying his best to sound reasonable. "This is for the best, yes? No fuss."

Carter picked up the table and added it to their makeshift defences.

The door bulged again as it was struck a second time, the hinges making cracking sounds as the wood started to splinter.

"The window," said Ben.

Just as the door crashed inwards, so Ben smashed the window outwards, covering his face with his arms to protect himself from the jagged shards. The chair and the table still blocked the door from opening fully and Ben saw a hand enter first. It was holding a pistol. And it was searching for a target.

Carter didn't hesitate. He threw his own weight against the door and there was a yelp as the Legionnaire's wrist was crushed. The bullet went wild and the Legionnaires were still stumbling through the door as Ben and his Watchers dived out the window.

Four Legionnaires were waiting for them in the street.

Carter cheerfully slashed at one with his claw. Nathaniel swung his quarterstaff, catching another in the belly and bending him double. That left two.

"You take the one on the left," Ben called to Lucy.

The Legionnaires had been expecting them to run, so this full-on assault took them by surprise. Ben was up against a barrel-chested man with tiny eyes almost lost in the fat folds of his face. If the man laid a punch on him, then Ben would be going down. Fortunately, for all his size, the man signalled his moves so clearly that Ben was able to avoid them with ease. The man swung a huge haymaker of a punch and Ben ducked neatly beneath it. Then, using a move which Mr. Moon had delighted in teaching him, Ben moved in close and gave an open-handed blow to the side of the big man's neck. The giant wobbled for a second, not comprehending what had happened to him, and then fell face down on the pavement, unconscious, landing with a splash.

Beside Ben, Lucy was finishing off her opponent. Her Legionnaire was lean and wiry, with whip-crack reflexes.

The man launched a volley of punches in quick succession, but each one met only air as Lucy weaved around his blows. Finding the weakness in his defences, Lucy unclenched her fists so that her hands were held out in front of her as if she was waiting to receive a Christmas present. Then she jabbed her hands upwards, keeping her fingers locked straight as they hit the Legionnaire just below the ribcage.

The man would live, of course, but that wasn't much consolation when he was rolling in pain and watching his sworn enemies disappearing up the street into the distance.

The Watchers put on a spurt of speed and, by the time the Legionnaires got out of the house, they were half a street away.

Ben caught Lucy's eye as they ran.

"You'd be an amazing dancer," he said.

Lucy laughed, did a cartwheel, and kept on running.

* * *

Inside the staff tent, Brigadier Carnehan looked down at the sleeping figures, tucked up beneath thick, army blankets. The little girl and the brave crippled lad, not forgetting that dog, nestled in beside the boy. Survivors against the odds. *What's going to become of you?* he wondered. *The orphanage? The workhouse?* Neither option held much hope for the future. Carnehan tiptoed over to the girl's bed and paused, adjusting her blanket slightly so that it didn't cover her nose and mouth, then he returned to his field chair beside the stove, deep in thought.

He had written to his wife about Molly and Munro, the waif and the stray that he had rescued from the rubble, but he hadn't given the letter to the dispatcher yet. It was a foolish letter in many ways and Carnehan was surprised that he had felt so compelled to put pen to paper at all.

The Legion had ripped the heart out of London. Civil war was always the war that a soldier dreaded – where was the victory for an Englishman in killing another Englishman? Carnehan desperately wanted some good to come out of this, for there to be some legacy of the conflict of which he could be truly proud.

That was what he had suggested to his wife. When they were first married they desperately wanted to have children but they had never been blessed, and so they let that dream die. Had this blasted war given them a second chance?

Carnehan pulled the envelope out of his pocket and held it between thumb and forefinger, staring at the address written on the front as if somehow the answer were contained there.

It was stupid, he decided, and he hooked opened the door on the stove revealing the crackling fire inside. He should toss the letter into the flames and forget about it.

He leaned forwards and watched as the paper started to discolour, turning from white to cream as the heat reached out to grasp it—

Molly rolled over and gave a small moan. She sounded so small and vulnerable. These children *needed* a protector, needed a father…

Carnehan snatched the letter away from the stove and shoved it into his pocket almost angrily. He needed to smoke his pipe and think.

It was going to be a long night.

CHAPTER 19

THE PUPPET MASTER

The Watchers were gathered beneath a canvas tent on the roof of St Bride's church. The rain was pelting down, finding every hole in the old fabric and falling on them in fat, cold drops. And there the Watchers slept fitfully, taking what rest they could. They would need everything within them if they were to rescue Ghost and Moon and then see Revolution Day through to the end.

When Ben woke his right hand was throbbing faintly. He sensed that it had something to do with the never-ending storm. If only he knew what.

Since Mr. Sweet had taken control, Ben had decided that it was vital for the Watchers of London to know where they could go if they were lost or alone and needed to regroup. Monday, the British Museum; Tuesday, the Temple; Wednesday, Westminster Abbey; Thursday, Tallow Chandlers' Hall; Friday, Fenchurch Street Station; Saturday, St Bride's; Sunday, Christ Church Spitalfields. Ben had made every Watcher learn the list by heart. It had served them well, so far.

Carter was there, with Nathaniel and Lucy, and maybe fifty or so other Watchers from across the city. But they could also see that their numbers were dwindling day by day. That was yet another reason why it was so vitally important to rescue Moon and Ghost. They would need everyone they could get for tomorrow, Revolution Day.

The canvas lifted and their eyes lit up to see Valentine.

"You got out," said Nathaniel. "Well done, mate."

"What about the escapees?" asked Ben, clasping his hand.

"Never let it be said that I let a chap down in their hour of need," said Valentine. "Managed to get them all into the hands of some thoroughly decent Watchers running a safe house on Pye Corner. Close run thing though, don't you know."

Ben clapped Valentine on the shoulder.

"Must say," Valentine continued, "emotions were running pretty high. Heard some things about what

Sweet's been doing that would make your hair curl. Seems he's even been executing every red-headed boy that he comes across just in case the blighter is you, Benjamin."

Ben shuddered.

Valentine went on. "You can be sure that every man jack of our escapees will be fighting alongside us when the uprising kicks off."

"They won't be the only ones." A deep voice reached them from outside the tent. Ben's heart missed a beat.

It can't be...? "Pa!" shouted Ben, slipping out from under the canvas and running to him.

"It's Saturday," said Jonas. "So, St Bride's."

Nathaniel joined them too and both boys spoke over each other, not giving Jonas time to reply or even draw breath between their questions.

"We saw your flare."

"How's Molly?"

"What happened to the Liberator?"

"Are you hurt?"

"I've missed you."

"We need you."

Jonas enjoyed their embraces and attention. "I'm as right as rain," he said, running his hand through his sopping hair. "But I'll catch my death if we stand out in this – can't we at least get under cover?"

The Kingdom boys happily yielded and brought their father back under the shelter of their makeshift tent.

"Right," said Jonas. "First things first, Molly's fine."

Lucy smiled.

"She's being looked after by the troops – they've sort of adopted her as a mascot – and there's this brigadier, Carnehan his name is, commanding office of the regiment of Coldstream Guards. Really decent sort. He's taken Molly under his wing."

"And the Liberator? We saw the explosion."

"She won't fly again," said Jonas sadly. "Hardly a matchstick remains, but she did the job. As far as I know, we didn't lose anyone on her last flight, everyone got off in time. A little crisp around the edges maybe, but alive."

"What of London beyond the Wall?" asked Carter.

Jonas breathed heavily through his nose. "People are in shock. The army is waiting to attack, but with the Queen still captive Sweet has got their hands tied. That's the official story anyway. However…" Here Jonas grinned and Ben recognized his own expression in his father's lopsided smile. "I've got some good news. Carnehan has brought in the sappers."

Ben had heard of them; they were military engineers and explosives experts.

"Right now," said Jonas, "the sappers are under the

death zone preparing to blow open the tunnels again. The army can't advance across the Dead Man's Land without being seen, but when the revolution starts they are going to open up a dozen points of entry—"

"And sneak in under the Legion's noses!" Ben finished the sentence.

"We still can't win unless Ben destroys the Crown of Corruption," Carter reminded them.

"That's why we have to rescue Ghost and Moon," said Ben. "The rebels are going to need Watchers to guide them or the revolution will be a shambles." He clenched his teeth. "We've got to get them out of Sweet's circus."

"I can help with that too," said Jonas, pulling out the poster that Munro had given them. "Ben, you once told me about a hunchbacked boy you met in the Under—"

"Munro."

"That's the lad," said Jonas. "He's left the Legion and he's safe with Molly and Carnehan. He's been able to give us lots of information about what's happening inside Sweet's headquarters at the Tower of London – numbers of guards, shift patterns, those sorts of useful details. He also brought us this." Jonas spread the poster wide.

"One o'clock today," said Valentine, reading down.

"At the Lyceum," said Nathaniel.

"Right," said Ben. "Then let's get moving."

* * *

Hans Schulman, the Watcher spy, was tied to a chair in Sweet's private chamber. Mr. Sweet examined him with the cold precision of a surgeon. Hans could not bear to meet the fierce gaze which bore into him through the silver sockets of Sweet's mask.

"Do you think you are cleverer then me, boy?" asked Sweet.

Hans said nothing.

"Did you honestly believe that I wouldn't be able to sniff out a traitor in my own ranks? You Watchers are so arrogant! You probably thought that you were a brilliant spy when you overheard me talking about the crossbones key. It never occurred to you that I *meant* you to hear me. You fell straight into my trap." Sweet laughed. "And now you are going to betray Ben Kingdom."

"Never," said Hans. "I'll die first."

"You don't have any choice in the matter, boy," said Sweet. "I wear the Crown of Corruption. I can make you do *anything*."

Before Hans could react, Sweet grabbed the boy's face in both hands. Sweet brought his own face in close, the beak of his mask scratching Hans's skin, his eyes piercing into the German lad's mind, stripping away all mental defences.

"I. Am. Your. Master," hissed Sweet.

Hans tried to screw his eyes shut to avoid Sweet's hypnotic stare, but as the words bored into his skull he found that he was unable to resist.

"I. AM. YOUR. MASTER."

The words exploded inside Hans's head, pushing every other thought aside, until only Sweet's voice remained.

Hans spasmed, like a medium at the seance table overwhelmed by a spirit that is not their own.

"You are my master," he repeated.

"You will obey me."

"I will obey you."

"Take this to Ben Kingdom," said Sweet, placing an iron key in the boy's hand. "Give him this message and then return…"

Hans had no choice but to listen. Mr. Sweet's lie ingrained itself in the wet clay of his mind so that he would be able to repeat it word-perfectly when the time was right.

"Now go!" Sweet ordered.

"Yes, master."

The Watcher's own spy was now working against them. Hans Schulman was Sweet's puppet and he jerked away on his errand like a good wooden boy. Sweet licked his cracked lips in delicious anticipation.

The voices inside Sweet's head kept telling him that Ben Kingdom would defeat him, but with the German boy under his control, Sweet had sealed Kingdom's fate once and for all.

It was almost too simple. Propelled by his schoolboy sense of patriotism, Ben Kingdom would never allow Queen Victoria to rot in a cell if he had been handed the key. So it was a given that Kingdom would come running, place the key in the lock, turn it and…

Sweet slammed his hands together gleefully.

The Watchers, in their earnest naivety, always failed to see the depth of cunning that resided in the souls of the Legion. The Under had many secrets, most of which could inflict pain.

The dungeon doors had *two* keys. One which opened the lock. And another which released a vicelike trap – steel spikes which would spring out from their hiding place in the wall and put an end to any rescue attempt. For ever.

Guess which key he had sent to Ben Kingdom?

CHAPTER 20

THE CRY
FOR BLOOD

"It's too much of a risk," said Carter. "You should stay behind, Ben."

"It's almost Revolution Day," Ben protested. "Even with the promise of help from Brigadier Carnehan, Ghost and Mr. Moon are *crucial* to the plan."

"Not as crucial as the Hand of Heaven," said Carter. "We lose you, we lose this war."

"The professor has got a point," said Lucy. "Now that we know Sweet is executing red-headed boys at random…"

"I know the risks," Ben snapped. "But I'm not going to allow Ghost and Mr. Moon to be thrown to the lions!"

His eyes rested on Lucy's backpack and without asking for her permission Ben began to rummage inside. He withdrew a tin of boot polish, popped the lid, dug his fingers into the waxy contents and then began to smear it through his hair until his usually shaggy ginger locks were plastered to his head. Then he plonked his billycock hat down on top and stood there defiantly.

"Satisfied?" said Ben.

"Not really," said Carter.

"I'm coming anyway."

They headed for the Lyceum and the circus in silence, avoiding other people as much as possible, and sticking to the side streets where they could. The rain acted as an ally, forcing heads down and keeping collars turned up. Carter, who was every bit as distinctive as Ben, walked with his hands firmly in his pockets, hiding his giveaway claw. So far, they hadn't attracted so much as a sideways glance.

Ben let their party string out so it didn't look as though they were a group. Lucy and Ben were at the front – they would head for the cheap seats, where they could get an overview of the whole theatre. Carter had also suggested that might keep Ben out of the thick of it. Valentine followed twenty paces behind, then Nathaniel. If they could, they were to get backstage and see if Ghost and Moon could be found earlier. Jonas and Carter brought up the rear. They would take position as near to the stage as possible. If it came to a full-frontal assault, then it was down to them.

Jeers and shouts made Ben glance over his shoulder and he saw a huge crowd following them down Gray's Inn Road. They seemed to be full to the brim with anger and ale, and Ben's party wasted no time in cutting a swift right onto High Holborn and out of their path.

Unfortunately there was a similar rabble gathered at the other end of the street. There'd be no escape that way either.

"What now?" said Lucy, obviously doubting that Ben's disguise could hold out under the scrutiny of so many hostile eyes.

Within moments they found themselves surrounded by a crowd heading in the same direction, and they had no choice other than to allow themselves to be driven along by the mob. They clasped hands as they were swept down the road on a tide of hatred.

"Death to the Watchers!" shouted a man with a boxer's broken nose and a spider's web tattooed inexpertly across his face.

Ben and Lucy exchanged glances. *What can we do?*

"Death to the Watchers!" Ben added his own voice to the throng.

The crowd carried them all the way to the Lyceum Theatre. A huge Legion banner hung down between the Roman columns: the black gauntleted fist on a field of white, the symbol of Sweet's oppression. The theatre had always seemed so glamorous to Ben in the past, but today it filled him with disgust.

Many was the time Ben had sneaked in to watch Dan Leno, "the funniest man on earth" as the billboards proclaimed or Paul Cinquevalli, "the king of the jugglers", who would catch a cannonball on the back of his neck. But under Sweet's rule, the theatres had changed their bills to suit the new mood of their audience. Where you might once have listened to Marie Lloyd chirping out "The Boy I Love Is Up In The Gallery", you would now be treated to a freak show, where the deformed and unfortunate were paraded for cruel titillation. There were no more plays by Oscar Wilde or comic operas by Gilbert and Sullivan. Instead, actors performed stories of murder and revenge, filling the auditoriums with screaming and always climaxing with the spilling of stage-blood and the hacking of fake limbs.

Ben dreaded what they were about to find inside the Lyceum.

Although there were commissionaires in attendance, in their smart red uniforms and white gloves, the crowd paid no attention to their requests to *"Walk this way, please, sir"*. It was every man for himself as the mob pushed and barged each other to get the best seats in the house. Ben gestured to Lucy with a nod of his head, and the pair made their way to the stairs which would take them to "the gods", as his pa always called them – the highest circle of seats that would give them the best view of proceedings. They had their crossbow pistols, they had rope, and height always gave Watchers the upper hand. Ben imagined himself swinging in to rescue Ghost and Moon and snatching them from the stage. Well, that was the plan anyway.

Ben and Lucy were able to get themselves seats in the front row on the left-hand side of the theatre. From their vantage point they could see everything. There was an orchestra in the pit, and a conductor with a prominent Legion armband waiting with his baton. It was a full house, with every seat occupied and angry-looking men, boys and women standing in the aisles. The only empty seats were in the royal box on the other side of the auditorium.

Ben searched for Carter and his pa and found them right at the back of the stalls, too far from the stage. Both men were trying to work their way through the crowd but they weren't having much success. One scuffle had already broken out, men and women exchanging blows as they fought over the last remaining seat.

Ben had been in some rough music halls but he had never sat in an audience like this. These people hadn't come just to be entertained; they weren't after a laugh and a sing-song and a break from it all. These people wanted blood.

Just then the conductor tapped on his music stand and an expectant hush fell upon the audience. Pausing for effect, the man flicked his baton with a flourish, leading the orchestra into a rousing march.

With a squeak of pulleys, the red velvet curtains were slowly drawn aside as the house lights went down. The bloodthirsty crowd roared its appreciation as the stage was revealed. Ben felt sick to his stomach.

A huge cage had been erected on the stage against a painted backdrop of a Roman arena. The cage was ten feet tall and thirty feet wide. In each corner there was another smaller cage holding one of the savage beasts that the crowd had been promised. That left a large cross of empty space in the middle – presumably where the fighting would take place.

In one corner was a lion, pacing back and forth and

roaring hungrily at the crowd. In another was a huge black bear, standing erect on its hind legs. In the third was a gorilla, a massive ape with a white stripe down its back, huge fists pawing the floor. Where Sweet had found the creatures, Ben could only guess. London Zoo seemed likely. In the fourth and final cage was a Feathered Man, crouched on its haunches, its long limbs ready to slash and claw.

Each of the animals was wearing a stout collar attached to a length of chain. These chains fed out through the bars to where gangs of four strongmen in leotards, their muscles glistening with oil, held them in their iron grips. These men were also responsible for controlling an array of levers and pulleys, which Ben assumed must control the gate of each animal pen. With this set-up, each team of men could control their own beast and either allow them access to the centre of the stage, or haul them back into their corner.

In his mind's eye, Ben could see how this wicked sport would play out. The victims would be placed in the middle of the open area of the cage. Then one of the animals would be released. If the victims survived that, then another pen would be opened, and so on...

Ben knew that there were men of all classes in London who loved to see animals fight, and win or lose money on the outcome. Bear-baiting had been outlawed for years, but there were still places you could go if you knew who to ask. Men would watch cocks tearing each other to pieces or dogs fighting tooth and nail – even rats. It was grisly. It was cruel. And Ben hated it.

Movement in the royal box caught Ben's eye and he nudged Lucy. It was Mr. Sweet, flanked by burly Legionnaires.

Damn, Ben cursed inwardly. *That changes everything.*

Now what should he do? Try to rescue his friends or maybe go straight for Sweet and try to end this war here and now?

"He's certainly dressed for the occasion," whispered Lucy, her breath soft in Ben's ear.

She was right. Sweet was wearing a flowing cape with a scarlet silk lining, its collar elegantly trimmed with fur. His face was concealed by an ivory mask in the shape of a bird's skull, wreathed with raven feathers. And on top of that, gleaming and malevolent, sat the Crown of Corruption.

Ben knew what he must do.

Sweet lifted his hand in a regal wave, a gold signet ring flashing on his finger. The crowd cheered lustily, and satisfied with this show of adoration, Sweet signalled his permission for the applause to cease.

His voice rolled out over the auditorium like black tar. "Let the circus begin!"

A drum roll sounded from the orchestra pit and for the first time Ben's eyes made out the faint square of a trapdoor in the middle of the stage, equidistant from the four savage contestants.

The trapdoor fell away and after a few seconds a platform rose into view. Standing on it were two figures. One armed with a trident, the other with a short Roman sword.

The audience erupted with glee. Except for Ben and Lucy.

They had found Ghost and Jago Moon.

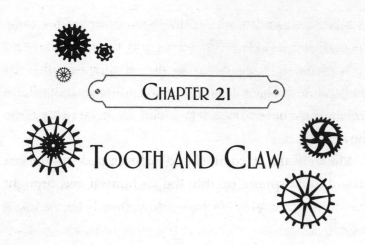

CHAPTER 21

TOOTH AND CLAW

Although Jago Moon was blind, many Legionnaires had learned to their cost that he was a dangerous man to put into a corner. Moon had trained his ears to such a level of sensitivity that his lack of sight ceased to be a setback at all. Moon brought his right arm back in a V-shape, holding the short stabbing sword horizontal with the floor. Shifting his weight onto his right leg, Moon slid into a martial arts stance, his open left hand stretched out before him for balance. At his side, Ghost held his trident in a double-handed grip, ready to lunge.

Moon heard the squeak of the hinges as one of the four animal pens was opened, followed by the rattle of a chain as a beast was released into the open centre of the cage. Recognizing its relative freedom and the meal that had been placed in front of it, the lion channelled all of its energy into its back legs, preparing to pounce. Its fierce amber eyes never once left Moon as it launched into the air.

Moon heard it coming and sidestepped at the last instant, then sprang up into the air himself and brought the round pommel of his sword down firmly on the lion's muzzle. Ghost leaped back at the same time, bringing up the trident, but the lion was too wily to allow itself to be speared that easily.

Stinging from Moon's blow, the lion gave a mighty roar which filled the theatre to the rafters. Ghost plunged his trident towards the animal's face but the lion batted the weapon away and then retaliated by slashing at Ghost with its claws. Ghost took three rapid steps backwards, which brought him out of the arc of the lion's paw but unfortunately within reach of the silverback gorilla. With a guttural roar, the giant ape reached through the bars of its own cage and caught Ghost squarely on the side of the head with a huge black fist, knocking him to the floor. Ghost jumped back up, but his head was spinning and he staggered again, stumbling perilously close to the lion. The crowd gasped with excitement.

Moon heard all of this and threw himself into a diving roll, which brought him up behind the lion. This time using the flat of his blade, Moon delivered a powerful strike to the lion's back leg, making the creature turn its attentions on him instead.

"You're Sweet's prisoner, just like me," Moon breathed. "I don't wanna hurt you, but I'm not gonna let you eat us, either."

The lion shook its shaggy mane in discomfort and then sprang at the blind man. With astonishing agility, Moon dropped down onto his back so that he could halt the lion's attack with his feet, bending his own legs and kicking out. The lion took the full force of Moon's kick in its sternum and fell back, yelping.

Ghost ran to Moon's side and helped the old man back up. Together they returned to the middle of the arena, panting with exertion.

"Is that all you've got?" Moon yelled.

The crowd jeered and booed. The winded lion paced back and forth, its tail flicking ceaselessly. Its chain was still slack; all it had to do was wait for its moment for revenge.

"Release the bear," ordered Sweet from the safety of his royal box.

The bear was as old and irritable as Moon himself.

It stood on its hind feet and rocked slowly like a heavyweight boxer choosing when to land the killer blow. It lowered its head in a fearsome growl, drops of hot spit spraying as it did so.

Ghost looked over his shoulder and saw that the lion had started padding towards them. Moon and Ghost stood back to back, silently turning in a circle, facing death in every direction.

The bear made the first move. It dropped onto all fours with such weight that the whole stage shook. Then it ran towards the Watchers, its gums drawn back to reveal a mouthful of savage teeth. There was nothing that Ghost and Moon could do except fall back. Moon stumbled as his legs tangled with Ghost's and the crowd drew in a collective breath. The bear only stopped because it had reached the end of its chain. Its handlers groaned with the effort as they struggled to hold it back.

The bear lifted its front legs again and swung at Moon, this time catching the blind Watcher a glancing blow that sent him reeling. Moon slumped to the ground, his hand going to his forehead and coming away red with blood. Which was when the lion sprang again.

In a flash, the enormous cat was standing over Moon, its jaws wide. Instead of backing away and surely being bitten, Moon flung his strong arms around the lion's neck and attempted to get it in a headlock. The lion flung its head from side to side, throwing Moon with it. The old man clung on, but his grip was loosening... Moon's face was deep in the lion's fur, away from the fury of the snapping teeth. He could smell its musky scent, could feel the blood pumping through its veins, the muscles rippling beneath the skin. It was a beautiful animal, Moon thought as his strength failed. There was no shame in losing this battle...

Ghost had no choice. Moon couldn't hold on much longer. Keeping out of reach of the bear's swinging paws, the young Watcher leaped high and sadly thrust his trident into the lion's side in a last ditch effort to save his friend.

The lion's roar of agony was deafening.

Perhaps animals have their own language. Or perhaps the sounds of pain need no translation. Either way, all the beasts responded. The bear bellowed. The gorilla pounded its fists against the drum of its chest. The Feathered Man lifted its head and shrieked a horrible curse.

"Release them all," roared Sweet.

"Lucy, you've got to try to help them. Carter and Pa are making their approach now."

"What about you?"

"I've got to face Sweet," said Ben, surreptitiously drawing out his crossbow.

"No!" Lucy hissed between her teeth. "It's too dangerous."

"I might never get this close to him again," said Ben. "I could destroy the crown now."

"Or you could get yourself killed."

"That's the risk I have to take." Ben gave her a wan smile. "You know the prophecy. Does it read as if the Hand of Heaven is a long-term job?"

"What are you going to do?" asked Lucy.

"Make it up as I go along," said Ben. "The same as always." He loaded his crossbow with a bolt which had a coil of thin rope attached. "I'm going to fix this rope into the ceiling, swing across the gap and destroy the crown before anyone can react."

The crowd exploded into cheering as the Feathered Man took to the air and hovered over the two ailing Watchers. Moon's head was bleeding freely and Ghost's leg had been raked by the bear's claws. Ben could see Carter and Pa in the midst of the mob, both desperately trying to manoeuvre themselves towards the stage without starting a fight on the way. Valentine and Nathaniel were hopefully backstage somewhere, but at that instant Ben knew that it was all down to him and Lucy.

"Shoot him then," urged Lucy. "You've got the crossbow, just do it."

"And then the crown will be picked up and placed on some other lunatic's head and we'll be no better off. It *has* to be this way, Lucy. Don't try to talk me out of it."

Ben carefully aimed the crossbow at the ceiling and let loose his bolt. It flew straight and true. He climbed up on the rail, readying himself to make the swing before any of the audience realized what was happening.

Lucy planted a small, soft kiss on his cheek.

Like all Watchers, they had been trained to run across rooftops, to jump the gaps, to land like cats and live to tell the tale. Now they had to put those skills into practice. Lucy clambered up on top of the rail and began to run along it like a tightrope walker, scampering along the lip of the scalloped boxes and finding footholds in the gilt plasterwork, until she was within jumping distance of the stage. When she could go no further, Lucy leaped out and grabbed the curtain rail over the stage. At the same time Ben grabbed the rope in both hands and flew over the audience like a trapeze artist. And the spectators loved it.

"More!" they applauded.

Lucy swung herself from the curtain rail across to one

of the beams that ran horizontally from one wing of the stage to the other and pulled herself up on top of it. Sandbags were stored on the rafters, used for raising and lowering backdrops. She worked one free, aimed carefully, then dropped it down on the bear's head. The huge animal was dazed, buying Ghost and Moon precious seconds.

Meanwhile, Ben's swing carried him down and then up, until he was in line with the royal box. Time froze. There was only him and Mr. Sweet in the whole universe.

Even through the disguise of Ben's blackened hair, Sweet recognized his nemesis.

Ben saw the blaze of fear in Sweet's eyes as the tyrant understood that this could be the end of his reign.

Then the crossbow bolt came loose from the ceiling.

And Ben fell.

With a cheer the crowd broke Ben's fall, assuming that his entrance was all part of the show. But the hands that reached for him did not come with kindness. Ben found himself tossed up in the air and pulled in all directions, as if he was a stick being fought over by dogs.

Above the stage, Lucy continued to aim her sandbag missiles, alternating between bombing the beasts inside the cage and the animal handlers outside. The gorilla was the master of the cage now. It stalked the central open cross and then climbed the bars, while the Feathered Man smelled the blood of the ailing lion and swooped in to finish what Ghost had started. Egged on by his drunken friends, someone in the audience threw an empty beer bottle at the gorilla. The glass smashed against the bars of the cage and the huge ape roared, shaking the bars in a furious attempt to reach his assailant. The strongmen in their leotards looked on with terror as the bolts that pinned the steel cage to the stage started to strain in their sockets, the wood splintering with each jolt.

Moon and Ghost were just about holding their own against the bear, but Lucy could see that they couldn't go on much longer. One blow from the bear's huge paws or one bite from those jaws and that would be the end. Valentine and Nathaniel still hadn't appeared – they had to be having problems of their own. Jonas had given up trying to get to the stage surreptitiously and was racing forwards, using the backs of the chairs as stepping stones and ignoring the cries of protest. Carter had found his own unique way, using his formidable claw to swing beneath the boxes.

No one had seen Mr. Sweet draw his revolver.

"Die, Ben Kingdom. *Die!*" Sweet shouted. Then he pulled the trigger, letting off round after round into the crowd.

The gorilla howled. The bear roared. The audience screamed.

And the Lyceum Theatre descended into pandemonium.

Shots rang out and all around Ben there were cries of agony as Sweet's bullets struck his own subjects. Ben dropped to the floor and shielded his head with his arms to prevent himself from being trampled as the crowd began to surge towards the exits like a herd of startled animals. First one man then another was knocked over the balcony in the confusion, but the mass evacuation didn't even slow.

Carter reached the stage and leaped over the heads of the confused musicians in the pit. "This is your cue to run," he suggested to the bemused conductor, even as the orchestra threw down their instruments and rushed to get away. Jonas barrelled into the nearest of the animal handlers, grabbing him with both arms and hurling him to the ground. Another of the strongmen moved to intercept Carter and made a huge show of rolling his fists in the style of a bare-knuckle boxer. The professor looked at the man with something close to contempt and then floored him with a single swinging punch.

"Next!" snapped Carter.

A faintly echoing *click, click, click* told Ben that Sweet

had run out of ammunition and he scrambled back onto his feet. If he could climb the velvet curtains…

Overhead, Lucy released the last of her sandbag missiles. Her aim was good and it landed squarely on the head of one of the animal handlers. The man staggered in ever decreasing circles and then collapsed. Now with no more missiles to drop, Lucy launched herself instead. She landed neatly on one of the mustachioed men, locking her legs around his neck. The man struggled to shake her off but Lucy only increased the pressure until he fell unconscious and slumped in a heap. She didn't have time to enjoy her victory though, as two more of the strongmen approached her. Lucy extended her quarterstaff with a flick of her wrist. She rapped the first strongman soundly on the temple and then jabbed the second in the solar plexus. Four men out of action. Lucy dusted her hands with satisfaction.

The remaining strongmen took this opportunity to make a break for it. They ran straight into Valentine and Nathaniel, who were just emerging from the wings. The Watchers were ready with their quarterstaffs, but the men didn't want to fight, they just wanted to get away. Lucy didn't blame them.

The Feathered Man was screaming. It had grown bored of the taste of lion. Now that it was no longer restrained by the strongmen tugging on its chain, the fallen angel flew up to the roof of the cage. Lucy saw the sinews on its long, spindly arms as it used all of its strength to strain against the bars. With a shriek that was part effort, part triumph, the Feathered Man was able to bend the bars in the roof just enough for it to snake its body through the gap. Once out, it unfurled its wings and flew up to squat on the balcony, dragging its chain behind it. Lucy shuddered. The horrible creature gave the impression that it had finished its theatre supper and was on the lookout for dessert.

And all the while the bear and the gorilla closed in on Moon and Ghost.

The only way to get the trapped Watchers out was through a doorway of iron bars at the front of the cage, secured with a sturdy padlock. Valentine searched the unconscious strongmen for a key, but Carter couldn't be bothered to wait. Three chops from his claw and the padlock gave way.

Carter opened the gate and stepped into the cage, extending his hand to Jago Moon. "I can't believe I'm doing this."

Anger had steadily been building up inside the bear and it chose that moment to charge. Moon performed a rolling dive, which took him out of the bear's path, but landed him beside the gorilla. The huge silverback flared its nostrils and pushed out its chest as it started to advance on the old Watcher, forcing him to retreat into the furthest corner.

Ghost had troubles of his own. The bear was growing berserk, swinging at the young Watcher with insane fury. Ghost ducked, but not soon enough. The bear caught him a glancing blow which sent him flying. Nathaniel jumped in through the open cage door and whacked the animal soundly on the snout with his staff – he didn't want to hurt it, but he had to get his friends out of danger. The bear yelped and staggered backwards, giving Ghost just enough time to dart out through the open gate, where Jonas was waiting to help him to safety. Ghost's big brown eyes said everything that his silent mouth couldn't.

Meanwhile, the gorilla continued to advance on Moon. The animal was snorting heavily and its black lips curled back to reveal pink gums and sharp white teeth. It was quick too. Each time Moon made to get round it, the ape blocked his path...

While this was happening beneath him, Ben was halfway up the stage curtains, climbing hand over hand. There was still a chance that he could get to Sweet...

With a fearsome roar, the bear spotted the open gate and loped towards it. The young Watchers dived aside as it burst through. The bear shook its mighty head, gave another roar and then blundered away towards the wings, knocking over a limelight in its hurry to be free.

Ben saw the lamp spill its burning contents. There was a long second of silence, followed by a *whump* as the velvet curtains caught fire. Moon heard the awful sound of the conflagration before he felt the heat.

It took half a heartbeat for the pillar of flames to reach Ben's feet. Ben had no choice. He threw himself clear, landing awkwardly and painfully on the stage. A scream filled the theatre, but it didn't come from Ben's lips.

It was Sweet who was wailing, arms up to protect what remained of his face, reliving his worst nightmare.

CHAPTER 22

BRINGING DOWN
THE HOUSE

The Lyceum was falling down around them.

Ghost was out of that hateful cage but he had only gone two paces when he lurched haphazardly.

"He's concussed," said Carter, "the bear has knocked him senseless. Nathaniel, Lucy, Valentine, get him out of here... Go! All of you. There's nothing more you can do here. I'll save Moon, trust me."

Valentine and Nathaniel supported Ghost between them. They began to move and Ghost moaned with pain. "Easy does it, old chap," said Valentine. "We'll soon get you out of this bally place."

Burning swathes of curtain were falling to the stage,

starting yet more fires. The wings were already impassable. In a few minutes, the theatre would be an inferno.

"Look sharp!" said Jonas, giving one of the unconscious strongmen a kick in the side to wake him. "We can't let them burn." Ben joined his pa and together they roused the animal handlers so the brutes could make their own escape.

Ben flicked his eyes towards the royal box. Sweet was gone.

All Ben wanted to do now was rescue Mr. Moon, but an awful creaking sound drew his attention upwards. Flames were already racing across the ceiling and it took Ben a moment to realize that the noise was coming from the impressive crystal chandelier. The fire had weakened the rope that held it up and the huge weight of the cut glass was about to go crashing to the floor. Nathaniel and Valentine were almost directly in its path, cradling Ghost between them. Lucy was only a pace behind.

"*Look out!*" Ben shouted.

Lucy reacted first. She pushed the others out of the way, but put herself in the line of danger.

The chandelier smashed to the ground, trapping Lucy's legs beneath its metal arms and sending a hundred broken crystals scattering. Jonas jumped down off the stage and ran to her. Bracing himself, he took the chandelier in his big hands and heaved it up. The effort showed on his contorted face and the proud veins on the side of his neck.

Ben was torn. He wanted to go to Lucy but Mr. Moon was trapped inside the cage, the gorilla standing squarely in his way.

The theatre gave another groan and a length of balcony collapsed, eaten away by flames. Valentine and Nathaniel were making good progress with Ghost, and Lucy had dragged herself out from under the mess of metal and crystal. Jonas let the chandelier drop and helped Lucy to her feet. She was limping but alive. That settled it for Ben.

"I'm coming to get you, Mr. Moon."

"Leave me, Ben," the grizzled Watcher called, sensing that the fire had spread around three sides of the cage. "No sense in all of us dying."

"I'm leaving with you or not at all."

Reassured that the other Watchers would make it, Ben knew that it was down to him and Carter. The heat was pressing in on them, as if they were in an oven. Moon was backed up as far against the bars as he could go and his path to the doorway was blocked by the massive ape. Carter, meanwhile, was approaching it cautiously from behind.

The gorilla pawed the ground as it prepared to attack. It wasn't looking good.

"Go," said Carter. "I'll get him out, I promise." The professor grinned like a wolf. "I'm a Watcher now."

"You can sling your hook an' all," Moon called to Carter. "I can handle this."

Trying to prove his point, Moon feinted left, and then moved quickly to his right in an attempt to get around the colossal ape. The gorilla rose up on its back legs and drummed its chest in fury, blocking Moon's escape again.

Undeterred, Carter cupped his hands and slapped them rhythmically on his own chest. The gorilla stopped…

Ben watched in amazement as Carter slowly approached the animal, his arms spread wide. To Ben's surprise, the professor started to make a series of small grunting noises, puffing out his cheeks and releasing short coughs, then snorting down his nostrils, until, step by heavy step, the gorilla shuffled away from Moon and turned to face Carter instead.

"Go now," Carter said to Moon. "While I've got it distracted."

"What do you think you're playing at?"

"Rescuing you," said Carter patronizingly. "You blind old curmudgeon."

Moon made a snorting sound of his own, and the gorilla swung its head back towards him.

"Please go," said Carter, with more compassion this time. "Ben needs you."

That was the persuasion that Moon needed, and he began to edge towards the open gate while Carter kept the gorilla distracted.

The professor made another deep sound in his chest. The gorilla grunted in return and Carter took a step closer, his forehead lowered and his eyes level with the beast's. Something about the noises that he was making seemed to pacify the animal.

"*Unk*," said Carter, and the gorilla responded, sitting heavily on its backside.

The man and the animal were face-to-face, Carter's breath mingling with the ape's as they peacefully searched each other's eyes.

"*Unk*," Carter repeated. "*Tanto munguni, unk.*"

Moon made it all the way around the cage to the safety of the gate, the squeak of its hinges as clear as a foghorn to his sharp ears. "Nice trick," he admitted grudgingly.

"I spent a month living among the gorillas in the cloud forests of the Virunga volcanoes," said Carter. "You can't help but pick up some of the dialect."

Carter put out his hand and the gorilla took it meekly, rising back to its feet.

"What are you playing at now?"

"I'm not leaving this magnificent creature to the mercy of the flames," said Carter firmly.

Moon was suitably put down. "I don't think I'm ever going to get the measure of you," he said, as they fled from the burning building.

"Few people do," said Carter as he ran. "And you're welcome, by the way. For saving your life."

Moon muttered something which was probably *thank you*.

"That'll do," said Carter with a smile.

"I don't mean to be rude, Professor," said Ben as they reached the foyer, and exploded into the rain-sodden street beyond. "But what *are* you going to do with your new friend?"

"Have you heard of Mr. Jamrach and his menagerie?"

"The old German geezer with the most dangerous pet shop in the world?"

"The very same."

Of course Ben had heard of him. *Every* East End boy had heard of Jamrach. Charles Jamrach was famous for his private collection of animals; he had an exotic pet emporium on the Ratcliffe Highway and a warehouse on Old Gravel Lane which Ben and the other lads used to sneak into for dares.

Ben was fascinated. "Is it true that one of his Bengal tigers escaped and carried off a small boy in its jaws and would have eaten him if Mr. Jamrach hadn't come to the rescue with his bare hands?"

"That's not even the half of it," said Carter.

Ben grinned; it made sense that a world traveller like Claw Carter would know a man like that.

"Jamrach's dead," said Moon, with a distinct lack of good grace. "Last September."

"I know," said Carter, "but his sons inherited the business."

"Got an answer for everything, haven't you?" said Moon.

CHAPTER 23

HERE LIES AUGUSTUS MOON

Ruby could feel Ben Kingdom all around her; the street breathed of him.

She was on Old Gravel Lane, the place where Ben had lived and grown. This was where she and Ben had met, just before Christmas last year. She had been using Ben then, gaining his confidence so that she could part him from the last of the Judas Coins. Look where that had got them.

Although she couldn't see it, Ruby knew that she was being followed by Grey Wing. The fallen angel was up there somewhere, among the storm clouds, watching her every step. She had been searching for the Gehenna Key all day and her quest had finally brought her here. Ruby paused outside St Peter's church opposite the Jolly Tar, the public house where Moon used to peddle his second-hand books. It was possible that another of his forefathers had been laid to rest here.

She'd changed since she met Ben. Ruby wasn't sure whether that was a good thing or not, but she did know that she couldn't keep on living the same old life.

Get the key. Get her stash. Get out.

She couldn't stand the thought of even one more day under the Legion's cold fist.

Ruby picked the lock and slipped inside St Peter's. As usual, she went looking for church silver first. In the vestry she found a rather nice plate which was for taking the collection, plus a St Christopher's medal on a chain that was tucked away at the back of a drawer. She hesitated and then put the plate back where she had found it, but she slipped the necklace over her head. St Christopher, the patron saint of travellers. Superstitious nonsense, but pretty, and she *was* going on a journey so...

The fierce black clouds overhead made it almost as dark as night inside the church and Ruby lit a stump of candle so that she could begin her search in earnest. So far the other members of the Moon family she had found had all had plaques marking their resting place inside a church, either in one of the side chapels or in the crypt. Ruby was hoping that would be the case again here. It was foul weather to be hunting round a graveyard.

After a few minutes, her flickering candle settled on a modest stone set into the floor.

AUGUSTUS MOON
SERVANT OF A HIGHER POWER
1515 - 1549
NOT DEAD, MERELY SLEEPING

I hope not, she thought with a shiver.

Ruby's fingers trembled as she caressed the memorial, searching for the Watcher symbol and the secret compartment that she knew it would release.

After a few seconds, she found what she was after and smiled.

The panel opened and Ruby was treated to a waft of stale air. She hesitated. Would there be another insulting message from beyond the grave or would she finally be able to give Grey Wing what he wanted and get him off her back?

There was a bundle inside the recess. Oiled cloth had been used to wrap a thin object about seven inches long.

Tremulously, Ruby picked it up and carefully unfolded the cloth, terrified of what lay beneath.

It was cold and black, and even the heat of her hand could do nothing to warm the metal. The teeth of the key took the form of a broken hand, a desecrated version of the Watcher symbol, and the bow at the end of the long cold shank was moulded in the shape of a skull.

There was no doubt that this was the Gehenna Key.

There was some writing engraved on the shank but it was too small to make out. Ruby pulled out the jeweller's eyeglass that she always carried – another of the tools of her trade – and pushed it to her right eye, closing the other.

Even then the script was hard to decipher.

There was a name: *Alasdair Valentine.*

When she had shared a barracks with Alexander Valentine, the boy had often told them of his ancestor, who was the original architect of the Under. Ruby knew the story well. Sir Alasdair was a priest turned bad, a man who had given up searching for God and decided instead to devote himself to the service of evil...

She read on.

The end of days, the death of light.

Release the creatures of the pit and revel in the night.

Ruby dropped the key as if it was a hot coal.

The creatures of the pit were just a legend, surely? A story told to Legion children to keep them in line.

Every Legionnaire knew that Sir Alasdair had designed the sanctuary of the Under, with its carved columns and vast throne. His blackest creation was the pit, a supposedly bottomless hole into which victims of the Legion could be thrown. The sanctuary was conceived to be the opposite of a church, a cathedral to evil, and the pit was the opposite of the spire – an anti-spire, as it were – intended to be so deep that it would lead to Hell itself. Ruby shuddered at the thought of a mind that could conceive that kind of plan.

Legionnaires digging the pit went down into its depths and never returned, or so the story went. There were rumours about "things" that lived in the darkness; appalling, abominable things. Even the Legion were scared by what they had awakened. It was quickly decided that the bottom of the pit should be sealed off. A huge gate was built, a mile down, operated by a system of hidden levers and controlled by a lock in the sanctuary itself. That lock had only one key – quite literally, the key to Hell.

Obviously the Watchers had stolen the key… And now it was lying on the floor in front of her.

Ruby had the urge to wrap it up and bury it again;

just pretend that she had never found it. But a flash of lightning suddenly illuminated the church and Ruby shrieked as she saw the black shape of a Feathered Man silhouetted against a stained glass window. The fallen angel gave a hideous cackling laugh. *It knew.*

There would be no way she could deceive Grey Wing. And no hiding place from his wrath.

Unless Ruby stayed here in the church. She was safe here, after all. Grey Wing and his fallen angels could not step over the threshold.

But she had no food. And all Grey Wing need do was send a patrol of Legionnaires to roust her out.

Ruby needed another plan. But what?

As she tried to think, she was distracted by a slurping, sucking sound. The rain had been so constant that she no longer heard all the varied sounds of water as it found different ways to punish the city and its people. However, this splashing sound was something new.

Although the church echoed, she was able to pinpoint the source to the resting place of Augustus Moon. Ruby bent her ear curiously to the open panel. The sound of water was rising up from inside. Pulling a crowbar from her pack, Ruby worked the edges of the gravestone free from the floor. Then, using all of her weight, she levered the stone up and out.

It wasn't just a secret compartment hidden beneath – it was the entrance to a tunnel!

"So the Moons have always been crafty beggars," said Ruby softly.

The noise of water was louder now and Ruby guessed that the tunnel must have flooded. Where it led and whether it was still passable were other questions entirely.

"There's only one way to find out."

Every step that Ruby took away from the Feathered Man felt like a step in the right direction. She had failed Ben once before when she allowed Sweet to get the last of the Judas Coins. She could not – she *would* not – be the one who let Grey Wing take the Gehenna Key.

Suddenly there was something in Ruby's life that was bigger than she was. She had purpose, and that purpose was to deny Grey Wing the key. Her stash seemed trivial in comparison. She could have all the gold in the world, but if Grey Wing had the key there would be no world left to enjoy it in.

With that thought driving her on, Ruby descended the stone stairs that spiralled downwards from the church floor. Floodwater was lapping at the bottom steps and Ruby shuddered as she stepped in up to her thighs. The tunnel only led in one direction, so that was the way Ruby went. It was a tight passage, not at all like the grand vaulted tunnels of the Under. Her shoulders almost brushed both walls and she had to stoop over to keep her head from rubbing the ceiling.

Water dripped on her through a hundred cracks in the brickwork and she cupped her candle protectively. What if it went out...? What if she met someone – or some*thing*?

Too many ifs, Ruby Johnson. She concentrated instead on putting one foot in front of the other.

When she reached another spiral staircase at the far end, Ruby felt elated. She knew that she was not out of the woods yet, but it felt better to be heading upwards again. The top of the stairs brought her to a trapdoor in the ceiling. Ruby pushed upwards with both hands and panicked when she found it wouldn't budge. The Gehenna Key in her pack felt impossibly heavy; she had to find a way to get it to Ben and the Watchers – they would know what to do.

Ruby climbed nearer to the trapdoor. She put her shoulders against it, then she used the strength of her legs in an attempt to force the trapdoor open. She felt the hard wood bruising her neck and shoulders, her thighs burning with the effort.

The wood did not budge.

Ruby put her heart and soul into it. *Come on... Please.* With a screech of protest, the door cracked open enough for her to be able to fit the edge of her crowbar into the gap.

Encouraged, she pushed again, and this time the trapdoor opened wide enough for Ruby to be able to wedge her jemmy in vertically and then squirm out past it.

She was in a mouldy basement. But where?

Two smells rushed to her nose with the answers. Beer and tobacco. Ruby could have almost cheered with joy. She was in the cellar of a pub. The tunnel had brought her across Old Gravel Lane to the Jolly Tar!

There was no time to congratulate herself though. She had to move quickly while she was still one step ahead of the Feathered Man. The Jolly Tar had a back door, she knew. Maybe she could sneak out that way...

The wood above Ruby's head splintered even as she was thinking those thoughts. She scurried backwards for protection as one of the floorboards was ripped away by a taloned hand. A pointed beak was thrust into the gap, snapping angrily. The Feathered Man tore two more floorboards away and shoved its head through the hole.

"Come with me, girl," Grey Wing screeched.

Josiah, the angel. Josiah, the Weeping Man.

In the dungeon, the water had been rising steadily throughout the day. Josiah could no longer sit on the floor but had to stand, only his head and shoulders above the surface. In her cell next door, his much shorter fellow prisoner was standing on her bed. It was only a matter of time.

But that was not the reason for Josiah's tears.

The Gehenna Key had been found. Josiah sensed it in his spirit and by that same visionary power he saw the girl, Ruby Johnson, in Grey Wing's clutches.

The Legion had dug too deep when they built the pit and even they feared what lay at the bottom of it, in the very bowels of the earth. But with the key, the creatures of the pit would no longer be restrained in its depths.

They were coming! Josiah could see them in his vision now, advancing towards the ancient gate that held them, in anticipation of its opening.

For centuries they had been brooding and hatching their nightmares of destruction. All mankind was their enemy. The Uncreated One loved these humans; that was why these demons hated them so bitterly. And when they were released they would not rest until the world was laid to waste and humanity was no more.

What horrors the Weeping Man foresaw!

The tentacles. The teeth. The limbs with no name to describe them. Barbs, hooks, suckers, tendrils. Eyes with no lids. Tongues with hands for grabbing. Everything that was monstrous and foul.

"Nooo!" Josiah bellowed, tugging again on his chains, to no avail.

And still the water rose.

Still the creatures of the pit began their ascent. Racing towards the light so that they could bring an end to it.

"Noooooo!"

DAY FIVE
1ST MAY, 1892

CHAPTER 24

REVOLUTION DAY

Midnight. Sunday. Christ Church Spitalfields.
Revolution Day.

Ben's right hand felt strange. It was not the occasional throbbing sensation that he had become used to, this was something new. Something powerful was stirring…

He surveyed his troops, cold and tired beneath their makeshift tent.

Nathaniel Kingdom, brother in arms. Alexander Valentine, Legion expert. Lucy Lambert, born for this moment. Ghost, the silent soldier, fit and ready for action again. Jonas Kingdom, the rock. Jago Moon, the hard place. Claw Carter, the secret weapon. Forty other Watchers, the brave remnant.

"Someone's coming," warned Moon. "It sounds like—"

"Hans!" said Ben, as the Watcher spy shuffled over the rooftop to join them. He seemed in a bad way. "Are you alright?"

The German boy turned his head slowly, his eyes swimming in and out of focus.

"What's happened?" asked Lucy. "You're not hurt, are you?"

"Not hurt," Hans repeated.

"Come and sit down," said Valentine. "He's obviously gone through the mill to get here, poor chap."

The Watchers gathered round their comrade. Moon thrust a tin mug of tea into his hands, straight from the small stove. "This'll warm you up, son."

Hans held the mug and stared at it, uncomprehending. The boy was a shadow of what he once was. His cheeks were gaunt, his expression pained.

"I have found the Queen…" Hans began the speech which Sweet had scratched onto his brain. "She is in a dungeon beneath the Tower of London…"

"Her Majesty!" Lucy gasped. "How is she?"

Hans ignored her question and continued. "I have a map that will take you to her, Ben Kingdom. And here…" Hans opened his hand to show the key clenched between his fingers. "This is the key to her cell."

"How did you manage it, son?" asked Moon, thumping Hans affectionately on the back.

Ben dragged Hans to his feet and threw his arms around him. "You've done it! You're gonna be the most popular German since Prince Albert!"

Ben felt Hans go stiff, and then, with a sudden jerk, the German lad promptly fell back down, his head lolling on his neck. A puppet with its strings cut.

"He's out cold," said Lucy. "The pressure must have been too much." She went to rouse him but Carter stopped her.

"You won't wake him," he said. "I've seen this before on expeditions. Extreme exhaustion resulting in a state close to coma. Best to leave him."

"You rest, Hans," said Ben. "You've earned it." He smiled broadly. "We can save Queen Victoria," he went on, his head spinning with joy. "Hans has given us the key to victory. When all of London hears this...well, let's just say, if I was in the Legion, I'd start running now."

Lucy made a pillow of her jacket and tried to settle Hans in a more comfortable position. She brushed the boy's forehead. It was cold with sickly sweat.

His heart still racing with excitement, Ben's mind went into overdrive as he worked out who could save Victoria. "Lucy, Mr. Moon, I want you to rescue Her Majesty.

Hans is in no state to lead you, but we've got his map."

Carter ran his eye over the crumpled piece of paper and then handed it to Valentine for his opinion.

"I never even knew that these tunnels existed," said Carter.

Valentine shook his head too. "These are new."

"No matter what happens to the rest of us, Lucy," said Ben, "you have to get Queen Victoria to safety." He placed the stolen key in Lucy's hand. "Take this," he said. "If anyone can get her out, it's you.

"Valentine, can you stay and watch over Hans, just until he wakes up? We can't have any Legionnaires finding him here and attacking him. Pa, Nathaniel, Ghost, you're my generals. When the army blast through those tunnels they'll have plans of their own, but the free Londoners will need leadership. Be on the lookout for signal lights – three flashes means a friend. Everyone who is coming to join us should shine a signal light at two this morning. You all have your streets and lists of targets; gather your troops into a unit, and then set to work. Guard towers have to be put out of action, street patrols have to be stopped. Every Legionnaire has to be incapacitated or distracted for long enough for me to complete the most vital part of the operation…" Ben spoke with an authority beyond his years; he almost didn't recognize his own voice.

This was his destiny, he understood, this was him being the Hand of Heaven. It was never about power for him, it was simply about finding the truth and standing up to defend it. Sweet was evil, pure and undiluted. Evil had to be resisted, so this was Ben resisting.

"Professor Carter, you're with me. I need you to get me to Sweet and keep him occupied while I put the Hand on his head and destroy the Crown of Corruption."

Ben knew full well that his part in the mission was the most dangerous. He might not get out of this alive. However he was equally certain that he wouldn't want to live the rest of his life in the knowledge that he hadn't tried.

"This is war," Ben went on, "but we are still Watchers. The Legion symbol is the gauntleted fist, ours is the open hand. If the Watchers win today—"

"*When* we win," Lucy encouraged.

"*When* we win," Ben echoed, "this has to be a day that no one is ashamed of. 1st May 1892 will be recorded in history. This is the Watchers' story for the next generations to read, this is when the world learns who we are. Mother Shepherd taught me the words to the Watcher creed." Ben coughed to cover the tremor that entered his voice. He began to recite the words which bound them all together. One voice became seven as Carter, Jonas, Nathaniel, Valentine, Lucy and Moon joined Ben; and then *forty-*

seven as all of the other cell leaders recited the Watcher creed with them.

"Love makes us wise.

Tears make us strong.

Patience makes us steadfast.

Justice makes us humble.

Forgiveness will bring us victory."

Ghost nodded his silent agreement. Forty-*eight*.

There were no more words for any of them to say. And so, instead of "goodbye" and "good luck", the Watchers hugged each other and shook hands, and enjoyed each others' company. Even Mr. Moon deigned to clasp Claw Carter by his hand.

"I hope you live through this," said Moon.

"You too," said Carter.

Ben held his pa and brother tighter than he had ever held them before. Then he stood awkwardly before Lucy. Lucy made the first move and put her hands on his shoulders.

"Promise me you won't do anything stupid, Ben."

"When have I ever done that?"

They stayed like that for as long as they could, just looking at each other.

Big Ben chimed one.

In sixty minutes, the revolution would begin.

"Right," said Ben. "Here we go."

Silently the Watchers went their separate ways, taking their packs, freshly stocked with everything they might need: matches, tools, climbing rope. Valentine busied himself making Hans more comfortable, leaving Carter and Ben standing thoughtfully on top of the British Museum, their own packs strung across their bodies.

"I'm glad I'm not fighting against you," said Ben.

"The feeling is mutual," Carter replied.

A fork of lightning chose that instant to shatter the night. Ben didn't know whether it was a good omen or bad. Either way, it was too late to do anything about it.

In his private rooms, Mr. Sweet stared into the gilt-edged mirror above the fire. He had changed his raven mask again. The new one was made of hand-stitched black leather. The Crown of Corruption still sat on top of course, nestled against a headdress of inky feathers. The beak was not as sharp as the iron mask's, but the overall effect was more stylish, he thought. Befitting a king. *But king of what?*

Two eyes blinked back at him from the eyeholes of the mask and it took him a second to realize that they were his.

Sweet continued to examine those eyes, looking as deeply into them as he could, searching for evidence of the man he used to be. And all the while he tried and failed to ignore the other figures that he could see stirring in the glass. The distorted faces of his constant companions, laughing and jeering. Taunting him for his failures. The shadows that enticed him into deeper and more desperate wickedness.

You aren't real, Sweet assured himself as he spun round to find that he was alone, as always.

Yes, we are, they hissed when his back was turned.

Sweet swayed and put his hand on the mantelpiece for support, his signet ring glinting. He had been suffering from these bouts of dizziness with increasing regularity; as if his grip on his body was slipping along with his hold on his sanity. Rage overtook him then, like a volcano erupting. He balled his hand into a fist and smashed the mirror to pieces, his lips beneath his mask twisted into a snarl.

Ben Kingdom is coming for you, said the voices from the jagged shards of fallen glass.

He might be struggling to remember other things; even his own name was starting to slip out of reach. But Sweet would not forget the name of Kingdom. Neither forget, nor forgive.

"You're going to pay for what you did to me, boy."

And he knew how.

When Sweet had used the Crown of Corruption to invade the German boy's mind, he had plucked two words from the quivering jelly of his brain.

"Revolution Day," said Sweet, rolling the words on his tongue just as he would a fine brandy.

The words had come with a date. 1st May. Today.

And a time: two o'clock.

And a ridiculously flimsy plan.

The Londoners were going to rise up apparently. They were going to flash their lanterns and gather in the streets and then Ben Kingdom and his merry band were going to overthrow the Legion. They weren't even going to use bullets to do it. Such naivety, really, it was so precious. Violence won the day every time in Sweet's experience and violence was exactly what the Watchers could expect. Massive, overwhelming, soul-destroying violence.

The one trump card in Ben Kingdom's plan had been the element of surprise and, by the power of the crown, even that had been denied him.

"So you think this will work?" whispered Ben, his back pressed against the wall, the rain making streams down his face.

Ben and Carter had been working their way cautiously through the abandoned streets towards the Tower and Mr. Sweet. Neither of them spoke, both deep in thoughts of their own. They had made it all the way to Lower Thames Street without being spotted. Ben's right hand was throbbing, the sign that meant that he was about to be used as an instrument of the Uncreated One, the source of good at the centre of the universe.

Claw Carter ran his hand across his unshaven chin pensively. The professor looked so tired, Ben thought, drawn tight like wire.

Thunder had been boiling in the clouds and periodically London was brought to vivid life by a flash of lightning.

"It might work," said Carter. "It just might."

For a brief moment the professor's wolfish face was lit up by the storm and Ben was shocked by what he saw – the raw hunger of a predator. Carter still had a score to settle with the Legion, and there was no doubt that there was about to be a reckoning.

"We have to try it," said Ben, putting from his mind the uneasiness that had begun to nag at him. "We can do it," he encouraged them both. "What other choice do we have?"

The stamp of heavy boots advancing from the direction of the Tower alerted them both to a brigade of Legionnaires on the hunt for curfew breakers. Ben pushed himself deeper into the shadows of a side alley, Carter beside him.

Keep your head down, Benny Boy.

If they could just make it past this patrol there was a fair chance that they could get to the Tower...where their troubles would really begin. Ben was relying on Carter being able to get them inside, using the professor's knowledge of the Legion against them. Without that edge, they were probably finished.

Ben felt Carter's hand land firmly on his shoulder and give a squeeze of reassurance. A cannonade of thunder rolled across the city, shaking windows in its fury. The Legionnaires were level with the alleyway now, their own heads tucked down against their chests as the rain lashed down.

Just a little further…

They were almost past.

Made it! thought Ben with relief. *They haven't seen us.*

"Here!" shouted Carter at the top of his lungs. "Over here!"

"What are you doing?" gasped Ben as the Legionnaires swivelled, their rifles raised.

Carter kept a firm grip on Ben's shoulder and shoved him out into the open, his claw suddenly resting on Ben's naked throat.

"Well, well, well," snarled Captain Mickelwhite. "If it isn't Claw Carter?"

"The very same."

Mickelwhite did not lower his gun. There was something different about him; it took Ben a moment to realize that the boy's long nose had been broken and now twisted to the right. "You know what we do to traitors, Carter," he said with a cruel smirk.

"I do," said Carter. "But I'm not a traitor. I'm the man who brings you Ben Kingdom's head on a plate."

"What are you doing?" Ben said desperately.

Carter shoved Ben hard in the back and sent him stumbling. The brigade of Legionnaires joined in a chorus of mocking laughter.

"Oh, Professor," mimicked Mickelwhite. "Why are you being so mean?"

Claw Carter roared with approval. "I'm doing it because I want to; because I can." He turned to Ben. "You thought I was your *friend*..." He drawled the word, making it sound weak and foolish. "Well, I'm sick of listening to your endless drivel about hope and forgiveness and love. I've travelled the world and never found those things."

"But you said that you believed in the Watchers, in what we stand for..." protested Ben.

"Let's tell him what we believe, shall we, lads?" Carter gestured to the watching Legionnaires. "Perhaps if we shout it loud enough, we might drum it into that thick, ginger head of his?"

Ben felt sick as they marched him to the Tower, chanting as they went.

"No weakness in our hearts!

No mercy for our enemies!

No law to bind us!

No prison to hold us!

No grievance to go unavenged!

No Watcher to be left alive!"

Carter brought his face down level with Ben's while Mickelwhite looked on and smirked.

"Do you see where *you* fit in that picture, boy?"

CHAPTER 25

THE BATTLE OF LONDON

Big Ben tolled two.

"It's time, Pa," Nathaniel whispered.

Jonas Kingdom nodded. Ghost extended his quarterstaff and held it in a double-handed grip. They were as ready as they would ever be.

The Watchers were hidden on a roof on Whitechapel High Street. It was a vital strategic point, set at a crossroads, with a clear view up Commercial Street and down Leman Street. London was shrouded in an unnatural darkness. The clouds that had been gathering over the city for days seemed to be alive, stirred by hidden winds until they were circling overhead. The rain fell like a waterfall, not in drops but in continuous streams.

"It's gonna be alright, son," said Jonas, realizing that he was reassuring himself too.

They waited for the signal lights, the sign that their hope would not be in vain.

Nathaniel spotted it first.

"Look, Pa," he said pointing. "Do you see it?"

"I see it," said Jonas; the flicker of light in a window as a lamp was brought close to the glass. The curtain was drawn over it, then back again, three times, to send three brief flashes of light. Further down the street the message was repeated in another window, then another and another. Jonas smiled. Every way he looked he could see a light twinkling in a window.

"We aren't going to be alone," he said. "Londoners believe in the Watchers...and in your brother."

"That's probably because they haven't had to live with him," said Nathaniel, although his chest was swelling with pride as he dropped the rope ladder over the side of the building and clambered down to the ground.

The three Watchers returned the signal and gradually people emerged into the rain-drowned night. Jonas could see the mixture of emotions on their faces. There was fear, but determination too. More and more ordinary Londoners defied Sweet's curfew and came out into the street, carrying clubs, walking sticks, pickaxe handles, even a frying pan.

One young man ran up to Nathaniel eagerly and grabbed him by the shoulders.

"Are you with us?" the man asked.

"Damned right," said Nathaniel.

"Listen up!" called Jonas, getting the attention of the crowd and holding out his own quarterstaff horizontally, like a shepherd rounding up his flock. "The first thing we need to do is secure these streets, then we can start moving out from here. There's a Legion guard post at Aldgate Station, that's our first target."

Abruptly a brilliant light scorched through the black and the revolutionaries were all lit up as bright as day. Jonas listened for the following rumble of thunder, but it didn't come. It was then that he spotted the source of the illumination – a searchlight at the end of the street, aimed directly at them.

"RUN!" Jonas shouted, just as the squad of Legionnaires began their charge, guns blazing.

"Gunfire," said Lucy, as the sounds of the battle reached them on Lime Street.

"It's not good," said Moon. "The army uses Martini-

Enfield rifles and .455 calibre Webley revolvers..." He inclined his head to listen more intently. "Those shots are from Winchester lever-action rifles and a few Smith & Wesson Model 3s – gangster weapons imported from America."

"It'll be a massacre," Lucy gasped.

"Keep your mind focused on the mission, Lucy. The night's not lost yet."

Lucy forced all her emotions down and checked the map, sheltering it as best she could to prevent it from disintegrating in the rain. "Right," she said. "There should be an entrance to the Under right...*here.*"

She disturbed some bins behind a fishmonger's, sending a stinking mess of fish guts and bones spilling across the cobblestones, and together, Lucy and Moon heaved open a metal hatch.

It opened onto absolute black, ringing with the sounds of running water and the shrill conversation of rats. Lucy checked her pack, making sure that she had matches and that they were wrapped as best as she could manage inside waterproofed cloth. It took courage to descend into the Under at the best of times, but the idea of being stuck down there with no light terrified her.

And if the uprising failed, then the light of the Watchers would be extinguished for ever.

Moon patted his trusty swordstick, the walking cane with a sword hidden inside. His battered face filled Lucy with confidence – there was no room for doubts among those strong lines – but Lucy couldn't stop herself from wishing that Ben was with her instead.

More shots sounded.

Lucy was halfway down the iron ladder when a series of enormous booms rumbled right across the city. The ladder shook as the ground around her shuddered with the aftershocks.

More gunfire followed.

"It sounds as if Carnehan's boys have arrived just in time," Moon grinned.

Brigadier Daniel Carnehan led from the front.

Munro had been able to show them exactly how they could use the Legion's own tunnels against them. The sappers had set explosive charges – blasting through the defences that the Legion's work teams had built – and now Carnehan's Coldstream Guards could take the fight to the enemy.

His troops were dressed in civilian clothes; Carnehan knew that Sweet wouldn't hesitate to execute Her Majesty if he saw just one soldier inside the Wall. This was against

every army regulation but desperate times called for such desperate measures. The brigadier was well aware that this operation would either earn him the Victoria Cross or a court martial...if he made it out alive, of course.

Three Feathered Men swooped down in formation to intercept them, talons raised and ready for the kill. The soldiers opened fire, peppering the creatures' wings with bullet holes, but this merely slowed them down.

Carnehan was unfazed. "Special gun crew!"

Two soldiers ran to the front, cradling a heavy weapon, like some sort of portable cannon. The first man kneeled, tube on his shoulder, hands on the trigger. The second man loaded a brass shell from his backpack into the breech, tapped the gunner's arm and stepped clear. With a roar of gunpowder a weighted steel net shot out, entangling the leading Feathered Man so that it plummeted to the ground. One down...goodness knew how many more to go.

"Reload!" ordered the brigadier.

The Battle of London had truly begun.

Mr. Sweet was in the sanctuary – the centre of the Un and the black heart of everything the Legion stood An underground temple of evil.

The focal point of the chamber was a vast golden throne, with a back which towered ten feet into the air. It was there that the leaders of the Legion across the centuries had sat and allowed themselves to be adored. In front of the throne was the pit. A hole of impossible depth and impenetrable blackness. And at the bottom of that hole – kept there by the gate which had been locked centuries ago with the Gehenna Key – were the creatures. Awake and restless and tired of their prison.

Sweet almost fell into the arms of the throne, grateful that it was there to catch him. The Crown of Corruption was so very heavy that sometimes Sweet imagined his forehead must be bleeding just from the pressure of it. Then there were the Others, the spectres who stalked him day and night. Inside his head, whispering and laughing.

As ever, the vast hall of the sanctuary was illuminated by a thousand candles, revealing the huge carved columns that reached up to the vaulted ceiling and outlining the black lip of the pit. With every second however, the darkness was breeding. Water was dripping from between the stones of the roof and extinguishing the candles beneath. The hissing reminded Sweet of some enormous serpent, feeding in the shadows.

The vast doors of the sanctuary opened and a brigade

of Legionnaires trooped in. There was a smaller figure in the midst of them. A red-headed boy.

This was the guest who Sweet had been waiting for.

This was the boy who had left him in the flames.

The boy who had stirred up London against him.

The boy who led the Watchers and threatened to destroy him.

"Ben Kingdom!" he roared.

Mickelwhite, Bedlam and the brigade slammed their fists to their chests in the Legion salute.

Claw Carter bent down and whispered in Ben's ear. "I said I could get us to Sweet, my boy," he said with a wink. "I'll create a diversion and you get that crown." And with that, Carter shoved Ben viciously, sending him reeling.

Ben released a deep sigh of relief even as he staggered. *You had me going there.*

"I've brought you Ben Kingdom," said Carter, raising his voice.

"*I* brought him," said Mickelwhite petulantly.

"Hold your tongue, boy," said Carter. "Let the grown-ups talk."

Carter kicked Ben in the back, propelling him forwards again.

Blimey, that hurt, thought Ben, as the professor's boot made contact, but he could see what Carter was trying to do. Ben had to get close enough to Sweet to place the Hand of Heaven on the crown. Carter's method was on the rough side, but it had been effective so far.

"Well?" said Carter. "Do you want to kill him or not?"

Ben allowed the next shove to knock him to his knees and he fell to the ground. He began to crawl towards Sweet. *Just a little closer…*

This was the moment. This was his destiny. It was now that he would defeat the Legion. Or die trying.

A rumbling sound sent tremors through the sanctuary. Ben could feel the vibrations rising up through his hands and knees as the floodwater continued to eat away at the foundations of the Under. But as well as the gurgling water and the ominous groans from the stonework, Ben could hear other noises… Disturbing noises he had never heard before, not even in nightmares, although that was where they belonged. Discordant clicks, eerie rattles. Noises of bones and teeth and claws.

First things first, Ben told himself firmly.

His right hand had been pulsing ever since he entered the Under. This close to Sweet and the crown, Ben could hardly control the trembling in his fingers. Part of him dreaded what would come next. What would happen when the Hand of Heaven made contact with the most evil object in—

Ben wasn't able to complete that thought because a kick in the ribs from Mickelwhite knocked the wind out of him and sent him sprawling. No acting required.

He lay flat out. The hammering of blood inside his head and strange unnamable sounds that scratched at the edge of his imagination threatened to keep him there, but he could not, *would not*, stop now. Get in close. Grab the crown. Use the Hand to destroy it. That was all that mattered.

"You tried to kill me," Sweet accused Carter.

"Snap," Carter replied. "But surely bringing you this gutter-rat makes us friends again." He punctuated his sentence with another sharp kick for Ben. The professor wasn't using his full force, Ben knew, but it still felt bloomin' realistic on the receiving end.

Ben used the opportunity to throw himself closer to Sweet.

Nearly there…

Still giving the impression that he was crippled with pain, Ben clambered up onto his hands and knees, gasping. He was right in front of Sweet now, but the throne was elevated and, even seated, Sweet was a tall man. Ben would need to move faster than he had ever done before… Carter and Sweet were still talking but their words disappeared as Ben focused everything on this leap. There wouldn't be a second chance…

Calling on every ounce of his energy, Ben thrust himself upwards, reaching out with both hands…

Sweet's face turned towards Ben as he lunged for the crown. Ben saw the unadulterated hatred in Sweet's eyes as the big man twisted his body away from Ben's trajectory.

Ben's fingers came within inches of the crown but they clasped empty air. He fell against the throne and before he had time to recover, Sweet's muscular arms were wrapped around him from behind. Ben was trapped in a bear hug that squeezed the air from his lungs. His arms were pinned to his sides and, as Sweet continued to increase the pressure, Ben felt a fluttering of panic inside his chest. Any moment now his ribs would break. Ben had no doubt that Sweet would keep crushing until there was no life left in his body.

"Ben Kingdom," Sweet whispered. "I've dreamed of this moment."

Ben tried to break Sweet's hold, but every time he managed to twist in the big man's grasp, Sweet only tightened his deadlock. Ben changed tack. He used his legs to kick at Sweet's shins, even throwing his head backwards in an effort to catch Sweet a glancing blow.

Sweet laughed. "Please struggle," he said. "It makes it much more fun for me."

Lack of oxygen was making Ben's head swim. He knew

that he would be unconscious soon. This wasn't how it was meant to turn out...

Just as Ben thought he was going to black out, Sweet changed his grip and flung Ben roughly to the ground. Ben sucked in a huge mouthful of air but he had no time to gather his wits before Sweet pulled him up by the hair and began to drag him towards the pit. They reached the edge and Sweet forced Ben to his knees before it, his fat fist still clenched in Ben's hair.

"Look!" snarled Sweet. "When your Watchers are no more, all the world will be as dark as this."

Ben didn't want to look – hardly dared to – but he couldn't help it. Although he scrunched his eyes shut, Ben found them opening...looking down into the pit. It seemed to call out to Ben, as if wishing him to fall.

Suddenly, Ben felt Sweet's grip loosen. His stomach churned and Ben braced himself for the inevitable plunge. This was it...

But the death push never came.

Instead the meaty hand which had been clutching Ben by the scalp lost grip completely. With relief, Ben scrambled out of reach. Sweet was staggering in small circles. His murderous fingers fumbled at the back of his neck, until they finally plucked a tiny missile from his skin.

"Deathstalker scorpion venom," said Carter cheerily,

taking a blowpipe from his mouth. "An old favourite. Sweet made it too easy for me, though. Leaning over you with his fat neck exposed like that, he might as well paint a target on it."

Mickelwhite nudged his fellow Legionnaires, drawing his own sword. "Don't just stand there, you imbeciles," he snarled.

But Carter was prepared, and moved to intercept. "Now's your chance, Ben!"

Sweet fell to his knees as the poison spread through his system. Sweet's eyes blazed *death* at Ben, but the big man's body would no longer obey him. The great and mighty King Oliver the Merciless was helpless.

Ben took a step forwards... He reached out with both hands...and seized the Crown of Corruption from Sweet's head.

Instantly Ben felt the shock of holding such a foul and evil object. Just touching the thing made Ben's skin crawl. Made from the thirty Coins of Judas. Steeped in misery and blood, imbued with the selfish longings of generations. It radiated wickedness.

Ben had carried one Coin for a while and its influence had almost destroyed him. He had hurt people, and enjoyed it. The Coin had made him feel angry and spiteful and viciously alive.

The crown had to be destroyed.

Across the room Ben could see Carter hacking through the Legionnaires with his claw, sending them running in terror for the door. Standing beside the pit, trembling with raw emotion, Ben let go of the crown with his left hand so that he was holding it in his right hand alone. The Hand of Heaven.

And then the power hit.

Ben had no idea where the light came from, but it was so intense that he had to shield his own eyes while it blazed. This was the light of the sun, the fierce light of metal in the furnace, light so bright that it hurt. In the grip of the Hand of Heaven, the Coins began to bubble and liquefy. And scream. Ben hadn't been expecting that.

Even as they melted the Coins resisted their fate, the silver twisting and turning as if it might escape. Worse, as he squinted through his fingers, Ben saw faces appear then disappear on each of the Coins. Men. Women. Young. Old. Their tormented expressions showed their desperate longing on the particular Coin that had entrapped them.

Ben saw one Coin morph into a face which terrified him: his own.

He realized then that these were the faces of the Coin carriers. All the people down the ages who had betrayed the good inside themselves for the empty promises of the Judas silver.

Ben's face dissolved and became Ruby Johnson's. Then her face faded to be replaced by Mr. Sweet's. Then, with a final hissing spit, all of the Coins melted away into nothing.

Ben lowered his hand and the last remnants of the Crown of Corruption dripped from his fingers into the depths of the pit.

Sweet gave an animal howl of separation and loss. He lurched to his feet and made a desperate grab for the molten droplets of silver.

Ben could only watch as the man who had terrorized London plunged into the all-consuming darkness of the pit, his cloak flapping behind him like broken wings.

Ben closed his eyes, exhausted and overwhelmed. He saw Mother Shepherd in his imagination. And Josiah. And his own dear mother. And for the first time he knew that they would have been proud of him.

Totally spent, Ben slumped down on his backside in time to see Mickelwhite and the last of his Legionnaires cowardly scurrying out of the sanctuary. Equally exhausted from his exertions, Carter walked around the pit and came to sit beside Ben.

"We did it," said Ben, retrieving his fallen billycock, a smile filling his face.

"*You* did it," said Carter. "This is *your* victory, Benjamin Kingdom."

Ben could have stayed there and basked in the moment, but he couldn't forget his friends on the surface and the battles that they were fighting. Wearily, he rose to his feet, extending his hand to haul Carter upright too.

The huge sanctuary doors creaked open and a chill ran through Ben's soul. A hulking presence entered the chamber...

"Grey Wing," said Carter.

The Feathered Man extended his battle-scarred wings above him until they filled the doorway. And beneath the shadow of those wings was a girl.

"Ruby!" Ben gasped.

"Ben!" she called to him. "Ben!"

That was when all Hell broke loose.

CHAPTER 26

INTO THE
JAWS OF DOOM

Hans awoke and found himself in a war zone. His ears were instantly assailed by shouts and screams from the streets below. He could hear all the sounds of battle: fear, anger, gunfire and, piercing through it all, the shrieking of the Feathered Men.

As weak as a kitten, Hans struggled to sit.

"I say, steady on, old chap," said Valentine. "You've had a bit of a rough time."

Hans had no clear memory of where he was or how he had got there. He screwed his eyes shut and saw Mr. Sweet's face leering over him. He cried out in pain as he felt the long fingers of Sweet's domination raking through his mind.

And then Sweet's control was abruptly snapped.

Three images rose to the surface, filtering through the confusion in his brain as if they had been held on the seabed by heavy weights and had suddenly broken free.

Ben.

Key.

Danger!

Hans grasped Valentine by the lapels. "Where is Ben?" he shouted. "Tell me!"

"He's gone with Carter to pay a final house call on Mr. Sweet."

"The key? What happened to the key I brought?"

"Lucy and Mr. Moon have got it."

Hans was on his feet and running for the edge of the roof before Valentine could say a word to stop him.

"It's a trap!" Hans shouted. "We must stop them – they are walking into the jaws of doom!"

"So far, so good," said Lucy.

If you ignored the filthy water that they were wading through. And the rats that periodically mistook their legs for food. And the occasional body that they found, floating face down in the Under.

Moon rolled his blind eyes.

"Well," Lucy conceded, "you know what I mean."

What was definitely good was the map that Hans had provided for them. And the key. Lucy felt its reassuring weight in her pocket. It was the little things that made prison breaks so much easier.

But they had to get to Her Majesty first.

The floodwater had grown steadily deeper and the Under was groaning beneath the strain. The Under had remained secret and secure below the city streets for hundreds of years, but water had a power and a perseverance which nothing in nature could defy. Waves ground rocks into sand. Rain reduced mountains to foothills. And floods swept away everything in their path.

Even as they progressed down the tunnel, water was searching for a way to bring that tunnel down on their heads. Seeping through the soil. Squeezing between cracks, weakening mortar, loosening bricks.

With a shuddering rasp, a chunk of masonry came free from the ceiling a few feet in front them. It fell with a crash, sending a tidal wave through the floodwater.

Lucy let out a long breath. "That was too close for my liking."

Clutching the damp map in one hand and her lantern in the other, Lucy struggled on beside Moon, fighting against the water with every step. Their twisting, turning journey had shown them that the tunnels undulated. In one passage they might be up to their ankles and in the next up to their waists. But from what she could make out, the final passageway headed down into the deeper water again.

Lucy grabbed a plank of wood that was floating down the corridor and planted her lamp squarely on the top. "We might need this," she said.

Soon the water was at shoulder height and they pushed the plank ahead of them like a raft, their legs kicking out behind.

"Do you think that Her Majesty...?" Lucy couldn't bring herself to finish the question, her teeth rattling with the cold. Time was running out. It surely wouldn't be long before the water level reached the roof. But they were almost there.

"London breeds tough old girls," said Moon. His voice drifted off slightly and Lucy wondered whether he was thinking of Queen Victoria or Mother Shepherd.

A few more steps and, according to the map, they were in the right place. Half-submerged cell doors lined the corridor. Could an old woman really have survived down here?

They hadn't encountered any Legionnaires in the abandoned and waterlogged labyrinth and the moment for caution had passed. "Your Majesty!" Lucy shouted. "Your Majesty, we're here to rescue you!"

"Lucy Lambert!" a voice replied. A deep, powerful voice that struck a chord in Lucy's heart. It couldn't be...

Lucy and Moon swam for all they were worth. Lucy knew that she was crying but didn't really care. Was the Weeping Man alive?

"Josiah!" Lucy shouted, her voice cracking with emotion. "We thought you were...we didn't know... Where are you?"

"Here," said Josiah, and Lucy's torch found a familiar hand emerging from between the bars of a prison cell door.

Lucy ploughed through the water to the angel, taking his hand in hers and kissing it tenderly. "We're here for you now," she said.

"Lucy Lambert," said Josiah, "I was sent to watch over *you*."

Lucy's lantern lit up the Weeping Man's face. She hoped that her expression only showed how much she loved him and not the shock that she felt. It was clear that Josiah had suffered as a guest of the Legion. But in spite of it all, Josiah's eyes had lost none of their compassion.

"It's good to hear your voice again, old friend," said Jago Moon. "Now, let's get you out of there."

"Until a moment ago that would have been impossible,"

said Josiah, a smile spreading across his lips. "But when I heard you approaching, my chains melted away."

Lucy looked confused. "I don't understand."

Josiah's smile grew broader. "The witch-silver bonds that kept me here dissolved before my eyes. That can only mean that the Crown of Corruption which gave them their power has been destroyed."

"He's only gone and done it," said Moon, hugging Lucy. "Ben's done it!"

"There will be time for celebrating later," said Josiah. "Victoria is next door, but she is failing fast."

Lucy banged on the adjoining door, but there was no response. Were they too late?

She pulled out the key that Hans had bravely smuggled out and, tugging her goggles down to protect her eye, Lucy submerged herself so that she could get the key in the lock.

Her first two attempts were unsuccessful as her shaking fingers failed to find the hole. Finally she slid the key home with a sense of triumph and, with a twist of her wrist, she turned it until she could feel the bolts drawing back.

The *click* was the loudest sound that Lucy had ever heard.

* * *

Hans and Valentine hurtled through the streets in an attempt to intercept Lucy and Moon before...

"We have to warn them," Hans panted. But a sick feeling in his stomach taunted him; *they're dead already*.

Missiles *zinged* around them as they plunged headlong through open war. Guided by the Watchers, brave rebels threw stones and broken bricks from rooftop vantage points. Legionnaires responded with rifles and crossbows.

Hans and Valentine skidded around one corner and came face-to-face with an entire *battalion* of Legionnaires. So much for the Legion being caught by surprise, Hans thought as they hastily retreated, running zigzags through the rain.

Breathless, they ducked into a deserted side alley, managing to dodge the battalion on their tail. The Watchers had been so insistent that this uprising should be done without bloodshed but Hans found his teeth grinding together in anger and frustration. Had they set the revolutionaries up to fail? They certainly hadn't seen any signs of victory so far.

A flash of movement on the rooftops overhead caught Hans's eye and he felt a flicker of hope. Was this more Watchers preparing to attack the Legion?

That hope was shattered when a body dropped from the sky and landed on the ground in front of them.

It was the body of a lad in Watcher uniform. He was very, very dead.

Hans and Valentine looked up. A Feathered Man was hovering over the alley. Its yellow beak was streaked with red. It saw them and screamed.

Valentine brandished his quarterstaff. "You keep going, old chap," he said. "I'll give you as much of a head start as I can."

So Hans kept running, hoping against hope that he could save Lucy and Mr. Moon...

Ben turned to confront Grey Wing.

When is this gonna end?

He had nothing left to give. If it wasn't for the adrenaline pounding through his veins, he probably wouldn't have been able to stand. Even so, he rolled his shoulders with attitude, adjusted his billycock and stepped forward.

"I've destroyed your crown, your mate Sweetie is somewhere at the bottom of the pit, and I'm all out of birdseed... So you may as well just leave the girl with me and sling your hook, unless you fancy a taste of the same medicine?"

It was bravado, of course, and Ben knew that Ruby could see right through it. He was still getting over the shock of seeing her again. She seemed smaller than he remembered her, more vulnerable.

"Come on, Ruby," he said, holding out his hand to her. "I'm taking you out of here."

Ruby shook her head sadly and pointed to her ankle. Ben didn't understand until he saw the shackle. Grey Wing had Ruby on a chain; one end was attached to her ankle, the other was in the fallen angel's grasp. Ruby wasn't going anywhere.

Grey Wing threw back his head and screeched with laughter. "Your little girlfriend stole something for me," he taunted, holding up an ornate key. "Shall we see what it does?"

"The Gehenna Key!" said Carter, the shock of recognition on his face. "Don't do it! You'll destroy us all!"

"You say that as if it is a bad thing," mocked Grey Wing, stalking across the chamber dragging Ruby in his wake. The Feathered Man cocked his head and hissed at Carter. "From dust you came, and to dust you will return." With that, the Feathered Man put the tip of one of his talons beneath a flagstone at the edge of the pit and lifted it up. Ben saw an ornate keyhole set into the stonework underneath.

They faced each other across the pit. "Stop," said Carter, "I'm begging you."

Ben had never heard the professor speak like this –

Carter was afraid and that made Ben very scared too.

Ben ran through the options in his mind – he *had* to stop Grey Wing from using that key.

Jump the pit? *Too far.*

Could he make it round to the other side in time? *Impossible.*

"Stop, Grey Wing," Carter repeated. "Please."

"Never," said Grey Wing, lowering the Gehenna Key towards the lock.

Carter sighed resignedly. "I knew you were going to say that." The professor's head dropped and he turned his back on the victorious Feathered Man. The look of defeat on the professor's face was absolute – the misdirection that he had intended it to be. With practised dexterity, Carter flicked aside his coat, pulled a crossbow pistol from its holster, spun back to face the creature, and loosed off a shot at Grey Wing's heart.

Ruby had seen none of it.

She chose that moment to wrench on her chain, making a frantic attempt to grab the key. "I won't let you do it!" she shouted at Grey Wing. Ruby went to block him – and stepped straight into the path of the crossbow.

Carter's bolt flew straight and true.

Ben gasped as the missile pierced Ruby between her shoulder blades with a dull *thunk.*

Ruby turned, a look of confusion on her face. Her eyes sought Ben across the chasm of the pit.

"I'm sorry," said Ruby Johnson. Then she dropped to the floor. Dead.

Ben was frozen with shock. At his side, Carter had no more crossbow bolts and no more tricks up his sleeve.

Grey Wing shrieked again and thrust the Gehenna Key home, twisting it with a guttural scream of victory.

Numbly Ben heard an ancient mechanism rumble into life far beneath them. He could make out cogs turning and, from deep down underground, the heavy metal sounds of bolts being drawn back. Each *clunk* rattled against Ben's heart.

There followed a single second of empty silence and expectation.

"Listen," said Grey Wing. "Can you hear them? My cousins?"

Ben didn't want to hear.

At first he thought that the scratching noise was in his head. He once knew a boy down at the docks who claimed that a beetle had crawled into his ear while he slept and he could hear it always, scuttling around inside as it tried to find the way out again.

The noises that Ben heard were like that; impossible to escape.

Gibbering, clicking, scratching sounds, rising up from the depths.

"Run, Ben," said Carter. "Save yourself."

Ben had never known the professor to run from anything.

"*Humans* built the Under," croaked Grey Wing. "Foolish, spiteful, vengeful, wicked humans, like Sweet—" He listed these traits as if they should be revered rather than reviled. "And yet they lacked the courage of their convictions," Grey Wing continued scornfully. "They made their sacrifices so that the Feathered Men would join them, and then they were too afraid to allow us to be anything more than guard dogs on chains, monsters at their beck and call.

"They built this sanctuary, with its pit leading down into the darkest places that could be imagined. But the dwellers in the deep cannot rise up because *humans* placed bars across the pit, inscribed with words of binding.

"You are all so weak compared to us," Grey Wing mocked. "You mortals only ever think of yourselves – *my* needs, *my* dreams, *my* desires. Soon you will realize that the universe is very much bigger than you have imagined. Bigger and more powerful. Hungrier..."

Ben could hear the mad scramble as the *things* that had been imprisoned raced for freedom. The rattle of claws and barbs. The snapping of teeth and jaws. The slathering of a thousand mouths. The creatures had begun their climb.

"They're coming!" screamed Grey Wing.

CHAPTER 27

HELL ON EARTH

Jago Moon knew what a lock sounded like. He sometimes thought that he would have made an excellent safe-cracker if he hadn't chosen the more honest profession of bookseller – and freedom fighter, of course. As soon as Lucy had turned the key and the teeth came into contact with the first tumbler, Moon knew that she was in danger.

He heard the ratcheting within the stonework as the springs released their deadly load. He heard the whisper of the steel spikes as they emerged from their hidden home in the wall. And he heard Lucy's sad gasp as she recognized her mistake.

The trap snapped out for her.

And Lucy would have been impaled a dozen times if Moon hadn't clasped her by the shoulders and flung her out of the way.

Lucy went under the water as she was thrown backwards and in her panic she sucked the liquid into her lungs. But Moon's hands quickly hauled her back above the surface and her body went into a spasm of retching as she brought the dirty water back up again. When she was finished, she leaned her body against Mr. Moon, her head resting on his shoulder, drawing on his inner calm while her own heart pounded wildly.

"Thank you," she said quietly.

"I'd snatch you from the jaws of Hell itself, Lucy Lambert," said Moon with a grin. "Not much of a trap, at the end of the day," he sniffed. "They really want to get those cogs oiled."

"Lucy," said Josiah tenderly from behind his bars. "The thought of London without you watching over it would break my heart."

"Right then," Moon continued briskly before he got too emotional. "Get your jemmy out your pack, we've still got a couple of doors to open."

"Wait – now that my cursed chains have gone," said Josiah, "I can feel some of my strength starting to return." Lucy jolted with shock as Josiah's fist punched through his cell door, splintering the wood around the lock. The angel pushed open his door against the weight of water and stepped out of his cell for the first time since the Feast of Ravens.

Lucy threw her arms around him and then recoiled when her hands touched the angel's bare shoulders and felt the jagged stumps.

"What have they done to you?"

"Nothing that time won't heal," said Josiah. "Or that I haven't already forgiven."

Lucy had been so focused on the rescue mission that she had almost forgotten the threat of the floodwater continuing to wreak havoc on the Under. But suddenly the tunnel shuddered beneath their feet and an awful rasping sound echoed around them. All along the length of the corridor, stones began to break free from the roof and crash into the water. The lantern on its plank raft was still alight, but one close splash would leave them all blind.

"Follow me," said Josiah calmly. The Weeping Man put his hands to the metal spikes and, with a tremendous effort, he forced them back into their hidden housing in the wall, only stopping when they all heard the click of the spring lock snapping back into place.

"Victoria," Josiah shouted. "If you can hear me, please stand clear of the door."

The angel positioned himself in front of Queen Victoria's cell door and kicked it with such force that it shattered. The Watchers pushed their way through the broken wood and Lucy gasped when she saw a white shape floating on the surface of the water, arms spread wide. She swung the lantern round for a better look and breathed a sigh of relief when she saw that it was only a voluminous blouse. So where was the Queen?

The light found a tiny form right at the rear of the cell. As the floodwaters had risen it seemed that the Queen had taken her bed and managed somehow to stand it upright against the wall. Victoria was clinging to the top of it, her face above the surface, but her eyes closed.

Josiah drew closer and picked up the small woman as if she were a child. Victoria's skin was as pale and shiny as candle wax and her lips were almost lilac from hypothermia. Josiah breathed very gently on her face and the elderly monarch's eyes fluttered open.

"We're taking you home," he said.

Lucy barely remembered the journey out of those terrible dungeons. As they climbed higher, the water level dropped, but the Under itself had become one big mantrap, ready to crush them. All around them, above and beneath, stones that had held fast for hundreds of years were growing loose. Threatening to fall at any time.

When Moon punched open the last trapdoor, Lucy had never felt more grateful to be alive. Although they had emerged within the shadow of the Wall, she stood there and let the rain fall on her body, her arms spread and her head back, so she could catch the raindrops in her mouth. She stayed like that for a blissful second before pulling her flare gun from her pack, unwrapping the oilcloth that had kept it dry and firing it into the sky.

The green explosion lit up the clouds.

Mission accomplished.

Jonas pointed to the flare as it rose into the air and burst green over the city.

Nathaniel punched the air.

Lucy and Mr. Moon had rescued Victoria!

It was the signal that the army had been waiting for too and from all around the city, Victoria's army began their assault. Message received and understood; Her Majesty was safe. Now the gloves could come off.

The ground beneath Nathaniel's feet shook, the vibration followed a moment later by the sounds of cannon fire. "Looks like the Wall is coming down tonight, son," said Jonas.

Along with the brave men and women of London, Jonas, Nathaniel and Ghost had battled tooth and nail to wrestle their sector out of Legion hands. It had been harder than they had ever imagined. Good men and women had been forced to fight like the devil to protect the ones they loved. Jonas knew that even though they would be relieved to live to tell the tale, battles like that left deep scars inside. And the night was still not over.

Just as one brigade of Legionnaires was defeated, so another one emerged to take its place. Then there were the Feathered Men who were spoilt for choice when it came to fresh victims to devour. They seemed to have gone into some sort of feeding frenzy and the sound of their delirious glee echoed overhead, louder than the incessant rain, louder even than the artillery bombardment.

Jonas was painfully aware that the Feathered Men could still win if the free Londoners lost their courage now. He drew Ghost and Nathaniel to him.

"The Queen is safe," Jonas shouted above the mayhem. "God save the Queen!" Then louder, at the top of his lungs: "God save the Queen!"

Nathaniel joined in and they chanted with all their might.

Down the road another man joined in. Then another and another, their spirits lifting as they took strength in that good news.

The cry spread, house by house, ringing the length of Old Gravel Lane, then right across the East End.

"God save the Queen!"

"And God help us," Jonas added as the battle continued.

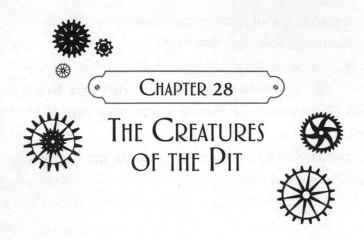

CHAPTER 28

THE CREATURES OF THE PIT

The noise of the creatures held Ben like a vice. Claw Carter was rooted to the spot too, equally mesmerized by the appalling sounds emanating from the pit. Ben had read about sailors whose minds were imprisoned by the sirens' song and then lured to their deaths on the rocks. The music of the creatures was a thousand times worse.

Grey Wing, meanwhile, was in ecstasy, hooting and howling in triumph. Water was streaming from the roof now, snuffing out the remaining candles and bringing with it a hail of masonry. Ruby lay discarded, like a broken toy, blood from her wound mingling with the water on the floor until she was surrounded by a halo of red.

And the tide of terror was still rising.

Squealing. Snapping. Slithering.

The sounds bombarded Ben, filling his heart with fear. He had no idea what sort of monsters might be climbing up from the darkness, but his imagination ran wild.

Ben couldn't help himself. Curiosity got the better of him. He looked down.

He saw teeth. So many teeth. Thin ones like needles. Long ones for ripping and tearing.

And eyes, glowing back at him with malice.

The *things* – Ben could think of no better word to describe them – were crawling and scrabbling up the sides of the hole that had held them for so very long. Some of the things seemed to change form as he watched them. Long tentacles would appear from dark orifices to taste the air. Freakish limbs swayed disturbingly before sprouting eyes or fingers or mouths.

Ben saw what looked like a human hand being tossed between the creatures. Then he spotted the signet ring and realized with revulsion that it was all that remained of Mr. Sweet.

Only a handful of candles still burned now and it felt as if the darkness was hemming them in on all sides, the circle of light dwindling with each passing second.

Ben gazed at Ruby and the sight of her motionless form stirred something inside of him stronger than his fear.

There were so many things that Ben still wanted to say to Ruby; that she was amazing; that she should be a Watcher. That he forgave her.

The Hand of Heaven began to thrum with power as the first wave of creatures started to spill out of the pit and scurry away into the darkness. Some of the vile things came scuttling towards Ben, chittering with laughter and gnashing their tiny jaws. Ben retreated, lashing out with his feet. As he did so he was struck with the urgent need to get Ruby out of their way; he couldn't stand the thought of these awful beings touching her.

Ben tried to skirt round the edge of the pit, but halted in his tracks as a new monstrosity emerged from the depths. It moved so swiftly that Ben only had an impression of a vast circular mouth and a mane of grabbing tentacles before they rose up and were lost in the darkest recesses of the roof. Ben stared in disbelief as it gradually dawned on him that the enormous swaying trunk now before him was just the creature's *neck*.

Grey Wing hopped up and down in a manic dance of delight.

Carter had obviously had the same thought as Ben, and while Grey Wing was distracted he managed to reach

Ruby and drag her out of the path of the creatures. *If any Legionnaire was worth saving, it was Ruby Johnson,* thought Carter.

As they retreated, one of the beasts sprung at Carter's throat, a long pink tongue flicking out and encircling his neck like a lasso. Carter promptly cut the appendage with his claw and left the creature to flap on the floor, squealing in pain. Carrying Ruby across his shoulders now, Carter tried to clear a path to the door but there were simply too many creatures blocking his way. The floor was a mass of writhing things, impossible to say where one ended and another began.

Ben was fighting a losing battle too and before long all three of them were crammed onto the only high ground available. Ben stood on the island of Sweet's throne, Carter beside him with Ruby in his arms, while the ghastly creatures surrounded them; a sea of undulating bodies.

"This is your end," Grey Wing shrieked triumphantly, flying towards them, the vast creature swaying behind him like a tree in a storm. "The Legion never knew the meaning of evil, but *I* will teach mankind that lesson today. While my Feathered Men rule the skies, the creatures of the pit shall lay your world to waste... And the purge will start with you, Ben King—"

Grey Wing never finished those words.

Without warning, the huge monster snatched Grey Wing out of the air and engulfed him. Ben winced as he heard the crunching of those enormous jaws. In a single gulp, Grey Wing was gone. The creature brushed against the roof of the sanctuary, bringing down a hail of masonry. Ben couldn't help but notice the shower of feathers that fell with the stones. Then the monster made a rattling sound in its throat and started to sway.

"Look out!" warned Carter. "It's going to strike again."

Ben stood his ground. All this time the power of the Hand had been building.

He raised his right hand and brandished it before him. The thing drew back with a hiss and the creatures around the throne retreated.

"That's right," said Ben. "You know what this is, don't cha?"

Ben had no earthly hope against such a nightmarish enemy, but he allowed the Hand to guide him, feeling its raw energy surging through his veins.

He lifted the Hand up towards the ceiling and then brought it down vigorously with a short, sharp tug. In response, a massive stone broke loose from the ceiling and smashed against the beast's skull.

The creature roared, opening its mouth wide... Ben

stretched his fingers towards one of the pillars, closed the Hand into a fist and then flung it out in the direction of the gaping mouth. An entire section of pillar flew through the air to wedge itself in the beast's jaws.

"Chew on that," said Ben.

He enjoyed a split second of success before the roof began to collapse.

Ben hadn't been prepared for the deluge of water and broken bricks that came thundering down through the jagged hole he had made in the ceiling. The floodwaters had been weakening the Under for days and now it seemed that the Hand had set in motion its ultimate destruction.

The last of the candles died and the darkness was absolute.

Ben could hear the creatures squealing in pain as hunks of masonry struck them, but Ben knew that the rockfall alone wasn't enough to drive the monsters back into the pit.

Only light could repel darkness.

Only the Hand.

Carter had taught him that a single candle flame can be seen for twenty miles. How much brighter would the Hand of Heaven shine?

As he thought that, the same brilliance that had

radiated from his fingers when the crown was destroyed began to return – a hundred – a *thousand* times brighter. It was like staring into the sun. Ben turned his own face away and shut his eyes, fearful that he might go as blind as Moon. The sanctuary was red, then radiant white.

The endless day…

There was a panic-stricken slithering and scuttling as the creatures tried to dodge the continued bombardment of masonry and escape the purity of the light. Even the gigantic thing was retreating, unable to avoid the crushing stones or stand another second in the light of the Hand.

It's just a shame that I'm gonna be buried too, thought Ben; the light fading as the last creature fled in terror, even as the Under continued to fall, brick by brick...

After everything he'd been through, was this really how it would end?

Buried in the dark? Pulverised?

Not if Ben had anything to say on it!

Carter, Ben and Ruby were still huddled together on the throne. "Professor," said Ben. "Can you climb off and hold Ruby while I try something?"

Another immense portion of the roof broke away. It hit the floor of the sanctuary with a noise which reminded Ben of stepping on snails; a sickly mixture of crunch and squelch.

"What are you going to do?" asked Carter.

"I'm going to tip this throne forwards so that we can shelter beneath it and not get our bonces caved in."

"I'd love to believe you can do it, Ben, but it must weigh tons."

"I've never let small things like the facts get in the way before," said Ben, making light in order to overcome the fear of death that was creeping over him.

It *was* impossible to shift the throne, Ben knew that, but he remembered Josiah telling him that *nothing* was impossible for the Uncreated One. Ben manoeuvred himself behind the throne, hooked his right hand beneath it, clenched his teeth, summoned his strength and heaved...

The throne lifted an inch...the Hand pulsed with otherworldly power. Ben lifted harder...and the throne toppled forwards. Ben and Carter made a mad scramble to get under the shelter it provided, dragging Ruby with them.

She groaned.

Ben found her fingers and laughed out loud. He had expected her skin to be icy cold but it was warm to the touch.

"Ruby," he said, trying to rouse her. "Ruby, it's Ben."

Ruby's fingers gave his hand the faintest squeeze.

"I knew you were trouble right from the start," she said weakly.

"I'm going to get you out of here," Ben promised, his hopes soaring even as the Under disintegrated around them.

"We'd best get down," said Moon. "That sounds like a twelve-pound muzzle-loading smooth-bore cannon to me."

Even as he finished speaking they all heard the whistle, and then a huge section of Wall buckled inwards just twenty feet in front of them, sending them hurrying for cover. Josiah shielded the Queen. Lucy covered her head instinctively as she was showered with shards of brickwork and the air was filled with the tang of cordite.

Another booming rumble followed and through the breach in the Wall, Lucy saw the flare of artillery.

Queen Victoria straightened in Josiah's arms – suddenly aware of how unbefitting it was for the Queen to be carried like a child – as a unit of what appeared to be London militiamen approached. Her clothes were hardly better than rags, her thinning hair plastered to her scalp. Josiah lowered her to the ground and Victoria did her best to stand erect – she barely came up to the angel's shoulder.

Lucy spotted her distress and took off her own scarf, wrapping it respectfully around Victoria's shoulders and over her head to protect the Queen's modesty. "With your permission, Ma'am," she added with a little curtsey.

The leader of the men came over to the Queen and saluted smartly. "Brigadier Daniel Carnehan, at your service, Ma'am. Please forgive our appearance, a necessary disguise I'm afraid. These men are Coldstream Guards, Your Majesty. Will you allow us the honour of escorting you to safety?"

Carnehan was guiding the Queen away when he turned on his heel to face Lucy and Mr. Moon. "I recognize your uniforms," said Carnehan. "Watchers, I salute you."

"Not so much as a 'thank you' from the Queen, though," sniffed Moon when Victoria was not quite out of earshot. "There's gratitude for you."

Ben, Carter and Ruby were trapped. The throne had kept them safe but they would never be able to get out from the ruins of the Under.

And still the Hand ached with supernatural power.

This was the end of the Under, the defeat of the Legion. Ben had done what the prophecy had said he would. The darkness had been defeated. Now it was time to return to the light. He reached up. He needed to see the London sky. He pointed to where the stars would be and closed his eyes.

An immense shuddering and groaning filled the sanctuary, followed by a rockfall that sounded like an entire mountain collapsing.

Ben, Carter and Ruby remained stock-still. The draught caused by the downfall was enough to stir their hair as it swirled through the chamber and enveloped them in a cloud of dust. But amazingly not one single stone hit them.

"Did you do that?" asked Carter.

Ben didn't answer but they all looked up.

There was a jagged hole in the roof of the sanctuary and above that a hole in the roof above and above that yet another hole.

Ben, Carter and Ruby stared up and saw…the sky.

On London's streets, the rain was stopping. A wind had picked up out of nowhere and was driving the clouds out of the sky.

"Two Legionnaires are coming," said Moon. "Sounds like they're in a right old panic."

He recognized the footsteps and smiled.

An arrogant tread, with a heavy heel. Tall, from the length of stride, but thin, almost spindly. Accompanied by a shorter boy with a rolling gait. Both running. Both scared.

Mickelwhite and Bedlam.

The two Legionnaires were so intent on escape that they almost ran into the Watchers.

Lucy moved in close to Bedlam, tucked her shoulder under his armpit, grabbed him by the arm and threw him over her own shoulder so that he landed smack on his back. The little yob tried to get back up again, but Lucy kept him down with a foot on his chest.

"When you're in prison, you can remember that it was 'Scarface' who put you there."

Moon meanwhile took the opportunity to floor Mickelwhite one last time. The old man took slightly too much pleasure in tripping Mickelwhite with his swordstick, sending him sprawling onto his face.

"Over here!" Lucy called to a group of nearby soldiers, who were handcuffing Legionnaires and leading them away.

"I think you've broken my nose again," Mickelwhite whined, as the soldiers bundled him away.

"I wish Ben was here for this," said Lucy. "You do think he's alright, don't you?"

"Ben's got the Touch," Moon replied. "He'll come through."

And that was when the street gave way fifty yards ahead of them. Houses crumbled and the road itself disappeared into the ground.

"Can you hear what I hear?" said Moon, heading for the crater.

When they were ten feet away Lucy heard it too; a familiar voice calling up from out of the ground. She ran the remaining steps, Moon and Josiah at her side, and then they all kneeled down and peered over the lip of the hole.

"See," Ben called up to them from the ruins of the sanctuary. "I knew I had friends in high places."

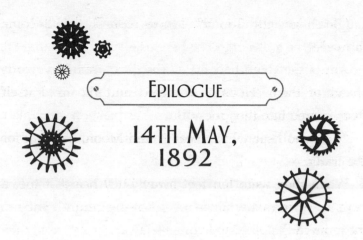

All the Watchers were waiting anxiously in the red carpeted corridor of Buckingham Palace. Only Carter seemed relaxed. This was all very new for Ben. He hadn't even been in a room with carpet before.

In the two weeks that followed Revolution Day, peace and order had gradually been restored to London, although it would take months, if not years, to repair the damage that the Legion had wreaked. And there were other, deeper scars which might never heal. The courts had been kept busy sentencing the Legionnaires who had been rounded up, and yet Ben didn't imagine for one moment that it was the end of the Legion. If the last few months of his life had taught him anything, it was to keep his guard up. However, he took comfort when Josiah confirmed that the power of the Hand had sealed the pit more permanently than any key ever could. And the Smutts family had all been found, thank goodness. But other questions remained. How many Legionnaires had gone into hiding? Had all the Feathered Men been dispatched?

"Of course," said Carter casually. "This isn't the first time I've been entertained by royalty. There's a tribe of pygmies in Papua New Guinea—"

"Shhhh!" said Moon. "We'd better shut up and look lively, the Lord Chamberlain's coming."

"I don't hear anything," said Carter.

The door opened and the Lord Chamberlain stood there, resplendent in his official finery.

"His wig makes a deafening rustle," said Moon in a stage whisper as the Watchers were ushered into the royal presence.

Seated on her throne before them was Her Imperial Majesty, The Queen Empress, Victoria. Ben felt his knees tremble as they approached down the long chamber and his hand grabbed hold of Lucy's. They stood in awestruck silence: Jonas and Nathaniel Kingdom, Alexander Valentine, Hans Schulman, Jago Moon, Professor James "Claw" Carter, Ghost, Lucy Lambert.

And Ben.

"It seems that we are deeply indebted to you," said the Queen. "Both our nation and I have cause to thank and honour your bravery and devotion..."

This is it, thought Ben. *I'm gonna get knighted.*

"For this reason, we have thought long and hard about how we might best recognize your gallant efforts..."

I'm gonna be bloomin' rich at the very least.

"You have our eternal gratitude and I wish to bestow upon you a gift. Lord Chamberlain, if you please."

The Lord Chamberlain bowed from the waist and then the Watchers retreated backwards out of Her Majesty's presence, as instructed.

"What's that all about?" whispered Ben.

"This way," said the Lord Chamberlain. "Follow me."

Five minutes later, the Watchers were standing on the roof of Buckingham Palace. Two figures were waiting for them there.

Josiah, the Weeping Man, standing strong again. His eyes were half shut in appreciation of the sunshine on his face and wind on his wings, and the stumps through his black coat showed the first feathery down of new growth.

And by his side, a girl with bright emerald eyes and chestnut hair cut like a boy's.

"Josiah said that you might be recruiting," said Ruby.

Ben grinned. "Ain't life grand."

There was more to be said between Ben and Ruby; between them all. They had survived a war and changed irrevocably. London was spread out before them. It too would never be the same.

The purring of an engine began to rise from behind them in the palace gardens, and Ben felt his excitement mount. It couldn't be...?

"Her Majesty felt that this was the best way in which she could repay your services," said the Lord Chamberlain, having to raise his voice as the Liberator Mark II rose into view.

"I take back what I said about her being ungrateful," muttered Moon.

The new airship was magnificent. Half as long again as the original Liberator and improved in every way. Ben's eyes grew wide. With its bowsprit extending from the prow at the front of the ship and raised poop deck at the rear, the new Liberator looked as if it belonged in the Royal Navy. The polished handrails gleamed and the row of harpoons which emerged from the gun deck looked ready to take on any Feathered Man. Most glorious of all, in Ben's opinion, was the Watcher symbol emblazoned in brass on the ship's side.

"She's beautiful," Lucy gasped.

"She's not the only one," said Ben, smiling at her. "Come on," he said, repositioning his billycock and running across the roof to the gangplank, which a British Naval Officer had extended over the side.

"The ship comes with Her Majesty's blessing, but not with the crew," the Lord Chamberlain added.

The sailors trooped off and the Watchers climbed happily aboard. Jonas took his customary position at the helm and they soared up into the clouds, high above battle-scarred London. Nathaniel stood proudly alongside his pa. Lucy joined them, the wind toying with her summer-gold hair. Valentine and Ruby stood a little apart.

Carter, Ghost and Moon went to examine the gun emplacements.

Ben went to the prow and climbed out onto the bowsprit.

They soared over the city. Ben held out both his arms like wings and relished the feel of the clean, fresh air rushing around him, almost as if it were washing away the last stains of his war against the Legion.

The sky was blue, for the first time in what felt like years, and far below the Liberator Ben could see signs of new life. Rubble being cleared, new houses being built... The city was so much a part of him and Ben delighted in seeing it from this bird's-eye view. Through his Watcher goggles he could see Big Ben. He could see the docks. He could see Old Gravel Lane. It was exhilarating and he wished that he could stay here among the clouds and never come down.

Josiah came to stand beside Ben.

"So," said Ben. "Job done."

Josiah smiled, although there was a tear forming in his eye.

"Evil never sleeps, Ben. You know the Watchers cannot rest either."

"Is there more trouble brewing?"

"We are needed in the East," said Josiah.

Ben brought his telescope up. "Whereabouts?" he said. "Is the Legion making a last stand on the Ratcliffe Highway?"

Josiah shook his head.

"Blackwall?"

"Quite a lot further east," said Josiah.

"Where?"

"India."

Lucy and Carter had moved a little closer and both pricked up their ears.

"That's a long way," said Ben. "Isn't it?"

"The other side of the world."

"Here we go again," said Ben Kingdom, a broad grin on his face as he adjusted his billycock. "Hang on to your hats!"

THE WATCHERS

THE BATTLES OF BEN KINGDOM

THE CLAWS OF EVIL

ANDREW BEASLEY

CATCH UP WITH BEN'S FIRST BATTLE IN

THE CLAWS OF EVIL

EVERY COIN HAS TWO FACES.
EVERY WAR HAS TWO SIDES.
ONE BOY HAS TO MAKE THE RIGHT CHOICE.

The year is 1891, and LONDON is at war. High up on the
rooftops lives a ragtag band of orphans and spies – the
WATCHERS – PROTECTORS of the city. But below the cobbled
streets lurks the LEGION, a ruthless gang of CUT-THROATS
and thieves, plotting to unleash the darkest forces of HELL.

When a MYSTERIOUS coin falls into his hands, cocky street
urchin, BEN KINGDOM, is flung into the midst of this ancient
BATTLE. The fate of the world rests with Ben, but which side
will he choose? An army of angels...or THE CLAWS OF EVIL.

ISBN: 9781409544005
EPUB: 9781409557258   KINDLE: 9781409557265

THE BATTLES OF
BEN KINGDOM

THE FEAST OF RAVENS

ANDREW BEASLEY

READ BEN'S ACTION-PACKED SECOND STORY

THE FEAST OF RAVENS

LIGHT CAN SAVE THE BLACKEST HEART.
DARKNESS CAN POISON THE PUREST SOUL.
ONE BOY HAS TO LEAD THE FIGHT.

The year is 1892, and LONDON is in the grip of EVIL.
A demonic terror stalks the streets, wreaking chaos as it helps
the LEGION, a vicious underground gang, to raise Hell on
earth. Only the WATCHERS, a secret society of urchins and
warriors, can stop them.

An ancient prophecy claims one boy, BEN KINGDOM, has the
power to end this war. But Ben has a secret so deadly it could
DESTROY everything the Watchers have worked for.
Can he find the courage to fulfil his destiny...or will
the city fall at THE FEAST OF RAVENS?

ISBN: 9781409546245
EPUB: 9781409557357   KINDLE: 9781409557364

Ben's Guide
to London Watcher Slang

An unorthodox glossary for some of the more unusual or unfamiliar words and phrases to be found in this book.

ballyhoo: uproar, noise, an ear-splitting racket. A most common sound to be heard on the streets of London when the Legion were at large.

billycock: a felt hat with a low, rounded crown, like a bowler. The best sort of hat there is, naturally.

blighter: a person who blights; basically someone really irritating, or possibly anyone annoying who may also be pitied – like a younger brother or sister (e.g., poor little blighter).

brigadier: a senior military rank. A brigadier commands a brigade, usually consisting of three battalions of about 3,000 troops.

by jingo: what toffs like Valentine say when they want to shout "by Jesus" but are too polite to do it.

cordite: a smokeless explosive, used in ammunition. There's been quite a lot of it about recently...

cosh: a short club made of wood or metal, used for fighting. Should you ever find yourself unfortunate enough to be walloped on the head with a cosh by a Legionnaire, it is very likely to hurt. A lot.

every man jack: you, me, that chap over there, the Watcher on the roof and the Legion in the gutter – basically every single person you can think of.

haymaker: the wildest and fiercest of punches; a real belter.

jemmy: a short crowbar used as a lever for prying things open. One of the standard tools of the trade for a professional thief like Ruby Johnson, but equally essential in Watcher rescue missions.

limelight: the first theatrical spotlights, created by heating lime (a white substance consisting of calcium oxide) by burning jets of oxygen and hydrogen. The actual lights are technically called limes, not to be confused with the small green fruit. They require constant attention to keep the calcium oxide burning, and as you've probably gathered from events described in this book, are also highly flammable.

Marie Tussaud: French founder of Madame Tussaud's waxworks, who took wax death masks of people who'd had their heads chopped off during the French Revolution. Luckily the Watchers escaped such a terrible fate on 1st May 1892. Marie Tussaud toured Britain with her wax models, eventually opening a permanent exhibition on Baker Street in 1835. Her museum is still going strong, although it's moved to Marylebone Road now.

Marquis of Queensbury rules: a code of fair rules in boxing, published in 1867 and publicly endorsed by the Marquis of Queensbury. He didn't write them though – a bloke called John Graham Chambers did that. They are the first rules to mention gloves in boxing and are rather gentlemanly, all things considered.

Mayfair: one of the poshest areas of West London, although slightly less swanky after the Legion moved in.

put the wind up somebody's nightshirt: imagine a draught blowing up your nightshirt and exposing your knobbly knees! It would make you feel a bit defenseless and anxious, wouldn't it? Well, the Watchers aim to put the wind up the Legion's nightshirt.

quarterstaff: a shaft of hardwood measuring several feet used for fighting and defence against the Legion. Collapsible variations are preferable as these can be shortened, both to conceal the weapon, and to increase Watchers' speed and dexterity when running across rooftops.

rendezvous: both the agreement to meet at a specified time or place, and the location where you are meeting. The French origins of the word make it sound wonderfully secretive and mysterious.

The Savoy: the first luxury hotel in Britain. Totally top-notch with electric lights, electric lifts and hot and cold running water. Most of the rooms even came with their own bathroom when it opened in 1889 – can you imagine! Not somewhere you'd expect to find the city's most ruthless criminals.

Sherpa: a member of a Himalayan group living on the borders of Nepal and Tibet, famed for their skill in mountaineering. Rest assured that Claw Carter has never eaten a Sherpa. The man just has a very strange sense of humour.

solar plexus: all the nerves right in the pit of your stomach. A horrible place to get hit, but a good place to aim for on a Legionnaire.

stoker: the person in charge of tending the furnace on an airship, steamship or steam train.

tramp steamer: a merchant ship operating without a schedule, travelling wherever is required to deliver its cargoes. Potentially quite a good method of transport for stowaways.

Acknowledgements

I've poured a few years of my life into these stories now…
and I've loved every single minute of it! My lifelong
dream has come true in the last twelve months and I just
wanted to make special mention of some of the wonderful
people who helped to make it all happen.

I must start with my agent, Anne Finnis. Thank you,
Anne, for all your kindness and wisdom – you really are
the one for me! Thanks also to Caroline Hill-Trevor for
taking Ben out into the world. I'm also deeply indebted to
my friend, Helen Greathead – I'll *always* remember my
first editor.

The Battles of Ben Kingdom have allowed me the
privilege of speaking in schools, libraries, festivals and
bookshops across the country. Big thanks to The Edge of
the World Bookshop for my first front window; to all at
Foyles for their support; and to my friends at Waterstones
Plymouth – especially the lovely Libby Allman. Special
thanks, as always, to the staff and children at SDPS.

Everyone knows how proud I am to be an Usborne
author. Firstly, I have to thank Rebecca Hill – I couldn't
wish for a more supportive publisher. Sarah Stewart
and Becky Walker – I'm grateful for your eagle eyes.

Big thanks also to Amy Dobson and Anna Howorth – I still get goosebumps when I see our books on the shelf.

Thanks go to the talented Hannah Cobley, Neil Francis and Sarah Cronin – I continue to be thrilled by your breathtaking design; Ian McNee – *love* the map; and the amazing David Wyatt – Best. Cover. Ever.

Very special thanks, as always, to my brilliant and insightful editor, Stephanie King – from start to finish it has been an absolute joy to work with you, dear editor. We did good. *Thank you, so much.*

Mum and Dad – I don't know what I would do without your limitless love; thank you for always believing in me. Darling Amanda – you still bring laughter into my life. Mum and Jack – I love you loads. Trè and Christina – big love, always. Colin, Stuart, Richard, Martin and Charles – my band of brothers, I treasure our friendship. Ben and Lucy – I don't have enough words to say how much I love you. My darling Jules – every day you give me a new reason to love you; my best friend, my helpmate, my gorgeous wife, I couldn't do this without you. And my Loving Father – all the glory is yours. *I love you all.*

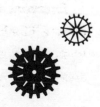

About the Author

Andrew Beasley was born in Hertfordshire, and has spent most of his life with his nose buried in a book.

As a student he read law in Bristol, but was disappointed to discover that life as a lawyer wasn't as exciting as books had led him to believe. He then spent a number of years travelling extensively across Europe for work, although he didn't see much of it because he was usually reading a book.

Andrew is now a primary school teacher, where he shares his passion for storytelling with his class. Andrew lives in Cornwall with his wife and their two children, Ben and Lucy.

THE BATTLES CONTINUE AT
WWW.BENKINGDOM.COM

HOW TO SELL

A former owner of a variety of [jewellery] operations in Texas, Clancy Martin is presently an [Associate] Professor and Chair of Philosophy at the University [of Missouri] in Kansas City. He has translated Kierkegaard and N[ietzsche, has] written several books for Oxford University Press, [and has pu]blished many essays, reviews, [and short] stories.

'Dirty, greatly original, and very hard to stop reading'

Jonathan Franzen

'A bleak, funny, unforgiving novel about how we buy and sell everything – merchandise, drugs, sex, trust, power, peace of mind, religion, friendship, and each other'

Zadie Smith

'The feeling you get from the moment you open *How to Sell* is one of inevitability. This is the inevitability of truth-telling, of tragedy, of the set-up to a good joke, and, very possibly, the inevitability of the classic'

Benjamin Kunkel

'A tender yet hardboiled coming-of-age story, a vivid, sometimes philosophical portrait of yearning and greed, of human love and human spoilage'

Sam Lipsyte

'A funny, quirky takedown of the American dream. A bastard child of John Updike and Mordechai Richler, *How to Sell* grabs you by the tuchus and doesn't let go'

Gary Shteyngart

'Succeeds in the most important way a novel can: it makes a previously unimagined world as real as your own. A wonderful debut'

John Niven

HOW TO SELL

Clancy Martin

HARVILL SECKER LONDON

Published by Harvill Secker 2009

2 4 6 8 10 9 7 5 3 1

Copyright © Clancy Martin 2009

Clancy Martin has asserted his right under the Copyright, Designs
and Patents Act 1988 to be identified as the author of this work

First published in Great Britain in 2009 by
HARVILL SECKER
Random House, 20 Vauxhall Bridge Road
London SW1V 2SA

www.rbooks.co.uk

Addresses for companies within The Random House Group Limited
can be found at: www.randomhouse.co.uk/offices.htm

The Random House Group Limited Reg. No. 954009

A CIP catalogue record for this book
is available from the British Library

ISBN 9781846552885

Designed by Jonathan D. Lippincott

The Random House Group Limited supports The Forest Stewardship
Council (FSC), the leading international forest certification organisation.
All our titles that are printed on Greenpeace approved FSC certified paper
carry the FSC logo. Our paper procurement policy can be found at
www.rbooks.co.uk/environment

Mixed Sources
Product group from well-managed
forests and other controlled sources
www.fsc.org Cert no. TT-COC-2139
© 1996 Forest Stewardship Council
FSC

Printed and bound in Great Britain by Clays, St Ives PLC

For Rebecca

PART ONE

FIRST COPY

Our father told it that Jim was caught dressing up in my grandmother's black Mikimotos when he was scarcely two years old, but the first time I considered jewelry was the morning I stole my mother's wedding ring. It was white gold. A hundred-year-old Art Nouveau band with eleven diamonds in two rows across the finger, garnets that were sold as rubies in the centers of tiny roses on both sides, and hand-engraved scrollwork on the underside where it held the skin. It was the only precious thing she had left. It was never from her hand. But there it was on the sill of the window, above the kitchen sink, next to a yellow and green plant she kept.

I needed the money. My girlfriend was leaving me for a grocery store produce clerk named Andrew, a high school basketball forward, and I knew I could buy her back. So I took the ring and put it in my pocket. I removed the red rubber stopper from the drain so that my mother would believe the ring had flushed into our plumbing. For good measure I ran the water to wash it down. She might be in the other room listening.

There was a pawnshop I trusted on Seventeenth Avenue, two blocks from my high school. Woody's Cash Canada. It had a banner in the front window that read WE BUY BROKEN GOLD. It was on the first floor of a three-story building with a barbershop on the second floor and a pool hall on top. We were told never to go into that pool hall. Of course, I should have gone to a pawnshop farther from home but I had not yet learned to reflect in that way. The barbershop was on the second floor and there were stacks of *Cheri*, *Fox*, *Club Confidential*, and other shiny porno magazines on the wooden side tables next to the chairs where you waited. Some men fingered them while they were having their hair cut. When my brother and I were kids I was afraid to look at those magazines, then when I was older and went in alone I pretended to be uninterested.

Woody's was the authentic variety of pawnshop, the sort I would come to love: three full jewelry cases with real bargains on minor-brand Swiss watches, early-twentieth-century American fourteen- and sixteen-karat rose and copper gold watch heads, Art Deco Hamiltons and Gruens, and odd antique pieces—this was the kind of place where you might even find a natural pearl or an unrecognized tsavorite garnet or a piece of really good old orange citrine—mixed in among crap like gold nugget bracelets and blue topaz pendants and amethyst rings.

"I know it's not much. It's an old ring, I guess."

"It's not so bad. Let's see what it weighs. Is that platinum? Or just white gold?"

"I don't know. What's platinum?"

That was not a question for the seller to ask.

"I know those are diamonds, though. Those must be worth something."

"Take a look under the loupe. Full of carbon. See those black specks? That's called carbon. That's what it is, too. Carbon molecules that never crystallized. Imperfections. Really hurts the value. Lots of inclusions, too. Internal flaws. But at least no cracks. That's something. I couldn't touch it if there were cracks. Too risky."

He knew his business. Didn't steam it, didn't clean it at all. We were looking at sixty years' worth of dirt, hair, and skin.

He gave me three hundred dollars for the ring, which was about correct. Given his position.

"I hate to sell it. I inherited it, you know. My grandmother."

"I can loan against this," he said. "This is a loan, no problem. Normally I will do better for a loan. But on this I advise you sell it outright."

Then I wished I had said it was a friend's. In case he called my parents or something.

"But there's this girl."

"Love is a good reason. The best reason. Think about it. That's why your grandmother left it to you. She didn't think you were going to wear it, did she? No. It was for a girl. If you need to sell it for the girl, that's what she would have wanted. Women understand these things. What matters and what doesn't. You should hear all the love stories they tell me in this place. A pawnshop is the place to learn about love."

He took the ring into the back.

"Your grandmother had good taste in jewelry," he said after he returned and paid me. "That won't be here long."

5

Good, I thought.

Today that ring would retail for seventeen, eighteen thousand, but at that time I imagine it brought three grand.

Don Strickland, who ran Woody's, was an old guy and not a friend of mine but he had bought several things from me, including a heavy walnut box holding sterling flatware I had found in the bureau of an actual friend's home. In fact it was not the friend's home but a friend was babysitting there and a few of us got together to steal drinks from their liquor cabinet and watch a video. While the popcorn was popping I wandered into the dining room and found the silver. My friend Tina, the babysitter, came around the corner and caught me. But I had not moved it. I had only opened a drawer. So she could not say anything. She raised her eyebrows at me and said, "Bobby, what are you doing?" I explained that I was looking for a bowl for the popcorn. Before we left, after several drinks, while she was kissing the other friend of mine in a corner, I returned there and hurried out with the heavy box full of silver in my arms. I lost two friends that way. But I wasn't ready to blame myself. They were not diligent about it. They could have spared all three of us the harm, if they had tried.

Often, at night, when I was twelve, thirteen, fourteen, and it was winter and the snow was falling, I would leave our neighborhood and climb the hill up into Mount Royal, to walk through their streets and look into the illuminated windows of the houses. You know what that's like: when it is very cold and motionless, because the snow is coming straight down, it hangs in circles in the streetlights, and inside the houses there is calm

6

or happy movement, as though people are eating and laughing, and their lamps by their windows are like gold and jewels. I would listen to the snow under my tennis shoes, and fold my arms deeper into my coat. These houses were enormous: three, four, five times the size of ours, with larger and faster cars, yards like fields, and they were made of stone and brick, but nevertheless they seemed welcoming, they were warm places, you could see that easily enough. My father had grown up in a house like one of these. My mother, though, was raised in an apartment.

When we were down in Florida at Christmas my father would tell me, "You can have a poverty-consciousness, son, like your mother, or you can have a wealth-consciousness. It's up to you. Some people are bound to be poor. Your mother and that idiot she married. They can't help it." That was a reason for those walks. To work on my wealth-consciousness.

Even with many seasons of practice I have never been adept at stealing and when they kicked me out of high school it was stealing that did it. A case of class rings for the graduating seniors. When I got them to the pawnshop—after my mother's ring I was using a different one, a dark-cornered place by the Alberta Liquor Store on the south edge of downtown, where you always stumbled over a couple of drunk Indians on the sidewalk and the aroma of human urine was strong—they proved to be base metal mock-ups. Brass and iron lightly electroplated in ten-karat gold and sterling silver.

The principal, Mr. Robinson, and the high school security guard had been after me for three semesters, so it was an excuse for them to play detective.

"But they aren't even worth anything," I said. "You cannot expel me because of some fake rings."

"You don't belong here, Robert," Mr. Robinson said. "This place is for good people. You are not a good person. You are a thief, a liar, and a coward."

That made us quiet for a moment. Across his desk we sniffed each other. I suspect we both knew I smelled better than he did.

I sat outside on a curb in the parking lot and read *Siddhartha*. I kept that book in my backpack for occasions like this. Sometimes I would switch it out with *Jonathan Livingston Seagull*, or *On the Road*, or Norman Vincent Peale's *The Power of Positive Thinking*, or *Journey to the End of the Night*. These were all favorites of mine I had read many times.

When I called my big brother, Jim, to tell him about my expulsion he tried to sell me on the jewelry store. I should have known that as soon as the pitch started Jim believed the lies he was throwing me. It's like being an actor or prime minister, you get all worked up with the audience and you think you can say nothing false or unbelievable.

"It is not your fault," he said. "The same thing happened to me, more or less, it was just drugs instead of thievery. Head south. The U.S. is where all of us should be, Bobby. That's what I'm saying. Move down here with me. I'll pay for the ticket and you pick it up at the counter at the airport. Dad knew what he was doing when he moved to the States. You and me lead the next charge. Let me handle Mom. I'm making five grand a week down here. That's twenty thousand dollars a month. Plus the company car. A Porsche! Next year I get the convertible. You would live rent-free. I am practically a gemologist now. You can take the classes, too. Live with us. That's college! You do it in the mail. You could be a gemologist in a year. You won't believe what those guys make. The real GIA gemologists. That's the Gemological Institute of America. That's a whole lot better than university, Bobby. Paychecks. Not to mention the prestige."

"I don't really want to go to university, anyway," I said. "I hate school."

"Me, too. I always hated school. That's natural."

"What about my girlfriend?"

"Of course you'll meet girls! You'll meet a thousand of them. That's what Mr. Popper hires if he can. Half the sales force is girls. College girls, too. Coeds! You know what they're like. And customers. Girls love jewelry, Bobby. That's most of the market. And women, of course. But lots of girls. You should see the girls! Everybody knows about the girls in Texas. They are the best girls in the whole country. These do not look like Canadian girls. You wouldn't think they were the same kind of animal. And they are all over Canadian guys. They love the foreign accent."

"What I was saying was I met a girl up here. A girl in one of my classes. I guess she's my girlfriend."

"That's great! I say give it a try. You can have ten girlfriends. Plus you can always go back. Make some real money and fly her down for Christmas. Think of the presents you can buy her. That's another thing. You can buy any jewelry you want. For employees it's all twenty percent over cost. You don't know how cheap it is until you're on the inside. You can buy jewelry for nothing! I had no idea. It's triple key, quadruple key, five times. That's industry language. Triple key means you sell it for three times what it costs. You'll learn all that when you get here.

9

It's called Fort Worth Deluxe Diamond Exchange. Like a stock exchange. Only better, because anyone can buy. Anyone can walk off the street and get something for their money. And jewelry goes up in value! It's an investment! That's what I am telling you. I am not trying to talk you into anything. You have to make your own mistakes."

Jim hung up. I called Wendy. I wanted to speak to her while I was enthusiastic.

"Why don't I come over?" I said. "What are you doing?"

"I have too much homework," she said. "I have chemistry homework and physics."

"That's joke homework. Do it before class starts. I'll sneak into the library and help you with it. I'll meet you in the parking lot. I can do it there if you want. I know that stuff."

"I'm not learning it that way. We can't do it like that anymore. Anyway, I have to get off the phone. I can't see you tonight. I am supposed to go to the grocery store with my mom."

"The grocery store?"

"I said I would. I said I would go with her."

"I could come over afterward."

I knew about the grocery store. Andrew. He went to high school by Wendy's house. It was the high school she was supposed to go to before we met. Then she decided to go to my high school, which also had the honors program she wanted to be in, which was the reason she went there, and not falling in love with me. But whenever anything went wrong at Western it was on account of me that she had come to this lousy school. Now I was kicked out and she was hanging around the high school by her house. She even went to their basketball games. She was going to the grocery store with her mom to see Andrew in the produce department. She imagined herself spinning on his cock in the iceberg lettuce bin. He might stick a cold cucumber up her ass. I remembered that when I was in third grade Jason DeBoer had said that to me, "You walk like you've got a cucumber stuck up your ass." I understood the remark.

Wendy was not a virgin but she preferred anal sex. She said it was because she could not take chances. As a matter of method she lied to herself first before lying to other people. Or she would lie with a truthful statement like, "I can't get pregnant if you come in my ass." That was a fact but concealed her genuine agenda.

"Fine. I get it. Go see grocery boy. I'll just see you tomorrow."

"No, that's not what I'm saying. What I'm saying is maybe you shouldn't come over anymore."

"You said you were going to the grocery store with your mom."

"I said I was but I won't. Fine. I'm staying home. I don't care. That isn't the issue. You are not listening to me."

"Is your mom mad at me?"

"My mom is not the problem, Bobby. Okay. I didn't want to say this. But you are giving me no choice. You made me say it. We shouldn't see each other anywhere. At all. And don't say what I know you are going to say. It's not about anyone else. It's about us."

I listened to the telephone. I reassured myself that she did not understand the words that were coming from her mouth, and maybe did not even hear them.

"Us and Andrew, you mean," I said. I hated to remind her of his name. But I wanted to hear her deny it.

"You're not even in high school anymore, Bobby. I mean,

what are you doing with yourself? What are you going to do? Just be a dropout? Sleep in the mall every day?"

To keep my mother in the dark, in the morning when I was going to school I would just take the bus down to the zoo or to the mall. I did not really sleep there. Wendy said that because I had fallen asleep in the food court once and been kicked out by a security guard. I only started going to the mall in the first place because Wendy liked the Caesar salads from the Copper Creperie and I would bring them to her for lunch. I had to sneak in and out of my own high school, because Mr. Robinson had his eye out for me. He had chased me right down the main hallway and out the front doors only a few days before. I later told people that the reason I was expelled was that he had caught me in the hallway by one shoulder and I turned around and clocked him one, right in the nose, and he keeled over like a cut tree. Flat on his back, right there by the cafeteria doors. My old man had been a boxer and he had taught me how to throw a right cross and a few combinations, I explained. That part was true.

"Maybe I should leave," I said. Let's see what she says about that, I thought.

"Where are you going to go? When? Are you going to live with your brother? That's a good idea."

This was not the response I had expected. I did not even know how she might have guessed about that.

"I thought you loved me," I said. That did not come out right, either. "I mean, don't you love me?"

"I would only want you to go to Texas because I love you. Because you need a change. I wouldn't want you to go for any other reason."

"You want me to go? Because I will go if you really want me to go. But I don't think that's what you honestly want. I think if you ask yourself honestly you will know that's not what you want."

"What I'm saying is I know it's for your own good. Even though I don't want you to go. You could go and then you could come back. That's what I'm saying."

"If you say you don't want me to go then I won't go."

I did not understand how it had happened that now I was going. Before this conversation had begun I knew I could never move down to Texas. What was I going to do, sell jewelry for a living?

"I think it's important that you go. That is what I am trying to say. I will miss you but sometimes it is good to miss a person. Then when you come back things will be different. Better."

There was silence on my end. I wondered if she was in her bedroom, alone, or if she was in the kitchen with her mother listening.

"Is your mother there? Is your mother making you say that?"

Wendy's mother had liked me for the first several months. It was not difficult to arrange. I flattered her, dressed cleanly, and smiled often. "You have such nice teeth, Bobby," she told me. "I just can't believe you never had braces." But then, a month or two before this conversation, she had found some pornographic letters I had written Wendy—it wasn't my idea, she insisted on them, it was a job I had to do in order to have regular sex with her—and, like I say, her mother had found the letters, which in itself might not have been disastrous, but one of the letters was about a mother-daughter-boyfriend thing, and since then she could not tolerate me.

"No. I am in my bedroom. You need to go. It will be good for us," she said. She made that yawning noise she always made when she was lying.

"You are yawning," I said.

"I am yawning because I am tired," she said.

"No, you are yawning because you really don't want me to go," I said. "Because you are lying when you say you want me to go."

She yawned again.

"You are right. I don't want you to go. But I think it is really important that you go."

"I'm going," I said. "To go, I mean." Now I had her where I wanted her.

"Good," she said. "I'm glad it's decided. I'm proud of you. But now I have to go. I have to go to the grocery store with my mother."

"What? You are doing what?"

"I slipped when I said that," she said. "I didn't mean to say that last part. I am staying home."

"Stay on the phone, then," I said.

"I have to go, Bobby. I have to do my homework. I am turning off my phone so I can do my homework. Otherwise you'll never hang up the phone. You'll just keep calling back and you won't let me work. I love you but I have to get off the phone now."

"I love you, too," I said. "I'm sorry," I said. But I knew she had hung up as soon as she told me she loved me. She always hung up before I could. That was how I preferred it.

My mother was out of the house, walking our dog with my stepfather. That was part of their regular routine. I waited until they had been gone ten minutes or so, to be sure they would not duck back in for something they had forgotten. An old plastic bag for the dog poop, for example. Then I called my dad.

"The hell with that, son!" he said. "Don't be silly! You aren't supposed to be a jewelry salesman. Let your big brother hold down that end of the fort. That's not the right situation for you. If you're ready to leave the nest and move to the States, come live with your old man."

My father had never asked me to live with him before. He had often insisted that I could if I wanted to, but he had never requested it.

"Come on, Robby!" I loved it when my father would use that name for me. "The real South! Sunshine and oranges! You don't want to waste your time in Texas with all those cowboys and rednecks. I've got grapefruits growing on the tree in the backyard! I eat them for breakfast."

"Florida?" I grinned and blinked back the tears.

The next day, during another of my mother's dog walks, I called Wendy. When I told her that I had changed my mind about Texas and now I was going to move to the States to live with my father she agreed to see me again. Because it was my father, I think, and not my brother. That made the plan sound real.

"Take me out on a date," she said. I was making a plate of microwave nachos while we talked. "I want to see you before you leave. You weren't going to leave without saying goodbye."

At the end of the date she said she didn't want to go home yet. "Let's drive out to the field," she said. I knew what that meant.

We suffered the sex on an oily blanket in the back of my borrowed tow truck.

"This is your goodbye present," she said. "Your so-long fuck."

Why does she have to use the expression so-long? I thought.

"This is too much work," I told her after several minutes. "You are never going to come. Maybe if we move to the grass."

I had my legs wrapped around the armature of the towing apparatus for leverage.

"No, I am close, don't stop now," she said.

"My jaw hurts," I said.

"I'll make it worth your while. Don't stop. You're next," she said. "There. But softer. Right there."

The tow truck came from an old job of mine, the Shell station on Sixth Street, which was down the street from the Safeway where Jim had first taught me to steal Du Maurier cigarettes. My friend still worked at the Shell station, and because I got him the job he would often allow me to borrow the tow truck for a few hours in the evening after Erik Jensen, the white-headed Danish owner, left.

After Wendy came and the two or three minutes of my sex were over, we wiped up and rested on each other. That was frequently the only part of our sex that was thoroughly happy for me.

"Can I have your jacket? It's getting cold out here."

A few years ago her parents had moved to a new development on the north end of the city and we were parked out at the end of it in a long pasture where new houses would eventually be. Beyond there were pine trees. We could see the sun going down behind the mountains. All the mosquitoes were dead from the cold and it was nice to be in the field with the last bits of sun on the sparkly white tips of the mountains. I gave her my jacket. I was grateful that she had asked for it. I was in a short-sleeved T-shirt and the hairs on my arms rose with the wind.

"It smells like it's going to snow," I said.

"I'm excited for you about your dad. I wasn't surprised but I was excited."

"I was surprised," I said. "You can come down too. We can lie on the beach together."

"Do they have a beach in Palm Springs? I thought that was in the desert."

"No, he's back in Florida. He's got a new church there." At this time my father was a kind of minister or guru.

"He moves all the time," she said. "That must be great. I wish I lived in California and Arizona and Florida."

17

"I know. Me, too. I mean, I guess I will be."

She was quiet then and ran her hand across my stomach. I flinched because I did not want to have sex again. But she did not notice and she continued to stroke my stomach. Then she put her hand under my T-shirt. Her hand was hot and gluey.

"When he was still in real estate he used to live in this house right next to John Lennon," I said. "Once we were out on the balcony, Jim and I had a balcony right off of our bedroom, and I remember there were mirrors on the closet doors. We were out there and my dad was smoking his pipe and he pointed to the other balcony, the next house over, and he said, 'Do you boys know who the Beatles are?' I didn't know but I said that I did. And my dad said, 'That fellow over there is the one who started the band. That's John Lennon. He's a famous musician, boys. He's my next-door neighbor. Let that be a lesson to you, boys. You can be anything you want to be. He was just some poor kid in the streets of Liverpool and now he is famous and lives right next door to your old man.'"

"That's a good story," Wendy said.

"I know it sounds made up. But you can ask my dad. When you come to visit."

"I'd like to meet him. You should invite me."

Wendy was beautiful but I was not sure my dad would think so. He would think she was a bit thick in the ass.

"That is a good idea," I said. "Maybe he could even pick up your ticket. He does that kind of thing. He is making a lot of money these days."

She had her hand in my underwear now. She was patient and she knew what she was doing. She applied her intelligence rigorously to sex, unlike most people.

"I'll give you a present if you ask him," she said.

"I'll ask him," I said. "I will sure try. He would like you."

She laughed. "I am sure I will like him," she said.

I knew she would, of course. Every woman did. That was another reason not to invite her. Because of the comparison, I mean.

A few days later, on the weekend, my dad called back.

"Son, it's not right for you to move to the States. Not now. This is an important time for you. Listen to what your mother is telling you. This is a time to finish high school and take care of your responsibilities. Your mother's right, for once in her life. I don't like it any better than you do, son."

I silently listened to the betrayal develop. He was a parent and so was expert at it. The deception was comfortable for me, too. I did not mind having him to blame.

"The truth is I talked to the boys about all this last night."

That one made me take the phone away from my ear for a second to look at it. I knew he would pull that kind of thing when it did not really matter. But I did not expect it on something as important as this.

"The boys" were astral beings my father soul-traveled to while the rest of us were sleeping. He relied on their advice for many of his decisions. He would also take counsel from a woman named Priscilla, who was not precisely an astral being but lived on a parallel plane. My father's deep confidence in the existence and wisdom of these otherworldly advisers had convinced me, when I was younger, that they were real. By this time I wouldn't say I believed in them, but maybe I didn't disbelieve, either. My beliefs on the matter were troubled.

"The boys have been keeping an eye on you for me. And

they all agree. You need to stay in Calgary right now. The States is a dangerous place for you for the next few years, son. It was a unanimous vote. I fought like a tiger for you to come down with me. But when the big boys upstairs all have the same idea, you shut up and listen."

I did not want to say even one word to him or hear his responses.

"You're being dramatic, son," my father said. "Talk to me."

At the airport the snow melted in the parking lot and Wendy stood with her hand on the open car door.

"Aren't you coming in?" I said. "Will you walk me to the gate, at least?" I hated to sound like that but I had no choice. I couldn't say goodbye to her yet.

"Aren't you cold?" she said. I wore shorts and a T-shirt because I was going to Dallas. I had a backpack and a book she had given me to say goodbye. In the cover she had written, "Friends forever."

I tore the cover off once I was on the plane and stuck it in the pouch on the back of the seat. I was angry and tearful. The old woman seated next to me inspected me with skepticism.

"That's not a trash bin," she said. "Is this your first flight? Are you afraid of flying? I don't want there to be any accidents."

"No," I said.

21

"Are you going to get sick?" she asked me. "Use the vomit bag if you are going to get sick. Maybe I should change seats. You look like someone who throws up on airplanes. I don't like that. I am older than you are."

It was sunrise. From the windows in the airport we could see the runways and the fields beyond, and beyond them the dark line of the mountains. The snow was more shiny than usual. I had only hoped that Wendy would stop me so that I might turn around and stay with her. But she called my bluff. On the jet bridge I had paused. I turned, and as I turned I saw the look of fear on her face. She was afraid that I would come back.

On the other end, over Dallas–Fort Worth, we sat in a stack. I could see our fellow planes circling above and below us with their faint red wing lights against the clouds and gray sky like some kid had pushed all of the buttons in an elevator. The captain explained that a freak ice storm had struck Dallas and coated the runways and the wings of the aircraft on the ground. I knew the cold weather was only my luck following us. Planes could not land or leave. The stewardesses distributed free drinks and even I had a glass of champagne. The old woman sitting next to me was drunk. She complained when I unpacked the two pieces of fried chicken Wendy's mother had wrapped in tinfoil for my lunch. That's how eager Wendy's mother was to get rid of me.

"It's your favorite," Wendy said when she gave it to me in the car. "She wants you to know she isn't mad at you. She thinks you're doing the grown-up thing."

Running away from home and high school to go into the jewelry business with my big brother. That was the mature plan of action. But I took the chicken.

"Are you really going to eat that?" the old woman next to

me asked. There was an odor to her enormous mouth. Her lipstick was smeared from drinking and it looked like a live animal might jump out of that red hole and bite me on the cheek.

From all the circling and rising up and down, I finally vomited, twice, but missed her. She rose and tried to join another aisle but people were drunk and impatient. Then she fell and the stewardess insisted she return to her seat.

"I could have broken my leg," she told me. She pulled up her dress but I would not look at her white calves and knees. "I have osteoporosis. My son is a doctor. This is your fault," she said. "If I get a bruise."

She massaged her legs and I leaned my forehead on the plastic window so that I would not vomit again.

At last we landed. The Texans in the airport were bundled in overcoats, boots, and scarves, and they gaped at me in my shorts and T-shirt.

"Hell, that fella there thinks it's summertime."

"You been outside, boy? It's cold enough to knock a maggot off a gutwagon."

I saw Jim. He waved to me from the baggage carousel. I almost did not recognize him in his blue suit and red tie. The tie had bright orange rhinoceroses on it. Later I would see that Mr. Popper, the owner of the jewelry store, wore the same one.

"I don't have any bags," I said. "Just my backpack."

"Come on, you are going to freeze," he said. "Here, take my coat."

We stepped outside and he lit a cigarette.

"You smoke now? No? That's good. But seriously, you might want to take it up. For the productivity. It's been proven. Help you stay on your toes. Competition. They have the free market down here. Hey, here's the car, get in. Christ, these Texans. A little snow and they think it's the North Pole. We should set up a stand and sell fur coats. We'd be rich in an afternoon."

It was a white Cadillac limousine. I had never been in a limousine before. The driver was wearing a shiny black cap like in a movie. He held the door open for us.

"Sorry about the limo," Jim said. His big smile made me want to tell him about Wendy and leaving her and the jet bridge but I could not do that, either.

"This is Lisa. Lisa, my little brother, Robert. Or Bobby, really."

Seated in one of the white leather seats of the limousine, with her back to the driver so that Jim and I could sit together on the bench, was a woman.

"Hi, Bobby."

That was nice of her to use my name like that.

I did not know what to say to her. I tried to smile.

"I wanted to get a Rolls but apparently there's a convention in Dallas. Cosmetic surgeons. They sucked up all the best limos. I guess we better go shopping. I knew you wouldn't have the clothes for work but I didn't figure you'd show up in Bermuda shorts." He laughed. "I'm just kidding. I understand. Ready for a change. I been there. You know that. But you can't walk into the store in that outfit. And we got to get back. It's slammed down there. Customers were standing half a mile around the block when I came in to work this morning. With the ice storm and everything. People got the day off work, maybe. At seven o'clock in the morning. But it's one helluva sale. This Christmas is going to be something. I am really glad you're here. You're going to love it. You are in a real country now."

He showed me a small brown glass bottle about the size of

24

half a thumb with a black plastic top, like something a doctor might use to inspect your eyes.

"Here, take a bump. This way." He turned the bottle over twice and inhaled sharply into each nostril. "There you go. You'll like it. Go ahead, do a couple more. Warm yourself up. That's probably enough for a start. Oop, slow down. You gotta be careful with that stuff. Here, pass it over, I'll join you. Lisa? Your turn. I trade it with a fellow for help with his watches. He sells Rolexes in brown-town to all the small-timers. Crap, mostly. Gold nugget bracelets, that kind of thing. He moves some merchandise, though. There it is," he said. "Hot in here. See those towers? That's Dallas. Downtown Dallas. We are going to make a quick stop and pick up some watches from Granddad. He's a good old boy. Half dead from his liver. Keeps a submachine gun on the wall behind his desk. But he's the best secondhand Swiss watch dealer in the South. Then we'll go shopping and get you a suit, a pair of alligator shoes. We can still get back to work by three. I have a diamond appointment at three we can't miss. Here, pass me back that one-hitter. Okay. Your turn. A five-carat radiant. I've got it right here. Take a look at this."

He opened his briefcase and took a small white paper from one of the suede pockets. He unfolded it. Inside the heavy white paper was a slender blue paper, like wax paper, but more delicate, and in the blue paper rested a diamond. It was the size of a nickel.

"Hold out your hand," he said. He picked it up with his fingers and dropped it in my palm.

"That's thirty thousand dollars you're holding. Thirty thousand dollars our cost. If I sell it today it's a two-thousand-dollar commission. Not bad, eh? One day's work, two grand. On top of my regular salary."

"That's your brother," Lisa said. "It's not like that for everyone at the store."

I inspected the innocuous glassy stone. My palms were sweating and the water and oil coated the diamond.

"Hey, give me back that bottle, would you, Lisa? Here, Bobby." I didn't know where to put the diamond while I sniffed the cocaine. "Go ahead and hit it one more time. No, get them both. Both nostrils. Pinch the other one as you do it."

He took the diamond from me, cleaned it with a yellow cloth, and placed it back in his briefcase. "Then we better slow down. We've got a big day. This is your first day at work."

"He has to work today? Why don't you just show him the store today? He's fresh off the plane, Jim."

Jim took the bottle of cocaine from me, handed it to Lisa, and laughed.

"He's a Clark," he said. "He'll be fine. Won't you, Bobby? You want the day off? Hell, you haven't even worked yet and you want a day off? I doubt it."

I did want the day off. But I could not disappoint Jim. Especially not on my first day. In our family you are eager to work. But I did not want to seem ungrateful to Lisa. I was awkward.

"You're both working now? Today?" I said. I directed the question to Jim but I looked aside at Lisa to see if she had heard me.

"Of course we're working. Lisa here is one of my top sales-women. She has a deal on a pink gold Patek today. Patek Philippe. That's the best Swiss watch in the world. Best brand, period. Skeleton back, moon phase. You'll see when we get there. That's why she's coming to Granddad's. I wanted you guys to meet. You would have met anyway at the store but I wanted you to meet just the three of us."

26

She smiled at him easily and looked out the window.

"It's snowing," she said. "I love the snow."

"Inside and outside!" Jim said, and laughed. I was embarrassed for him in front of Lisa about the joke. For years he embarrassed himself and me both that way. Especially in foreign countries. "Hell, we may as well just finish this bottle. There's more where that came from."

I kept looking back over at Lisa. I tried not to. But she looked like a woman in a magazine. She didn't look like an everyday normal woman who might be sitting in a car with you. Though it was a limousine. She did look like a woman in a limousine. Like a dream woman in a dream limousine.

She opened the window, with the electric button, and the cold rushed into the cozy warm red and white leather compartment of the big car.

"Oops. Sorry, Bobby," she said, and smiled at me again. Very gently and deeply, it seemed to me. "I just wanted to catch a snowflake on my hand."

"With a big deal like that it helps if you talk to the wholesaler," he continued. "Plus this old guy, the customer I mean, is sick as a dog in love with Lisa—"

"That's not true," she said.

"Of course it's true," Jim said. "Like every damn guy in our store, for that matter. Myself included." He laughed.

"Don't listen to your brother," she said. "He's being ridiculous. He's joking with you."

"Granddad can show Lisa things about the watch that he could not explain over the phone. Plus she needs to see how he holds it, how he treats it. How he cares for it. This is not an ordinary watch. The only sad thing is that there's not much juice left in it. It's a twenty-thousand-dollar deal that we won't make three grand on. Hell, I'll show him the invoice. That's how you have to do it with these big collectors. They're practically in the business themselves. But you take care of them on these deals and the diamond studs at Christmas, the tennis necklace for the girl-friend, the steel Rolexes for his best employees, all the cherry stuff comes your way. Once you catch a crow you never let him go. Isn't that right, Lisa?"

"That's what he tells me," she said to me. "You're making your poor brother dizzy," she said to Jim.

She was correct. I was disoriented and my mouth was dry. For a minute longer I tried to seem lively. Then I gave up and rested the side of my face against the cold, pleasant glass of the dark limousine window. I watched the long stripes of snow and the frozen highway outside. We were in the fast lane passing cars on our right. Everyone else was driving slowly and unsurely in the snow. Like they were walking and we were skiing past.

"Texans," Jim said. "You all right, buddy? Have another bump and then maybe take a little break. We'll stop for lunch after Granddad's and you can have a beer. That always helps me when I'm a bit coked up. A beer is what you need. Still getting over the flight, I bet. He's always had a nervous stomach," he explained to Lisa. "Can't fly worth a damn, can't get on a boat. Can't even ride in the back seat of a car."

"I'm okay," I said. "Really I'm fine. I feel great."

"Close your eyes for a minute," Lisa said. "Hey, why don't you come sit by me?"

That sounds like a very good idea, I thought. I looked at Jim, but he didn't seem to mind. He was smiling like he was simply excited to see me. I switched seats, leaned back, and closed my eyes.

"That's enough for right now. There's no hurry. You could

put your head in my lap if you like." Did she say that or was I already asleep? I was not sleepy, though. But with my eyes closed and my head lying back in the already-hot-again car it seemed like I had disappeared.

"Relax and we'll be there before you know it. Take off your tennis shoes," she said.

No, I was wide awake. I did not want to take off my shoes because my socks were wet with sweat. I did not want Lisa to smell my feet. I am in the United States in a limousine with my head on the legs of a woman with black hair, I thought, and her fingernails on my eyebrows and ears. I opened my eyes again to look at her.

"Close your eyes. We'll be there soon."

"You're spoiling him." Jim laughed. "It's not fair."

"Let him go to sleep. You don't have to torture him all the time. That's how my brothers always were."

"Still, you are kind of boyish," Jim said.

"It won't work. I am playing with Bobby right now," Lisa said. Her fingernails scratched an itch I didn't know I had deep in my scalp. "Rest a minute."

I could not fall asleep but I pretended I had. I did not like to deceive her. But I wanted her to keep on talking in those same words.

*T*he hands on the watches in a showcase are motionless. Even with the quartz watches you withdraw the crown so that the watch will stop and the battery will last. It stimulates the customer when you give an automatic watch a twist before placing it on his wrist and it begins to run. Popping in the stem with a quartz has the same effect.

My first job at Fort Worth Deluxe Diamond Exchange was setting the Swiss watches at ten past ten. With automatics the hands are still unless the watch is moved, and winders you only wind every few months, so that the oil does not settle and clog the movement. They are set at ten to two because years ago Rolex began displaying their watches in photographs with the watches set at that time. If you try different hand positions on the watches you will see they got it right. A watch looks best set at ten to two. Many years after this a Rolex man in Zürich,

Switzerland, told me that the V made by the hands is V for Victory. "But it does not work in German," he said, and laughed.

At the end of the day in any jewelry store many of the watches have been shown and so their hands have moved, which means that in the morning someone must reset them. Also the automatics may be quickened into motion by being shuffled in and out of the cases. They rest in trays, and the trays are placed in plastic tubs that stack when you put them in the safes. They move again when you remove them from the safes in the morning.

Another task was polishing the brass numbers that were kept on the table at the entrance to the store. As you entered you saw a tall, narrow hexagonal table, about as high as your bottom rib. The table was elaborately constructed of long brown and white steer horns and darkly stained, brightly lacquered cowhide straps. The top was a solid piece of polished cherrywood. On the table was a brass stand, and on that stand hung two hundred brass plates, each about the size of a regular Christmas card, with numbers on them in black enamel from one to two hundred. To get a salesman or saleswoman you had to take a number, like at the seafood counter at the grocery store. That's how frantic the store would get. "Like a shark pit, Bobby," Mr. Popper once told me with delight. "That's why I do the free giveaways in the paper. You have to create a feeding frenzy. Who wants to eat in an empty restaurant? It's un-American. They got to fight for it. That's the secret of marketing, Bob. Like stags in the rut." I made sure these numbers were all in order in the morning and I polished them at night before we went home.

•

The front-of-the-house was the glamorous half of the store but, as in a restaurant, the real work was done in back. That's where the safes were, and the phones, and the steam cleaners and the stand-up polishing wheel, and Jim's and the other managers' desks. Their trash cans had to be emptied every morning.

"You're doing a great job on the front," Jim told me, after my first week. I vacuumed the carpets, and cleaned butts out of the sand-filled ashtrays with a slotted spoon. We had a wooden hand press you used to flatten the sand and make a diamond imprint in it once the butts were out. "Everybody says so. But you have to take the same care with the back-of-the-house," Jim said. "That's what Popper will really notice. Take special care of his office and his stairs."

I vacuumed the stairs to Mr. Popper's office every morning before the store opened. In the darkened stairwell yellow light shone from beneath the door and, with the security of his extra lock, which opened with a special key like a credit card, it seemed like the cave of Aladdin, or the lair of a sleepy dragon.

One morning, two weeks after I started, I was on the stairs on my hands and knees when I felt a tap on my back. I looked up and saw Mr. Popper.

Mr. Popper was short. He had a round white face and a huge potbelly. He was wearing a pink Hermès tie. He always wore Hermès ties, which were purchased for him by his wife, Sheila, who was hated by everyone at the store. Except for Jim, because he did not hate anyone, and because she had made Jim her protégé.

"Good morning there, young fella," Mr. Popper said.

I wondered if I should turn off the vacuum cleaner or keep vacuuming. Mr. Popper held his green ostrich cowboy hat in his hand. The hat had a feather.

Mr. Popper gave me a look and I realized I was blocking the stairwell. So I turned off the vacuum cleaner, stood, and pressed myself against the wall.

I was pleased that now Mr. Popper knew who vacuumed his stairs.

*I*t was not what you think of when you think of a jewelry store. There were not those stretched-out, noiseless, frightening afternoons we would come to know later, in our own store, when only one or two customers wandered in—tire-kickers, you understood with a look—and waved away the salespeople, rubbed their sweaty fingers across the top of a clean showcase or two, and then walked out again without asking even to see a wedding band or a pair of diamond studs. There was always business in The Store. We had more customers than salespeople. And we had lots of salespeople. Nearly one hundred, during the season, when Mr. Popper brought in college students from TCU and SMU. All day, every day, there were boxes being wrapped, receipts being written, credit card machines singing. When we opened in the morning it was like a soccer game in South America or the first morning of the new school year.

"Son. Let me see that watch, there, son. That big daddy there. The gold one."

I was Windexing the Rolex case. It was Monday morning after the weekend Halloween sale. I had done the trash, the ashtrays, and the vacuuming but I was behind on the showcases because Jim had sold one hundred and eighty thousand over the weekend, so he slept in and we drove in late.

"We'll get there at nine," he had told me. When I woke him again fifteen minutes later, nervously, he said, "Nine-thirty. Take the car if you want. Maybe I'll take the day off." I saw his coke next to the bed and because I could hear his wife, my sister-in-law, Lily, downstairs in the kitchen I quickly did a line myself and then made him a line and fed it to him. After a minute he sat up in bed and said, "Cut me another one of those, would you? Go ahead and have one yourself if you want." I cut us both two fat lines and he did one and said, "I'll save that one for after my shower." I did two more small lines while he was in the shower and tapped a couple of bumps into a piece of foil from his pack of cigarettes for later. Lily met us at the bottom of the stairs in her blue flannel pajamas. They had sheep and rabbits on them. I had had a crush on her for years but now that I lived with her she held less interest. She smoked too much and her teeth were yellowing. She had thin lips and large, clumsy hands. But when I looked at her I also thought about how I once saw her in her underwear leaving the bathroom after a shower. Her hip bones were narrow and angular against the cotton of her white underwear. Her face was wide but the bones of her skull were visible beneath her wet hair.

"Are you two going to be coming home late tonight? Should I make some dinner? I was thinking of roasting a chicken."

"I don't know," Jim said. "The same as always, I guess. If that's late. We'll eat at work."

"Well, I can't eat a whole chicken by myself."

She smiled at me and then frowned at Jim.

"You look nice this morning, Robert," she said. She bent over and rubbed her thighs. Her breasts swung beneath her pajama top. Then she crouched and stretched out her arms like a bird. "I need to get a job, Jimmy. My muscles are sore. I'm bored. I don't have anything to do except smoke pot and exercise all day."

"You don't have a green card yet," Jim said. We both had green cards because our father had got them for us when he first moved to Florida. He guessed, correctly, that we would want them later in life.

"I want to go home, then," she said. "I want to see my parents."

"Maybe after Christmas," Jim said. "Or you could go anytime, I guess. We'll be all right." He grinned at me. It was a very brotherly grin.

"You two stay out of trouble today," Lily said. "Don't let my husband boss you around too much," she said to me.

Then we were in the car, coming west on I-30 in the rushhour traffic we normally missed because we drove in before dawn, and there was downtown Fort Worth bright in the morning sun.

"Come on, son, get with the program! Ain't you had your coffee yet this mornin'? I want to see a watch! That gold one there. That there Rolex. The big one."

I didn't have case keys. I knew if I went to borrow a set of keys whoever I borrowed them from, even Jim, would ask me why I needed them, and then if I said there was a large black man in a red suit with three gold teeth and a white tie with a diamond tie stud at the Rolex case who wanted to look at a men's President I would be back to Windexing cases and someone else would be selling him. The reason I didn't have case keys was that I was not on the sales floor yet. They didn't even let me work the phones. But then I saw the case was open. All of the cases were open. One of the last things you did before opening the doors in the morning was push all of the locks on the showcases. But this whole side, even the men's jewelry, all the way to the diamond room, stood open.

The men's President Rolex was displayed on the beige suede stand in the original walnut box all the men's Presidents were housed in. It had the silver plastic crown on its gray silk cord and the original green hanging tags. Underneath the suede stand, I knew, were the original warranty, books, and authenticity papers. I handled the heavy watch carefully. I had almost dropped it as I slid it from its stand.

"This one, sir?" I asked, and handed him the watch. I did not know to unbuckle it before handing it to him, and I did not know that it was short-links so that it would not close on his thick wrist.

He smiled at the watch. He slipped it onto his fingers. Then he turned it and looked at the back of the bracelet.

"What's the trick? How do you get it open?" he asked me.

"They call that an invisible buckle, sir," I said. "See that crown there? That little gold crown? Just flip that with your finger."

He struggled with the bracelet of the watch for a moment and then popped it open with his thumbnail. I took a quick look around the showroom but no one seemed to be paying us any attention. Seven or eight customers browsed the diamond jewelry counters. Lisa was showing cluster rings to a fat woman with white hair, a tall man in a cowboy hat picked malachite, lapis lazuli, and rose quartz beads at the bead board, and a young man with two children stood patiently at the buy counter. His baby cried from the little home in a backpack on his father's chest. There were only three salespeople on the floor—everyone was still in back eating donuts—and it was so early we had not even put out the brass numbers.

I looked back at my customer and he had the watch on his wrist. He was trying to close it but it wouldn't fit.

"I didn't figure they made these things so damn little."

"You have got a big wrist," I told him. "You're lucky. Look at it on me."

I took the watch from him—something I would never have done a year later—and placed it on my own wrist and closed it. It hung there like a hoop. I shook the watch around my wrist.

"See that?" I said. "I would love to own one someday. But I could never wear one even if I could afford it. You need a man's wrist for one of these. My father always teases me about my wrists. He used to be a boxer. But really he's got these same girlish wrists I've got." I took the watch off and handed it back to him. "It looks silly on me. I mean, it makes me look silly. It looks proper on you."

He slid the watch back on again. It almost fit his wrist with the buckle open. It would take five more links to fit him properly, I figured. I knew how to fit the links. You always started with fewer than you thought you needed. But this man's wrist was enormous.

"How's it feel?" I asked him. "I was surprised the first time I held one, how heavy they are." That weight, the heft of quality, is part of the pitch.

"What did you say is the price on this watch? Is this the one I saw advertised in the paper?"

We were selling men's Presidents for four thousand nine hundred and ninety-five dollars. $4,995.00. They were selling down the street at Waltham's—Fort Worth's registered Rolex dealer—for eleven thousand eight hundred. I did not know the details yet. I thought we were simply more honest and competitive. I thought we were just the best deal in town. That's what I told him, too.

"That's the one. Yes sir. Forty-nine ninety-five. A brand-new Rolex men's President, solid eighteen-karat gold, lifetime warranty."

You spend the rest of your career trying to recapture that

innocence. Sinlessness and candor like that is a fierce advantage. But you can't fake it.

"So your old man was a boxer," he said, rolling the head of the watch through his fingers. "He must have had a few pounds on you," he said, and laughed. "Well, you going to save me any money on this watch, son? What's the best price? You ask the boss-man what his best price is for cash money. If you can save me a little money I think I'll take this one home."

I left the watch in his hands. I didn't do it because it was the right thing to do, though it was, but because I was afraid to ask for it back. I ran into the back-of-the-house and went to the safe room to find the link box, which was a clear plastic fishing tackle box, with a white label on the side that read ROLEX, that was kept full of men's and ladies' stainless-steel and stainless-and-gold jubilee and oyster links and eighteen-karat white and yellow gold links for the Presidents, and even some diamond pave or bezel set links for the diamond Presidents, and pulled out five President links, made sure they were all the same size and all had screws, grabbed a screwdriver off of the Watchman's desk, and hurried back onto the sales floor before an authentic salesperson could approach him and steal the sale. He was standing there admiring the watch on his wrist in a case mirror that he had found. Next time bring the customer a mirror. Especially a black customer, I knew. The more you serve them the better.

Later I found out that this, too, was false. In fact just the opposite is the case. But it takes years to learn how to sell.

"What did the man say? You work him over for me? You give him the old one-two? The combination?"

I knew we had four thousand and fifty dollars in the men's Presidents we were running for forty-nine ninety-five. These watches were truly loss leaders for us. To bring in the big fish.

"He said forty-seven hundred," I told him. I knew Jim would cut them down to forty-five fifty, sometimes, to close a deal. "For cash."

"That's no sales tax, then," he said. "For cash. That's forty-seven tax, title, and license. Out the door."

"Yes sir. Forty-seven hundred out the door."

"Sold. You going to fix this so she fits me? I'll just wear her out. This thing come with a box? I can put my old Seiko in there. See what my wife thinks about that," he said, and laughed again.

"Hell, that's not a bad way to start your Monday morning, is it, son? What did you say your name was?" He was counting hundred-dollar bills onto the counter. My Windex bottle and my roll of paper towels were still sitting there on the glass. "I bet there's a fine commission for you on this. I sure hope so. You look awful young to be selling jewelry, come to think of it. You old enough to be out of high school? Course there ain't no shame in working for a living. I never finished high school myself. And look at me now. Work hard and you'll be wearing one of these yourself someday, son."

"Yes sir," I said. "I hope so, sir," I said. I finished installing the links and handed him the watch. I counted the money. There was forty-seven hundred dollars. I tucked it into the outside pocket of my jacket.

"Now I'm going to need an appraisal for this watch. You can't wear a watch like this uninsured. Write me up a receipt, young man. There you go, write down all the details. Lifetime warranty, you said. Put it down in black and white. I'm gonna keep that piece of paper in a safe place. Safety deposit box. With that insurance appraisal."

He shook the watch down to the end of his wrist, before the

wrist joint. It fit. It was snug but it had just a bit of slide. You should be able to slip the end of your pinkie finger between the bracelet and the base of the wrist.

"Put that box in a bag for me, would you, son? Stick that old Seiko in there. Worn that watch for twenty years. My son will get it now. How's that look? Now that's a bit of sunshine. Look at that light up." He laughed again, that large laugh of the older southern black man. It made you happier to hear it. "That there's the real deal. What will this appraise for? Eight, nine grand?"

"Eleven thousand eight hundred," I explained. "That's brand-new retail list price. If you had to walk into Waltham's today and buy a new one out of their case, that is what you would pay. So that's what we appraise them for. Retail replacement value."

"All right, well you get that in the mail to me tomorrow. It's been a pleasure. A real pleasure. You'll see me again. Yes sir. You're my jeweler now. You got a card? Hell, you haven't even told me your name."

"Bobby Clark, sir," I said. I shook his hand. I had not wanted to do that because my palms were wet with sweat. "I'll put a card in the appraisal, sir." I did not have cards yet. After he left I went along the line of watch cases and made sure all the cases were locked. I went into the diamond room and sat there for a minute in the red leather chair that was fashioned out of white and black bulls' horns, just like the table the brass numbers sat on. Besides newspapers on my paper route growing up, which didn't really count, and credit card applications I had sold at Sears for a few afternoons before they found out none of my applications were going through, that men's President was my first time, my first sale.

In the back-of-the-house Jim was waiting for me. He was in the hallway next to the customers' bathroom, what we called the executive bathroom. It had Frette hand towels and the expensive toilet paper. There was another bathroom in the back that we were all supposed to use. But the saleswomen tended to use this front bathroom on the sly, and it was the one I used, too, because if I had to I could pretend I was only replacing the toilet paper or cleaning the mirror. I always had my Windex with me. It was a safer place to do a line.

For years bathrooms were sanctuaries for me. In time I learned that the best ones are not private bathrooms at all, because in these someone can destroy the solitude by knocking on the door. Then you are on their schedule. The one you want is not a big, alienating public toilet, the ones in an airport, but a smallish-sized restroom with three or four stalls, where you can take one next to the wall and sit there as long as you please. Your boss, your wife, the police, they are all far away from that toilet and that space. It is like being on an airplane, but happier, because you are alone.

The hallway to the executive bathroom was also a confidential space insulated from the rest of the store. The steps to Mr. Popper's office led to this hallway. The walls were papered in a green-and-silver-chevroned fabric, there was a row of porcelain-framed mirrors on one side, and it was dimly lit by a row of five small, round, pink glass chandeliers that Jim said Sheila had bought on an island off the coast of Venice. The hallway was not an easy way to get from the front to the back so you were supposed to stay out of it. But there was no official rule. I liked it because it was private and there were no cameras, I liked how my skin looked in the pink light and those old thick lead glass mirrors, and I liked those chandeliers that had flowers around the hidden bulbs. I often found

Jim pausing there, too. Like me, he liked to use the executive bathroom. He was allowed to, though, because he was a manager.

"Did you sell that watch? Did you sell that President? That was the display. You didn't sell the display, did you?"

I took the stack of hundred-dollar bills from my pocket and handed it to him.

"I got forty-seven for it. Forty-seven is all right, right? He asked for a better price for cash. I didn't charge him sales tax."

"That was the display, Bobby. That was the last men's Prez in the store. We were taking orders off that watch. We don't have another one. We can only take orders on Presidents at that price. Did you write him a receipt? You have to charge sales tax if you write him a receipt."

"No, I didn't write him a receipt." Sometimes you know to lie simply by the way a person asks you a question. It is a defensive reflex, like running.

The store's copy of the handwritten receipt I had given my customer was in my breast pocket. I could just tear it up and flush it down the toilet.

"You didn't write him a receipt? Okay, that's good. Okay. Let's go tell Sheila you sold the floor model. At least you got cash. At least it's not a charge. She's going to shit. But it's all right, it's just Sheila. I'm not saying it wasn't a good sale. You didn't know. What were you doing out there? Why didn't you come get me? You did the right thing. You sold the watch. Nobody can say you didn't do the right thing. You made the sale. Good man. Hell, we shouldn't have the damn thing out there if it's not for sale. How could you know any better? It could have happened to anybody. Who would have guessed you would have sold the damn thing? You didn't even come to me for a price. That's the instinct. That's the Clark blood."

42

I wanted to hug him. I didn't, of course.

"It's funny," he said. "Remind me to tell you the story about how the Polack sold her first big watch. I was there. I was a customer, actually. It was back in my vacuum cleaner days. But I helped her sell it. It was a Patek Philippe, not a President, but it was like this deal of yours. She needed an assist, though. She couldn't swing it on her own. Nobody else in this store could have sold that watch the way you just did. Nobody except me and Mr. Popper, anyway. Hell, I don't even know if I would have had those kind of balls, Bobby."

This was more or less the same pitch he gave Sheila in the bookkeeper's office. He was just rehearsing it for himself. She started to yell and then Jim showed her all the cash provided by my customer. She settled down. That was why he told her the story before he showed her the money. Because he knew once she saw green her volume would lower.

Nevertheless Sheila explained that I had broken company policy and cost the store money. None of this made sense to me at the time, but the thing was, with Christmas still three and a half months away, we were already not selling Rolex watches, we were only selling Rolex orders. We took the money and promised the watch, that was it, you got a piece of paper in the mail saying that your watch would arrive as soon as possible. In fact, I learned years later, we never even intended to order any more Rolexes. Or maybe we intended to but never did.

In the middle of Sheila's speech Mr. Popper entered the office and she stopped.

"Did I hear right?" he asked. He barely let a smile come through. I tried to look at the pink and purple raccoons on his tie, so I wouldn't smile too big myself. I didn't want to seem proud.

"Did I hear what I think I heard? News around here is one of these Clark brothers sold himself a men's President first thing. Before he even ate his scrambled eggs for breakfast. Now which one of you done it? Not this little one?"

He patted me on the shoulder. Then he took two one-hundred-dollar bills off the pile of cash from my Rolex sale on the bookkeeper's desk and folded them in half and tucked them in the breast pocket of my jacket, in with the receipt.

"Hell, Sheila, sounds to me like we got another genuine twenty-four karat Clark here. Jim, why is this fella still stocking the box room? When were you planning on putting him on the floor? When he beats you on the boards? Looks like he's gonna sell whether you put him there or not!"

He took a stick of ChapStick from his pocket and rubbed it quickly around the inside of each nostril. He had delicate skin and his lips and nostrils chapped in the dry Fort Worth air. As strange and disorienting as this habit of his was, the first time you saw him do it, because he was Mr. Popper you wanted to line your own nose with ChapStick, or maybe to carry a stick of ChapStick with you so that you could quickly do it for him when you saw him reaching in his pocket.

"You just listen to your big brother," he told me. "When you're ready, he'll let you sell. Sheila here is right. We got pro-tocols for a reason. You just do like Jim here does and you'll be all right. Hell, that's something, though. Doesn't even have a set of showcase keys and he's already sold his first President."

Jim had green eyes, green eyes like our father's, eyes as green as a bird's. His shoulders were broad and he had been California's number one gymnast when in high school living with Dad. Before then he had attended Shattuck Military Academy in Faribault, Minnesota, where our dad had sent him when he was first getting into serious trouble back in Calgary. "It's where Marlon Brando went to school, son," our dad had told Jim. At Shattuck Jim met the fellows who helped him to become a drug smuggler and a dealer. That was when he became a salesman, he said. When he realized he had a talent.

He enjoyed the same ease with women our father had, but because he lacked our dad's energy he did not have sex with nearly so many of them. He could talk, though. He lied less than our father did. He was reasonable.

He did not know how to dress. He did not say hurtful things to other people.

He was my big brother but for me when I was a kid and a teenager he was like someone else's big brother, one I had read about in a book.

When I knew him better, from hotel rooms, three-day Ecstasy-and-cocaine-fed drunks, shared rooms in whorehouses, and overnight international flights, I learned that he would whimper in his sleep. By then, of course, I understood what he might have to fear.

In the cold early mornings before opening, the store was quiet. First thing as we walked to the back we turned on the heat. It was off during the day, even in the coldest months of winter, because of all the bodies. When we entered we could often see our breath. The best part about Jim having a key was that we usually got in before the other employees arrived. Then it was just the two of us, we had the whole store to ourselves.

The white leather of the showcase interiors and the display stands, the risers and the stair-step displays for the rings and the bracelet rolls, looked like the vacant interiors of many shiny-clean, rich, and glamorous apartments.

Lisa and I were putting out the showcases together. She liked to do the wedding rings while I did the men's jewelry in the case next to her.

"I don't believe you won't read your mother's letters. That's awful. Your own mother. She is probably crying when she writes those letters. You can probably smell her tears on those letters."

Not reading my mother's letters was revenge because Wendy was not calling. She could blame that on the cost of long-distance. But she would not write me letters, either. I wrote Wendy a letter every day at first. Then as we got busier at work I wrote two or three a week. I would lie in bed when we got home in the evening, at eight or nine, smoke a joint, and write her part of a letter or a letter.

Later that day Lisa brought it up again.

"You should try reading one," Lisa said. "Just pick any letter she sent you. Open it and read a few sentences. You never know, she might surprise you."

We were having lunch together at a Mexican restaurant we liked over on Third and Main, just a few blocks from the store. Jim was not with us.

"You're saving them for a reason," she said. "When was the last time you read one?"

We were on our second margarita and had ordered only a guacamole and a plate of blue corn tortilla nachos.

I was anxious about the hour we had been away but she was placid. "It's so busy they will never notice," she said.

"Can we talk about something else besides my mother?" I said. I couldn't think of anything else to say.

There was something about her neck and her collarbone that made you really want to have sex with Lisa. In addition to her many other sexy qualities, I mean. But even if she let me, which I knew she wouldn't, that would be cheating. On Jim and Wendy both. Not that I could ever ask her, even if she would have let me. Jim was married but Lisa was his girlfriend nevertheless. Having sex with your brother's girlfriend was worse than cheating on your own girlfriend.

I had strong opinions on this whole cheating business because of what our father did to our mother. I asked him once how he could have cheated on Mom. I could always ask him any question. He used to say, "Hey, son, want to take a drive?" Or, "Are you in the mood for a cold drink?" Then we would get in the car and drive around and talk.

"She told you I hit her?"

"Didn't you?" Jim had told me, but I wasn't going to let Dad know that.

"That was a difficult time, son. It was when I was drinking. I'm surprised she told you that. That is disappointing."

"I still don't see how you could cheat on her like that, Dad."

"It's complicated, son. Sometimes one person's sex drive doesn't match the other's. Your mother is what is technically called frigid. That's not an insult, it is a scientific term. It is not her fault. It's your grandmother. That bitch. She never held her when she was growing up. That's why you boys have had the problems you have had. She never held you. She couldn't even hug you

47

when you hurt yourself. It wasn't her fault. She didn't know how. In your case, Bobby, she weaned you too soon. It was on an airplane. Because she was embarrassed of her own body. Sad."

"That doesn't sound like a good excuse, Dad. I could never do that."

"I hope that's true, son. You might look at it differently later. Try not to be too hard on your old man."

"I don't think so, Dad," I had said. "I don't think there's more than one way to look at it."

Lisa said, "I understand." She ate another bite of the nachos. I tried not to watch the way she placed the chip into her mouth. I could see her lips and her tongue and her white teeth. I was afraid that if she saw me watching she would understand what I was thinking.

"So let's have a new conversation now. You start. What should our conversation be about? It's your turn. You think of a subject."

She was easy to talk to until I began to consider her sexually. Well, I had always considered her sexually, ever since I had met her, but she had seemed remote until the past few days. Now the sexualness of her kept happening every time I looked at her, like I would reach out and grab her at any second and start having sex with her, right here under the table, without having any control over it, and that drove everything else out of my head. Not one word that I might speak was in my brain.

I took a sip of my margarita.

"Now you're just going to sit there and look at me?" She laughed. "Sometimes you really remind me of your brother. And then sometimes I swear you are complete opposites."

I wanted her to explain that. So I could fix the opposite parts, I mean.

*E*very salesman had to write his own appraisals, so as part of my training Jim gave me his to do. We did them at closing before going home. Often Lisa and I would hang out at Jim's desk and do them together. Though normally she let hers sit for a few days before she sent them out. Jim nagged her about that.

"It's crucial they go out in the morning mail," Jim said. "It's called confirming the sale. When the customer gets this appraisal in the mail a day or two after he bought the piece and reads it and sees the appraised price, it reconfirms his decision. Then he tells himself he made a good decision when he spent that money. An investment."

"What did we pay for these, Dennis?" I was appraising a pair of diamond studs, three carats total weight, set in fourteen-karat yellow gold with push-backs. As a rule when you did an appraisal the jewelry was already out the door with the customer, but Jim was having these studs converted to screw-backs.

"What would you call these for color and clarity?"

Dennis Panier, the manager of the back-of-the-house, was also in charge of diamonds. "Most diamonds we just use our own made-up grading system," Dennis explained to me once. "We can't use GIA. It would discombobulate the average Texan."

I showed Dennis the ear studs. He looked up at them, in a hurry.

"I'd call 'em K SI3s if I were you. That's close enough for lookin', anyhow. I pay twelve hundred a carat for goods like those. Pull them and weigh them and you'll know what we paid."

I looked at the diamonds more closely myself. It seemed to me that Dennis was right. But Jim had told me "white, eye-clean," which should translate to H or I, and SI1 to SI2.

"Are you sure? I mean, I'm sure you're sure. I'm sorry to ask. But Jim said they were—well, something else."

He laughed. Dennis's startling, musical laugh was one of his best selling tools. Any person who heard his laugh started to laugh after him, a beat or two after he began. He may have deployed it as a tool or it may have been entirely natural, you could not tell. It was like the pied piper. He looked a bit like the pied piper, too. He was from the swamps of Louisiana and he had the rubber-band-like body and the milky coffee-colored skin of those old French Creoles. Popper had found him tending bar at the Dungeon in New Orleans. He was five feet two or three inches tall, and he had a long nose, slightly pinched at the sides, with a broad round tip. He had a lot of brown hair, and stray curls at his temples, like a girl.

•

When I gave Jim the appraisal he was confused.

"Look, Bobby, the appraisal is not a lab report. I know I told you it is important to get it exactly right. But there is more to being right than being good at arithmetic. We are not calculators, we are people, and so are our customers." When he had first shown me how to write one I made the mistake of comparing it to writing up a lab in IB chemistry or physics. "This is not a scientific thing. It is a sales tool. Plus it protects the most important person in the transaction. Who is that? The customer. It protects our customer, Matthew, here. Matthew Randolph." He tapped the appraisal and looked at me seriously. "Mr. Matthew Randolph is protected from the insurance industry if his wife's new diamond studs are lost or stolen. You know what those insurance bastards are like. They'll take your money all right but they don't want to give it back to you. So we have to make sure that Matthew has plenty of money to work with if something does happen. Do you want to explain to Matt that his wife has to downgrade her diamond studs, now, even though they were appraised and insured, because the cost of diamonds has gone up and we failed to account for that in the appraisal? Or that god forbid we appraised the studs too low? Would that be fair to Matt? Would that make him a lifetime customer? This business is about building relationships, Bobby. Relationships of trust. What if some joker pulled every stone on his new tennis bracelet? Those things can weigh out half of what's on the tag. For crying out loud. We have to trust them to treat our expertise with respect. They have to trust our expert opinions. This is how we do it. Stick to the store's grading system. Take the information from the tag. That's why we tape the tag to the original store copy of the receipt. So there can be no mistakes. Then, whatever he paid for them, whatever he actually paid, times it by three. Your retail replacement value. Some customers will ask you to lower this number because of the cost of the insurance. If they ask, fine, it's their business, their decision. The point is we want his wife to see this appraisal and she'll think that's about what he paid for them. She'll be thrilled. But always call the customer to ask where the appraisal should be mailed. Never forget that. Or you can have a real mess on your hands. It can even turn legal. You understand." There was a blue pen on his desk. I picked it up and played with it between my fingers. "In case the studs aren't for his wife, say. And you accidentally send them to the home address. You make that mistake once and you never make it again.

"Okay, sit down," he said. "It's my fault. I've been letting Lisa show you. Nothing against Lisa, but she doesn't always follow policy. Let's write this one together, step by step. Carats total weight? Three, right? Three-point-oh-seven. That's accuracy, Bobby. That's what I am trying to teach you. Just like it says on the tag."

Lisa was good on the floor, and I watched her to learn, but the best saleswoman we had, and Mr. Popper's personal favorite, was a woman—almost a girl—named the Polack. She sold without lying, and she had an energy you admired. People said she was the most beautiful woman in Fort Worth, Texas. She had won contests. Except for her eyes she could have been Jewish, or Moroccan. There was something about her that reminded you of a wide, shadowy desert. She had a thick eastern European brow and greasy lips. There were hail dents on the roof and the hood of her big green Mercedes. One time she took me to lunch in her other car, a wine-colored Cadillac convertible.

I was jealous of her. Jim treated her with an odd respect, because she was the one who had convinced him to come into the jewelry business. Jim was only a customer when he first met her. This was three years before I joined Jim in Texas. He was twenty-one years old and Kirby vacuum cleaner's youngest regional sales manager. He was buying a stainless steel Cartier for an institutional client of his, Jim said. And he thought he would buy a case of Montblancs for his top sellers if they would make him a quantity discount. It was almost Christmas and the sales floor stood ten deep with buyers. It was the fat time. Jim stood in a corner away from the entrance doors next to a tall marble pedestal ashtray and smoked.

I had heard him tell the story a hundred times. After a while Jim grew bored of watching all the selling and he shouldered his way to the Patek and Breguet case. There was the Polack. Industry people said that the Polack took her first job as a jewelry salesperson because she liked the sex that went with jewelry. But that was not it. She was there because she liked the way the money smelled. "She didn't know the first damn thing about jewelry," Jim always said when he told the story. "Back then she didn't even know how to sell. That was the first thing I noticed about her, in fact. Money. She even smells like it. That woman knows money better than anyone I've ever met."

She was showing a platinum Patek Philippe to an elderly Vietnamese man in a black suit. Jim stood next to the old man.

"You don't want one of those," Jim said to the customer. "No name recognition. You want the Rolex. The Rolex is what you need. See?" He pulled back his cuff to show the old man. Jim had won it two years before. "Ten thousand Kirbys in one year," he said. "That's more than thirty vacuum cleaners a day. Five million seven hundred thousand dollars gross." It said

Kirby right on the dial. Not every company can do that with a factory dial. Kirby had a special deal with Rolex USA.

"That looks pretty good," the man said to Jim. "But I prefer this one."

"What do you think? The Rolex or that one there?" Jim asked the saleswoman.

"Let me take the links out of your watch," she said to Jim. Jim always wore his watches loose, the same as I did. That's where I learned to do it. The Polack probably planned to keep the links for the store or for herself. "To wear it like that is not good for the watch. This man knows what to buy."

The Patek cost as much as five Rolex Presidents. But Jim did not know that, then.

"It's comfortable that way," Jim said. "Let's see it on his wrist. I bet that watch looks great on him," Jim said to her.

"It is a handsome watch," the Polack said. "Old," she said.

"Not old," Jim said. "Distinguished."

"That is what I said," she said. "Sophisticated. You listen," she said.

She wiped the Patek she was selling with a diamond cloth. The salesman next to her winced. But he did not correct her. Dust from the diamonds would scratch the soft metal of the head and the sapphire crystal.

"Try it on," Jim said to the man.

The Polack put the watch on the man. She handled the man's fingers and wrist like she was fixing a broken machine.

"Do you have a mirror?" Jim asked her.

"Of course," she said. "I have a mirror," she said. She went to find one. Jim nudged the man with his elbow as she walked away.

"Look at that. That's something."

They smiled at each other. The old man was missing all of his top teeth except two, one on either side, which looked like yellow fangs. He admired the watch on his wrist. He had slender, muscular wrists and the elegant Patek looked right on him. The pale platinum belonged on his leathered skin. He could see himself feeding his enemies to the crocodiles in the moat behind his mansion. The Polack returned with the mirror and angled it on its brass stand to show him the watch on his arm. There they were, the three of them, together in his own country. The deep jungle. Tigers coiled and watchful beneath the shadowy canopy. Hot wind in the saw grass. The rain boiling in the low clouds.

"*Oui, c'est ça,*" he said. "That is the one."

"Power," Jim said. The old man looked at him. "That's what it says. Achievement. Victory. That's triumph right there. Strength, too."

The old man studied the watch.

"When's the last time you bought yourself a Christmas present?" Jim asked him.

He fought the smile, but it appeared on its own. "I admit this is the first time," he said.

You wait for that smile. You come to doubt you ever saw it. Then some customer lights it up at you and you recollect that you are not duping them at all, but helping them.

"I like this watch," the man said. He nodded to the Polack.

She ran his credit card and then found Jim on the showroom floor.

"Good going, Mr. Suit," she said. "But you are a suit. I can throw you out. I do not need a man to do it."

"Nice sale," Jim said.

"We have good watches," the Polack said. "These are my own watches."

55

"A guy like that is hard," Jim said. "He worked for his money. Doesn't trust anybody. Orientals are tough, the toughest."

"So, Suit, you sell for Rolex? You are here to arrest me?"

"Arrest you? I sell vacuums," Jim said. "But today I'm here to buy. You want to make another sale?"

"You don't look like a vacuum cleaner man," she said. "You are too young. My mother is someone who loves vacuum cleaners," she said.

"Sensible woman," Jim said. "But don't kid yourself. Everyone loves a good vacuum cleaner." When I was thirteen and fourteen, visiting him for the summer, I drove around with him and heard this pitch over and over. It was one of my favorites. "Love is the word. A good vacuum cleaner is an investment. A good vacuum cleaner you own for life. Pass it down to your grandkids. Save it for the next generation. Change the belt once a year and it will never age a day. Hardwoods, concrete, carpet. Everyone wants clean floors. Clean floors are like expensive shoes. Walk into someone's house, what's the first thing you notice? The shoes and the floor. They go together. Nothing worse than a dirty floor. White trash. Slovenly. It doesn't matter if you have a maid, you still need a good vacuum cleaner. You can't expect her to get your floors clean with a Hoover. You think a Hoover will last twenty years? Cheap plastic, too many parts. You can buy one at Target. Can you buy a Rolex at Target? Manolo Blahniks? Kirby vacuum cleaners have been the world's leading professional vacuum cleaner for the home for more than half a century."

The Polack laughed. "Ha!"

I remember the first time I heard that laugh. Like a dog's bark. At first it disoriented you, then it made sense.

"I don't really sell them anymore," Jim told her. "I teach

other people how to do it. But I'm proud I can. Never be ashamed of being a salesperson. It's one of the few honest trades. Jesus Christ was a salesman. Muhammad. Allah. World's greatest. Paul. Those Jews. Think about Christ without Paul, huh? Ron Hubbard. Santa Claus. You ever think about him? Think about a mother telling her child about Santa Claus. She's not lying. That's selling. So where are you from? Would you like to join me for lunch?"

The Polack was never a customer, though.

"Today you buy a watch, yes?" she said. "We do business, vacuum man."

It was one of Jim's best stories, and the whole thing was true.

Lisa had a pale blue silk comforter on her bed. The comforter was very warm, much warmer than you expected it would be from looking at it.

We opened the windows and listened to the thunderstorm. Texas has thunderstorms like no place in the world. Because the sky is so high. We were curled up under the comforter.

"I bought it in Vegas," she said, petting it with her hand. "I love it."

"I like it too," I said.

The thunder rolled. The rain was falling underneath the sound of the thunder. We could hear it on the pavement and on the roof.

"Do you think Lily is prettier than me?"

"Lily is my brother's wife. I don't think about her like that."

Maybe this was a lie, I'm not sure, but as the days went past and Lisa and I spent more time together, it was becoming less and less a lie. And yet it was not a very salable lie to tell my brother's girlfriend.

"You didn't answer the question."

"I don't know if I can explain that properly. You are very pretty."

I still had a list of people I tried not to deceive more than necessary.

Lisa kept bamboo in clear glass containers on her bedstand next to her phone, by her windows, on her bathroom sink, and next to her refrigerator. The water was trapped in black rocks in the glass. It was green and growing but it was untidy bamboo. Ever since, I have associated bamboo, especially the disorderly, un-Japanese kind, with guilty sex, crystal methedrine, and simple unfeigned affection.

"Are you sleeping with me because I sold that Rolex?" I asked her.

I was lucky she was a kind person. She might have said this sort of thing, too, when she was only sixteen.

"Yes. That's exactly why I am sleeping with you," she said. "Because you sold that Rolex. One lousy Rolex that we lost money on." She laughed. "I'm sorry," she said. "I didn't mean it like that."

"I guess that's what Jim would think. If he knew about us."

She was quiet. I watched her. She was hard to figure out.

"Here," she said. "Take another. Take some more." She handed me the pipe. I reached for the lighter. "No, let me light it for you," she said.

Jim bought his methamphetamine from her and they both shared it with me. She liked to smoke it, but he told me only to sniff it. "Never smoke meth with Lisa," he told me. "Once you start smoking it you may as well inject it. You'll never quit."

"I need a new haircut," she said. "I wish I had different hair. I was born with the wrong hair. It is my father's fault. He had nice features and perfect teeth, like yours, but not very good hair. It's my baby hair, my mother used to say." I was quiet. I knew her mother had died when she was young. Jim had told me that. "It never changed. To my grown-up hair, I mean. It's the hair I was born with."

"Your hair is nice. It is soft."

"You can touch it if you want to. It's soft all over. Yours is thick. It is one of your better features. I wish my skin was as nice as your hair."

"I don't want to mess it up," I said.

My face felt hot from the crystal, and I worried that my ears were red. I wanted to ask her for a beer. But I was shy to. I could hear each of the raindrops outside, one by one, as they struck the roof and the sidewalk and the leaves of the trees. I could even hear them as they fell.

"There's something I want to tell you," she said.

I'd been waiting for this. Not waiting for it, but I had known it was coming, and I would try to prepare for it, when I would let myself think about it, which was not often and not for long. I tried not to panic. What if she's already told Jim? I could handle her telling me that we couldn't have sex, even, so long as she hadn't said anything to Jim. That might be best, in fact.

"It's that store," she said. "You have to be careful of that place. It has a bad effect on people. It makes some things too easy."

Wait. I was confused. Is she talking about Jim and me?

"Jim says I should go home for Christmas," I said. Then I wished I hadn't introduced his name. She hadn't said "Jim" yet. "My girlfriend Wendy is back there."

"I know you have a girlfriend," she said. "You don't have to tell me that. It is nice to have a girlfriend. I don't mind your girlfriend."

She lit the pipe for herself, smoked it, and then quickly handed it to me while the drug was still bubbling in the well of the glass.

"It's the cash drawer," Lisa said, releasing the smoke very slowly and talking over it. I couldn't do that. "Have you ever noticed how no one keeps the cash drawer? They say they reconcile it but they don't, really. That's what Jim says. They just add up the receipts. But we take in money a lot of different ways. Plus what if you don't turn in your receipts? What if you just hide them and take them home? Or what if you tore them up and flushed them down the toilet? Then on a cash sale no one would ever know about the cash at all. It would just be like invisible money. We only do an inventory once a quarter. As long as what you sell isn't anything big, no one would even notice. No merchandise, no paperwork, no money. Who would know the difference?"

This isn't about me and Jim at all, I thought. That was a relief. But this was a different problem that I had not even imagined. She knows something, Bobby. I had been taking money from the drawer for several weeks.

I wondered if this was a trick of Jim's to trip me up. He could have asked Lisa to mention it to me first. It was only lunch money I took. Twenty or fifty dollars, once a day, sometimes twice. Jim might have found my hiding spot in the closet. Seven hundred and sixty dollars, a gold Seiko for Wendy, a rope of pearls, a pair of carat-and-a-half-total-weight diamond studs, an emerald ring for her birthday in May, a half-ounce gold Krugerrand for her father for Christmas, a fourteen-karat cloisonné bangle for her mother, a white gold box chain with a white gold panda pendant for her little sister. If he found that, would he accuse me or observe me? Or seek a confession? Had Lily snooped it out?

"Let's do it again," she said. "I like doing it with you more. If you want to know the truth."

I didn't want to hear anything about how she had sex with my brother. I said so.

"I wouldn't say anything about that," she said. "I wasn't going to say anything like that. Give me some credit, Bobby."

I looked at the pipe. There was a bit more to smoke in the bottom, before she reloaded it.

"I love your brother," Lisa said. "But I like it better this way. I can love him from a distance. It feels natural to love somebody who can't really love you back the way you might want. We should probably slow down with this stuff. I don't want to. But I'm talking too much."

"That makes sense," I said. I didn't want to slow down, either. I was in the mood to go faster, in fact. "I understand that. It is the same way for me."

"That is the crank," she said. "Crank makes you smarter. Everybody knows it. Even Einstein did crank," she said. "Not to mention Jack Kerouac.

"Here, let's do some more," she said. "Let's do as much as we want. I always want to do that and I never do. Let's actually do it. Let's smoke a big bunch together and then make love for an hour. We can be like whales. They make love for a week in the water."

She climbed out from under the comforter.

61

"Come out here with me," she said. "The cold air feels good. God, listen to the storm."

She added more crystal to the pipe. We knelt naked together on the bed with our knees rubbing and smoked.

"My ass is like a whale's," she said, and laughed.

"Is that right about Einstein?" I said. "I think you are thinking of Freud. And I think it was cocaine. Or Sherlock Holmes, maybe. He was a big cokehead, too."

"Was there a real Sherlock Holmes? I don't like cocaine," Lisa said. "That is your brother's drug. For me it's over too soon." She laughed again. "That's funny," she said.

She laughed too often, especially around sex. That was probably the only thing I did not like about her.

When the buy counter was slow or our regular man on the runs—a fellow who called himself the Wizard of Oz—got overbooked, Mr. Popper told Jim to send me out to bat cleanup. I wore a backpack, like a high school kid, full of diamonds, checks, bullion, sometimes cash, Swiss watches, and other precious goods that we ferried back and forth between Fort Worth and Dallas. Much of our business was conducted this way. I kept a pair of blue jeans at the store for when they sent me on the runs because you did not want to attract attention. The regular runs guy, the Wizard, drove a bruised Toyota pickup truck for the same reason. But with all the cars in his collection Popper owned only one that was anonymous, so I usually took Jim's company Porsche or the big four-door Audi. I enjoyed driving these cars and wished I could wear a suit. That would impress the girls at gas stations when I was filling up the car.

Elie Kizakov was our main memorandum supplier of diamonds ten carats or larger, and most of our fancy stones, especially the rarest fancy colors like red, orange, and green. Jim, Dennis, and Mr. Popper referred to him simply as the Jew. He took a liking to me because the first time we met, at his fifteenth-floor office in the Murray Savings Building on Preston Road in Dallas, where all the serious diamond dealers were— not just the Jews and Israelis but the Indians and South Africans as well—I was reading Spinoza's *Ethics*. I always brought a book with me to Murray Savings because they liked to make you wait. Not Mr. Kizakov, though.

"Spinoza. He was a pantheist. You know what a pantheist is?"

I nodded.

"He was the most famous intellectual ever to be excommunicated from our faith," he said. "Other than Jesus Christ. But then Jesus was not an intellectual. A real mistake the rabbis made. Spinoza, I mean. A great man. But, to be fair, not a religious man. Pantheism, atheism, they are one and the same. What is your name?"

I told him.

"You are not related to Jim Clark?"

I nodded again.

"But you are not selling? Why not?"

I lied and explained that we were short-staffed on the runs.

"Deliveries are not so bad. It is honest work. You perform a useful service. I often tell Idan selling is a dangerous business. Better you should work construction. Do something of use to your fellow man. At least postpone selling for a year or two. Until you see it for what it truly is. This way you avoid selling yourself."

•

As Kizakov began to trust me he took time with me.

"You want to learn something, Clark? Come here. Look at this."

He was my favorite stop. Kizakov and another man, an Indian named Namil, whose wife gave me samosas. I hadn't even known I liked Indian food until I tried those.

"In this business, always trust your eyes," Mr. Kizakov taught me. "There are always lies in business. That is nothing to complain about. But in some businesses, like this one, you can see what you are buying. There is money in the paper businesses. That is true. My father was in insurance. In Berlin. And Prague. A very successful man, my father. But personally I like to see what I am paying for. I like to show my customer what I am selling him. Now, after he sees everything I can see, it is his responsibility.

"Take a look at this diamond." He took a diamond from his inside jacket pocket. It was a very unusual place for a wholesaler to secure a diamond. It was not even in a paper. He cleaned it with his shirtsleeve. It was bright pink, and the table of the diamond alone was the size of a quarter, never mind the crown. It must have been twenty carats or more.

"Go on. You have a loupe? No? You carry all these diamonds for Ronnie Popper and you do not even carry a loupe? You going to trust some other man's loupe for checking in the diamonds? Don't tell me you don't loupe them when you sign for them? You put your signature there on that memorandum paper on another man's word? On a contract? *Bist du verwirrt?* Crazy? Who do you think they are going to blame when you come back to the office with the wrong diamond? They got your signature. Until they make titles for diamonds, Robert Clark, like they do for automobiles and airplanes, there will always be trickery and deception in this business of ours. In diamonds it is too easy to cheat another man, and the money is very large. So you must rely on your eyes. Here, you keep that one, that loupe. It is my gift to you. Put it on a chain so you don't forget it. You tell Popper I said to give you a gold chain to wear around your neck and hang it on. He can bill me if he wants to. God knows what the man owes me. Inspect the diamond. Use the loupe. Let me see how you look."

I opened the teardrop-shaped device so that the lens was extended from its cover. I tried to hold it casually, with my forefinger through the case, like Jim did. Then I took the tweezers from Kizakov and lifted the diamond. I pushed the slide forward and locked the tweezers.

"No. Please. You are hurting me with handling the stone like that. Give me the tweezers. Never use that slide to close them up. You should not even use such tweezers. And keep both eyes open. You never close one eye when using a loupe. What is your brother teaching you?"

I did not remind him that they were his tweezers.

"Let me show you. This is how it is done. You never start from the top of the stone. If you were buying the diamond, already the man you are buying from knows he can cheat you. Start from the bottom. Then the side, the profile, all around the diamond, like this. Then you look through the crown. Finally the table, but there you will learn very little. The diamond is designed to hide everything one might otherwise see. That is the specific virtue of the cutter. That is the function of the diamond. Like a woman's beauty. To hide its own flaws. Now look again. In the manner I have shown you."

The diamond was flawless. There was nothing but facets,

angles, and light. But then, looking through the pavilion from the bottom, I caught a kind of S-shaped glitter near the center of the stone. I looked for it again from the side, again seeing into the pavilion, and turned the diamond by rotating the tweezers in my fingers as Elie Kizakov had shown me, and I went around twice very slowly before it appeared again, a different shape, but tracing from it was another line that branched off in a kind of X. If you looked for it turning it at an odd angle to the light it flashed illumination at you like a bright red figure for an instant and then vanished. You blinked at it when it appeared. I could only make the diamond do it twice and then somehow it evaded me. There may have been a change in the light of the room, a cloud outside could make that difference, or a shadow interfering, from Kizakov perhaps.

"You see her!"

I looked for the minute inclusion again through the crown and the table but it was gone.

"I named the diamond the pink ballerina. For that inclusion. If you see her thoroughly, looking many times, you will see she has a figure like a dancer."

"What does it look like under a microscope? Under thirty power?"

"The microscope? Don't be ridiculous. In the microscope it is gone. Ten power is the correct magnification for inspecting the brilliant cut. That is the reason we use the ten power. Not because they did not have microscopes in the nineteenth century or some other GIA nonsense. Anyone can make a stronger lens if he can make a lens at all."

The buzzer rang in the outside office. Kizakov looked at his video monitor. He took the diamond from me and put it back in his pocket.

"Now you learn something else," he said. "Idan!" he shouted down the back hallway. "Your appointment is here."

Idan was Elie's son. He was a dark-haired, dark-skinned man about ten years older than me who had once taken me for a ride around Highland Park and down Lovers' Lane in his Corvette convertible. "Let's stop in at Gucci," he had said, and bought a shirt, a tie, and two pairs of gray socks. "You want anything, Bobby?" he had said. "I'm buying." I knew better than to take him up on it. Plus I was shy to ask. When he came to the store, all the saleswomen talked about him after he left. "His eyes," they said. "Have you ever seen such eyes on a man?" It was true that he had unusually large, pale gray eyes, like the color of platinum, in fact. But much prettier. I believed it was his eyelashes they were actually thinking of.

It could not have been easy to be Idan, I thought. His father was part of the generation that founded modern Israel. Kizakov had even known the great Ben-Gurion, and worked under Berl Katznelson in the Labor movement. But I never saw Idan show any resentment toward his father.

Kizakov waited until Idan had pushed the button to open the electronic door for the two men waiting outside. They came into the large Plexiglas mantrap in the outer office and then waited while Idan buzzed them into the main office. We watched them on the monitor. They were young men and one carried a briefcase. The other one wore a baseball cap. They did not look like the sort of men I associated with Kizakov's office. If I had seen them in this building at all I would have expected to see them in the gold and colored-stone showrooms of the newer Pakistani and Chinese wholesalers on the second and third floors. Kizakov watched his son greet them and shake their hands. Then he took me by the arm and we walked up front.

"This is my father, Elie Kizakov," Idan said. Kizakov nodded to them both but he did not offer his hand. One of them held out his hand for a moment and then dropped it. But he did not seem dismayed.

"Danny Johnson says you guys are the man," the fellow with the briefcase said. I could not see his feet but I thought, I bet he is wearing tennis shoes. He had yellow teeth. He kept pulling his lips back. His yellow teeth looked frightening against his white skin.

"Who is this?" the one in the baseball cap said, and shook his thumb at me.

"Daniel Johnson is a very good customer of ours," Kizakov said, ignoring the question. "Idan tells me you have a diamond to sell."

"Damn right we got a diamond to sell," the man in the baseball cap said. His partner gave him a look. "I mean, yes sir. Danny says you are the man for it. I mean, he says you guys can pay. Cash. We ain't interested in no check."

"Why don't we have a look at your diamond?" Kizakov said. "Idan?"

Idan unfolded a diamond cloth on the showcase and placed a set of tweezers and a brass hexagonal loupe beside it. He carefully turned the small, portable diamond scale on the showcase to face the two men. He quickly recalibrated the scale. The one man put the briefcase on the showcase and opened it. He took a bulging, oddly cardboardy diamond paper from the briefcase and opened it on the showcase. He turned the paper and spilled the diamond out onto the diamond cloth. It was an oval. It looked like five or six carats to me.

Elie Kizakov pulled his lips between his teeth and opened his eyes in that way he had. It was an impatient expression.

"What does it weigh?" Idan said.

"Six carats," the man in the baseball cap said. "Six on the money."

Idan cleaned it with the white cloth and then placed it in the diamond scale. "Five sixty-two," he said. He looked at his father.

"Why did you ask me what it weighed if you was just going to weigh it? Don't you take our word? Don't a man's word count for something with you? I don't like that. In America we take a man's word as his promise. I think you ought to take a man's word for something," the one in the baseball cap said.

Idan started to reply. His father raised his hand to silence him. The diamond lay there on the scale and watched us. The man in the baseball cap rubbed his hands on his sides, on the hips of his jeans. A second or two ticked by. Then, without any flinch or change of demeanor that might have warned us, the other man, the one not in a baseball cap, shouted, "I am sick of this shit! Up with your hands, Jew-boy!" and pulled a black handgun from the briefcase. We could not see into the briefcase because he had kept the lid turned toward us. To hide the handgun, I realized. He waved the handgun in the air oddly and loosely, like a flyswatter, and then pointed it at Idan. Idan reached for something—I never learned what he was going for—and the man with the weapon grabbed him by the side of the head and slammed his face down onto the showcase. It was glass but it did not break. Baseball Cap shouted, "The cash! Where's the safe, old man? He'll kill him! He'll blow his brains out!" I saw that the other man had pulled Idan over the showcase and onto the floor and, kneeling with one knee on top of him, like a hunter kneels on a deer he has killed, had the barrel of the gun pressed into the socket of his eye. Idan was silent and lying there, still.

Then a totally unexpected thing happened. Kizakov, who was seventy years old and perhaps five feet tall, five feet tall in his boots, and who had a white beard halfway down his chest, vaulted the showcase we were standing behind, grabbed the gun from the man who was holding it in his son's eye, and pistol-whipped him to the floor. He continued pistol-whipping him as his buddy Baseball Cap looked on in astonishment. For a moment Baseball Cap looked at me and in our eyes we briefly shared a kind of recognition that, had the circumstances been different, might have made us friends, or at least would have started us laughing. Then he turned away and ran for the door.

"Stop!" Elie Kizakov commanded.

But he didn't stop. He made it into the mantrap and that stopped him.

His partner was unconscious or dead. His face, his neck, and his T-shirt were covered in blood. Kizakov was bloody also and had blood on his glasses. I looked for blood on Idan but did not see any. There was a surprising amount of blood all around, however. Later I saw it in odd places, like the magazines on the table next to the sofa on the back wall and in the candy dish on the coffee table.

Kizakov stood up. He put the gun on the showcase. He cleaned his glasses with a handkerchief from his pocket.

"I'll call the cops," Idan said.

"Do not be a fool," his father said. Baseball Cap struggled and shouted in the mantrap. He was very frightened. He looked like a sparrow trapped in a room full of closed windows.

Kizakov picked up the diamond, squinted at it quickly and closely with it held between his forefinger and thumb, and then placed it in his pants pocket.

70

"Put that one in the mantrap with him," he said. "You!" he shouted at Baseball Cap. "Quiet down! You want I should shoot you? You want I should hit you on your head?" He was breathing heavily and he sat down, suddenly, in a green leather chair I often sat in on that side of their little showroom.

"Use the gun, Idan," he said. "Wipe it off. But hold a gun on him while you put his partner in there. Robert, no, you do not move." I was walking around the showcase to help Idan. "This is our business."

Idan had dragged the unconscious robber into the mantrap. His friend huddled in a corner. I expected Idan to menace him a little with the gun but he was all business. Then I remembered that after high school Idan had been in the army like all Israelis.

"Let them go, Idan," Kizakov said. "We don't bother with them anymore."

Kizakov bent over and untied and tightly retied his shoelaces. He pulled the black leather laces so hard I thought he would break them. Then he sat up straight and brushed his hand back across his head.

"Bring us some vodka, Idan. How is your eye? All right? You will have a black eye for the girls. You can tell them it was a prizefight! Come look at this diamond and tell me what you think. It is better than I would have guessed. They must have stolen it also. It is probably three thousand a carat, I am thinking. Come on, Robert, have a glass of vodka with me and my son. We are all three of us comrades in arms now."

This was one of my best times in the jewelry business.

Once the story got around town, the joke was that only Elie Kizakov could be robbed and turn a twenty-thousand-dollar profit on the deal.

"You saw it, Bobby? Did he really pistol-whip that nigger?"

"He wasn't black. They were two white guys."

My role in it as eyewitness made even me a minor celebrity. That added some fun to the runs.

Several years after this incident Idan married an Israeli diamond wholesaler's daughter, one of the biggest in the business. I was at their wedding in Tel Aviv. Clouds of live doves were released from great hidden nets during specified times in the ceremony. Soon she caught him in an affair with a man and made it very public in the industry. She went door to door with the story. That kind of spectacle, enacted by his wife, was not well received. They divorced, and last I heard he was selling cars.

Sheila wouldn't let me sell until after Thanksgiving, so along with my Dallas runs I spent the next six weeks on the buys and the repair counter. These were the last two showcases on the east side of the store, behind the bead board, the rice pearl case, and the men's jewelry. It was also where we did our give-aways, the coupons for free amethysts, topazes, or "Authentic Two-Carat Cubic Zirconium" that Popper ran across the bottom two inches of the big full-page *Star-Telegram* ads every Friday, Saturday, and Sunday.

Everyone except for the elite among the sales force, the real top-of-the-boarders, had to do a turn on these counters once a week. But new people started there before they went on the floor. Most of the salespeople—and the salespeople in training, like me—preferred the buys to the repairs. You could make the store more money faster on the right buy than on any sale. The buys, during the early eighties gold boom, were how Ronnie and Sheila made their stake.

I had been instructed on these facts, yet I avoided buying because of the young mothers, the edgy-eyed blacks and Mexicans, the poor and discouraged people. When a sad buy approached the counter I went to the bathroom, or bent and tied my shoelaces very methodically and patiently, and someone else picked it up.

It was Friday morning and I had just taken in a clean, oil, and adjust on a ladies' Rolex two-tone. I walked my customer through the crowd to the door and thanked her. That was unusual with a repair but I took special care of the Rolexes. As soon as the door closed behind her Jim caught me by the arm.

I thought I was in trouble for dawdling. I had been taking my time with her because I had been eating Lisa's speed all morning and I felt that if I took a step the world would tilt over on its side. Probably onto my head.

"Is that a Rolex? Is that a ladies' two-tone? Is that her leaving? In the suit? The black suit?"

"It's a COA. I got her for four hundred." On a nice COA Jim told me to try to up-sell them into jewelry if I could. So when he grabbed the job envelope I thought he was looking for a few extra items or a second invoice.

"It wasn't my fault," I said. "She wasn't buying. I even showed her twister beads and silver charms. She only cared about her watch."

"We need the COAs. You get a hundred bucks on a COA now."

"Right." I saw he was not angry. "I know. Give it to the Watchman, right?"

"We can do it. Why waste the job envelope? Let me take a look."

He poured the virginal stainless and gold watch out of the paper and cardboard envelope. It was a pretty ladies' two-tone.

"Perfect. It even has the right dial. Come with me. Hurry."

We squeezed our way through the crowd to the back-of-the-house.

Before we were past the diamond desk, Don Frazier, the bullion and auction man, seized Jim by the arm.

"Whose watch is that? Where did you get that?"

Jim laughed. "Sorry. My deal."

"You're not shipping that watch."

"Don't be an asshole."

In back the phone girls were clustered around lunch, eating. The fat girls standing at the catered sandwiches, their hands full and their mouths wet, looked like animals at a carcass.

I followed him around the safes and through the rows of desks to the little jewelry cleaning room. Behind a half-finished aluminum-beam and Sheetrock wall, on the opposite end of the store from the bookkeeper's room and the stairs to Mr. Popper's office, there was a bench and sink and the various messy tools you need for cleaning jewelry. We had six ultrasonics, of various temperatures and strengths, lined up in a row and always humming and bubbling like scientific cauldrons, and two big red and blue Swest steamers. Beyond the steamers in what had once been a coat closet was the polishing wheel. There was no vent hood or dust screen. They had simply put it on an old desk safe, screwed it into the wall, and plugged it in. Only the older guys were allowed to use this machine. It was dangerous and you could destroy a piece of jewelry in an instant. The most common mistake was wrapping a bracelet or necklace around the wheel. Then it would spin ferociously until you could shut the machine off. This would stretch the gold, pop out diamonds, and shatter color. The

Watchman had once notoriously destroyed a seven-carat black opal, a fifteen-thousand-dollar gem at cost, just this way.

Working very quickly, Jim removed the bracelet from the head of the watch, changed the wheels on the polisher, and began to work on the outside steel links of the Rolex bracelet.

"What are you doing?" I asked him. "I thought the jewelers do that. While Benny's servicing the head."

"Set it," he said, and handed me the head of the watch. "Give it a good wind. And wipe it down. Clean next to the lugs. That's where the dirt will be. We want to make it look brand-new."

First I cleaned the interior of the lugs with a toothbrush we kept at the steamers. Inside the lugs, at the corners, a black and green wax or dirt gathers like the grime you might find under a fingernail. It is made up mostly of human skin and oils. Then I used a Q-tip and alcohol to clean the rest of the head. Finally, after checking the crown to make sure it was tight, I held the head in rubber-tipped metal tongs like I had seen the watchmakers do and steamed off the watch.

"Hurry," Jim said. He already had the band hung on a wire in the ultrasonic. It was buzzing. He lifted it out, inspected it, rinsed it off in the sink under the tap, and dried it with a paper towel. Then he carefully reattached it to the head. He performed this operation with the patient affection and ease of a mother placing a diaper on her baby.

"Get me a Rolex box," he said.

I still did not understand what he was up to.

"I thought we were out of Rolex boxes."

"We are out of real Rolex boxes. Get me one of the Watchman's boxes. Tell him you don't want a Chinese one. You want an Italian. One of the green leather ones. The good ones. If he's not there, look under his desk. That's where he hides them. Get the whole thing: the exterior box, the books, the papers, everything. Tell him it's for me. Tell him a hanging tag and crown. The whole damn package."

He slipped the open-buckled watch over his wrist. He compared it with his own watch. He was checking the timing.

"Look at that bracelet," he said. "It looked brand-new before I even hit it. This watch isn't a year old. Look how smooth and tight it is." He fondled it between his fingers. "Like silk."

It was very hot in the room with the steamers. Or maybe it was the speed. I knew I had taken too much, but I wanted some more.

"This watch is right on the money," he said. He took the watch off his wrist and folded up the buckle. He pinched in the soft steel edge of the buckle slightly to tighten it up. It snapped shut with a soft click.

"Why did she bring it in, did she say?" Jim asked me. "Did she say it was running slow? Or it stops?"

For the laugh I said loudly, "She said it stops when she doesn't wear it."

Several salespeople around me laughed. There was a line of them waiting to use the steamers.

Many Rolex and other customers who own automatic watches do not understand that for the mainspring to stay wound you have to wear the watch. You run into this at least once a week. The customer takes off her watch because she is going to play tennis or go to the spa and forgets to wear it for a couple of days, and when she puts it back on because they are on their way to meet friends for dinner she is dismayed and confused to see that the watch has stopped. It starts running again as soon as she has it on her wrist so she quickly resets it before her husband notices—why worry him, it was such a nice gift?—and then hurries down the next day to see us. We sell her the four-hundred-dollar COA and explain that it's not uncommon that a Rolex might require the procedure, even in a new watch, because one never knows how long the watch may have been in the factory in Switzerland before being shipped, and in any event it is part of the regular maintenance of such a fine, rare, and expensive timepiece, which is why it will stay in the family for generations. "Like owning a leopard or a tiger," you say. "This is no housecat. A bit more in care and feeding but well worth it for the exquisiteness. For the uniqueness." Then, only after we return the watch to her, we explain how an automatic movement functions, so that we do not see her again in a couple of weeks.

I went to fetch the box.

The Watchman protested.

"Nope. Not an outer box," he said. "These are the last. You can have the inner box but not an outer. Use one of the big white Taiwanese boxes. We just got in a whole shipment of them. The ones for the big South Sea ropes. The inner fits in one of those. They are almost snug. You can't have that Rolex outer box. I only have three ladies' outers left."

I said, "It's for Jim," and he said, "He better be selling a goddamn President. Tell Jim I said it better be nothing less than a goddamn ladies' President, little brother."

When I returned with the Rolex box Jim hung the real Rolex tags on the watch and placed it in the counterfeit box. He inspected the real Rolex books and the counterfeit papers and placed them carefully under the leather box in the counterfeit cardboard outer box. It was a lovely green box, untouched, it looked like it had been made a few minutes before, with that Rolex oyster artwork printed all over it. Then he placed the gold crown on top of the leather box and closed up the whole package.

"Okay, follow me," he said.

We went back out on the sales floor. He elbowed his way through the throng of salespeople lining the counter toward the diamond room.

Lisa waved to me from the pearl showcase and winked. She was showing a long double rope of pearls. I waved back to her. She waved again and smiled, and I realized that the first time she had been waving to Jim.

Jim stopped outside the diamond room door.

"Okay, Bobby, you only listen. Not one word," he said. "Stand in the corner, be invisible, and learn. Don't even ask him if he wants another drink. Let me do that."

He opened the sales door to the diamond room and put his head in.

"Good news," I heard him say. "I found one," he said.

I followed him in and stood in the corner. The customer, an obviously important customer, sat at the diamond table. Jim sat down next to Dennis and placed the Rolex box showily on the table, a large antique desk with spindly legs. The legs did not look like they could support the desk. In the center of the desk was a diamond pad, and on the silk pad was the alexandrite necklace.

The alexandrite necklace was a white elephant Sheila had bought at the Jewelers Circular Keystone Las Vegas show a year and a half before. It was tagged at four hundred thousand dollars and I knew it had a twenty-thousand-dollar bonus plus the regular ten-percent-of-the-net commission. It was fifty-two carats of perfectly calibrated square-cut natural Siberian untreated full-color-change alexandrite set in eighteen-karat green gold. The center stone was six carats and, loose, was worth fifty thousand dollars. In natural sunlight the necklace was bright green,

green like five-thousand-a-carat Colombian emerald. Here in the artificial light of the halogens it was pigeon-blood red. On the way outside, if you were carrying it in your hands or wearing it on your neck, it would pass through half the colors of the spectrum, each one individually recognizable.

But it was impossible to sell. Alexandrites have no sparkle, and if a husband or a lover has spent half a million dollars on her necklace a woman wants her friends to know that her necklace cost half a million dollars, and one can only be sure of that with big diamonds. At the very least she wants some rubies or emeralds. Something they recognize. Alexandrites you have to explain, and that defeats the purpose. That was why, unlike all of our other showpieces, the necklace never went to any society parties. It was perhaps the most beautiful piece of jewelry you would ever see, but it lacked the crucial quality of all jewelry: bang for your buck. Flash for your cash. Like a Fabergé egg.

I had seen this customer in the store before but did not know his name. He was a large, strangely pale man, wearing black crocodile boots and a leather baseball cap, with very dark eyes, eyes that looked black until you looked at him from the side and saw they had many dark brown rings around the pupils. As white as his skin was, he nevertheless had the exaggerated jaw and facial features of an Indian, like the Iroquois you would see sleeping in the bus stations or by the train tracks back in Calgary. But here with his beaded belt and his cowskin vest he was an American cowboy.

He wore a platinum President and a platinum wedding ring with a seven-carat emerald-cut in the center. I remembered when Dennis sold that ring, just a few weeks after I arrived at the store. Jim had bragged about it during a sales meeting. It was sixty thousand dollars, and the customer had paid in cash.

"I didn't think we could do it three days from Thanksgiving," Jim told him. "Everybody's out. There are just no new ladies' two-tones available right now. I called all over. Not even Rolex USA in downtown Dallas has them. But I have a friend across town who saves a few back for occasions like this. To sweeten a deal. He drove this over for me. His last ladies' two-tone. He was planning on giving it to his wife for Christmas. Brand new in the box. Books, papers, everything. Fresh from the factory."

"What the hell does a jeweler's wife want with one of these?" the customer said. "Shouldn't she have a gold Rolex? I wouldn't put my wife in a three-thousand-dollar watch. Not if I was in your line of work."

He opened the box. The gold plastic Rolex crown fell out and sat next to the necklace.

"You know how it is with women. They are just the thing right now," Jim said. "This guy's wife has a couple of Presidents, she has a Patek and a Cartier. But now she wanted a ladies' two-tone. She wants what she knows her friends want and won't get this year."

"Looks like she won't get it, either," Dennis said. His curly hair, along with that bright-toothed smile of his, made him look like an elf or a devil. "The shoemaker's wife." He laughed.

"Hell, I imagine she'll get her turn," the customer said. "Her husband's in the business."

"After Christmas," Dennis said. "A few months after Christmas Rolex will loosen up on them."

Dennis and Jim fell into their own imaginary world of the made-up jeweler and his wife who was supposed to get this watch for Christmas, the watch that I had taken from the wrist of my customer only minutes before. I could almost see the worried jeweler and his disappointed wife. And I could feel the story working. It made even me want the customer to have the watch. Just so that other fictional woman who was supposed to get it couldn't. It was ours now. In our hands. She would have to wait.

"You boys do come through. I gotta hand it to you, Jimmy. Well, Dennis, let's get down to business. How much you gonna sell me this little dude for? This one of those nineteen ninety-five specials you fellas run in the paper?"

"Let's think about it as a package," Dennis said. "You know Mr. Popper wants to move this necklace. You know what it's worth. You know he needs the money. Make him an offer. I'll take any fair offer up to him. Make him a cash offer, Glen."

The customer looked over at me. His black eyes were supple and healthy. You would have bet he was an honest man. But he's rich, I told myself. He must be cleverer than he appears.

"Make yourself useful, would you, son, and refill my drink here? I think these boys are about to mug me."

He shook the ice in the empty glass.

"The Macallan, Bobby. The thirty-year-old," Dennis said without looking at me. We did not have any thirty-year-old scotch, but we did have Macallan, and I jogged out to the bar cabinet behind the bookkeeper's office. As I passed the stairs to Mr. Popper's office with the fresh drink I saw him coming the other way. He caught me by the shoulder.

"What's happening in there?" he asked. His face sparkled with happiness and anticipation. "Is he buying it? What's he buying? He's buying it, isn't he? Is he buying the necklace? The alexandrites? Is he going for it?" Mr. Popper was bouncing in his shoes. He was shorter than I was and his round belly and the bouncing made him seem like a red rubber ball bouncing in a playground. You wanted immediately to hold him or hug him. He was that enthusiastic. He was one of those geniuses. I've only met three or four of them over the years. He was not human like you and me.

"I don't know," I said. "I think so."

"Well don't stand here jawing with me," he said. He pushed me by the small of my back while holding my shoulder. We shoved our way into the salespeople around the watch counter, who when they saw I was with Mr. Popper parted a way for me to the door of the diamond room. "Get in there, son! Get in there!" Then he leaned forward and whispered, "If he buys it, it's a thousand cash for you, too. A thousand dollars! Today! Close him," he said. "Get him, Bobby, get him!" he said. Then he laughed. "Isn't this wonderful?" he said, and held open his arms as though he would lift the whole showroom between them. "It's almost Christmas, everyone," he said. "It's the most glorious time of the year!" Customers and salespeople laughed aloud with him. The air grew golden around us. We all shone together. The halogens brightened even whiter. The music of the voices of the salespeople and the customers in the showroom lifted like a chorus. There was music playing, of course, on the Muzak, Christmas music. The Chipmunks' Christmas album. I looked for Lisa and saw her there spotlighted in the halogens with the big pearls she was selling around her neck. She was facing the other way and her customer, a narrow-shouldered man in an elegant gray suit, was helping her with the clasp. I bet that is a sale, I thought. The way he's fingering her neck he looks like he's buying. Then I opened the door and was in. Mr. Popper closed the door behind me.

"There he is," the customer said. "There's your boy. Boy, we got a job for you."

All three of their faces looked at me.

"This is a time for champagne," the customer said. "Here, hand me over that scotch. There's a good fella."

"I'll get the champagne," Jim said. "Bobby, you take this Rolex and have it gift-wrapped. Wait for it. Ask Lisa if she wouldn't mind wrapping it, she's the best. I am going to give this necklace one more steaming and then we'll take a last look at it in its case. I better get Ronnie. We'll be right back. Let's start with the champagne and go from there. Congratulations, Mr. Redback."

Jim and I left with the Rolex and the necklace.

"So he's buying it?" I said to Jim.

"He bought it. He already bought it. He bought the alexandrite necklace. Dennis, that son of a bitch, sold it. He sold it." I looked at him to see if he was jealous but he was delighted. This was perhaps my older brother's most compelling virtue: he enjoyed the luck of others, particularly if he loved them. He would never understand envy or resentment. I worry that I am wired the opposite way.

"Get that woman's watch wrapped," Jim said. "Your customer closed the deal. Her COA sold that necklace. You sold it, really, Bobby, when you sold that clean, oil, and adjust."

In my excitement I had almost forgotten that the watch was not ours.

"This watch?" I said. "Wait. I thought we were just showing it. You want me to wrap up her watch?" I cannot say, now, whether I was feigning innocence or I was genuinely confused. But that was what I said.

"You know of any other like-new ladies' two-tones lying around? Think you can get on the phone and have one here in the time it takes for Ronnie and Redback to count the cash?"

"No, I was just asking," I said. "I didn't mean it like that."

"Don't worry, your customer will get a watch," Jim said. "She may have to wait awhile, and it won't be that watch, but she'll get a watch. Meanwhile, she can wear around one of our Bertoluccis. She may even get attached to it. Bertolucci is really a much nicer watch." Even I knew that was false. "Hell, we would even be willing to trade her, which is an upgrade for her. Come to think of it, I know a used eighteen-karat Bertolucci we could lend her. Dennis paid too much for that thing, but she probably figures her watch is worth five, the Bertolucci lists at eighteen, you tell her we give her a discount apology to our cost which is nine thousand, that's easy math. You can sell that. Just return her phone calls promptly. Make her earn every inch of it. She has to think she is beating you up. I'll walk you through it. If that beat-up old gold Bertolucci is still here after Christmas that's a perfect solution. We can tighten the bracelet with Teflon spray. It won't last, but it will be perfect for this deal." He was losing me in the whirlwind of the imaginary pitch I was going to have to deliver to the irate, cheated customer.

"I don't really want her as a customer. I mean, you can have her."

"Bobby." Jim looked at me earnestly. It was like the time on the bus when I was five and he caught me crossing my legs at the knee. "Boys never sit like that," he had told me, staring me straight in the eye. Another one was, "Never start a fight, but never back down from one, either." I don't remember how that came up, because I was not in many fights. "Bobby. It is time to stop pretending to learn the business and really learn it. Do you want to make real money or not? Do you want to be a salesman? Yes or no?"

I didn't think about my answer. I mostly wanted to get out from under that gaze of his. It was like a microwave. He did not use it often.

"Black Friday is in four days," Jim said. "Black Friday you go on the floor."

At that moment Lisa appeared, as though she had been listening to the whole thing, took the watch from my hands, and left with it. I understood she was going to wrap it for me. Often, this happened to me, when some angel descended to solve a problem, as if I were wired with a secret microphone. But she should have taken me with her.

"This is your first real season," Jim said. "Christmas is expecting you. Come on, time to play Santa Claus. Santa Claus and his band of merry elves."

That's Robin Hood, I thought. But I did not correct him.

"Feel these shoulders," he said. He massaged my shoulders from the front like a manager would massage his boxer's shoulders. "That is too much tension. We have got to get you laid.

"Let's get through the weekend and Sunday night we'll pick up Lisa and one of her buddies and we'll go have some fun. Lisa will know somebody. Let's get through the weekend and we'll get you a girl.

"Come on, go grab that watch and let's get back in there," he said.

There was a bookstore on the edge of downtown that was open on Sundays. We were working seven days a week now, but we got off early on Sundays and if Jim and Lily were having a fight, or out shopping, I would drive over to the bookstore and then maybe leave my car there and walk into downtown for a hamburger and a Coke at Ted's. It was a nice place to sit and read a new book that you had bought. The first time I read D. T. Suzuki I was sitting at the red linoleum bar in Ted's, eating my french fries one at a time, with Tabasco mixed into the ketchup.

To get there I would walk a few blocks out of my way so that I could pass Lisa's building. I thought she might be outside doing something, taking out the garbage, say, or looking up and down the street, or taking a walk herself, and then we would bump into each other and we could get a hamburger together or go sit in a bar I knew she liked and have a drink. But she never was outside her apartment. The whole street was always empty, in fact. Just parked cars and the brown brick buildings. I should have called her and asked her to meet me. But I was afraid to call her. I didn't even know her number. She was always the one who asked me out, when we got together outside of the store.

Jim had not given me any cocaine for several weeks, so Lisa had switched me entirely to her speed.

"This is healthier anyway," she said. "You don't know what's in that cocaine. It goes through so many hands before it gets to Texas. But with crank it's manufactured right here in Fort Worth. I know the guy who makes it. It's practically like buying it at the pharmacy."

I was leaving the customers' bathroom, rubbing crank from the bottom of my nose with the side of my hand, when Mr. Popper caught me by the arm.

"Bobby," he said. "Come on up here for a minute. Come on up to my office. We need to have a little talk."

They must have a hidden camera in there, I thought. He's been watching me on a monitor in his office. I had masturbated in that bathroom, too. I hoped he wouldn't make me watch the tape. But I was going to be fired. Jim told me to be especially careful about drugs around Mr. Popper and Sheila.

"They are not hypocritical people," Jim had said. "They aren't Bible-beaters or anything like that. But they hate drugs. One time they did a big drug testing and they fired five or six people over it. They couldn't fire everybody who tested positive or they would have had to find a whole new staff. Dennis and I tested positive, of course, and the Watchman, and a bunch of other people. They looked past it. But we all had to promise to quit, and watch a video about the dangers of narcotics. They even made us sign a contract. They brought in a couple of speakers from AA. It was a big deal. We had to read some of those damn AA comic books at our regular sales meeting. 'Take them home,' Popper said. 'Commit them to memory.' Comic books. You remember the ones. The same damn ones Mom used to bring home from her AA meetings. I'm just saying, because you're you, be cautious." So I knew I was fired. But it did not sound like they were the type to press charges.

Popper sat down at his desk. The banks of video monitors were flickering on his credenza beside him, and there were more behind him. I tried not to look at them. I wondered which one had caught me.

"I don't know if you like to drink or not, Bobby. I am not much of a drinking man myself. But I will take a glass of good scotch from time to time. Have you ever tasted a good single-malt scotch? I go over to Scotland once or twice a year with a couple of buddies of mine, good old boys from the construction business here in town, and we play a little golf, go fishing for those powerful salmon they have up there, and hit the distilleries. They put you up in a castle. Here, you should try a glass. I drink it neat, but for your first taste you might want some ice and a splash of water."

Mr. Popper stood, so I stood, too. He laughed.

"Sit down, son! Relax! Boy you Canadians come nervous. Your brother's near half as jumpy as you are. You been up to something you don't want me to know about?" He smiled. The way he smiled, like we were in on the secret together, made me think maybe he didn't know about the drugs after all, or that if he knew he didn't mind. I sat back down.

He poured the drinks at the bar on the other side of his office. It was a built-in bar, made of brass and beveled glass, and I had polished and cleaned it many times, always while Mr. Popper was working in his office and on the phone. I stocked it, too, with ice cream and diet sodas. Mr. Popper ate two or three pints of Häagen-Dazs ice cream a day. All different flavors, though his favorite was strawberry.

"Here you are," he said, and put the pretty, golden drink on the desk in front of me.

"Drink it slow. You don't want to hurry through a liquor like that one."

I took a sip. It was strong. But like warm caramel and honey. It was nothing like scotch I had tried before. Because of the richness of the flavor I thought of it as the first properly American liquor I had ever tasted.

"Bobby, some of us got a gift. I have it. Your brother has it. And watching you on that alexandrite deal . . ." He laughed. "That was some kind of deal, wasn't it? I thought we were never getting rid of that sunuvabitch. The things my wife will buy. Anyway, observing you, I got a feeling you have it, too. An instinct for what the other fella needs to hear. What will clarify his own decision-making process for him. How to unify a man's will."

I knew he didn't expect me to say anything. I took a swallow of my drink.

"Look here, Bobby. I'd like to show you something. Something special to me. You might find it interesting."

He took a large red-and-gilt leather-bound book from a shelf beside his desk. It was the size of book you expected an old-fashioned Bible to be. It was obviously heavy and he carried it in both of his arms around the desk and laid it open in front of me. He turned through the thick, cream-colored pages. Inside he had glued copies of newspaper columns, pictures cut out from other books, newspaper ads featuring items from our store. Everything was jewelry.

"This is a scrapbook I keep. Gives me ideas. And reminds me of what works and what doesn't. It's a tool my own mentor showed me to use. He was a coin man. No interest in jewelry at all. But they are more or less the same business. Look at this here."

It was a headline from the *L.A. Times*, dated May 7, 1953. It read: "Five-Million-Dollar Fake Gem Plot Uncovered!"

"That there's the so-called Szirak Treasure. Some ole boys claimed they had found a collection of five-hundred-year-old crown jewels, orbs and tiaras and what have you, and sold the whole lot to a collector. Five million back then is like fifty million today. They got busted, but just through ineptitude."

He turned the page to a clipping from a paper in San Antonio. "Ten-Million-Dollar Coin Collection Revealed as Fake!"

"I knew that fella. I knew him rather well." He patted me on the shoulder. "What he used to do was, you took a new coin, changed the date with a little drill-and-stamp apparatus we employed, and then to get the look of age you blew cigar smoke over them in a paper bag. It was no more complicated than that. If he had stuck to counterfeiting he could still be the most famous coin dealer in the Southwest. But he fell in with an insurance man and a safe salesman and they conjured up this deal where they'd sell the coins, insure them, sell the security system, then wait a few months and steal the whole damn thing back from the customer. They got caught stealing their own coins— from some helicopter manufacturer, as I recall—and when the FBI brought in their experts they discovered all the coins was fake, to boot. Boy, that caused a commotion down in San Antone." He turned the page. "Take a gander at this one here. This is from the British National Archives. Calendar of State Papers, from the time of King James the First. Sixteen hundred and six."

He traced the lines of text with his slender, leaflike fingers as he read. Not with one finger but with two or three, like a priest or a magician.

" 'Query on the equity of a Chancery decision on fraud committed by Robert Davis, at the instigation of Richard Glanville, in selling counterfeit jewels to Francis Courtney.' That's beautiful, isn't it? 'At the instigation of.' That is the proper usage of the English language. Like poetry. Listen to that." He laughed and took another drink of the scotch. I took a mouthful, too.

"In these parts we're amateurs, Bobby. Those old boys were selling paste to the crowned heads of Europe while our forefathers were scratching their asses in the potato fields. Goes back to the alchemists. The first blue diamonds, sold by Tavernier back in the seventeenth century, were London Blue topazes with fancy faceting. Hell, he made the market for the damn things. Until he told 'em they were blue diamonds nobody had even heard of such a thing! You have to be extra careful when you're dealing with the Belgians and the Dutch. I avoid those fellas, they got too much expertise in contrivance for the likes of us Texans. Hell, the crown jewels of England are just plain old everyday garnets. Sheila and me have been to the

Tower of London to view them. I wouldn't pay ten bucks a carat for those stones. And these days, with the Thais and the Indians, even I can't tell half the time what's real and what's fake. Course that's my point. It don't really matter, so long as she's done right. I know a boy who got out of the museum business because he claimed he'd never sold a real painting. Nothing but counterfeits and copies. 'The dream of acquisition,' he calls it. One of the leading experts on German Expressionism in the world."

He took his ChapStick from his pocket and rubbed it quickly around his nostrils.

"I suspect the problem, Bobby, if you want to know the plain honest truth of the matter, is people getting hung up on this notion of intrinsic value. It's the silliest damn thing. There ain't no intrinsic value to a diamond except in a drill bit. And that's an instrument. Outside of religion you simply won't find a dadblamed thing that will stand up to the scrutiny of intrinsic value. Least of all the truth. What I'm getting at, Bobby, is you may notice, over time, as you study and learn, a certain amount of chicanery in this business of ours. But don't let that dismay you. It's just the nature of the business we're in, part and parcel of the good old capitalist system that's gonna make us both rich men before we die."

He paused on that and looked at me carefully. I understood it was time for me to speak.

"I understand, Mr. Popper," I said. "I mean, I believe I understand. If I have any questions I'll ask Jim. I sure hope I can do as well as you have done, sir. Half as well, I mean." The scotch had settled into my stomach and I felt comfortable and happy. I finished the last swallow.

"That's an excellent idea. If you have any questions, you just ask your big brother. He understands this business better than almost anybody I've got working for me. Reminds me of myself. Hell, you both do, I don't mind telling you." He stood, rounded the desk, and patted me on the shoulder. "I wouldn't worry too much, son. You and your big brother are going to be just fine."

*T*he 800 lines at the store only worked in the continental United States. You were supposed to use one of the dedicated lines if you were going to make a long-distance call. But there were no technological reasons you could not pick any line and dial whoever you wanted to call, in any country. So I usually called Wendy from the store. I would wait until Jim was up in Popper's office discussing the day's sales and then I had a free half hour or so. I would untangle gold chains with two pairs of tweezers, or package up loose color in their little plastic boxes, while I talked to her. That way if Jim rounded the corner I could hang up in a hurry and to his eyes I was hard at work at his desk.

"I think I'm in love with another woman," I told Wendy on the phone. "Not a girl, I mean. A woman."

"Uh-huh," she said. "What's her name?"

"I'm not lying, if that's what you think. Her name is Lisa," I said.

"This is a real woman. You are not making this up."

I was making up part of it. I did not think I was in love with her. At least, as far as I could tell.

"She is a jewelry salesperson. She's in college, too. Or she was. At SMU. Southern Methodist University."

"Some Christian school. Isn't that nice. I bet she's real smart. What does she look like? This Christian saleswoman. Is she skinny?"

"She has black hair. She is nice. You would like her. She knows all about you."

"Sure. I would love her, too. Is she skinny?"

She is believing me. She is buying it, I corrected myself.

That was an important distinction I had recently learned. "Don't take responsibility for other people's beliefs, whatever you say to them," Jim had told me. "For one thing, it's presumptuous."

"I don't know. I guess she's skinny. I haven't really noticed. You would say she's skinny, I guess."

"Are you fucking her? Are you fucking this skinny Christian? Or does she not do that? Because of Jesus."

"Wendy, it's not like you aren't doing the same thing. With Andrew."

"That's not the way you made it sound. It's a little fast, Bobby. I don't mind. It's fine. Do what you want. You didn't exactly make it sound like you were going down there to start fucking Christian girls. *Women*, I mean. Excuse me. You said you were in love with me. I never said I love Andrew. I said I thought you needed a change."

"I don't love her like I love you," I said. Back down now and the whole effect is lost, I thought.

"I can tell. I have to go, Bobby."

"Okay. We're pretty busy here, too." Wait. At nine o'clock at night? You can do better than that, Bobby.

"I have to go find someone to fuck. Maybe some nice Christian."

She hung up.

•

*T*hen our dad came to town. Now I can remember but it was hard for me to believe, at a certain point in my life, how happy Jim and I would both become when our dad unexpectedly arrived. "He's already in New Orleans," Jim said. "He'll be here on Friday."

Jim said we would borrow his former landlord's house for the visit.

"We can't show the old man our apartment, Bobby," he said. "It's not what he's expecting. I'll see if Sean's in town. He owes me a favor from the deal I made him on that rose gold Vacheron. Let's see if we can't get Sean Munrow's place for the week."

He was frowning his eyebrows in that playful, irresponsible way and we both loved the joke.

Sean Munrow owned a mansion on Kerry Place, just east of Forest Park Drive, on a faded but magnificent street. Jim and his wife had lived behind it in a small converted apartment, an old coach house and servants' quarters, when they first moved to Texas and he was selling vacuum cleaners door-to-door. Munrow was a DUI and fix-a-ticket attorney who had branches all over the metroplex. He owned a yacht and vacation houses and was rarely in Texas. So Jim tracked him down and Munrow said, "Sure, you know where the key is, it hasn't moved," but then we went over there together and it was too much work. He had pictures of his kids everywhere—he was divorced and had those dad's guilty portraits—and many of the rooms were closed up with the furniture draped or pushed up against the walls. It looked like he only lived in two rooms and the kitchen. I was astonished. Here was a rich, successful man. It was so forlorn.

"This will never work," Jim said. "We don't have the time. I've got a better idea."

We booked the Presidential Suite at the Mansion on Turtle Creek. Eleven thousand dollars a night.

"He better not stay longer than the weekend," Jim said. "American Express will cut us off if they try to run a second approval."

"What about Lily?" I said.

"You know how he is. He can't stand her. He only wants to see us anyhow. I'll tell him we're having problems. That will make him happy. He can give me a bunch of marriage advice. Plus it gets me off the hook for titty bars and the girls. I won't have to listen to the practice-fidelity-never-take-your-marriage-for-granted-keep-your-promises-look-what-happened-to-your-old-man bullshit."

That made sense to me.

"We have to tip the hell out of every valet parker, Bobby. We have to eat in the restaurant twenty times in the next week. Everybody has to know our names. Here's a roll of twenties. Anybody does anything for you, if they push a damn button on the elevator, hand him a twenty-dollar bill and say, 'My name's Bobby Clark. Thank you very much.'"

I felt like I was running for mayor of Dallas. We drove back and forth for breakfast, lunch, and dinner, and took a customer or a top seller with us every time. We hung out at the hot tub—it was too cold for the pool—and had cocktails in the evening. Lily didn't say much, we were already working sixteen- and seventeen-hour days. Lisa tagged along for dinner and mocked us both.

"You are not going to fool your father," she said. "He's your dad."

"He has a lot of imagination," Jim said. "All we have to do is provide the right setting. Plus this is what he is anticipating. I don't want to disappoint him."

"He thinks you live in a hotel? Like Howard Hughes?"

"Like Howard Hughes! That's good! That's perfect, Lisa. I had not thought of that. When he says, 'Jimmy, what the hell are you doing living in a hotel?' I'll say, 'You know, Dad, like Howard Hughes.' He'll like that. That's the kind of thing he would come up with on his own. Come to think of it, that's the way to play it. Better if he comes up with it in his own head. Like it was his idea. Bobby, when we are pulling up to the hotel, say something about airplanes. We're in Texas, for crying out loud. Say something about the airport and airplanes and making airplanes. It doesn't matter what. He'll think Howard Hughes and then when we show him our suite it will make perfect sense. Howard Hughes but without the fingernails, that's what he'll think."

We were at the store and Dad walked into the showroom with his arm around the waist of a woman. She was slightly taller than he was and I saw immediately how the other saleswomen noticed her. She was a redhead. Wendy was a redhead, too. It is true what they say, they are more sexual than other women and usually sexually deviant.

"That is mine," the Polack said when she saw them. We were side by side, working the buy counter. "That one I am cherry-picking."

"He's not here for jewelry, Polack," I told her. It had taken me weeks to grow comfortable with using that name. But she preferred it.

"You do not know, Bobby Clark," she said. "You have not the nose for the business. Look at that woman. You think she is here for her fun? Why is she with that short man? I tell you why! She brings the man to buy. She tells him, 'Yes, fine, I fuck you, Mr. Short Man, now I want my diamonds!' "

"He's my father, Polack," I said. "That man there. He is here to see Jim and me."

She looked from one to the other of us, back and forth.

"Okay," she said, "he is wasting my time. You, too." She returned to her buy.

After we showed him the suite we went down to the bar. We sat in the sofa and chairs that faced the enormous empty fireplace. I was drinking a margarita, Jim had a glass of wine, and our dad had his usual club soda with an extra slice of lime.

Our dad was getting a little gray in his beard, I noticed. It had a nice effect, though. It added to that wise-man impression he wanted to make. He truly did seem like a wise man at times. A wise man in the sense of a yogi, I mean, or a Christian mystic. Like a Thomas Merton kind of wise man.

"Listen, boys, this is important. We need to get you both into the Masons. Bobby, how old are you now?"

"Sixteen. Seventeen in May."

"That's too bad. You have to be twenty-one, son. You can join the DeMolay. But Jimmy, we can sign you up immediately. Let me see who I know in town. You'll need a sponsor. What's the name of that fellow who owns your jewelry store? Cooper?"

"Popper."

"He's probably a Mason. We had better make sure he's a Mason. Is he Scottish Rite? I expect you to know these things, Dindy. These things matter." Dindy had been Jim's nickname since he was a baby.

"How's his reputation? In business. And around town. Is he an honest man?"

The waiter brought us our check.

"On your room, Mr. Clark?"

"Thanks, Steve." Jim signed the bill.

"You'll meet him tomorrow, Dad. He's brilliant."

"Reason is a limited tool, son. There's a lot more to a man than his brain. I am asking you about his consciousness now. Is he an old soul? Is he developed? I can see the influence this man is having on the two of you." He looked pointedly at our jewelry. Maybe we were wearing a few too many pieces. I worried about my quarter-ounce Chinese panda pinkie ring. The diameter was too large for my pinkie, so I wore it on the ring finger of my right hand. "I want to see if the man has character. He's successful in business. That is a good sign. But not always, son."

On the way back to the suite I saw a young woman at the front desk look at my dad carefully from behind a large stand of those white and purple orchids that expensive hotels like to erect. My dad saw her, too. The redhead whom he had brought into the store, a doctor's receptionist he had picked up in Baton Rouge, was already on a bus back home.

"I'll meet you upstairs, boys," he said. "Go on up without me."

I held the elevator door so that I could watch him for a minute. He stood at the front desk and smiled that smile at her. He leaned across the counter and whispered something in her ear. She laughed. It was a thick laugh full of musical notes like a lioness's cough.

By the time he came up, two hours later, Jim and I were full of champagne and in the suite's side-by-side oversized marble tubs.

"I'm going to bed, boys," he said. "I'm exhausted." He winked at us both.

The next day over dinner our dad confronted us. We were eating Steak Diane in the private dining room. Jim and I were splitting a second bottle of Montrachet—he always preferred whites—and our dad was drinking a Fresca. Then he ordered a near-beer.

"Okay, boys, enough. You two set this up just to impress your old man. This is foolishness. Come on, son," he said to Jim firmly.

I stepped into the background and focused on my steak. As a younger brother that was my expertise and my privilege.

"You need to start covering your nut. Put this cash aside. When are you going to go out on your own? You'll never get rich working for somebody else. This ought to be part of your seed money, son."

Then he turned his attention to me.

"Let's have a talk just the two of us, Bobby. Dindy, I need to talk privately to your brother."

"We're in the middle of dinner, Dad," I said.

"Finish up, then," he said. He pushed his plate away. "Come on, Rob, let's take a ride. Dindy, you go chase a skirt in the bar. Find one for us both. For that matter go find three of them, son. We're in a hotel, aren't we?"

While the valet brought up his car my dad took me by the biceps the way he sometimes would. I tried to flex, subtly.

"Look, your old man's not a fool. I visit you guys astrally. That's the best way for me to keep tabs on you both. And not just at night, son. I can keep an eye on you anytime I meditate. Something the monks taught me up in Srinagar. I won't tell you how often I come take a look. It's more often than you think. You have to remember I spend thirty or forty hours a week in samadhi now. Like William Blake. These days I spend most of my hours in paradise, son." I had a photo of him from the time he was in Srinagar glued in the inside cover of my copy of

Jonathan Livingston Seagull. His head was shaved and he was wearing an orange down parka. I thought that was odd. I had expected him to be in robes. In my wallet I had a similar photo, but without the parka, from his last trip to Tibet.

When the valet handed him the keys he passed them on to me.

"You drive, son," he said.

We got in the car.

"I told your mother it was not the right time for you to be down here. Your brother is an old soul, it's less dangerous for him."

"There's nothing going on, Dad. I am still going to go to college. I am still going to finish high school. I am just making some extra money."

"There's something dishonest about this business, son. I'm not worried about Dindy. But you know the problems you've had. With honesty. Not to mention stealing. You know the old saying, son. Opportunity makes the thief. You don't want to be caught hiding your hands in your pockets again. I know you remember what I'm talking about."

He was referring to a time when I was five years old at a car dealership. He was buying a new Lincoln Continental and there was a dish of pink and purple candies on the salesman's desk. No one offered one to me, so while they were talking I grabbed a couple or three or four and stuck them in my pockets. But then later when we were looking at the new car and the sales manager had come out to congratulate my father on his purchase, he looked down at me and said, "Why do you have your hands in your pockets like that, young fella? What are you hiding in there?" He was only joking but I did not realize it and I showed them the candy. It got a big laugh. But later my father wanted to moralize about it, and he brought it up again when I was first caught shoplifting in second grade, and on other occasions that had presented themselves over the years.

"What about that Lisa girl? You want to tell me what's going on there? What's your brother up to?"

This time he raised his glasses and gave me the real green-eyed stare. I tried to concentrate on my driving. Now he was not messing around. I did not know if he was bluffing because he already knew about me and Lisa or if he only wanted me to tell him about Jim's extramarital affair.

If I could have, I would have asked him if he could see anything about Jim and the Polack. Lisa had said that Jim and the Polack were up to something. "Nothing romantic," she said. "But one of his other deals." I figured she was jealous. It was good news if Jim was seeing the Polack. But I didn't like the fact that Lisa was so interested in whether or not it was true. There was a good use for Dad's extrasensory perception, I thought. To decipher a few clues for me about Jim and the Polack. But since Jim was married it wasn't the kind of thing I could ask Dad.

"Nothing, Dad. She's a friend of ours. She's like a sister."

"A sister. Right. I had a dream about that girl. It was not a good dream, son."

We were silent for a few minutes. I picked up a Cat Stevens tape that was lying next to the ashtray where he kept his pipe and put it in the tape player. Then that song about the father and the son came on so I turned it off again.

"Pull over, Robby," he said. "Over there. Under the overpass. I have something to show you."

We were wandering around central Dallas—I didn't know

precisely where he wanted me to go, but we were just driving to drive—and I turned onto Lovers' Lane. We had just passed that eight-foot painted statue of Lenin that stands there in the spotlights in front of Goff's Hamburgers.

"You know he was a Mason," my dad said.

"What?"

"Vladimir Lenin. He was a Mason. Any great man you have ever heard of. Even Martin Luther King, Jr. They made a special exception for him."

"Here, Dad?"

"Right over there on the shoulder. Below the underpass. That's safe. Up there, son. Be careful. Slow down. It's night, son! Watch what you're doing! I've got something to show you."

I stopped the car.

"Pop the trunk."

Other cars slowed to eye us as we walked around to the back of my dad's Honda. It was not a place you could really stop, especially after dark. There were a few honks. They were short, friendly honks, though, offering help. Maybe our car had broken down. It was windy and cold. I wanted to get back in the car. Trash and paper lifted in the air.

"Look at this," he said, unzipping a black leather tie case. "See that?"

He handed me a check, without letting go of it. It was a cashier's check for three hundred and sixty thousand dollars.

"That's from Ruth Moody. Now, that's trust, son. That's how we're going to open the new church," he said. He squeezed my arm with his other hand. "That's what a real salesman can do if he wants to. There's a lesson in that for you."

I wondered why he had not cashed the check yet.

We got back in the car.

"I can't bear to sit in that hotel and watch your brother piss away all that green."

I drove through the side streets of Highland Park so that Dad could admire the gigantic houses. I wanted him to see that Dallas was as good as Palm Beach and Coronado and the other cities he had lived in.

"It's some hotel, though, isn't it?" he said. His expression was proud and happy. "Of course, he's only a kid. You can't see that right now. But the fact is your big brother's still just a kid."

Those words made me anxious, because Lisa had used the same expression just the other day. She had said, "You and your brother are both just a couple of kids, Bobby." I did not mind being called a kid, or even hearing Jim described as a kid. What I didn't like was Dad repeating Lisa's words.

*T*wo days later, in a Denny's on the west side of downtown, the icy morning he left, my father changed. I think this was the first time I met the man who would become my new father. He was angry with me because I was not responding to remarks of Priscilla's. I had known Priscilla for years. She was not a normal imaginary friend. She was an important resident of a foreign planet. The planet existed in a parallel universe. When he first told me about her, when I was seven years old, he said he had met her "just through dumb luck" on an astral trip during his initiation as an Eckankar trainer. I suppose she was in the audience. My father consulted Priscilla on personal and sexual concerns of his clients and parishioners. He insisted he was a mystic, not a psychic, which meant that he never charged for his consultations with Priscilla. He did, however, charge for his counseling. He had a PhD in counseling from an outfit in southern California.

Around the time I turned twelve Priscilla became a person whom my father could see and converse with, though she remained hidden to me because of my spiritual condition. But by now my father had abandoned this distinction and demanded that Priscilla be treated with ordinary social courtesy. So he was shouting at me in Denny's because I was not answering Priscilla's questions. This time I felt I had to admit to myself that my father was not merely playing at being a crazy person like he might otherwise have done, for the pity. Maybe he really was a schizophrenic, or worse, like our mother had insisted for years.

Naturally I do not know what questions Priscilla was asking. They were probably simple questions about my mother, the store, my brother, my sex life, hopefully not Lisa, et cetera. I knew Priscilla had good manners and common sense. I pictured her in her forties, with graying blond hair and glasses. She might have worn a button-down sweater over a T-shirt, and come from a college town in British Columbia or Washington state.

Maybe it is only his blood sugar, I thought. He had severe diabetes.

The scene ended when my father threw his glass of iced coffee at me. Then he left without paying the check. The glass broke when it hit my head. I had milk and coffee on my face.

The waitress came with a clean rag and some paper napkins. She mopped up the table.

"Your eyebrow is bleeding," she said. "He's your dad?" she asked me. I nodded. I was grateful for some sympathy.

"You should be respectful of your dad," she said. "What did you say to him?" She shook her head.

"It's seventeen dollars," she said. At Denny's you pay at the register. I asked her to refill my Coke and for a second bacon scrambler. I knew he would drive around downtown for half an hour and then come back. It was his last day in Texas before getting back on the road. He would come back to say goodbye before he hit the highway. Plus I had left my wallet at the store and I didn't have any money.

"After you pay your check," the waitress said.

"Put it on this check," I said. "I'm not finished."

"Oh, yes, you are," she said.

Years after, when Jim and I were partners in our own store, I might tell a version of this story to one or another customer I liked—they do exist—and the customer would say something along the lines of: "So that's when you finally knew your dad was insane?" Then I felt an unfamiliar obligation to assert myself: not in defense of my father, and not for my own sake, either, but on account of the truth. I wanted to reply: What the hell makes you think he was crazy? Because you've never seen another world, you know it doesn't exist? That's called an argument from ignorance, and of all the twenty-two logical fallacies it's the easiest to understand. Look, I don't expect that when the curtain goes down, and I am alone in the hospital room, with the lights fading, and the world, the whole world, is vanishing into the dark, that, suddenly, like the best birthday surprise you ever got, the fluorescents will spark back on and everyone will shout, "Surprise!"—all the dead people I've ever lost and thought I'd left behind, there, ringing my bed, with gifts in their hands, or with their arms open to receive me—and I will rise from the white hospital sheets and they will give me my complimentary custom-made gold-vermeil-and-carved-ivory wings. With Jesus standing there in a silver diaper. But I do not know it cannot be true. And if in another life I meet my father and he is waiting with his I-told-you-so-son-but-you-never-listen smile, I might ask him questions, but I won't be any more astonished than I was when, say, Wendy first kissed me and then let me take off her pants and fuck her.

How are you so sure he was insane? I wanted to shout at my customer and seize him by the ears and neck, or by the hair on the back of his head, and shake his shitty face off. How the hell could you possibly know?

Mike Bloom, formerly Ezekiel Blumenstein, known to me and Jim—and Lisa, too—as Granddad, taught me those logical fallacies, and many other tricks of both rationality and motivated irrationality. Years later he became like a mentor to me. There was a short list of us who could call Mr. Blumenstein Granddad and he called each of us Grandson. Granddaughter for Lisa, of course. He was the only person I ever met in the jewelry business who told me to ask myself about the karmic implications of my actions.

The jewelry business is rich with optimistic people.

Unlike my father, Granddad was cynical about human nature, but he had led the kind of complex life that stimulates the mind. He was, for example, the only real person I had ever heard of who lost his parents to pirates. His father had been a yacht builder, a speculator, who also owned a chain of used-car lots across Texas and Oklahoma. They had been in the Canary Islands and were boarded by African pirates, and they macheted his mother and father and dumped him, the two-and-a-half-year-old, on a beach on the coast of Spain. He remembered it all quite clearly. He was raised by Basques and spoke and read nine languages. He studied phenomenology with the students of Husserl, the big boys, at Leuven. Then he moved back to Oklahoma, in honor of his father, and lived there for twenty years before taking an interest in Swiss watches and opening his present outfit in Dallas. Everyone said he had had a long, long-distance affair with Lana Turner. Because he supplied everyone, he was the best gossip in the Dallas–Fort Worth jewelry business. "I should have been a barber, Grandson," he would tell me. "Or a fry cook. That's an honest living. Back in the old days a barber always heard the news first. A man makes friends on that kind of information. Money, too."

Behind his desk he kept an old Russian machine gun on a shelf. It was not because he was Russian mob. He hated the Russian advance into our market and prominently and dangerously refused to do business with them. It was the machine gun he had used when he was a teenager and fought with the Basques in Spain. If he liked you, Granddad might tell the story of the gun.

"This gun has lived up more excitement than either of us, Grandson," he told me. "It's one of the guns the Russians brought in before Franco, when Spain was supposed to become the Communist South beach club of Europe. The regular fucking Costa del Pinko."

He leaned back in his chair and patted the gun with his large hand in a familiar, almost sexual way.

"I got it from a woman, a Gypsy woman. You should have seen this old woman. Uglier than the south end of a northbound dump truck. She had it from her lover, a man who died on a hill in Spain during the resistance. They bombed him and his whole band—they were all guerilla fighters, those boys, commies but tough as blood—working behind the lines. She climbed the hill afterward to find his body but all she found was this weapon. She lost it to me in a bet. If I lost I would have had to fuck her. Can you believe that? Crazy Gypsy woman. I fucked her anyway, of course. She was a good old gal. I couldn't have been eighteen at the time and she was seventy going on a hundred and twenty-five. She liked it slow. Of course, you don't want to hear this shit. Let's get down to business. Very nimble in bed, though, the Gypsy race. They take it seriously. Many of them are bullfighters and flamenco dancers. The flamenco dancers, those are the cowardly ones. Can't say I blame them, though. You probably never killed a bull." I shook my head. "It ain't very much fun."

Granddad was a still, restful man, like you imagine an ancient Chinese emperor might be, but his hands were always moving. He shuffled the watches around his desk while he talked, writing up my memorandum invoice as he proceeded. I had the job of wrapping each watch carefully in tissue paper before placing it in my briefcase. The boxes and papers, when he had them, went in a separate cardboard box. Granddad never dealt in any counterfeit boxes or papers. Everything was original. The watches, too, naturally.

He preferred to sell men's watches.

"For a woman a watch is just another piece of jewelry, Grandson," he told me. "There's a reason the best watches are made for men. Women don't understand the aesthetic."

There were Patek Philippes on their straps, the finest watches in the world, repeaters that chimed the hour and quarter hour, moon face complications and platinum heads; there were the stainless steel Blancpains and IWCs, watches that the men in the industry all wore, because they were much more expensive than they looked; there were the old reliable sure-to-sell Rolexes, the bread and butter, which bored even me already; there were Breguets, with mysterious complications, modeled after the pocket watch Breguet himself had made for Marie Antionette and delivered long after she was dead; there were glamorous and fantastically expensive Ulysse Nardins, Vacheron Constantins, and Franck Mullers, the ones you sold only to Arabs, wealthy gay men, and the true connoisseurs, several of them with crystal backs so you could view the elaborate multicolored movements, and the tiny sapphires and rubies within the gears that helped them revolve; there were the square-headed Boucherons, mostly yellow gold and on gold mesh bracelets, that Granddad told me the French preferred; there were the coin-headed Corums, which my father always complimented when he noticed them on other men's wrists, and which I had planned to buy for him one day, and never did. My dad wore his own watch with the head against the underside of the wrist, so you had to roll your arm over to see the time. "The only way a gentleman wears his watch, son," he told me. "Because a gentleman is never in a hurry, and he does not need to know the time except when he desires to." Granddad wore his stainless steel Patek the same way.

"Time, Grandson," he explained to me one slow afternoon, when he insisted I wait for a shipment of sixty back-of-list Bulgaris on crocodile straps that Mr. Popper was running in a Saturday sale. "That's why I love them the way I do. A watch puts you in the middle of the stuff of ordinary being. That's what I like about them. They remind us of our position in the universe. Stranded in the goddamn seconds the way we are. But between our rounds here—in life, I mean—we get a taste of the other stuff. That's why the Chinese call this the middle kingdom."

I loved to sit and listen to him when he spoke in this way.

"Well, enough of this metaphysical bullshit," he said, after the UPS man dropped off the watches. "Let's send you back to the real world of buying and selling. Finish your sandwich, there, and get on I-35."

He often waited for me and then we ate lunch together. He loved Reuben sandwiches. But he rarely ate more than a couple of bites.

"I bet ole Ronnie will make a killing on these Bulgaris," he said. "Don't think much of them myself. But it's a good price point on a watch. People know the name."

I watched him take one of the colorful Bulgaris out of its box, place it on his wrist, set it, and then put it back in the box again.

"You know the only thing I miss about retail, Grandson?" I did not believe he had ever been in retail. But since he said it, it reflected the facts. "Credit cards. I miss sliding those credit cards. A dollar has romance, no doubt about it. But a credit card can fuck."

I'm not hungry," Lisa said. "Anyway I'm broke. Let's go down to the Caves."

"I can buy you lunch," I said.

"I know where you get your lunch money," she said. She meant from the cash box on the floor that we used to make change for our cash sales. But now I was pretty sure she stole from it, too. Everybody did.

"I have real money, too." We had been paid last Friday. It was funny that she was already out of cash. "But we don't have to eat if you don't want to."

At lunch Lisa and I often snuck down into the old box room, what was called the Caves, which was behind the rows of jewelers' benches with the dirty, silent men in safety goggles and grimy aprons bent over their clamps and tweezers, with blue torches lined up one after another in their wire torch rests, hissing, barely audible, back to the very end of the basement where there were rows and rows of cardboard boxes holding thousands of silk pouches, seed pearl necklaces and earrings and rings—things Mr. Popper had bought from China for a hundred dollars a crate—and the counterfeit Rolex papers, and the counterfeit "Rottexx" watches we sold for fifty bucks a pop, and knockoff Mexican Swatches that looked exactly like the real thing (even the Swatch rep couldn't tell the difference), and the hundreds and hundreds of empty jewelry boxes, in our signature forest green with red interiors, Christmas colors we kept all year round, waiting to be filled and sold, waiting to be unwrapped, admired, opened, and discarded.

We had sex with her sitting on a piece of dusty metal shelving and her legs around my waist. "Isn't that cold on your bottom?" I said, and she said, "It's called my ass, Bobby. Shut up and fuck me. I like it on my ass. It hurts. It feels good. Come on. Make me remember it. Really fuck me!"

Afterward I didn't want to go back upstairs and face those swarming, oily customers, but then, smoking the crank, I felt like cleaning something. "I love to do it down here," Lisa said, and the way she said it made me think she had done it with more than only me down here, so I changed the subject. We smoked the crystal off a square of tinfoil. I wanted to get on the floor and empty some ashtrays. Plus I was getting paranoid. Jim was surely looking for us.

"Let's finish this last and go back upstairs," I said. I knew if I told her I was worried about Jim she would make fun of me and become stubborn.

"Don't worry about Jim," she said. "He's busy, too. He's not always looking for us, believe me. He's got more than enough to take care of right now. Plenty. Don't be silly. Anyway, you shouldn't exaggerate your own importance. It's not attractive."

She tapped out a little more powder onto the tinfoil and lit the lighter again. I could see how hot it was getting and worried about her fingertips burning. But she did not seem to notice. I wanted a glass of water.

"I wish we had more time like this," I said. "Just the two of us. It seems like I never get to see you. Not enough, I mean."

"Bobby." She laughed. "You are sweet. Don't be crazy. We spend about twenty hours a day together."

"I tried to call you from Dallas last night when I was on my runs." I had called from the phone in Kizakov's office. "I thought maybe if I got back early, if I hurried, we could have a late dinner. You weren't around." Jim had been out, too. More and more I had been noticing that about the two of them. How they went missing at the same time. I couldn't ask Jim where he was, of course.

She ignored me. She was focused on cooking the drug.

"Jim is a schemer. I don't mean that as a criticism. It's because he's an entrepreneur. He's always busy cooking up something for Jim. That's what keeps him out of trouble. Kind of." She laughed. "His plans. If he doesn't include you in all of them it's for your own good. Trust me on that one. I'm older than you are."

"It's not that," I said. "It's not like I'm trying to impress him. I just want to do a good job. I want to be a good employee."

"He's already proud of you, Bobby. You don't have to prove anything to him. He loves you because you're his brother. Because you are the person you are. Not because of anything you're doing."

That reminded me of something my mother once told me. It was after an award ceremony for the safety patrols in elementary school. I had cheated on the national exam and won "The Smartest Safety Patrol in Canada" or some such crazy Canadian award. After I received my new ten-speed bike and carried the flag down the Seventh Street Mall, my mother took me aside and said, "You see that? That's what success does, Bobby. No one is going to like us for who we are. You have to make people like you. They will never like you just you on your own."

That was not what my father would have said. He thought human beings loved one another, truly, all the way down.

Black Friday had come and gone and I was still not on the sales floor.

"That was the promise," I told Jim. "I am back-of-the-house and the buys until after Thanksgiving and then I go on the floor."

"It's true, Jim," Lisa said. It was after hours, almost midnight, and the three of us were sitting at his desk sorting diamond melee. The Watchman was still there, too, a few desks away, checking in diamond bezels, counterfeit buckles, and other Rolex accessories that we had shipped in from all over the world.

"It's Sheila who is holding you up," Jim said. "You know how it works, Bobby. Sheila's in charge of all the employees. In the end it's her call."

"She shouldn't lie. She shouldn't break her promises," I said.

"I don't think it's Sheila at all. I think it's Dennis," Lisa said. "It's because you are Jim's little brother."

"Whatever," Jim said. "Who knows? It doesn't matter. It's politics. Dennis wants my job. He's sick of running the back. We'll get you on the phones and then he won't be able to keep you off the floor. Sell some silver contracts. That's how the Po-lack got everyone paying attention. Other than her tits, I mean."

He said that for Lisa. She was small-chested and complained about it, often, especially after sex. I looked away from both of them, afraid that they would read something on my face that they should not see. Each of them something different.

"Nice, Jimmy," Lisa said. But she was smiling. "Real funny."

"Sheila started her out as a hostess," he continued. "Then she nailed some big bullion contracts, working the phones, and she was on the floor two weeks later. If you really sell on the phones Sheila will know she is wasting you in the back."

What you did was, you sold the customer a quantity of pre-cious metal as an investment, and sold him the security of storing it for him in your safes. When silver was at $5.60, a customer could buy a thousand ounces of silver at five dollars an ounce. "We can sell the metal at below the market price because we buy it off the street and smelt it ourselves, and it is in our interest to sell it be-low market value to you, sir, because then when you want to buy a diamond tennis bracelet for your tenth anniversary you will call me first." Customers paid a nominal fee of fifty dollars per year, per thousand ounces, to store it in our safes. We never actually bought the metal. And that was how you made money in it. The official story around the store was we stored the metal off-premises but even the phone girls knew that was bullshit. So it was pure profit, and you were paid a straight ten percent commission on any metal contract. A ten-thousand-dollar contract meant a thousand-dollar commission. We were selling them by the hundreds.

"Okay, that sounds good," I said. "I want to learn how to sell metals contracts. I want to be one of the silver guys."

"I still think you'd be best out on the floor," Lisa said, and smiled at me. Those wide-open smiles of hers were one of the best things about her. "And you shouldn't compare your brother to that woman, Jim. What is it with you and her lately? Bobby is nothing like her."

"We'll start you out on my Rolex calls," Jim said. "That will soften up your phone manners. The phone is an art, Bobby. They can't see what they're buying. You have to learn how to pitch your voice. That's all you got on the Rolex lines. The sounds of your own mouth."

Bobby, we need to talk to you."

It was three of the saleswomen. They hot-boxed me in the old safe room, the little closet-sized room near the front where we kept the appraisal folders, wrapping paper, pearl folders, and recent mailers now. Tracy, who was pretty, this old yellow skinned bitch Rita, whom everyone hated and feared, and a fat woman, one of the hard-core phone saleswomen who used to train everybody but now had gone to part-time because of health problems, whose name I didn't know. The Polack disliked her, because of a battle between the two of them from years before, and she called her simply "Pig." She would say it directly to her face, with other people around, too. Even customers, if she was out on the floor looking for a piece of jewelry for a client on the phone. When you worked the phones the rule was you always held the article of jewelry you were trying to sell. If it actually existed, that is, and wasn't only a picture in our catalogue. It's surprising how much that helps with the sale.

The fat saleswoman stood at the door and kept an eye out so that no one would overhear.

"We don't think you should be seeing Lisa," Tracy said.

"She is not a nice person," the fat one said. "Okay, she's nice enough. But she's not the kind of person you think she is. Not nice in that way. She's a slut."

I did not know what to say. Why did anyone know about me and Lisa?

"She's Jim's girlfriend. I am not going to have sex with my brother's girlfriend."

"What? What did you say?" Tracy said.

"Oh, you didn't know?" Rita said. "For about a year now. Inseparable. No one knows what all they are up to. That's what I would say. More than just you-know-what."

"Wow. This is good," Tracy said. "This is juicy."

"I think it's illegal for both of them," the fat one said. "Remember that schoolteacher? And the high school boy? That was just last year."

"That's because the boy murdered her husband," Rita said. "A minor cannot be prosecuted for statutory rape."

"What about two sixteen-year-olds? What if they had sex? I used to do it all the time," Tracy said. The fat one laughed. "I mean, like with boyfriends. A boyfriend. Not like this. Like we were both sixteen. Or eighteen, maybe. Maybe we were both eighteen. So that would be different. Because we were adults."

"I suggest you be perfectly candid, Bobby. Then I could take your side when the truth comes out. I would rather do that. I am not fond of liars. We are keeping an eye on you, Bobby," Rita said.

I looked away from her and tried to remember exactly what I had just said.

If Rita, Tracy, and that fat saleswoman knew about Lisa and me, I wondered whether Jim had heard. I doubted it. It was a big store, I told myself. Jim didn't like gossip. He might have heard something and dismissed it. Or defended me and Lisa, even.

I found Lisa in back at Jim's desk changing tags for a sale Sheila wanted in the men's jewelry case. Even at Christmas men's jewelry is a tough sell. Lisa was replacing the tags with new tags that were twice the price, so that Sheila could put ALL MEN'S JEWELRY 50% OFF NOW UNTIL CHRISTMAS EVE! signs throughout the men's case, and Mr. Popper could run a black-and-white banner across the bottom of one of the big full-page Christmas "Rolex and diamond" ads in the weekend *Star-Telegram*. Now and through the rest of the season Ronnie Popper was the biggest customer the *Fort Worth Star-Telegram* enjoyed.

"Hey," I said. I sat down and started removing the paper-and-string tags. This was before computer tags.

"No, not like that," she said. "Do it one at a time. Write the new tag up and then take the old one off. Otherwise you get mixed up."

I took a pink message pad from the desk and wrote a note to Lisa. It said, "Do you think Jim could know?"

She read it, folded it back up, and fed it into Jim's paper shredder. Because he ran the Rolex files he had the industrial-sized paper shredder, not one of the little ones like everybody else had that sat on top of a trash can. His had its own separate trash receptacle.

"Why don't you ask him?" she said. "Or I can ask him if you want." She smiled at me in a mysterious way that let me know she was smarter than me, but it didn't bother her, she liked it that way.

"I don't want you to ask him. You can't be the one to ask him. I don't even know what to ask."

"Ask who?" Jim pulled a chair over from Dennis's desk and sat down. He surprised me from behind the filing cabinets. He couldn't have heard what we were saying back there. And we weren't saying anything, I thought. I looked for the note but then remembered I had just watched Lisa put it in the shredder. It was never getting back out of that shredder alive, I thought.

"Ask you," Lisa said.

"Ask me what? Ask me," Jim said. "What is it, Bobby?" For a moment he looked concerned. Then Lisa shook her head and looked at him carefully, but with a small smile. I saw the communication pass between them. Jim laughed. He seemed relieved.

"Oh," he said. "That. You had me worried for a second. Okay. Good. I gotcha. Come on, Bobby," he said. "Let's take a walk."

Then I knew that he must know, but I continued to lie to myself about it until we were out of the store and in the street.

"Here," he said, and handed me his one-hitter. "Do a bump. Cup it in your palm like you are blowing into your hand from the cold. Just do it quickly and no one will notice."

I pretended to do a bump to satisfy him, but I didn't turn the knob to put the cocaine in the chamber. I couldn't walk in the street and sniff cocaine.

He looked at the bottle when I handed it back to him.

"You didn't even do it," he said. "You didn't get any. Here, I'll load it for you. Just be careful. Don't spill it when I hand it back to you."

We were walking toward a little park Jim liked downtown that was a few blocks from the store. In the summer it had fountains, but in winter they turned the fountains off, usually, and it

120

was just a square of black granite surrounded by trees on all sides. It felt protected when you sat there. Like a grove.

He put one hand on my shoulder. Not his whole arm, we weren't that kind of a family, but his hand, like he would steer me with it.

"Listen, don't worry about this Lisa thing," he said.

"Jim, I don't, I mean, she is. I wanted to tell you."

I realized that if Jim told me that I could not see Lisa anymore, I wouldn't. He was more important than any person. He was my brother. You can break up with your girlfriend, you could divorce your wife if you had one, but your brother is always your brother.

"Don't even worry about it, Bobby. This isn't something you and I are going to be concerned about. Here, do another bump. Hit the other nostril. Careful. It's loaded."

I did another bump. It was fun, walking through the quiet cold streets, in the open like this, sniffing cocaine. It was like we were the ones making the laws. Or the laws could apply to the other people and we stood above them.

"I'm married, Bobby. Lily and I have enough problems as it is. You are a free man. I am happy for you. Not much has been going on with me and Lisa lately, if you want to know the truth. It's all ancient history. Pretty much." Then he did another bump. He handed the bottle back over to me. "She told me immediately, anyway," he said.

"She told you?"

My hands started shaking. I was afraid my eyes might be getting wet. That could just be the cold. I didn't know where to look. I tried to focus on the trunk of a tree on the other side of the park. I could not imagine what he might say next. It was going to be awful, I knew that much.

121

"When? I mean, when did she tell you?"

"Don't be mad at her. That's how she is. She told me when you two started and she wanted to tell you, too. But I asked her not to. There wasn't any reason. You needed some time. You came down here without any confidence at all. It was that girlfriend of yours. She had you like a whipped puppy. But look at you now. You're becoming a man. So, deal with it that way. Like a man handles things."

He was not accusing me of anything.

"I wouldn't take this thing with Lisa too seriously, Bobby, if I were you. Sometimes it's better to stay on the surface with somebody. You know what I mean?"

I nodded. I wasn't sure that I understood him, but we both enjoyed it when he gave me advice, like this. He didn't do it often enough.

We sat down on a stone bench. We passed the one-hitter back and forth. Above us was the noise of the traffic of downtown, and beyond it the deep-lunged breathing of the two enormous highways, I-30 and I-35, that intersected at the southeast corner of downtown Fort Worth. For about five minutes we sat there together. My fingers hurt with the cold. Suddenly I worried that the time was awkward rather than natural. I couldn't decide. I blamed it on the cocaine.

Jim patted me twice on the back. He stood up, and put the one-hitter away in the breast pocket of his jacket. Even if I was upset I could have used one more, I thought.

"Okay, Bobby," he said. "We're squared away. Let's get back to work."

*E*veryone liked to watch for the Neiman's deliveries in the afternoons. They came in once or twice a week. More often at Christmastime, when the money was really flowing. Sheila went shopping in the morning at the Fort Worth Neiman's and had everything sent to the store. They had three children, two sons and a daughter, but as far as I could tell they were never at home. I didn't even know their kids' names, and there were no photographs of them, not even on Sheila's desk. They kept their dry cleaning in a big armoire in Mr. Popper's office. Sheila changed in the office if they were going out in the evening.

I was taking a break from the phones, working the buy counter—the Polack was there, too, in a dress that fit her like a ballerina's leotard, working the buys beside me—and a young mother came in with a kid under one arm and another in a stroller. I noticed her all the way from the entrance because the regular Neiman's delivery guy came in just ahead of her and, with his hands full of bags, held the door open for her with his foot. I guess she wasn't even twenty years old. A teenager, same as me. I hoped she would pick someone else but she saw me looking at her and came straight for me. She wanted to sell her wedding ring. She took it from her ring finger and handed it to me with a hopeful expression. But not too hopeful.

"It was his mother's," she said. "It is supposed to be worth a lot of money."

Even before I cleaned it I could see it was a real diamond. But after it soaked in the ultrasonic for a few minutes and then I steamed it off it blazed. I needed to show it to Dennis before I made an offer.

Dennis was at his desk. When I handed it to him he gave me one of his standard lines: "How we lookin'? Are we cookin'?" Then when he slowed down and saw the ring he was quiet. He louped and handled the diamond ring greedily. Now he was all business.

"Where is she?" he said. From his desk you could see the buy counters through the one-way mirror. I pointed.

"Okay. Listen to me. I am going to let you handle this one, Bobby. If you're goin' to stay in the flood you got to swim sometime. But don't you fuck this up. Offer her five grand. You hear me? She hesitates, up to six. Six thousand. Tell her it will be cash money. Cash today. But take it real slow. Do not let her walk. She does not leave the store with this ring."

I nodded. I was not convinced.

"Hell. Maybe I should handle this one," he said. "If it's all the same to you. What's the hurry? You can grab the next one."

I started to agree with him. Then Jim was there at my shoulder. He took me by the arm.

"What?" he said. "No. We all have to learn, Dennis," he said. "Give him a chance. Let me see the ring," he said.

"Wow," he said when Dennis handed it to him.

"I know," Dennis said. "That's what I have been saying."

Jim grabbed an ashtray from Dennis's desk and rubbed the ring around in the ashes. He looked at it, spat on it, and rubbed it around again. Then he cleaned off the shank and handed it back to me.

"Offer her five hundred bucks," he said.

"What? No," Dennis said. "No, no, no. No sir. No way, nohow."

"Look at her, Dennis," Jim said. "She's got two little kids with her. She's a kid herself, for chrissake. She doesn't know what that ring is worth. She's selling her wedding ring and her husband's not with her. What does that tell you? She'll just figure he lied to her about what it was worth. As usual. That's what she'll think. She'll be so mad at him she'll sell it for five hundred just to get back at him."

I did not want to do this buy at all.

Then one of the phone girls ran up and put her arm around Jim's shoulders. They all liked to fold themselves onto him. It irritated Lisa.

"You've got a Rolex call on seven," she said. "It's a hot one. I think you better take it."

"Okay," he said. He frowned at me. "Go on, Bobby. Show them how it's done. Show them how the Clarks do it. Five hundred. Five bills. We'll make seven, eight grand on this deal. We'll walk it up to Popper's office together. Watch this, Dennis. Just watch."

125

I went back onto the floor and told the woman we could offer her five hundred dollars. Her children were struggling and giving her trouble.

"Five hundred? Oh, no," she said. "That's not going to help. We need at least a thousand. I have to get a thousand dollars or I am in real trouble. Can you make it a thousand? It was his mother's ring. It's very old. It's like an antique. It is supposed to be worth thousands and thousands of dollars. Couldn't you do a thousand?"

"We can't pay that," I said. "But listen to me. Across the street from us just a block up Houston is a place called Edelstein's." I leaned across the counter. I handed the ring back to her. That was something you were never supposed to do during a buy. I tried to block her out with my back so that they could not see what I was doing from behind the mirror. "This ring is probably worth at least five thousand dollars. But we will only pay five hundred. Take it over to Edelstein's. They are Jews and they are smart buyers but they are fair. I bet you can get five thousand dollars or more."

"Wait a second," she said. She was angry. "What are you saying? You are saying I will get more money somewhere else? Your ads say that you pay the best price in Fort Worth! You mean I came all the way down here with my kids just so you can send me somewhere else? If it's worth five thousand dollars, then you should buy it for five thousand dollars!" She was getting loud. This was not the reaction I had expected.

"I understand," I said. "You are going to get me in a lot of trouble. I'm just saying. Believe me. I can't explain it right now. I am trying to help you. It's only a block. One city block that way." I pointed with my thumb. "Take your ring there and say you need seven thousand dollars. Just trust me, okay?"

She looked at me for a second like I was a person rather than some enemy behind a tie and a glass-and-brass counter and she saw I was telling her the truth. The truth went between us, I think you could say.

"Okay," she said. "I'm not saying thank you."

"Go," I said. I tried not to look over my shoulder. "Hurry," I said. She would not be safe until she was physically out the door. I knew those two. They would run down the street to catch her.

I watched her and her kids walk out into the cold morning. When I started to help another seller—I was so young that I hoped this would be the end of it—Jim caught me by the elbow and dragged me in back. He pulled me into the room where we kept the ring boxes, the same room where Rita and her friends had corralled me.

"What the hell just happened out there?" he said.

"She changed her mind. She said she was going to think about it."

"You little—" For half a beat he couldn't say it. Then he did. "You little motherfucker." He was so angry his eyes were wet. His cheeks were white and his chin and his ears turned red. But the terrible thing was the look on his face. I had never seen him wearing an expression anything like the expression he had on. "I heard the whole thing. This is my job, too, goddammit," he said. "You are fucking with two jobs here, Bobby. Do you get that? Do you fucking understand that?"

Later that afternoon he caught me in the box room. I was making it very tidy.

"Dad's in the hospital," he said. "His roommate called the ambulance. Apparently he was naked in the front yard, pissing on the neighbor's Mercedes."

We both had seen him like that before.

"Where? In Palm Beach?"

"Scottsdale. He's back in Arizona, apparently. Just fucking typical."

Growing up Jim had lived with our father and his craziness for years. He blamed our father for his physical and mental diseases, in fact. But for me it felt like God was attacking all three of us.

"He acts like he's some kind of saint. He thinks he can do whatever he wants. So now we have to interrupt our lives. He's not thinking about us when he does things like this."

"It's not like he wants to be in the hospital," I said.

"Oh, you don't think so? Don't be so sure, Bobby. He treats hospitals like they're goddamn luxury hotels. You know how he does it. He checks in every chance he gets. Welcome to the James Clark Resort and Spa. Clean sheets, fresh drugs, sleep till noon, free food, nurses who love all of your stories. Lay in bed and watch television all goddamn day. Between naps. I am seriously sick of this shit, Bobby. I love Dad. But this is about it for me."

We couldn't leave on Friday, so we flew out the following night after closing and had Sunday, Monday, and Tuesday morning off of work. We would go straight from the airport to the store when we returned. In first class we got drunk on free brandy-and-sodas and Jim gave me some Ecstasy.

"It's not a drug," he said. "It's like an herb. But wait until you try it. Doctors use it for therapy. But you buy it at a head shop. Lisa found it. Her friends are all taking it now. She has been taking it before she comes to work in the morning. She says it helps her sell."

I did not tell him that Lisa and I had been taking it to-gether. But she would only give me a half at a time because she was worried that otherwise people would notice.

Jim and I swallowed two each. Then after an hour or so, as we were getting ready to land, he said, "This is fun. Let's take another." When we got off the plane we were in very good moods. We took a taxi to a topless bar. "We want some girls," Jim told the taxi driver. He was a Mexican fellow and he shook his head at us. There was a crucifix hanging from his rearview mirror. But then he smiled. "Maybe there is a place," he said. "But it is a long drive. It will cost you maybe one hundred dol-lars. Each way. But I can wait for you. I wait in the car."

We stopped for a six-pack of beer and took some more of the pills. We had our arms around each other and explained how we felt about our childhood. Jim was embarrassed. He checked on the driver by looking in the mirror. But the radio was playing tinny Mexican music.

"It's the drugs talking, Bobby," he said. "It's okay. I know."

"No, no, this is how I always felt," I said. "I was just afraid to say it."

When he woke me we were at a warehouse in the desert. There were pickup trucks and old cars parked around it. It was dark except for one shy spotlight and the illuminated sign above the front door: CHILLI WILLI'S. Later I learned that this was not the original Chilli Willi's. The real Chilli Willi's is not in the United States at all but twenty miles back in the scrub south of the slums around the city—not the resort—of Cancún, Mexico.

"Is he all right?" a bouncer asked my brother. I had my arms around his neck and shoulders like a little kid.

"He will be fine," he said. "He's had a nap. I'll sit him down. He doesn't want anything more to drink."

Inside it was dark and there were rows of seats like in a theater, but in front of the seats were long tables, like the tables in a school cafeteria, so you had a place to put your drink. There were no waitresses; you went to one of the bars or a dancer brought you your drinks.

Jim brought us two beers. "Take it easy," he said. "You should do one more X," he said, and gave me another pill. "It will sober you up. Chew it up. It will go into your bloodstream faster."

There was competition, so Jim gave a bouncer, a big Mexican with a beard, two hundred dollars and then we had a girl immediately. This was the girl Jim wanted, a Mexican, short, like our mother, but athletic, and with big breasts. She was about my age but had a square chin that made her look older. She grabbed my leg.

"So it will be two? Two of you? Sounds like fun to me, man," she said. "Three together is what I like. That works good for me, man. Is he okay?"

"He's good," my brother said. "He's just had a little too much to drink."

"Here," he said, and took out his little brown bottle. "This will help him. Come on, Bobby, this will perk you up." He started to tap out a line of cocaine on the table.

"No, man, you can't do that in here," she said. "Let's go up to the room. We can have all the fun you want up in the room, man. Put that away. Let's go."

"Hang on. We need a girl for my brother."

"Okay, two girls, no problem, man. I got a friend. I get my good friend. He is going to like her. You going to like her," she said, and put her hand between my legs.

•

Upstairs, the cocaine revived me. We laughed and cut long lines for the women on the wooden coffee table and fed them the rest of the Ecstasy.

"Don't worry," Jim said. "I'll have Lisa FedEx some more out tomorrow." But he was only reassuring himself.

There was beer brought to the room and then the woman with me, the friend, took me to a different room. She was not attractive but she was kind and interesting, what I could understand of her words. She explained her family, who were not in Arizona. There were no children, only nieces and nephews and her mother. Her father was dead. She did not speak much English. I took out my wallet and showed her my green card. She did not have one yet, of course.

Ours was a small dark room. I wanted to talk more than I wanted to have sex. She was on top and eventually we both agreed that that would not work. She got on her hands and knees and I struggled from the back. We needed to do what we came to do so that we could sleep with good consciences. We were determined, fit, young, and in time we succeeded.

In the morning the taxi driver was waiting according to his promise. We drove slowly down the desert road. There were rocks in the road, the sky was yellow, and long Sonora cacti inspected us from above. Those are the cacti like in the Road Runner cartoons, the ones with round arms reaching up. Twice I had to tap the driver's shoulder to pull over so I could vomit. Jim slept heavily.

At my father's apartment his roommate or girlfriend told us we could not stay.

"I can't have you sleeping around here," she said. "You are grown men. It doesn't look right." She had red hair and was wearing a bikini. I tried not to look at her too closely. Jim was eyeballing her breasts. He did that entirely innocently. If you told him later he was staring he would not even believe you.

"I am going out to the pool now," she said. "I have to lock up."

"Give us a minute," Jim said. "I want to bring him a couple of things. Bobby, find his binders. Look on the bookshelves. I'll get his shaving kit and some clothes."

"I'll get him a couple of books, too," I said. The woman sat on the sofa. "Maybe he would like a couple of his medals for next to his bed?"

"This better not take long," she said. "Is your dad all right? I hope he's okay and everything. But seriously."

My father always kept a special room, his study, for his framed press clippings, ribbons, and medals. When we were little, bored at home alone while he was at work, we would look through them, Jim and I, especially the ones he hadn't hung yet, in their frames on the floor. Mostly they were press clippings. "Local Boy Breaks Ski-Jumping Record." "Jimmy Clark Wins Hill Climb." "Freshman Scores Record Six Touchdowns." "Boy Wonder Takes Gold in Wrestling, Shot Put and Diving." He had won every athletic contest you can imagine. He played goalie for Canada in the Olympic Games. He still held the Shattuck Military Academy record for the hundred-yard dash. In early adulthood the success continued for several years. I remember one of the big ones, the color cover of *Maclean's* magazine. He and my uncle Robert—whom I was named after—were both on their motorcycles, and the headline read "The New Millionaires."

That was when they were doing real estate development together in Calgary. When I was three and four—which would make Jim ten or eleven—he would drive us around town and show us the cedar-shake apartment buildings they built. He loved those false-mansard cedar-shake roofs. Even today in run-down parts of Calgary you can identify his apartment buildings by those roofs. "That's quality, boys," he would say. "If you always build quality you will never lose money."

I picked a few books from the shelves, Ram Dass's *Be Here Now*, two of the orange-covered Sai Baba readers he loved, and a kind of photocopied manual or training book from the Rosicrucians, and off a little Chippendale lyre table that I recognized—he liked to tote it around with him; it was small enough to fit in the back of the car, and it was from my grandparents' house back in Winnipeg—I took the invitation to the wedding of the Prince of Monaco in its green fake malachite frame. Then I asked his girlfriend where the bedroom was.

"Your brother is already back there," she said. "Why do you want to know? Go ahead. It's not like you're rummaging through my bedroom. I hope your dad gets better and everything but tell him I said he needs to find a new place to live. Peeing all over the neighbor's yard. Peeing all over the kitchen. The stuff I had to throw out."

I found his sandalwood meditation beads next to the bed where he always kept them, and his reading glasses and his extra pair of regular glasses. I took some incense, too, some of the special sticks I was never allowed to burn that he kept in a carved box from Tibet. This was all part of the regular routine. I looked in the closet for a cardboard box and put everything in there. He moved so often I even knew where he kept his packing boxes. One stack beneath the bed and another stack in the closet underneath his shoe boxes.

"Where are his keys?" Jim said.

"I don't know. I don't think I should give you those. I need his car. That is my only car."

"Listen carefully to me. Our father is in the hospital. We came from Texas. We do not have a car. I will make this easy for you. I will not say it again. Give me his keys."

It was the only time I ever heard him speak like our mother.

She went and brought the keys.

Then the car wouldn't start—"It's out of gas," Jim said—and we had to call the cabdriver back.

At the hospital our dad was asleep. The skin of his face was as orange as earwax. But his arms on the blue blanket were white and thin. I looked away from him.

"Shouldn't we wake him?"

"No, let him sleep," Jim said. He took his wallet from a drawer next to the bed. "Let's write him a note, though. Put his medals on that chair so he can reach them. He'll want to look at those."

I put his sandalwood beads by his water glass so he would discover them first. Then we put the note under the beads.

Outside, our cabdriver was taking a nap. He had his hat pulled over his face. I admired the fact that he could sleep like that. I knew I would never be the kind of man who could sleep on the bench of his cab with his hat down low over his eyes.

Jim patted him gently on the shoulder.

"Take us up Camelback Road," he said. "You know the

Phoenician Hotel? That's where we want to go. It's right at the base of Camelback Mountain. Not Superstition. Camelback."

I hoped we wouldn't be driving through any mountains. My stomach was still bouncing around.

"I always wanted to stay at this resort," Jim said. "When I was in high school my buddies and me used to sneak into their swimming pool. We would listen until some guy ordered a drink and put it on his room. Then once he left we would use his room number. It worked every time. They never caught us. We came back over and over again."

I watched the desert and the condo developments out the window. I was looking for a miniature golf course that I had loved when I was a kid.

"Putting us up at the Phoenician is the least Dad can do. Don't worry. I'll tell him it was my idea. But we won't mention it until we're leaving."

I remember how for a moment I understood my affection for him differently, then. I thought of how women will have sex with a man simply out of admiring and liking him so much. Not because they are attracted in a physical way. As a brother you could understand that.

"Okay," I said.

"And what's the only rule?" He rubbed his nose with his finger. He looked suddenly very happy. We both needed some sun. "There are no stinking rules!" he said.

Under different circumstances our father would have approved this attitude. It may well have been an expression of his. Jim often repeated Dad's expressions, likely without understanding he was doing so. I did not remember that particular slogan. But it was a good one.

When we left Dad was still in the hospital.

"I think they are going to amputate my feet, boys," he told us. "It's my diabetic neuropathy."

Jim looked at me, so that Dad couldn't see his expression, and rolled his eyes. He had been talking to the doctor, who explained that our dad's problems were "largely psychiatric."

"Maybe you can come out to Texas for Christmas, Dad," I said. "Or for New Year's Eve."

"I doubt it, son," he said. "I expect I'll still be right here in this goddamn hospital bed."

It was mostly the ugly and the overweight who worked the phones, and two of Sheila's cousins, twins, who were both in wheelchairs and could not navigate the showcases.

"Some of them used to be on the floor," Jim told me. "Rachel, for example. Then her husband went into the catering business and she put on all that weight. I should have paid to send her to Weight Watchers. She sells three times back here what she ever sold on the floor. That's why I'm sitting you across from her. When you're selling, sell with one ear on Rachel. Take in every word she says. Especially if she's selling a silver contract."

I faced Rachel and I was close enough to her that if she was eating a donut the particles from her mouth almost reached me. That was helpful because it kept my nose down on the phone. I could not watch her chew on her food.

My phone was plastic and red. On my phone I had eight regular lines and ten Rolex lines. The Rolex lines were not sales lines. They were problem lines. These were paid orders we had already taken but the watch was nowhere to be found. The bottom line was the line to Mr. Popper's office. You never used that line.

"We may as well get some blood on your hands, Bobby. Most of these guys are so mad you probably can't make them any madder. Well, that's not true. They can always get madder. Your leverage is the fact that they have paid. They have paid and they are not getting their money back. So use the watch. The watch they don't have yet and are begging for."

I nodded. I looked at the phone as though it were a live animal. A biter.

"Did you do what I told you? Did you watch the news this morning?"

"I said I watched it."

"Okay, fine, you said that. Now take a call. Think about what you are going to say. What was on the news? You need something big."

"There was a fire in Chicago. In a nightclub. A bunch of people died."

"For Christ's sake, Bobby. Don't pretend to be stupid. I know you are not stupid. You can't use a fire in Chicago, Bobby! Come on! Think! We need weather. Was there a tornado? A hurricane? You need international weather. You need— Oh, hell, it doesn't matter. Just grab a call. Do your best."

The Rolex lines were all blinking red. It was five after eight and already all ten Rolex lines were waiting, on hold. There was a special option on the voice mail you could select if you wanted to check on your Rolex. "Push 7 if you are inquiring about the status of your Rolex order." You could leave a message, too, but no one ever checked the message. I tried not to look at Jim, picked up the phone, and pushed a button.

"Fort Worth Deluxe. Thank you for holding. Mr. Myers? Nice to speak with you, Mr. Myers. Yes sir. I understand, sir, I am sorry about that, sir. Yes, I have your information right here, Mr. Myers. Bobby Clark. That's right, that's my name, sir. No sir, Jim is not in the office at the moment. I am his brother, though, and I am fully familiar with your order. Yes, that's right, I have it right here on my computer"—I opened the large filing cabinet next to Jim's desk and started to look for the Matthew Myers file, then Jim pulled it out for me—"a ladies' stainless and gold with a mother-of-pearl diamond dial. That's a beautiful watch, sir, my own wife wears one. The good news is it's here. No, not here in the store, not quite, but here in the country. The factory in Switzerland, that's right, sir, that's where the watch is coming from. But there's been a holdup in Chicago. The flight from Zürich connects in Chicago, that's right, sir, and that's where our customs agents are. That means we've almost got our hands on the watch. Yes, we very much appreciate your patience, Mr. Myers. The holdup is this fire they had there last night. The problem is our broker. His name?"

I looked at Jim. He shook his head. Shrugged. Gave me a thumbs-up sign. He handed me a pen and a pad of paper.

"Schopenhauer," I said. "Schopenhauer is his name. That's right, sir, like the philosopher, Arthur, yes, that's right, sir. I did not know myself until poor Schopenhauer told me. Impressive that you would know that, sir, if you don't mind me saying so. But our man is Swiss, not German. But the problem is this fire, you see. You would not have heard about it—oh, you have heard about it? Yes, that's right. Well, that's the holdup. Our man Schopenhauer was there. Yes sir, we just heard this morning, it's terrible. He was in the fire, you see. We don't know all the details yet. The owner is talking to his wife this morning. My understanding is that he was only injured. Yes, you are right, it's awful, just awful. Of course this is not your problem, sir. I understand that. But you see, he is brokering a shipment of about one hundred Rolexes for us at the moment, and your wife's new watch is in that shipment. There are about ninety-nine other people also waiting for watches, if that is any consolation, sir. No, yes, I see that, I have it right here, your ordering date. I know how long we've had your money, sir. The watch is here, sir, it is in Chicago waiting to be shipped to us. As soon as it clears customs it will be on the next plane to Dallas–Fort Worth. Yes sir. They have other brokers. We do need our regular broker, sir, you understand, customs is very complicated. I don't know if Schopenhauer's office is even aware of the situation yet, sir. The fire was just last night. Our owner is on the phone now solving the problem, sir. If you can just bear with us. I know how long you have been waiting, sir. But we have our health, don't we? Better than poor Schopenhauer can say. No, that was not a joke, sir. Do I recognize the seriousness of the situation? Schopenhauer is a dear friend of mine, I have known him for ten years. Well, thank you, sir, I appreciate that. I am sure Schopenhauer would say the same. Don't worry sir. Thank you, sir. Thank you, Mr. Myers. Goodbye."

"Perfect," Jim said. He was very pleased. He grabbed me happily by the shoulder. "Great! Now we can tell him the paperwork was burnt up in the fire. That guy—what is his name?—that Chicago broker could have accidentally taken the paperwork with him."

"It was a nightclub."

140

"Doesn't matter. We can all be mad at him! What kind of a moron takes his important papers to a nightclub? Where did we find this joker? We are never doing business with him again! But the watches are in limbo until customs gets the new papers. It could be weeks, even months. But it's not our fault. It's that damn broker. And hard to be too mad at him, after all, with his burns and recovery. There you go. That's exactly what I was trying to teach you. Let's use that same line on everybody this morning. They all get the fire story. What's that guy's name? Here, write it down for me. I like how it sounds, what did you say it is? French?"

I showed him where I had written it down on the page of legal pad that would go into Myers's file. "It's German," I said.

"Huh. That spelling doesn't help. How do you say that? Say it for me again. I like that name. Let's use that a lot. Poor ole Shoopenhauer."

"Schopenhauer," I said.

"Right, got it. Shoopenhauer. Burned up in the great Chicago fire of 1987."

He picked up a line. "This is Brad Reynolds on Rolexes, how can I help you? Mr. Branson? Oh, yes sir, one moment, let me look up your information on the computer, sir. No sir, I'm afraid Jim Clark is out at an auction today. But I can certainly help you, sir. A men's Explorer? Beautiful watch, I used to own one myself. Now, sir, your watch has arrived in the United States, but let me explain to you about the customs process. You see, there was a fire last night in Chicago. Oh, you heard? Yes, ghastly. Just terrible. Well, the problem is this."

•

Out on the highway, on the runs, was like working the back-of-the-house. The back-of-the-house had a camaraderie and ease that the sales floor lacked. In back you could feel that the customers were not people. Being out on the highway, doing the runs, you listened to whatever music you pleased, you could stop at Hardee's and eat an order of chicken strips with that mustard sauce, you could find a park and stop there for a while—there was a cemetery near Granddad's where I often stopped in the late afternoons—and read a chapter of a book or just lie on your back and watch the clouds. I wished Lisa could come hang out with me there. Even in the cold I would lie there, some afternoons, for half an hour, between the gravestones, and smoke a joint, and smell the winter air.

As Christmas approached and my phone sales improved they let me leave the store less and less. I was often at the top of the daily phone sales board, and a couple of times I made the top of the week. That meant a five-hundred-dollar cash bonus. So Sheila kept me on the phones all day long, but in the evenings I still did my Dallas runs.

This December night it was after eight and I called from Kizakov's to tell Jim I was going to drive straight home after I made the last Dallas drop. But he wasn't there. I asked for Lisa and she wasn't there, either. So I changed my mind about going straight home and thought I would swing by the store and see if they were back yet. They probably just went out for a quick bite of dinner, I thought. Maybe all three of us could go get a beer before we went home. And then Jim and I could ride home together.

In the parking garage I saw the two of them. Lisa was sitting on the nose of Jim's car with her hands between her legs and Jim stood a few feet away from her. It was dark and cold in the garage but light came through the open-aired space from the next building over. When you were getting into your car you could look into their office windows at night.

Jim and Lisa had not seen me. I had parked the car at the other end and was heading for the elevator when I saw it was them. I moved between two cars to watch them.

Lisa was crying.

I could hear Jim saying, "Oh, Lisa. What were you . . . ?"

I held my breath to listen more closely.

She said, "I don't know what to do now. I'm afraid to go home."

I listened closer still.

"I didn't even remember my stupid shirt," she said. "I'm such a moron. I didn't even want to tell you."

"I want to help you, Lisa," he said. He ran his fingers down the side of her face. "I mean, I'm here for you. That's not what I'm saying. But this time you need to clean up this mess of yours yourself."

I drove home. I should get on I-35 and drive back to Canada, I thought. Due north. While you two go enjoy your own private lives together.

It was the next night, after closing, and Lisa and I were alone in Mr. Popper's office. She sat on his desk. Her feet didn't touch the floor. Her yellow shoes dangled from her toes. Those curvy, high-arched feet of hers, in her black hose.

She brought it up all on her own. That was welcome.

"I need some money, Bobby," she said.

I had a little bit of money. It was money that had accumulated from my lunch-money borrowing from the cash drawer, and from a few larger receipts I had torn up and pocketed all of the cash. A tennis bracelet for nine hundred was my biggest hit. I had about fifteen hundred dollars hidden in a shoe box in the closet of my bedroom at Jim's. Along with the Christmas presents I had stolen for Wendy and her family, and a rope of pearls I thought my mom would like. The exact amount of cash was thirteen hundred and sixty dollars. I often counted it at night before going to sleep.

"I could give you some money," I told her. "I could give you five hundred. Actually, I have two thousand dollars I could give you if you wanted." I could steal the missing six hundred from the cash box tomorrow, if necessary. Or give her part of my paycheck.

I did not care about the money. I never cared about the money, in fact. It was just fun to have it for a while.

She laughed. But it was not her regular laugh.

"I wasn't asking you for money, Bobby. I was just telling you. To talk about it. I am in a little trouble. A real bit of trouble."

She pulled on her fingers that way she sometimes did.

I wished I could tell her what I had seen the night before. I could help her solve the problem as well as Jim, I figured. Better. He thought you needed to learn from your mistakes. He would do that to me when we were growing up. "Consequences suck, Bobby," he would say. I had been thinking up a plan. If Lisa and I went back to Canada I would get my old job at the gas station back. We might rent an apartment. If the police were involved they couldn't get her in Canada. Or whoever it was that was after her. Calgary is a long way from Texas.

"If you were ever, like, if you had broken the law or something, anything like that, I would want to help you," I said. "Any kind of help, I mean. Not just money."

Then her mood seemed to change.

She laughed again. But this time it was such a happy, kind laugh that it made me realize she hadn't laughed that way in weeks.

I was not sure what to say next.

"Let's talk about something else," she said.

Two gigantic light fixtures made of glass butterflies turned very slowly in the ceiling. They sent spots of every color across the room and the long, pale Arabian carpets.

"Don't take it so hard, Bobby. Don't worry so much." I must have looked crestfallen. "Come over here to kiss me," Lisa said. "Come give me one of those Bobby kisses."

We kissed while I stood and she sat on the edge of Mr. Popper's enormous metal desk with her knees bent around me, in her legs as I was, and her arms dangling like free tree limbs over my shoulders and neck and arms and my back.

It was not a complicated theft. Lisa wasn't why I stole the money. It was just there. I saw the ten thousand dollars on the bookkeeper's desk, so I placed five thousand dollars in each of my shoes. The shoes were too big, which helped. Jim had bought them for me that first day I landed, the day with Lisa and the limousine, and I had wanted big ones. I was timid to ask for the correct, smaller size with Lisa looking on. They were my black alligators. It was December 17 and I was standing in my socks in the bookkeeper's office with ten thousand dollars in my shoes on the floor. I tried pushing my feet in just as they were and it turned out there was no need even to untie the bows. They were that loose. Plus I was wearing silk socks.

With the cash under my feet the shoes actually fit better. I hurried down the back hallway and out into the crowd of customers, trying to be as inconspicuous as possible, while also trying to look like it was just ordinary me, on my way out the door to lunch. I couldn't look back over my shoulder to see if anyone saw me leaving. Then I was outside. I walked through the icy streets of downtown Fort Worth to the bank a few blocks from the store and wired half of the money to my old bank account at Royal Bank in Calgary. It would be safe, there, in Canada. Lisa needed the money, but it was a good idea to put a little aside for myself, too. This was my first bank account and I had had it since I was seven years old. I had opened it for my paper route. For my collections money. Plus that way once I gave Lisa the other half, all the money would be gone, and I didn't want any of it around. No evidence.

The only tricky part about the stealing was the wiring paperwork. I figured I should save it in case the wire did not go through. Then when I came back to the store I lost my nerve and tore it up and flushed it down the toilet. This was in the executive bathroom right outside the bookkeeper's office where I had discovered the money. The same bathroom by the stairs to Popper's office, that we weren't supposed to use that I always used. When I went back to the bathroom to check on the toilet, perhaps twenty minutes later—thinking I better make sure, because I had been afraid to look under the lid when I flushed it the first time—when I lifted the lid I saw the torn-up paper was still in the bowl. I tore up the wet paper smaller and flushed it again with some toilet paper. The third flush it finally went down. But if someone had found that paper that would have been it.

Mr. Popper sat behind his desk and Sheila paced around the room. She nearly tripped over my legs as she walked, and then again over my feet. But she didn't say anything to me. The bar fridges were on the floor, built into enormous Chinese lac-quered cabinets on one wall, so I was on my hands and knees.

I was stocking Mr. Popper's two bar fridges with Diet Dr Peppers, Tabs, Perrier, and gold-lidded pints of strawberry and coffee Häagen-Dazs ice cream.

Behind Mr. Popper a television was tuned to the news. It was on mute. There was a story about the ice storm that had closed much of the city. This was the big ice storm of 1987 and everyone said it was grisly news for the store because no one would come downtown in the ice, and we were only a week from Christmas. At this time of year we could see five hundred thousand dollars a day on the showroom floor. That was not counting the phones. But the ice storm could kill all of that.

Three salesmen, plus Jim, Dennis, and Popper's wife, Sheila, were seated at Popper's desk. Everyone faced Mr. Pop-per, watching him. No one noticed me. This was a good thing about being sixteen. They did not see me in the same way they saw one another. To encourage them not to think about me I kept my eyes on my stocking. If I seemed interested I would suddenly be less innocent. I endeavored to restock the contents of the refrigerator in the manner of a child who, with-out knowing how it had happened, found himself playing a boy's game among the legs, faces, and mysterious conversations of a group of friendly adults. But I also needed to stay in the office for as long as possible so that I could hear this conver-sation.

As a teenager I was not frightened. Perhaps I was jumpy.

"It wasn't Lisa," Jim said. "She reported it."

"It could have been anyone."

"She wants to take a polygraph."

"A polygraph won't catch an expert fucking prevaricator like that. Don't fucking kid yourself. They don't have a polygraph machine strong enough to trip up her kind of prevarication."

That was Sheila. She loved the word prevaricator. I asked Jim about it once and he said the story was that she had once accused her father of telling a lie and he had told her not to use that word because it was a hateful word—"Two words a Christian won't use," he had supposedly said, "hate, and lie"—so Sheila always said prevaricator, prevaricate, and prevarication. Apparently Mr. Popper had tried to switch her to dissimulation because it had a less rednecky ring to it, but no luck. She was always accusing everyone around her of prevaricating. That's the kind of person she was.

"She's a cokehead. Everybody knows it. A cokehead will do anything."

"It might have been a customer. Someone using the bathroom."

"They would have been with a salesperson. Don't be ridiculous. A customer is never back in that bathroom alone. Plus who would go into Cindy's office?"

"If the door was open. With the cash just sitting there."

"We can check the cameras."

"I can't believe Cindy would walk away from her desk with that cash on it. What was that woman thinking?" This was Mr. Popper. I glanced up and saw the way he glared at his wife. Cindy the bookkeeper was Sheila's responsibility. She reported directly to Sheila.

I never had the courage to look at my own wife that way, later. That was a look men used to have with their wives that we men today have forsaken, relinquished, or lost.

"There are no cameras in the bathroom."

"Not in the bathroom. To see who went in back. They have timers on them. We can check them against the time."

"I know it wasn't Lisa," Jim said.

"The cameras are on the showcases. There are no cameras in back. The cameras are all on the floor."

"It could have been Cindy. Why not Cindy? I would be tempted if I were her," Dennis said. What an innocent thing to say, I thought. You can learn from that, Bobby, I told myself. Dennis was that smart. That street-smart, I mean.

"It wasn't Cindy, you moron. For chrissake."

That was Sheila again. She always frightened me. She was not the sort of person who thought children—children like I am only a child, really, I wanted to remind them all—were naïve. Plus she did not even like her own children. She would have fired me over that first Rolex deal if I hadn't been Jim's little brother.

"Cindy was in the bathroom. That's why the money was on her desk."

"These fucking salespeople. No fucking gratitude." Sheila swore frequently. In Texas they call it cursing. "Why do you curse so much, Sheila?" Roger or Paul would ask her, and she would say, "Fuck you," to be funny. But to a Canadian it was unnerving.

"Ten grand. It takes some balls to stick ten grand in your purse."

"Or your pocket. Why does it have to be a purse?" Jim said. He was a defender of women. Or maybe he was still thinking of Lisa.

"A lousy ten grand," Popper said. "Why take the risk for that? Frustrating. I don't care about the damn money."

"Well I sure as fuck care about the money, Ronnie. And you should damn well care yourself."

"You're missing the point, Sheila. The point is there is a criminal among us."

He was Ali Baba in the house of a thousand thieves and he trusted these people. I have since noticed that both trusting and trustworthy people often have this problem of insufficient skepticism and investigation of the truth. It may be a laziness they share.

"Not even into that hallway? There must be a camera that can check that."

"They had to put the money somewhere. That's a good point. That much money wouldn't fit in your pants pockets."

"You wouldn't walk back into the phone room. Too many people."

"You would be too nervous."

"We might see if someone let a customer through the gate."

"Why take the cash off Cindy's desk when you knew it would be noticed? Why not just hit the cash box? You could hit the cash box every day and no one would ever notice." I glanced up because of a familiar sound in the way he said it and there was Jim giving me a close look. I arranged the cans of soda. Dr Peppers on the left, Tabs on the right. In the door were Sheila's Frescas and Perriers.

"I mean, if you are a thief," Jim said.

"You can't take money from the cash box like that. We reconcile it every night before we leave."

"Well, technically, I think you could. Come to think of it. That's something we better change. Shit, this is depressing."

"How many times do I have to tell you, Ronnie? You can't believe a word they say. Little pieces of shit."

"Plus the temptation. She should never have left it sitting there."

"It could have been anyone. We could polygraph them. The suspects. The ones who probably might have done it."

"What about the Polack? There's something sinister about that girl."

"She's not a thief," Popper said quickly. "No, it's not her."

I saw Sheila Popper give her husband a quick, sour glance. Jim and Dennis wiped their faces blank. But I saw them trying not to look at each other.

"Why this now?" Popper said. "Why did she just leave it on her desk? This is all we need." Mr. Popper hammered his desk with his brass Rolex paperweight. It was the signature Rolex crown but the size of a soup bowl. He was not angry. He was sad.

"We could call the cops. That might put a scare into someone."

"We are not calling the fucking cops, you fuckhead."

"Sheila! Control yourself!"

"If we polygraph anyone we have to polygraph everyone. Everyone who was here today, anyhow. That's the new law."

"I bet it was Roger." Roger was the Watchman. "I don't trust that guy. Plus he's getting divorced."

"How did they get the money out of the store?"

"It's only a few steps from the bathroom."

"Cindy couldn't have been in the bathroom."

"That's another reason why it couldn't be the Polack," Jim said. He looked at Popper as he said it. "The Polack was in the bathroom. That's what we said. We already established that."

"I thought it was Cindy in the bathroom."

"Do we know that?" Dennis said. "All we know is that somebody was in the front bathroom."

"I still think it could be Roger. Rita says it's a very messy divorce. Those are expensive. He isn't making any real sales lately, either."

Rita was an idea, I thought. The way she watched Lisa and me.

"Suppose for the sake of argument it was Cindy," Mr. Popper said. "She would have stolen something else. Why take just ten K? She could have hit us for tens of thousands. Maybe hundreds of thousands."

"Only a real dummy would take ten thousand dollars off the bookkeeper's desk like that." This was Jim. His tone was unpleasant for me to hear.

"We're not all thieves, Sheila," Dennis said.

"Dennis, just shut the fuck up," Sheila said.

There was a quiet moment.

"I bet it was Rita," I said. I said it very quietly, like I was speaking to the carpet and not the grown-ups in the room. I supposed nobody might even hear me.

Sheila said, "From the mouths of babes."

"I wouldn't want to think that. Golly, I hate to think that," Ronnie said.

"She's been disgruntled," Jim said.

"Hell, disgruntled! That's one word for it. Pissed off is another. Pissed off is what I'd call it," Mr. Popper said. "Ever since last Christmas. Or maybe it was the Christmas before that."

"She's been demanding a raise for three years," Sheila said. "I wouldn't put it past her."

"I bet you're right, Bobby," Dennis said. He looked back at me with the cold face of a lizard. You know something, you bastard, I thought. You know it was me. "I bet it was Rita."

"It's always the one you don't suspect, isn't it?"

"Rita. Huh. Who would have guessed?" Jim said. He was always the store's best closer.

It was late, the highway was black, and his cheeks and nose were green in the light from the speedometer and the other gauges. Jim and I were driving home.

"I am worn out," he said. "I hope all this is worth it."

The windshield wipers squeaked. I opened the window a crack. Outside, more sleet was falling. I thought about how our little black car must look on the black highway in the icy rain, from high above us, with the yellow beams of the headlights stretching out in front. The highway was already freezing over. Tomorrow the roads would be closed. But tonight, after Jim and Lily were asleep, I would drive to Lisa's.

I found the money, Bobby. I can't take this money."

After we had made love I crept out of the bedroom, very late, with her asleep in the bed behind me, and left the five thousand dollars where she would find it in the morning. To beat Jim to the store I would be up and at work before she was even out of bed. I wanted to be waiting for him outside when he got there. So that he didn't think I was hiding from him.

I understood that she would not take the cash if I tried to give it to her. This way she could pretend it was from Jim, or Santa Claus. But then she woke up in the early morning to get a glass of water or smoke a cigarette and found it. She woke me up with the light on and there she was, at the end of the bed, with the five thousand dollars out in front of her on the bed.

"It wasn't like that. I didn't steal it for you. I didn't mean to steal it at all, really. It was totally innocent. I'm serious. It was practically an accident. What happened was I was taking a short-cut from the steamer room past the Rolex desk so I could ask the Watchman a price for a ladies' all-stainless"—because we were so close to Christmas the price and availability on all-steel models changed daily, like bullion—"and I wanted to stop by the back bathroom on the way to do a bump. So the quick way was through Cindy's office."

"We are not supposed to walk that way."

"I know. That's what I am saying. It was just bad luck. So I'm hurrying through and I almost walked right past it. There were two stacks of bills, side by side, like bricks, you know, on the desk. I smiled toward where I expected Cindy to be sitting, to say, Gosh isn't that nice, a big stack of cash like that, and her chair was empty. So, you know, they don't have cameras in there," I said.

"I bet they will now, " Lisa said.

I wanted to say, Look, I know you need the money, and maybe you could even tell me why. But I did not want to interfere with her love for me in any way at all. I tried to recover control of the conversation.

"One thing about me, Lisa, is I was raised by bankrupts. That teaches you not to take property very seriously. Plus, being Canadian. You know. Socialism."

"Other people's property, you mean."

She had an odd look on her face that I couldn't decipher.

"Right. That's my problem. That's exactly what I'm saying. I don't treat other people's property with the proper seriousness. It's just a weakness I have. It's not like I had malicious intentions. It's my nature. My upbringing."

"Well, now they are polygraphing the whole store, Bobby," Lisa said. "The whole damn store. And you have brought me into it by giving me this money."

"You don't have anything to worry about," I said.

"What if I do? Bobby. This only makes things worse. Bobby, you don't know what they are going to ask about. Did you even think about why I need the money? That could come out too, Bobby. Anything could come out."

She reached over and grabbed one of the pillows. She wrapped her arms around it like it was a stuffed animal.

"It's not your fault. It's like your brother said . . . well, I mean, it's my own damn mess, not yours."

I watched her carefully. I knew that if I spoke she would stop talking. I strove to look like I was only there to listen.

"The thing is, Bobby, well, you know I have other people, other friends outside the store. They are not guys like you and Jim. They are a different kind of people. Not nice people. I mean, they aren't bad people exactly. But they are wild, you know?"

I could be wild, too, I thought. But I knew I couldn't say it.

"Anyway, I'm not going into it. But there was this party, and—"

"When were you at a party?" How did she have time to go to a party? "What people are you talking about?" Don't talk, Bobby, I told myself. She is trying to confess.

"Bobby, honey, listen to me. I am trying to tell you. You know, baby, this is really—well, it's not that it's none of your business, that's not what I'm saying. I'm just worrying about both of us, you know?"

She didn't understand that I could help her, if she would let me. That I wasn't concerned about anything except her.

"This is so ridiculous. I can't believe how stupid we are. Now that I'm talking about it, it was just like you. I'm sitting here judging you and it was just like you and this fucking money." She picked up the stack of bills and then put it back down again.

"I know you're not judging me," I said. "You can tell me anything, Lisa. I don't care." I wanted to say, I love you.

"You know, the funny thing is I wasn't even going to go to the stupid party. I was driving home."

"After work, you mean."

Was this Saturday she was talking about? But when I saw them in the parking garage it was Friday—so then it must have been Thursday. But on Thursday hadn't she stayed late and closed with Jim and me?

"You know how sometimes you just drive somewhere without even thinking, like knowing where you're going but not ever deciding to go there? And they were all fucked up, some of them had been partying for days. I kept trying to leave. Then the next thing you know it's me and this other guy and we are practically the only ones who aren't passed out. And there's a stash of drugs and money in this guy's place and nobody knows where he keeps it, but my friend said he wanted to show me."

"Your friend, you mean, the guy? Which guy?"

"Just listen for a minute, okay? I'm trying to tell you. Then, you know, whatever, and next thing he's passed out, too. It was just that easy. So I grabbed this stuff and I left and that was that. Just like you did at the store. I walked out. I mean, it could have been anybody, right? But they know it was me. They already went to my dealer and fucked him up, just because. They held him

157

down and burned him, Bobby. With the lit end of a cigar. Now I can't even be here. I shouldn't have even let you come over here. Oh, Bobby," she said, and for a second I hoped she was going to start crying. But when I reached toward her she stiffened.

"And even this five grand, even if I could take it. It would get me out of town. Maybe I could like leave half of it in my mailbox for them or something. You know, like, to calm them down. That might help a little, if they don't know where I am. But you stole this money, Bobby, and Popper's rent-a-cops are going to catch you. Now you've brought the store into this . . . I don't know, Bobby. And what about you? I can't have you going to jail because you were trying to help me. Oh Christ, Bobby. This is a real mess, you know? This is a real fucking mess we made together."

She wasn't looking at me. She was looking across the room at nothing. Her neck was as lovely as a person's wrist.

"Neither one of us can go back. That's the thing, that's the truth of it. This jewelry business is not the right thing for you anyway. It is just like how some people should not be married because they make each other worse. That's jewelry for you, Bobby. It's like Miracle-Gro on your failings. Mine, too. I've been wanting to tell you that anyway, and now—" She waved her hand at the money. "I'm staying up all night and packing and getting out of here."

"Good, okay," I said. "Let's go. Good idea. I'll come. I'll come with you." Then I laid my head down on her legs. I didn't want to see her face when I said it.

"Oh, baby. Come on. I'm sorry, but that is not something we can do. But you have to leave, that's for sure. Don't go to work. Make up some lie. You need to get on a plane back to Canada, as quick as you can get a ticket. That's what you should do. Go back to Wendy. Go home, Bobby. If you don't they could put you in prison. You have got to start growing up, now. Both of us do, I guess."

"I don't want you to go," I said into her folded legs. She scratched at my head very lightly with her fingertips. "I want to stay with you."

In the morning, when I woke up in her bed, with her blue comforter twisted around me, she was gone. I looked at her alarm clock. It was almost nine-thirty. Now Jim would want to know why I was late.

The lie detector tests began two days later, on December 23, so I stayed home sick with a stomachache.

"I think I need to go to the hospital," I said. "I think it's my appendix."

"You can't really take today off, Bobby," Jim said. "I mean, unless you're dying. It's the biggest day of the year. Christmas Eve is nothing like the day before Christmas Eve. This is it. This is the money day. Plus the polygraphs. That would look funny. They are doing them all day long. Don't you have an appointment? Did you sign the sign-up sheet? Everybody has to sign the sign-up sheet."

Dennis had given me the sign-up sheet with a look like he was passing a collection plate at church. I scribbled two mostly unrecognizable words that resembled the Watchman's name, perhaps, a bit, and passed it on.

"I'm on there," I said. "I'm interviewing tomorrow. You could sign up for today or tomorrow. I am really sick, here, Jim.

I feel like my appendix is going to burst or something. I am nauseated and I have this sharp pain in my side."

"Uh-huh. Okay," he said. "I am not making any excuses for you. This is the one day. This is the big day and you're blowing it. It's your call."

He looked at me with that look your mother gives you when she knows you are pretending to be sick.

"Better call an ambulance if it gets any worse," he said, and plugged in the phone by my bed. "Go ahead. Pull a James Clark. Pull a Dad on me. Don't blame me."

I had to stay in bed because Lily was in and out of the house all day but I didn't want to get out of bed anyway. I was trying not to think about Lisa. I smoked pot and reread *Autobiography of a Yogi*. I called Wendy but no one answered the phone. I counted my other, separate stash of hundreds and twenties in the closet, and looked over the Christmas gifts I had stolen for people I loved. I looked at the tourmaline-and-ivory ring I had put aside for Lisa. I couldn't give her any of her gifts now. It would be okay for Wendy, I thought. But you couldn't size it. And Wendy's fingers were fatter than Lisa's.

Jim was home after midnight. He was drunk and excited. He woke me up.

"Hey, I'm sorry," he said. "The way you were acting I half thought it was you. I owe you an apology. How's your stomach? Is it any better? Sorry I woke you up. I just thought you would want to know. You were right. It was Rita. I can't believe it. They did a few polygraphs and Rita was up early on the list and they caught her. They postponed the rest of the polygraphs until after Christmas so we can focus this last twenty-four hours."

He was sniffling a lot.

"Man, what a day I had. Fadeen called and bought that seventeen-carat. Six hundred grand. I already had it mounted and shipped. That's a thirty-thousand-dollar commission. One day. Ronnie and I have been out drinking Dom. He gave me that nephrite hippopotamus lighter, too. Just as a bonus. We rented a limousine and hit some Dallas bars." I hadn't seen him drunk very often. Maybe never before. "The Polack went, too. I should have asked Lisa, I guess. But she didn't show up for work. Two days in a row, now. Everybody was real suspicious about that until they caught Rita. I don't know where the hell she is. I guess I better call her."

I started to say something. I half sat up in the bed.

"Shhh," he said, looking back over his shoulder into the dark bedroom and the open hallway beyond.

"Lily's sleeping. We sure don't want to wake that up. Okay, go on back to sleep, buddy. I love you. Sorry again. Take the day off again tomorrow if you want. Tomorrow's Christmas Eve, it's not such a big day. Today was the day. But you needed the rest. Hell, it's Christmas, you've earned it. I love you, Bobby."

We didn't normally say that, because we were brothers. I knew he was only drunk but I didn't care.

"No, wake me up," I said. The relief of being innocent was hitting me like two lungfuls of crank. "I want to be there. I want to end the season with you and Mr. Popper and every-body. Don't let me sleep in."

All the highways were closed. There were semis and cars spilled around the city, on the edges of roads at odd angles, like someone had sprayed a deck of cards over I-30 and I-35. The big ice storm had broken very early that morning, Christmas Eve, but before we opened the doors the customers were stretched for more than half a mile down Houston Street.

Because of taking the back roads Jim and I were in late, at almost eight o'clock, and as we drove into the parking garage and witnessed it he said, "What the hell is going on, it's like a hockey game," before we understood that the line out front was for us, for the store. We made the news that day. But really as part of another, bigger headline, which I will now explain.

It was the biggest Christmas Eve the store had ever seen, and it was the biggest Christmas Eve I would ever see. The customers were packed in like kids at a concert. You could not walk through the showroom. If there had been a fire, hundreds of people would have died. The rent-a-cops didn't like it but Mr. Popper was back there getting them drunk. He was getting everyone drunk, putting champagne, Baileys Irish Cream, and Sheila's Texas Hill Country secret recipe of ninety-proof eggnog into the hands of anyone who would take a glass. "I don't understand how it doesn't curdle," people would say after taking a sip. But they drank it down. There was a line of salespeople waiting to get into the diamond room with their best crows waiting on the other side. Jim said afterward that Mr. Popper took in two million in seven hours. It was possible. These people were like women on the seventy-percent-off blue-tag day at Neiman's Last Call. But they were buying fine jewelry.

Around the middle of the afternoon Mr. Popper disappeared. That was unusual on Christmas Eve. Normally that was the one day of the year he would spend the whole day out on the floor with us, Jim said. About an hour later the crowd began to water down. There were drunks among the customers and the Watchman was passed out in his chair at his desk. Sheila was nowhere to be found, probably doing a last-minute shopping run herself. The rent-a-cops were blinking their eyes. One of them was twirling his leather-billed hat like a top on the banks of video monitors. They were waiting for their Christmas bonuses. Soon Popper would be down with the envelopes.

By shortly after five we had chased out our last panicky I-can't-believe-it's-Christmas-Eve-already husband, and locked the big double plate-glass-and-brass doors, and yet there was no Mr. Popper. People needed to get to their own families. But not without those December commission checks and the Christmas bonuses. We knew Cindy had been calculating and printing them all day yesterday and today. Mr. Popper signed them and then sealed them in an envelope, each with its bonus, which was secret and in cash. We were not allowed to discuss our bonuses. But I knew Jim was expecting fifteen grand or better.

With all of us gathered idly around the showcases and wandering in and out of the back-of-the-house, at last Jim said, "I'll go see what's up," assuming Popper was up in his office, but then Mr. Popper appeared at the front door. Outside the front door, I mean. We saw him through the glass. He had his keys in his hands and he opened the door. Then he stopped and opened the lock on the other door, the one we often did not bother to open, so that both doors could swing wide. He came into the middle of the showroom floor among the showcases. He was ringed with policemen and more serious-looking strangers, and then I knew with clarity what would happen next. They had lied to Jim about Rita to lure me back into the store. Or it might be, even, that Jim had lied. But no, that couldn't be. They had tricked him because we were brothers and now I was caught. Lisa was right. She knew not to come back. Why hadn't I listened to her? I thought I was so fucking clever. I outsmarted everybody. Now they would arrest me in front of everyone and take me to prison in cuffs. The doors were locked and there was no place to escape to. The salespeople and the rent-a-cops and the phone sales women and the Watchman and the other back-of-the-house guys and the Wizard and the gift-wrappers and the black-fingered jewelers in their aprons and the beautiful teenage hostesses and Jim all surged softly toward Popper, expecting. They didn't understand what was about to happen. They could never feel sorry for me, not on Christmas Eve. It was like a pack. I tried to drift to the back. But they were thick around me. I did not know where to run. My eyes were starting to fill with tears. And Popper spoke.

"Well, Merry Christmas, everyone," he said.

I thought perhaps I could feign fainting. Or faint for real, even.

"I have some bad news. Don't want to keep you good folks waiting around on Christmas Eve any longer than necessary. I really hate to do what I've been given no choice but to do." Run, Bobby. The doors are unlocked. Run! "Seems these fellas here"—and he waved his arm generally at the men around him, who moved in closer—"think we've—that is, I've—been up to some kind of wrongdoing. They aren't too specific on the particulars, and you all don't need to worry none. Don't worry about any single little thing. Our lawyers will have this solved in no time, you can rest assured of that." And he gave one of the men in particular a hard look. The man looked away at his shoes. "But they're closing us down." A wind went through the room. "And I'm afraid they won't let me write you your Christmas checks. These boys won't let me put a single damn dollar in your pockets for your families' Christmases. And I know better than anyone how hard you've worked and how much you deserve it. I'm sorry. I'm truly sorry. And, for what it's worth, Merry Christmas."

He was tearing up. He smiled this strong smile.

"All right, fellas, let's get this done."

There was silence. Someone started to cry. Then a couple more joined in. Someone said, "Goodbye, Mr. Popper." I expected a round of applause. They bundled him up and took him away. Three or four of the serious men in badly cut blue suits stayed behind to collect the store keys. They even collected case keys. The people who had safe combinations wrote them down. The men answered every question with a business card that had a lawyer's phone number on it. They would not even respond to the questions of the rent-a-cops, who were important regular off-duty Fort Worth policemen.

Jim handed in his keys and we drove home.

"I wonder how long I'll get to keep the Porsche," he said as we stepped cautiously up the icy steps to his door.

The day after Christmas I went back to Wendy and Calgary. Lisa had taken the money, that morning, but I had my stash in the closet, and the other five grand was waiting for me at the Royal Bank of Canada. I used it to buy Wendy a car, a preowned Fiat Spider convertible. I gave it to her for Valentine's Day. That was my first car. Then, a year or so later, Jim called and asked me to join him in his new business. We called it Clark's Precious Jewels.

PART TWO

We were sitting in Jim's office beneath the new Lalique crystal chandelier. "It will interfere with grading diamonds for color," Jim had said while they were hanging it, "but I don't give a damn. The thing is so expensive it will put people in the mood."

"Speaking of money, how are we doing? Did you call Donnie today?" I asked him. Donnie was our principal Fort Worth banker. Not for our loans but for our operating accounts. The borrowing bankers were all in Dallas. We called Donnie every morning to find out our balances. "Did you make that deal with Alan?"

"He'll be in before the weekend. You know Alan. He's very reliable when it comes to business. Plus the bracelet is right here." He shook a bulging job envelope on his desk. "He says he's got a big party this weekend. He won't show up without this bracelet on."

169

It was an eighteen-karat yellow gold Rolex-style bracelet with round diamonds bezel-set on the small outside links, and baguette-cut diamonds bar-set all the way up the center link. The clasp was invisible so the diamonds went all the way around the wrist. An ugly thing, bulky, inelegant, but technically successful and sturdily made.

Jim would sell Alan and our other drug-dealer and celebrity clients crap like this because it was what they wanted and it was very profitable. I made the mistake of trying to sell them what I wanted to see them wearing. I still believed I could be proud of my customers. The ones I liked, I mean.

We were sorting a package of the tiny round diamonds called diamond melee at Jim's desk. As he aged I noticed, more and more, how much Jim looked like our father. They carried their shoulders in the same way. Especially when he bent over the desk to inspect the diamond melee he might have been our father, viewed from behind, with a few extra pounds and with shorter hair.

"How did the sweeps come out?" I asked Jim. "Did you send Granddad his cut?"

"Great," he said. "Yeah, I sent it to him. I had Sosa run it over. He said he seemed nervous. Probably should have brought it myself. I've got your envelope, too. It's right here in my drawer."

At the end of every month we gathered the gold sweeps from the benches and the casting area and sent it over to the smelters. Half of that cash went to me and Jim, and the other half went straight to Granddad, in the same courier package with the profit-and-loss statement and the ledger on his merchandise accounts. Initially our system had made Granddad anxious. Like most multimillionaires, over the years he had learned to avoid cash.

"What about the IRS?" Granddad had asked. "I can't do a damn thing with this, Grandson. Can I deposit it in the bank?"

"Spend it! It's pocket change for you. It's the sweeps, Granddad," we told him. For us these days he was like that rich duck who visits Huey, Dewey, and Louie.

"It's untraceable income. You know how it works. We just sweep up the gold dust from the drilling off the floor. You sweep every night and this is what you have at the end of thirty days." We did not mention the extras that never went to the smelter, or that we kept half of every sweep for ourselves.

"But you probably shouldn't deposit it in a bank, no," Jim had said. "A safety deposit box would be fine."

"I don't think you're listening to me. I wasn't asking. I was telling. This is a great system you've thought up, Grandson. We all go to jail together," Granddad had said.

It was strange that Jim had not told me about the sweeps coming in.

"Glad you asked. I was about to tell you," he said, and gave me a look. He pulled the envelope from his desk drawer and slid it over to me. "Forty-four hundred. Almost twice what we got last month. I love it when we are building this much custom. The extra cutting and polishing make all that much more gold dust. Even the platinum was up this month. If we knew what we were doing we'd start our own smelting company."

That reassured me. He didn't sound like he was making that up.

"Wendy will be happy," I said. "Seems like that's the only thing I can do these days to please her."

He didn't look up as he spoke.

"It's just the baby. It's called departum depression. When the baby departs the womb. She'll come around. Concentrate on work, Bobby," he said. "That's what I do. Take one worry at a time. Focus on things you can fix. The other problems will solve themselves."

"She wants me home more, she says. But as soon as I walk in the door she hands me the baby. I feel like all I do is work, and then I work more when I get home."

"She won't even drive up here to meet you for lunch," Jim said. "I mean, I don't want to say anything. But she should make an effort, too. It takes both of you. I hate to say it, but I told you not to marry a Canadian. They don't understand the business environment. It's foreign to them. They don't understand what it takes to make it down here. Lily was no better than Wendy is, in that way. That's why this time around I bought American-made in the wife department. Look at Wendy's old man. He's a professor, for chrissake. A Canadian college teacher. He probably drives a damn Volvo. I bet he was home every day by three o'clock. That's what she's comparing you with."

I tried to remember if Wendy and I had been happy before the baby was born. But as far as I could remember the last time we had had sex was when she got pregnant. That was nearly two years ago, on my twenty-fourth birthday. Now I was almost twenty-six years old, and the baby was about to turn one.

Wendy hated the store and over the years she had come to dislike Jim. She would even come out and say it. "I hate that fucking store," she would say, and I would say, "Wendy, that store is our life." But I was trying to make us rich. This was what it took. Then we'd have time together. And great vacations. It wouldn't be like this much longer. I told her that, too. The night before, when we started to fight about it again, I tried to explain this to her. I had said, "I promise, it's temporary. I love you. Give me five years. I love Claire. I want to be home more." That last was a lie, but all the other parts were true.

"You never see Claire," she had said, and handed her to me. "You never even see your own daughter. When was the last time you changed a diaper, Bobby? When was the last time you bathed her?"

Claire started to cry. I did my best to hold her the right way. It is a tricky thing to hold a baby properly. Even your own baby. I handed her back to Wendy.

"Hush," she said to the baby. "That's enough, Claire," she said more firmly.

"She's just upset," I said.

This is not working, I thought. We had only been married for three years. It was too soon to get a divorce. My mother will love that, I thought.

Claire continued to cry. Her eyes and her fists were closed. Something about her mouth in its lonely curl reminded me of myself.

"Stop that, Claire! If you don't quiet down I'll give you back to your father."

"What did you just say?"

"Well, if it works," she had said, and walked out of the room.

"Come on, cheer up," Jim said. I looked up and saw him watching me carefully. His phone was ringing. It was after hours, so we had the ringers off, but I could see the red light blinking like the light on a police car. The private line. One of the women. Wendy, or Jim's new wife, or possibly his ex-wife. He sensibly never gave the private line to his girlfriends. His new marriage was going well, however: she was thoughtful and she did not call often. Or it could also be the Polack. The Polack had the private line, naturally.

"I'm cheerful," I said. "I'm just sick of sorting melee. Do you mind if we get out of here?"

"Let's put the rest of this package in the papers and go have some fun."

After the last of the diamonds we went to a dark topless bar in Euless Jim liked. The girls were not as pretty as in the Dallas titty bars but they worked harder. Lap dances were two for twenty dollars, and for fifty you could get a hand job in the back room. You don't get that kind of treatment in the upscale places. We each blew five hundred bucks or so of our sweeps money. It was a pleasant evening.

My first and my best crow at Clark's was Joe Morgan. I picked him up at a giant tent auction we held that summer under a circus tent we erected in the parking lot. The whole parking lot was beneath this enormous white and red tent that the rental guys inflated like an air balloon with enormous fans. We parked the twelve vintage Rolls-Royces we were auctioning at the far end on either side of the auctioneer's stage. It was the full-page color ad featuring those Rolls-Royces that brought in Morgan, he later told me.

Many crows are women, and the luxury jewelry business lives on them. Wealthy women who shop for jewelry in the way normal women gather shoes. But a rich male crow is even better than a woman, because women are buying for themselves, but men can at least pretend to be buying for their wives. It is easy for a husband to tell a wife that she does not need another diamond bracelet. But it is difficult, and very unusual, for a wife to tell her husband that she has enough jewelry. Even if she has more than she wants, she does not want to discourage his affection.

I was selling Morgan an eighteen-karat white gold diamond-and-emerald bracelet that had been assembled a few days before by our antique dealers over in Dallas. They had put it together for a "Grand Jewelry" event Neiman's was putting on—these two fellows were among Neiman's largest consigners—but they brought it to us first, because Jim and I had acquired a reputation for turning enormous pieces quickly if they were flashy enough. As soon as I saw it I called Morgan.

I did not own this bracelet, it was on memo, and I told Morgan that I was preparing to purchase it from a wealthy client and old friend of mine who needed some cash in a hurry.

"She needs some money that her husband doesn't know about," I said.

He gave me a sly look. "She's got something on the side, you think?"

He had a Jack and Coke in his hand. He was a tanned old Texas rancher who had made a fortune, young, in the Gulf, by building and leasing enormous steel barges. He liked to stir around the ice cubes in his drink with his large brown index finger. Usually he would have three or four while he was in the store, and I told the Polack to keep them coming and pour them strong.

"I don't think so, she must be in her late seventies." He was in his early sixties. I tell my salespeople: make the old ones feel young, and the young ones feel grown up. "I think it's for her daughter. She's in some kind of trouble." I knew that his daughter had left her husband and moved back home several years ago.

"Hell, that happens," he said, and took a drink. "That's kids."

I knew Morgan would buy this piece but the courtship period was crucial. It would take three or four visits before I would see the check, and in the meantime there would be other buyers he would hear about on the phone: someone would fly in from New York or Toronto, a dealer would ask if he could take it to a show, an expert on Colombian stones would appraise the emeralds. All this was theater, of course, I had only one customer who could buy this piece. And I only had the bracelet for a week.

He had the bracelet in his hand. He held it up like it was a fish he had caught by the tail.

"My wife, she does love platinum, don't she? That is some kind of pretty platinum bracelet. I don't think she has many emeralds, does she, Bobby? That's something she could use. I like those dark emeralds. Those ones with a bit of blue in them are the good ones, ain't that right?"

"That's right, Joe. You want that dark intense green with a blue undertone. Those are the very best."

In describing the emeralds, the diamonds, and the provenance of the bracelet—I was improvising a riff on a story I remembered by Jorge Luis Borges—I had forgotten to tell him that it was not platinum but eighteen-karat white gold. If I had dealt with that at the outset it was manageable. I could have explained that old South American pieces were always done in white gold in imitation of the grand European platinum pieces because they had not yet discovered platinum in South America at the turn of the century. That could have led us into a helpful conversation about the movie *Butch Cassidy and the Sundance Kid*, which was a surefire winner for a male customer, with Paul Newman and Robert Redford raiding gold mines in Brazil, robbing banks, riding horses, and jumping over waterfalls. But it was too late now. He had been telling himself for an hour that his wife would want it because it was platinum.

"Joe, let me give her a quick steam for you. All my saleswomen pawing the bracelet has put some oil on the stones. Of course, they are all dying just to try it on. Let me steam her off. I want you to see her in all her glory."

"Send that girl of yours, that Polish girl, in here while you're gone." Joe could never understand that the Polack was her name, not her ethnic origin. She wasn't Polish. I always thought of her as Kazakh. Something basically Russian, but more exotic.

"You got any more pickled eggs in back, Bobby?"

I kept pickled eggs in the fridge for Joe because he had once mentioned that no bars in the state of Texas kept pickled eggs on the counter any longer. I sent the Polack out to find a gallon jar of pickled eggs the same day. Turns out they are more available than you think.

"Send her in with a couple of eggs on a plate, would you, Bobby?"

When Ronnie went to prison, the store closed its doors, and we all went our separate ways, at first the Polack went out on her own, hip-pocketing. Mostly Swiss watches, turn-of-the-century large finished pieces, some counterfeit cut color, and loose diamonds. Jim offered her a job with us when she gunned down this young kid, a customer of mine, outside my office.

The customer was a heavyset redheaded guy from Mexico City. He wore glasses and looked more like a poet than a diamond thief. He was selling me a cheap four-carat diamond. It was stolen, brown, and full of carbon, and I planned to offer him a hundred a carat. Five bills tops. It would flip to Moshe or Western Trading for twenty-five hundred, maybe three grand. But before I made an offer I needed to show him a few diamonds of mine so that he would understand how bad his diamond was.

I had prepared several stones with fake cheap prices printed boldly on the diamond papers so that he would believe you could buy pretty four-carats for a thousand or less. I had bought from him before and I knew he was stupid and in a hurry, so I knew it would be easy. But in the middle of my explanation he jumped up, yelled some word that I didn't catch, and pulled a pistol on me. We had been robbed before, and the way he was bouncing on his legs I could see that he might shoot me accidentally. So I gave him the whole diamond box. I was already thinking of the numbers I had to call: first Paul, our insurance agent, then Jim at his girlfriend's, then the police, next Granddad (they were mostly his diamonds), then Amos at HDC about his memo stones, and Ken over at the bank, then Wendy. But as the Mexican ran out of my office the Polack was there and she took him by the shoulder and shot him briskly twice in the stomach. From my office it looked like she was holding him up to shoot him. But she fired so quickly you couldn't say. Then she stepped back and he fell. I looked for blood on her white dress. But she was as clean as a flame. She ignored the collapsed man, picked up the diamond box from the floor, and returned it to me. The poor kid was squirming on the floor. But he was oddly silent, like he was trying to catch his breath.

"Ha!" she said. "The young!" She was not thirty years old herself at the time. She sat down at my desk and opened her briefcase.

"Now you owe me, Clark! Ha ha! You better call the cops! The ambulances!"

"Hi, Polack," I said. My hands wobbled. I took off my wedding ring and put it on my diamond scale. I had never seen a real live human being shot before.

"Just a second, Polack," I said. "Hi. I asked could you give me one second."

That was the day I fell in love with her. I asked her out to dinner.

Jim later remarked that it didn't matter if she was my girlfriend for the next ten years, I would always only be a customer to the Polack.

Even after she came to work for us she continued her side deals. "I have money to make," she told us, as though that were the end of the discussion. At times it was convenient. If we were short on cash ourselves. Our sales manager, Lou Sosa, sold her his Blancpain for fifteen hundred bucks. That was a thousand shy of what it should have been. The Polack paid less than everyone else but she always paid cash. Sosa needed the money to square up with his divorce attorney. It was a dirty divorce with a child and the worthless remains of Sosa's old lawn-mowing business he kept on the side.

He asked me, "How can I turn this watch into cash in a hurry?" It was a beautiful automatic chronograph with a stainless head and a hobnail bezel. I had bought it off the street and given it to him as a bonus or a consolation when we first moved him from the shop onto the sales floor.

"I really hate to let it go, boss," he said. Sosa had these sloppy, worn-out shoulders that made you feel sorry for him. He always used a kind of pity-close on his customers. Told them his hard-luck stories. His lips were thin and his ears were white and small. "It represents my success to me. But I got to have the money. I mean, unless you guys can float me a loan? Like five grand?"

"I'd buy it if I could. You might ask the Watchman," I told him. "But if you're in a hurry, sell it to the Polack."

"I don't like that woman," he said. "No offense," he added quickly. Officially nobody knew the Polack and I were involved but it was one of those open secrets. You couldn't hide anything around our store for long. We worked too many hours.

"No big deal," I said. "I don't always like her myself."

"Frankly I wish Jim had never hired the Anteater," he went on.

That's a bit much, Sosa, I thought. But I knew he was angry at all women, then, because of the divorce, so I let it slide. I changed the subject.

Over the years she had acquired many of these unattractive industry names. One of them was the Anteater, because people said she had a practice, when inspecting diamond packages, of licking out the melee while your eye was turned and storing it in her cheeks like a goddamn hamster.

"Wouldn't that get her killed?' I asked Jim once, skeptically. "I mean, if it's true that she does that. Or thrown in jail or something."

"I don't think anyone has actually ever caught her at it, Bobby," Jim said. "Plus she does a lot of business with those fellas. It's like her commission, I guess. They're all too busy staring at her legs to notice anyway."

When Granddad heard we were putting her to work at our place he called me and told me not to do business with the Gypsy.

"I've known her since I was a kid, Granddad," I reassured him. "She helped me sell my first Rolex." That was not true but she had helped me sell plenty of them. She was the most dexterous liar I had ever met.

"She's Russian mob, Grandson," Granddad said. "We don't want those guys in your store."

He was a silent investor and he knew how to play by those elegant rules. But I could hear in his voice that he wanted to tell me I wasn't allowed to hire her at all.

She liked to wear oversized gold hoop earrings. You might have thought that was why some people called her the Gypsy. But they called her the Gypsy because of a different story that no one liked to talk about. It wasn't because she was a Gypsy, but because of something she was supposed to have done to some Gypsies.

I left Joe in my office and found her in back, at her desk, browsing through jewelry catalogues. She was wearing a bright green dress and her pale, snow-colored legs were bare. She was loveliest when she was concentrating on something, like she was at the moment. I stopped to look at her, for a moment, before she knew I was watching her. You couldn't help yourself. She makes Kate Moss look like a dog's belly, I thought.

She turned the pages in the catalogue. She would often tear out a page, look at it carefully, and then crumple it and throw it away. Like all independent custom jewelers, we ordered catalogues from every jewelry store and manufacturer in the world to get ideas for designs and to anticipate new trends. It didn't work particularly well, but looking for designs was a job our people enjoyed.

She started to show me a new Cartier design that she wanted to knock off, but I interrupted her and said, "Could you go sit with Morgan? Could you entertain him for a minute?"

I had the bracelet in my hand. I held it out to her to explain.

"Ha! Good. That old cowboy. He is horny," she said.

I did not know how to respond to that remark.

"Bring him a couple of those eggs on a plate, would you?"

"No, I won't. Those eggs disgust me. An Oriental person would eat them."

"Polack, come on. Would you help me out, please? As a favor?"

I took the emerald bracelet to Old John. I pulled him back to the polishing room, where we could speak discreetly.

Old John was a former helicopter gunner who held the first bench in our jewelry store. At Popper's Old John had always worked in the basement—"like the Roman god Vulcan," Old John used to say—but in our store he sat right up front. All of our jewelers worked in the front-of-the-house. Jim said the customers would worry about their jewelry less, while it was being worked on, if they could keep an eye on it. The best jeweler sat up front. From up front you could watch the teenage girls go in and out of Victoria's Secret through the big bay window next to the double doors. Tommy, our second-best bench man, sat behind Old John, and behind Tommy was Larry, et cetera, down to the back of the store, where the polishing wheels were. The exception was our wax carver, who always held the last bench because he claimed you couldn't carve waxes with people watching.

Although Old John used solder to fill the gaps in his channel setting he was a patient jeweler, and was the only one who could reliably work with platinum without costing us money. He never broke diamonds, not even the corners on princess cuts. He worked late like Jim and me. But we came in early and we never asked Old John to come in before noon. Often, after the store was closed and everyone else had gone home, he would tell me about his time as a gunner in Vietnam, or his year in prison in Mexico, or the seven years he did at Leavenworth, in Kansas, where he learned to be a jeweler. It's a fact many people don't know, that most jewelers and watchmakers learn how to sit on the bench while in prison.

Old John dyed his hair jet-black. He kept a jade-handled .45 chained to his bench. At Christmas he brought his boa in for the late nights and fed it mice in the store. He was five-foot-three. He drove a small, light, bruised Ford truck. His cheeks were as yellow and shiny as a tortoise's bottom shell. His lunch and his dinner came to work with him in Tupperware, and he brought his own special coffee in a canteen. He did not drink or smoke, and unlike almost every other jeweler I have ever known, he didn't take speed or other stimulants. I admired his asceticism.

"Old John, I have a problem," I said. "We need this bracelet to be platinum."

He inspected it dubiously.

"I don't feel very good about pulling those emeralds," Old John said.

"Me neither," I said. "Plus we don't have the time to re-make the whole thing. So, let's do it the old-fashioned way."

"Change the stamp," Old John said.

"I think it's for the best," I said. "He's not buying today, but we may as well do it right now. In case he wants to loupe the emeralds. I don't want him to notice the numbers. Be careful when you're polishing it. Then bring it back over to me on the other side."

"Is this a smart idea?" he said. "Does Jim know about this?"

"Old John, it's important," I said. "We're not going to make a habit of it."

What Old John was doing for me was grinding out the

"18kw," or eighteen-karat white gold stamps, on the bracelet—there were two, one on the tongue of the box clasp and one on the undercarriage—and restamping the bracelet "Pt," or platinum. He would rhodium-plate the whole afterward to give it that false brightness of freshly polished platinum. This was a common trick in the industry—restamping one karat weight or kind of metal as another—which I tried to avoid because it was amateurish, and easily discovered if the piece in question was ever inspected by another appraiser. Nevertheless, on certain occasions it was handy.

Back in my office the Polack and Morgan were laughing together. My favorite thing about the Polack was when I made her laugh. She looked much happier than most people. And, especially, happier than Wendy. But I wasn't crazy about it when other men got her laughing.

Morgan took the bottle and poured himself another bourbon. I always left the bottle on the desk, but not too close to him, so that he would never think I was encouraging him to drink. In reach, with a stretch.

"What do you think, girl?" He grabbed her knee with his hand. Then he winked at me and let go. "You taken a look at that old emerald bracelet? Your boss here is trying to rope me into another one of his hundred-thousand-dollar jewelry deals. What do you think, ole Polack? You think that bracelet would make a nice Christmas present for my wife?"

"This bracelet is for a woman of her kind. Your wife is the type of beautiful woman, Mr. Joe Morgan. So, yes, the bracelet."

Yes, the bracelet. I liked that. Good close, Polack, I thought.

"Mr. Morgan? Did you call me Mr. Morgan, girl? Mr. Morgan was my father! How many times do I have to tell you to call me Joe?"

"That's not a Christmas present, Joe," I said. We were half a year away from Christmas. I didn't have that kind of time. "Your anniversary is barely a month away. That's an anniversary piece. We'll figure something else out for Christmas. For anniversaries you want something that will stay in the family. Something your wife can pass down to your daughter. That bracelet is a Morgan family heirloom. At that price, especially. Here, Joe, let me see that pinkie ring of yours. When was the last time I cleaned that for you? Polack, would you mind taking this little diamond of Joe's next door and have Christian give it a tighten and polish?"

Joe Morgan wore a five-carat princess cut in a rose gold pinkie ring I had sold him a couple of years before. The stone was what is called top-light-brown, a kind of orangey-tan color, but set in rose gold with a rhodium plating beneath I had managed to make it look almost white. Cheap big diamonds like that are perfect for men's rings, because men feel it is feminine to inquire too closely about the quality of a diamond once it is set in a piece of men's jewelry. They are very particular about their wives' diamonds. But they are insecure about wearing diamond jewelry themselves, and they suppose that if they ask too many questions about their own diamonds you will conclude they are gay.

"Where the hell is she going? Where are you going, girl? Well if you got to go, go. But hurry back." He reached to pat the Polack on the bottom as she left, but she swung her hips and he missed.

"Man, that's a fine piece of ass, Bobby," he said. "You ever get yourself any of that action? Just a taste, maybe?"

We smiled that man's smile at each other, but I did not say anything.

"I wanted us to have a chance to speak seriously about this bracelet, Joe. You know I always tell people that you buy jewelry for the pleasure of owning it, not as an investment. But that piece is something entirely different. That truly is investment quality. It's like buying a Picasso. You don't see emeralds like that anymore, not even loose. But a hundred-year-old platinum bracelet that was formerly owned by an Argentinean countess? Come on. Plus the circumstances. If we sent that bracelet to Sotheby's or Christie's it would bring four hundred grand. She knows it, too. But she doesn't have the time. And the whole thing has to be cash. It has to be done with the greatest discretion. Margaret can't even wear that bracelet around town for a year or two. I'm dead serious about that. It will be recognized. That's one of the reasons I called you on this one, Joe. I know I can count on your discretion."

"Hell, there ain't nothing to worry about there. You know I can keep a damn secret. Code de macho. I sure as hell know you can, too." He laughed. Morgan liked to tell me stories about his wild days in the border towns. They were good stories.

"You in any hurry today, Bobby? Hell, I got some time today. Let's you and me relax a little bit, what do you say? Hit me again with that bourbon, would you?"

I poured him a cautious finger or two. I wanted him to want more than I was offering him.

"Keep going, keep going, there you go. That'll do her."

Well, well, I thought. This might be even easier than I thought. We might even wrap this one up today.

When I got home that night, still warm from the sale to Morgan, Wendy announced that she was going to fly down to St. Croix to seek my father's assistance for us.

"Maybe he can help. You always listen to your dad. We should both go."

"Wendy, you know how busy we are. If you are so determined, you can go, I guess. But you know I can't get away. Not to mention that you are crazy to think my dad will be any good. Jim's right. He's insane, Wendy."

"Crazy or not, I believe in your dad," she said.

"What about the baby?" I said. "What about Claire?" I was frightened to be left alone with that little baby of ours.

"I knew you would say that," she said. She looked so tired and even disappointed that I wished I had kept my mouth shut. But, really. "I already asked my mother to come watch her, Bobby."

"I have to work, Wendy. That's all I was saying. Somebody has to pay our bills."

"Anyway I already bought the ticket."

"Maybe it will be like a vacation," I said. "You could use a vacation. Get a little sun. We could both use a vacation." I had not meant to say that. I did not want her to think there was any possibility I could go or even consider going.

"It is not a vacation, Bobby. For crying out loud. Can you even hear yourself? Do you listen to what you say? I swear, what is wrong with you sometimes?"

Why don't you go ahead and tell me? I thought. What's wrong with me: if I am quiet for a few minutes you will be happy to instruct me.

"I am going to save this family," she said.

For the past few years our dad had been bouncing around even more than usual. When his last church had failed, in Coral Gables, he had been certified as a minister and a missionary for the Unitarian Church of Palm Beach and Boca Raton. The U.S. Virgin Islands was his first assignment.

"It's paradise, son," he told me on the phone. "Grab your big brother and hop on a plane. Bring your scuba gear. You boys will love it."

"We're running a business here, Dad," I said.

I sent a necklace with Wendy that our dad had ordered from us but never paid for. It had various esoteric Masonic insignia enameled on a large plate that went across the collarbone. I knew the necklace would roll on the neck and that plate would always wind up on the bottom. I could already hear my father complaining about it. But there was no other way to make the piece.

"Try to get the money," I said when I gave it to her. "It's just my cost."

Before she even checked into her hotel she rented a car at the airport and drove out to his church. He had not known she was coming that week. I had promised her I would call and warn him, but it stayed on my to-do list until after she was already back. I meant to call. But with Wendy out of town the Polack kept me on the run.

She sat in a church pew with the Rastafarians. During Dad's service the tall, bony man next to her stood in his pew, pulled down his sweatpants, and began to urinate into the aisle. He apologized to her.

"It is because of the Pope, ma'am," he said. "I'm sorry."

He took a very nice photograph of her, with her camera, standing and smiling with the open door of the church behind her and orange and purple bougainvillea beyond. It was a pleasant little chapel, from what I could see.

After my father finished his sermon, while the brass collection plate was going around, the Rastafarian invited Wendy to dinner. He was only being polite, she said. He was not making a pass.

"You can come and visit us," he said. "You don't have to stay for the meal. We have a nice farm. In the hills.

"I have to go now," he told her then. "I have to wash my hands."

When she met with my dad in his little trailer next to the church he wanted to do a reading on her.

"I have been watching him astrally," he told her. "He's fucking up. He has karma to work out with you. There may have to be a divorce."

She wept while he put her on the plane. "Don't give up," he said. "Fate!" he said, and waved from the bottom of the stairs. She took a picture of him waving up to her. He looked much better than the last time I had seen him. His color had improved and I saw he had added muscle tone in his face. She also showed me pictures of him on the beach, smoking his pipe, with the shallow Caribbean Sea behind him and storm clouds in the sky.

A couple of weeks after she was back he phoned me. Our 800 lines didn't cover the Virgin Islands, so he called collect.

"She just missed the hurricane. It's hurricane season down here."

A few days after she was back, Hurricane Boris struck.

"I straightened things out for you, son," he said. "Enough of this screwing around. You want to wind up like your old man?"

"Thanks, Dad," I said. I didn't want to say anything that might start a real conversation.

"My telepathy saw it coming. We got her out of here pronto. I felt the vibrations a week before it hit. We spent nine days inside playing ping-pong," he said. "Those niggers can play some ping-pong."

"Dad, please don't use that expression," I said.

"Oh, go screw yourself," he said, and laughed. "Those niggers are my parishioners. That's my flock, Bobby. We just about went crazy. Smoking dope, eating jerk chicken, and playing ping-pong. Holy snapping bald-headed eagles."

When I got off the phone I stood, slid open the pocket door, and leaned into Jim's office. There were no customers at his desk. He was picking baguettes for a custom job. It was one of his better designs, a Judith Ripka knockoff, a chrysoberyl ring in pink and white gold with the diamond baguettes on one side only. It looked a bit like a headless peacock with his tail fanned off to the side. But quite nice.

"I just talked to Dad," I said. "He doesn't sound bad. He sounds better."

"He's not coming to town, is he?"

"No, he's still down in the Virgin Islands," I said. "But I think it's doing him some good. He sounded like his old self."

"Did he ask you for money?"

"No, I'm serious. He really sounds like himself. Like the old Dad."

"I've fallen for that one too many times, Bobby. Believe me. It's an old trick of his. Next time he calls he will ask you for money. Speaking of which, have you looked at the gray account

191

lately?" The gray account was our estate-buy account, another one of Granddad's upside-down accounts. "We are down to a hundred grand in there. I ran an inventory and we only have three hundred at cost. That leaves us almost two hundred thousand short. We have to take better care of that account. I don't want to have to call Granddad. He's already asking about this quarter's check."

I sat back down at my desk and drew a picture of a bird on my desk pad. I put a little wave beneath it so it might be a seagull. The phone was ringing. No one on my sales floor was answering it. How much effort does it take to pick up the phone?

Before I left I would lie in bed at night in our dark bedroom and watch the red dots from my alarm clock reflected in the brass light fixture on the ceiling. I came home after ten, after eleven, my blood thin with the long day and night, and quietly, as smoothly as I could, slid my uncomfortable body beneath our covers. Next to me in the bed our baby daughter's head and small curls rested in a sweaty ring. Their breathing was shallow with sleep. I tried not to move. I kept my arms at my sides. But there was no point in closing my eyes. So I watched the red dots from the alarm clock on the brass chandelier above the foot of the bed. In the silence with the two of them barely breathing, like air among green leaves on their twigs, I could still hear the canned music that we piped in all day throughout the store. I listened for it and that listening in bed made me forlorn, self-pitying, and resentful.

I figure it out," the Polack said.

I looked up from the buy I was weighing. It was a Tiffany sterling set from the 1930s. It was a huge set, over four hundred pieces, soup ladles and onyx-handled hot chocolate tureens, and even a samovar. We paid four dollars an ounce—after deducting the estimated weight of the onyx, inlaid mother-of-pearl, and ivory—which was exactly what a smelter would pay us. We could have paid as much as twelve or even fifteen dollars an ounce, but it was brought to us by one of Jim's oldest and best customers and we knew she would take whatever we offered her. That's how it works with regulars: because they are already sold they are much easier to screw. But you have to screw them, to make up for all of the skinny-margin deals you did to get their business in the first place. If you don't screw your regulars you won't be around for long.

"I figured it. What I want for my present. My birthday."

I had forgotten her birthday was in a few weeks. Maybe she would like a nice pair of Manolo Blahnik boots, I thought. She did not spend enough money on her footwear. But I wouldn't get off that easy. A fur. That's what she's after. That coat is going to set you back, Bobby, I thought. It can't be just any fur coat. She will know the differences between them.

"You do not know?" she said. "Guess!"

"I guess I better know," I said. "Since I'm buying it."

"The Rolex. I want a Rolex," she said.

"A Rolex? Would you actually wear a Rolex?"

The jewelry business really is two things, in the end: diamonds and Rolexes. The truth is there is no other luxury brand, of any kind, that has achieved the same supremacy within its area as Rolex. It's a subject worthy of closer study.

"I change my mind about this. The Rolex is elegant. I want the boy's size. In stainless steel. We refinish the dial pink. To make it more feminine."

Pink? I did not understand this woman at all.

Still, I could rustle up one of those from the Watchman for a thousand, twelve hundred bucks. I was getting off cheap.

"You want to go out tonight?" I said. Thursday was our late day, we stayed open until eight, so Wendy was always asleep by the time I came home. "Want to go to Dallas, maybe?"

"Yes, I am going to Dallas tonight. But not with you," she said. "I have business to take care of. I leave early, in fact."

Okay, I thought. She has ordered her birthday present and now she is going to Dallas without me, leaving Jim and me with the cases to pull on her own, to do her side deals.

Maybe Jim will want to go have a few drinks, I thought. With Wendy already in bed it was a shame to waste the Thursday night.

I understood how grown men should view their offices. My office was supposed to be a refuge. This is my tree house, I ought to be thinking. But I preferred Jim's office to my own. My favorite place to sit was on the other side of his desk, in one of the customers' chairs, after closing.

"I'm moving out. I'm leaving Wendy," I said.

I watched his face as I said it. I knew he would be pleased. Not at my unhappiness, not at all. But between brothers, if you are close, it is a victory when your brother has serious trouble with his wife. Otherwise the wife divides the two of you, at least partially.

"What a shock," Jim said. Then he saw my face and he was gentler. "That's a good idea," he said. "You know what I think. That hasn't been a real marriage for some time now. You don't have to get divorced right away. Separate. That's what I like to do. It makes it easier when things turn legal anyway. They are less combative. But easier on both of you, I mean. Get a little distance. Clear your head."

Even at this desperate moment I did not like him criticizing my marriage. But I knew he was trying to encourage me.

We were sorting South Sea pearls on oversized pearl trays into calibrated colors and sizes for three matching necklaces. Jim had already sold one of the necklaces and made enough profit on the deal that the other two were free. They were astonishing. Twelve to fifteen millimeters in diameter, and white with that undertone of pink and gold that good South Seas have. You could see half a millimeter or so into the pearl, as though it were still alive in the oyster, as if it were the skin of a living human face.

196

"Listen to me, Bobby. The last thing you want to do is to run straight to the Polack with this," he said. "Keep that professional. She's your girlfriend at work, and that's the way you want it to stay. It would be better if she didn't even have to know you were moved out. When you're moved out Wendy will have a closer eye on you."

I wanted to say something but I felt too discouraged. I tried to concentrate on the pearls.

"What you need is a little clean honest fun. No connections, no worries. Remember Sylvia?" he said. "She's playful. She's got a healthy outlook."

I did not call immediately. But then one night, alone in the store with the layouts and artwork for our new catalogue, I decided I might. I found the number Jim had written hidden in the back of my main desk drawer, with the other numbers on pink and blue Post-it notes I used for phone sex. Her name was on the back of it with a comment about ear studs like she was a lead. In code, in case the Polack was digging around in my desk drawer: "2–3 carats, eye-clean and white, platinum bezels."

I had met with Sylvia once before, about a year ago, in May, at the motel behind our health club. That was my birthday present from Jim. But then on the drive back from a weekend getaway to Austin with Wendy—which was my birthday present from her—I noticed a crab on Claire's head among her thin white hair. She was in her car seat. I etched it off with my thumbnail before Wendy could see it. The baby yelled once and then laughed. It left a red mark on her skin near where her skull grew together. I bought a box of lice ointment at Eckerd's and did not plan on using Sylvia again.

Before I called her I called Wendy.

"How is the new apartment?" she asked me. "We came up to see you but you weren't there."

"I'm still at the office," I said.

"No, yesterday," she said. "Last night."

I had been in Dallas with the Polack last night.

"I was probably still at the office."

"We came by but the lights were off."

"I don't know. Maybe I was getting something to eat."

"I'm not trying to start a fight. We just wanted to see you. We wanted to see your new apartment."

"It's depressing. You won't like it."

"So come home, then. We want you to come home."

"You know I can't come home."

"But we want you to come home."

"I want to come home. But I can't."

"When do you think you can come home? By Christmas?"

"I don't know. I don't think so. Is the baby asleep?"

"No. We're watching a movie. You want to come watch it with us?"

"I can't."

"I was just joking. I was just asking."

It made me depressed to hear how much her voice had changed since I had moved out. Well, I was already depressed before I called, but more depressed. She was asking now, instead of telling.

After I hung up I sat and looked at my phone for a few minutes. The vacant store with its empty showcases and no salespeople at the desks was very quiet. The Muzak was playing. Jim was off with his new girlfriend, a crazy nineteen-year-old stripper. That would end badly. I stood and walked into the showroom. I turned off the halogens. Then it was dark on the showroom

floor and my office looked more inviting. I had a Tiffany drag-
onfly lamp on my desk—not a knockoff, the real thing—but the
bulb was burned out so I went in back and found a bulb. I replaced the bulb and turned it on. I looked at all the colored
glass pieces glowing like gems. They are prettier than jewelry, I
thought. People should just wear glass with electric lights inside. Then I called Sylvia.

She didn't pick up until the seventh or eighth ring. I almost
gave up.

"Can we get together for a drink? How about Birrapo-
retti's?"

"Hi, Bobby. It's nice to hear from you. How's Jim? I'm not
taking meetings anymore. But I have a girlfriend who is. You'll
like her. She's young. She's pretty."

"Is she a friend of yours?"

"She is taking over a few of my old clients. I am sure you
will like her. Call her."

The new hooker answered the phone on the first ring. She
wanted to meet at my apartment. I did not recognize the voice
because, of course, it was not what I was expecting.

"Shouldn't we meet at a motel?" I said. I knew we should
meet at a motel.

"No, thank you," she said politely.

I was nervous like you are before a date. I started to straighten
the apartment. Then I thought, No, you are not fixing up your
apartment for a hooker. I brushed my teeth. I opened a beer.
The doorbell rang. I looked through the peephole. A middle-
aged man in a jean jacket stood there. I did not know if I should
answer the door. He had blond bangs. He knocked and said
loudly, "I'm the friend. Sylvia's friend."

"Where's the girl?" I said through the door. "Who are you?"

"Open up," he shouted. I thought about my neighbors. I had not met any of them but they would hear this. I opened the door but left the chain on.

"What?" I said. "Who are you?"

"I just need to check out the apartment," he said. "Because you are a new client."

He was about forty years old. He had a pack of cigarettes in the breast pocket of his jean jacket.

"Are you carrying a gun?" I asked him. "This is probably not worth it," I said.

"Man, open up," he said, and the way his eyes turned down I saw that he was kind, like you will see on poor people and black people, so I opened the door.

"I need to make sure you are not some weirdo," he said.

"Look around," I said.

I was still in an Armani suit and a Zegna tie. I was wearing Bulgari plique-à-jour cufflinks. I thought that ought to count for something. There was a half-empty bottle of Creed Taba-rome on the breakfast bar. But the mattress was on the floor and I had no furniture. There were candles, wine bottles, an alarm clock, the cutaways I had brought home with me from the new catalogue, and a few books. There was a blue and green Favrile-glass Art Deco ashtray, which Jim had given me as my moving-out-of-the-house present, with two cigar butts in it.

"I just moved in," I said. "I just left my wife."

"I'm sorry," he said.

"No, it's for the best," I said. "She cries all the time."

"You have any children?" he asked.

"Just one," I said. "She's only a baby."

"That's sad," he said. "They say it's tough on the kids but

really it's toughest on the parents. My folks are divorced. It was always nice at Christmas."

"Mine, too," I said. "Two Christmases. Two birthdays, too."

"Don't divorce if you can help it."

I started to offer him a beer but then I remembered what we were doing.

"I guess you are a lonely guy," he said.

"That's fair," I said. "Just a lonely guy. Just like the rest of us."

"Speak for yourself," he said. "Have fun. Have a party. But remember I'll be down in the truck."

He left the door half open when he left. I started to close it but then jumped when the girl, on the other side, pushed it open at the same time. I let go and stepped back. For no reason, I felt embarrassed. Then she walked in. It was Lisa. I saw her before she saw me. Nine years had passed since I had seen her and here she was, walking in the door as the prostitute I had ordered. Boldly, like she expected to make me comfortable. I had noticed the confidence in her stride in the second or so before I even understood it was her.

Then she saw me. There was a moment while we waited. We might each have been seeing what the other one would do first. Or maybe neither of us knew what to do.

She abruptly covered her face with her hands. Like one of those three monkeys. She turned around and walked out of the apartment. I caught her at the bottom of the stairs.

"No," she said. "I did not see you. I do not know who you are. I am leaving. I am not who you think you called for."

"I didn't say anything. You have not even let me stop to say anything to you. Stop. Stop walking."

Then she turned around. She was over thirty now and I saw

that she was one of those women who, when the bones of the face finally matured, found the powerful beauty that had almost already been there in their teens and twenties, but not quite.

I grabbed her shoulder. Then I got both arms around her and I held her. She smelled the same as she used to. But I could feel her sinews and the darker hollows in her muscles. My face was in her neck and her hair. She stiffened. Then she touched the back of my head. But it was too gentle, like your mother would touch your head if you were sick, or like when you were little and she was leaving the house and you didn't want her to go.

"Bobby," she said, and pulled away.

"Where did you get my number?" she said. "How did you get my number?"

"From Sylvia," I said. "From that woman Sylvia." I almost added, From Jim. But I did not want to say his name right then.

She closed her eyes. She kept them closed. I watched her.

"Can you come upstairs?" I said. She opened her eyes, then. "Not to have sex. I didn't mean that. Can't we just talk?" Why did you say that, Bobby? Why did you say anything about sex?

She took one of my hands and held it in hers. It was hard, then, not to start crying.

"Lisa," I said.

"Your face is different now," she said while we were making love. It was the only further thing she said to me that night.

Some nights later, when we met again, but not at my apartment, at a hotel, after we had sex I said, stupidly, "Don't take this the wrong way. But why did you become a prostitute?" I didn't want to say how lonely it made me feel.

In fact I should have just said it, because the question did not bother her. She laughed. It wasn't a defensive laugh. It was an honest laugh.

"Bobby," she said. "You are still so sweet. You will always be young for your age."

"I don't understand. Why do you say that?" Already Lisa felt more like my girlfriend, again, than some hooker. I couldn't tell her that, of course.

"You sell jewelry for a living, Bobby. I was in that business once, too, remember? With what I do now, I sleep well at night. I don't have any complaints about my line of work. I like the way I look in the mirror."

I had no idea what she meant.

We were playing backgammon outside the coffee shop behind the store. Jim was beating me. I was down four hundred dollars. Sometimes as much as three thousand dollars went between us in those backgammon games. But we only cashed in the debt if one of us needed the money urgently. Otherwise we just let the bets flow back and forth from one game to the next. Usually he carried me, and not the other way around.

I had rolled double 3s and was trying out different moves in my head, watching the board, when Jim said, "Oh-oh." I looked up and saw his face. He looked like he might laugh, but in that way he laughed when he felt sorry for you. I turned to look behind me and there were Wendy and Claire. Claire was dragging her feet like she wanted her mother to pick her up. She had a stuffed lamb I had bought her at Neiman's in her free arm. Ever since her first birthday she had always carried a stuffed animal with her wherever she went. I could see Wendy was angry about something.

"You guys are working hard, I see," Wendy said.

"Hi, Wendy," Jim said.

"Daddy, I want something to drink," Claire said. I took her into my lap.

"I wasn't trying to interrupt your workday," Wendy said. "But I need some money. They are putting in that underground water filter today and I can't pay for it. You said we were going to pay for it in cash."

Jim gave me a look. Sometimes I would need a little more cash than he was ready to divide up. This water filter business had been one of those times. I'd agreed to it when I had the Polack at my desk and was in a hurry to get Wendy off the phone. I would have told Wendy yes to many things with the Polack sitting across from me listening to our conversation with the malevolence on her face that she wore only when I was talking to my wife.

"I'm sorry. I don't have that cash right now, Wendy."

"How much cash is it?" Jim was reaching in his pocket.

"No, don't worry about it, Jim," I said. I didn't want him to hear the number.

"It's thirty-five hundred," Wendy said.

"Thirty-five hundred dollars? For a water filter?"

"It's like an underground water filter," Wendy told Jim. "You never have to buy filtered water again. You even bathe in filtered water. I don't want to wash Claire in that water with all of that stuff they pump into it. Chemicals and detergents. That's not healthy. You should have seen our water when he tested it. It was really disgusting. It was frightening."

"Daddy. Thirsty." Claire squirmed in my lap. I started dancing her lamb on the table to distract her. With luck the lamb might bump the backgammon board.

"Bobby, why did Emily have your sunglasses on?"

"What? Who?"

Emily was the Polack's real name, but no one ever said it.

"That Polish saleswoman. Emily, Bobby. Who works in your store. I think you have met her."

"I better get back to the store, Bobby." Jim stood and folded up the backgammon board. "I'll see you back there. Don't you have an appointment at three? Isn't Morgan supposed to be in today?"

"Margaret," I said. "Margaret is coming in at three."

"Thirsty, Daddy! Thirsty, thirsty." She started to sing it.

"You do know who the Polack is, right? Are you willing to grant that much? She was wearing your sunglasses. Why would she be wearing your sunglasses?"

Why is she wearing sunglasses at all? I wondered. She is supposed to be picking sapphires for the Stein job.

"I don't know. I don't even know what you're talking about. How should I know what sunglasses she's wearing? They're not my sunglasses. They must be her sunglasses. They must be different sunglasses. You must be mistaken, Wendy. My sunglasses are in my car."

"That's true. She was driving your car, Bobby. She was driving away with the top down and your sunglasses on when I pulled in. Did you think she was wearing them in the store? Does she wear your sunglasses in the store while she works? She must be pretty attached to those sunglasses. Is there something you want to tell me, Bobby? I guess she is telling me. I think the Polack is trying to tell me already."

"Wendy, I don't know what you are trying to say, but I am going to get Claire something to drink. I don't want to fight right now. Seriously. I don't have time for this."

"Good, that's helpful. Walk away. Go on, now, and think of some lie to tell me."

"Come on, honey." I lifted Claire into my arms and carried her into the coffee shop. "What do you want? Milk? They have milk. Do you want apple juice?"

"Cookie, Daddy! That cookie! Pink cookie!"

After closing, the Polack told me the story herself.

"She pulls up in the car. So, she sees me. She is your wife, not mine! I did not know she was there. What am I hiding?"

Uh-huh, I thought. It was all just ordinary bad luck.

When I was with Lisa, later that evening, the suspicion occurred to me that the Polack and Wendy were collaborating in a plot to make me kill myself. Why they might want this I could not have said for certain. There was no life insurance money. It was all signed away to our investors in the buyout agreements. So just to get back at me, I supposed.

I watched Lisa across the table. She was sipping a blue margarita. This woman is a whole woman, I thought. She is who she appears to be. But those two. It was like they were the same woman, divided into two evil halves. You are getting drunk, Bobby, I thought. But there really was something to it. They understood and considered things I could not even speak if I knew them. They could see years into the future.

"Excuse me, Lisa," I said. She smiled at me. What a nice woman she is, I thought. She thinks about my pleasure, my state of being. She wants me to be happy.

I went to the bathroom and inspected myself, with kindness, in the mirror. I placed my palms on the red marble counter and sucked in my cheeks. That helped. I look a bit like Jesus, I thought, in a hound's-tooth pale yellow Armani suit. Or like John Lennon, but with slicked-back hair.

*T*here was a room at the Mansion on Turtle Creek that would become our regular room. But I think this was the first time we went to the Mansion together. It was a Friday night.

"Why did you call Sylvia? That's what I want to know. I don't really see you as one of these prostitute guys. I mean, I know you're married and all. But why not just go to a bar and get a regular girl?"

"You are my regular girl." We had been together for a month now and she let me say things like that to her. Probably she was only being patient with me. But she said it first. About a regular girl, I mean.

The summer was turning around, I felt. It could be a good summer yet.

"You know what I mean."

"That's how it seems to women. Because they can have sex whenever they want to. But for men it's not that way."

I could not see Lisa's expression because the light was behind her and her hair made a tent around her face. She bent over to kiss me and I could smell my bad breath in her hair. She whispered something to me. She straightened back up.

"It is because you are married. If you weren't married you would never have called me at all. That's kind of funny, isn't it? That we meet again because you are married?"

I couldn't tell if she was playing or if she was searching for something.

"That's not true. It's not just being married. I have a girl-friend."

"I know about your girlfriend. That Polack girl. What a waste."

"You have a boyfriend, too."

The blond with the bangs and the cigarettes was not a pimp. He was her boyfriend. Sometimes he still brought her to my apartment in his truck. But then I would drop her off at home. She did not like to drive herself.

"I have a real boyfriend who loves me. You just have me and a wife you cheat on and a weird eastern European girlfriend who has turned into some kind of mystery criminal. Not to mention that she was always a slut, even back in the Fort Worth Deluxe days. And I don't use that word. But I know."

"I'm not cheating on my wife. I moved out."

"It's still cheating, Bobby. Plus, whatever you say, you're cheating on that so-called girlfriend. With me."

"She's not exactly my girlfriend. She's a salesperson."

"That's nice. I bet she would love to hear you say that. That's a nice way to talk about her. Do you love her?"

That was a funny question to ask me. I couldn't tell how she meant it. But it seemed like a promising sign.

"She can be pretty nice. You might be surprised. She sure is a lot happier than Wendy is."

"Real nice, Bobby. The Polack. I don't understand you at all. I mean, I suppose maybe I do but I almost wish I didn't. She doesn't know about me, does she?"

"No one knows."

"Oh, I bet she does. That's what's really sad. She knows."

"No, she doesn't. You don't know her about this kind of thing. I'm telling you, she's dangerous. She's jealous, too. She would kill us both."

"You don't know anything, Bobby. You are just like a damn little kid. Why do you want all these mommies, Bobby? Wouldn't you be better off with just one mommy?"

Now she was being cruel, and I couldn't see why.

"Could we talk about something else?"

"We've got all night."

"Could we talk about something happy?"

"I'm happy. You should be happy, too. But you don't know anything. You can't even get a real girl. You had to call Sylvia."

That was something I had been thinking about. Since she brought it up. Since she was the one wanting to talk about these things. Just say it, Bobby, I thought. But as I spoke I couldn't quite ask her what I wanted to ask her.

"Sylvia," I said. "You know Jim gave me Sylvia's number." That was pretty close, I thought. Close enough.

"Jim, as in your brother, Jim?" She looked away from me. "No, I didn't know that. Why? I don't want to see Jim." She kissed me again, on my neck, and then rolled off of me. "Here, you want a fresh drink? I'll get us both one," she said.

211

While she was getting the bottle from the minibar she said, "You didn't give him my number, did you? Did you tell him about us?"

"No. Of course not. That's not what I was saying. He gave me Sylvia's number. That's all I was saying. He and Sylvia know each other. He doesn't know about you at all." That sounded odd. "I mean, I didn't know if you wanted me to tell him. I want to tell him about you. About us, I mean. About you and me. And that you are happy and everything. You know, I think he'd be glad to know. Like old friends and everything. Plus he cares about you. And me, too. He would be happy for us." Shut up, Bobby.

She had been watching me from where she was kneeling at the minibar but now she looked away from me. I couldn't tell why. Maybe it was that she believed I was lying and did not want to humiliate me by letting me see it in her face. I wasn't lying, though. That was the frustrating part.

"But maybe I shouldn't tell him. I don't know what you would think. You might not like him now."

"Maybe you think he wouldn't like me anymore," she said. She was turned away from me and the way her hair hung on her naked back, between those shoulder blades that belonged on an antelope, made me want to reach out and grab it with both hands. She was putting ice in the glasses. "It sounds like that is what you are saying. But do you really know him in that way? He might look at all this differently than you do. Do you really know what you're talking about, Bobby?"

"No, what I'm saying is you wouldn't like him now." I had to dig myself out and I would do it at Jim's expense, if necessary. I thought I was hurting her feelings. "He would definitely still like you."

She lit a cigarette. She came back to the bed.

212

"Here's your drink, baby," she said.

I took the cold glass of ice and vodka. I wanted to go to the bathroom to pee, but I didn't want to leave her alone to think. Also I was still a bit shy to urinate around her, and I couldn't close the bathroom door in the middle of this conversation.

"I hope you are not trying to trick me into something," she said.

"I said I don't want you to meet him, Lisa."

"That's what you said. I believe you. But this is how it starts with you two. I've seen it before. I've seen you two in action. It always starts with something. Something like this."

"What starts?"

"What do you think, Bobby? Nothing good, I'll tell you that much. Nothing that will make any of the three of us happier."

The three of us? But this time it is only about the two of us, I wanted to say.

I drank my vodka. Leave it alone, Bobby, I told myself. I tried to think of a joke to tell her. Something to get us on a new track.

"Let's not talk about Jim," I said. "I'm sorry I brought him up. That was one of your rules, right? No talking about Jim."

I couldn't help myself.

"Okay, that's it," she said. She started tickling me. "It sounds to me like you want to wrestle. You wanna wrestle?" she said. "I bet I can whip you. Let's wrestle." She took an ice cube out of her drink and put it in her teeth. She rubbed it on my chest. "You better watch out now," she said, with the ice cube in her fingers. "I can do some real damage with this thing."

When I woke up, in the morning, she was still there, where I didn't know if she would be. Outside my window I could see the shadows from the sun, not quite risen yet. There were birds out there, too, waking up, bouncing the branches just past the window. I didn't have a hangover. My first appointment wasn't until one. What a good day, I thought.

That same morning, a few hours later, the Polack came into my office and said, "A girl will speak with you."

The Polack was wearing one of my favorite thin silk shirts. The red one. She bought them for herself in one of those giant Chinese warehouses over on Harry Hines, where we sometimes bought cheap gold chain if we needed it in a hurry and didn't want to pay for Italian. They were only ten or twenty bucks apiece but they looked like they came right off a mannequin at Barneys. She knew I always wanted to fuck her when she wore one of those shirts. You could see all of the details of her body beneath it. I had told her so many times, and we had even had sex in the bathroom at the store while she was wearing it. I asked her to keep it on.

I understood who the girl was by the way the Polack said the words. I looked up from my work on my desk in fear. I knew I would see Lisa on the showroom floor. There were three or four customers out there, wandering the showcases. My salesmen were sitting on their asses as usual. But no Lisa. Dear God, that's one I owe you for, I thought. I knocked on the wood of my desk.

"She's waiting," the Polack said. "This girl. She is on the phone."

"A girl? A woman or a girl?"

"Yes, as I explain. A girl. She is on that line." She jabbed at the blinking light of the phone at my desk as though she were poking its eye out. I was afraid she was going to ask me to put her on speakerphone.

"Okay, Polack," I said. "Thank you." I shuffled the pink message notes on my desk until she left.

After I hung up, the Polack was back in my office. "She is who?" she said.

"She's a customer, Polack," I said.

"Okay. Customer. Fine. That's what you say. Who? Who from? How does she know to ask your name? I do not know this customer. She sounds like someone I know."

"She's a referral," I said.

"I said that. Whose?" the Polack said.

"Not now," I said. "Polack. Please. It's Jim's business. Okay?"

"Good. I talk to him about it," she said.

"No," I said. I almost called her Emily, to try to get through to her. But that would be a giveaway. "It's his personal business. Drop it."

At lunch I told the Polack that the customer who had called was an old girlfriend of Jim's, a girlfriend from the Lily days, who was now a hooker. I didn't tell her it was Lisa. You know, the useful cliché, keep the lie as close to the truth as you can.

"He does that? He pays these women to have sex with him?" she said. "So she asks for you. This is the story?"

The Polack ate her mozzarella-and-tomato salad. She was also having a bucket of mussels. Unlike me, she preferred the large ones.

"I kind of knew her, too," I said. "I mean, she left Jim just as I was coming in the business. That's why she asked for me. She wanted to know what Jim's romantic situation was. Like she had some kind of interest in him, I guess. Other than his money. I don't really know. But I cleared it up. I told her, you know, that she should just ask Jim. I told her that we didn't really get involved in one another's personal lives." I always had difficulty lying to the Polack. She was so suspicious that she made you feel like you were saying, Okay now I am going to lie to you, and then trying to tell the lie. It doesn't work. It's self-contradictory.

"I do not blame him. With this latest wife of his. Who would want to have sex with that? No. But, the hooker? For money? Do you ask, how many other cocks are in the hole? Now your cock is Mr. Lucky? We all fuck her at once! Shove in the cocks! More! Like a hotel. But we all sleep in the same bed!"

Lately the Polack wore her hair pulled back but today she had let it down and it made her look more human. She had angular cheekbones, long legs, and, when she wore short dresses or skirts, the kind of bony knees that made her look like a French or an Italian woman in a photo on a runway. But with the unjust and vulgar way she explained the motivations of other people, and more generally her outlook on life, she could seem almost ugly. For an unpleasant moment I wished a magical truck would leap the curb—we were eating outside, on the patio—and run her over right before my eyes. Stop dead with a huge rubber wheel crushing her belly and the crumpled chair beneath her. With that bit of white mozzarella squeezed from her lips. Then I thought, Bobby. You're cheating on the Polack, too. She's only trying to have a real relationship with you. She deserves your affection as much as anyone does. Or nearly as much. If you will just give her the benefit of the doubt.

"It's not such a big deal, Polack," I said.

"This is bad for a married man. You should be telling him

yourself. You are the brother. A married man should not go fuck some hooker. He breaks a promise."

"I'm married, Polack." Why do you say things like that, Bobby? Are you so determined to make your own life worse?

"I understand. And I am not the hooker. Or you forget?"

"What I'm saying is leave it alone. Plus if you say something then he would know I told you. He's my brother, Polack. He has to trust me. I should never have told you in the first place. But I knew, I mean, I thought you would show some discretion. This is important. I need to know I can tell you things, Polack. Without you running straight to repeat them to Jim. Anyway it's none of our business."

"Okay. No problem. I will tell it like a joke. We joke like that together. Jim and I, we have our friendship. I know him long before you."

"But I told you."

Her salad and her mussels were gone. She reached with her fork and started on my gnocchi. I didn't mind because I wasn't hungry. But it made me sick to watch her forking it up like that over the table.

"Go ahead and eat it," I said, though she hadn't asked.

I thought, Now I have to tell Jim the whole thing. He will want to call her, too. I did not think he would want to pay her for sex, like I was. But he would want to be friendly with her. He might even start dating her again. I didn't know what his status was with his current girlfriend. Plus his latest wife, of course. I could ask him not to call her, I thought. But who knew what he would think about that. He might just laugh about it. "Like you said. She's a hooker now," he would say. But he would call her anyway. Then he would tell her the story about the Polack and the lie I told her about Jim. She might think it was a sweet story. But they might laugh about it together.

Unless he has already called her, I thought. Then I didn't have to tell him anything. Or I could just say, Lisa called for you, earlier, and the Polack asked about it. I wondered if there was a way I could get the truth out of Sylvia. But she had been a hooker and a madam for years. She could keep a secret better than anyone.

There had to be a way to turn this to my advantage. It had that feel to it, like if I thought about it with my whole brain I could figure it out. Like a chess move that you know is there, and then you discover it.

What couldn't happen was that the Polack would find out about me and Lisa.

I could watch Jim's eyes when I told him. If he blinked too much I'd know they were already talking.

But then, if they weren't talking yet, and I told him, they'd start talking.

How could I keep them from talking? That's what I needed to figure out.

Lisa and I were about to go away for a weekend—she knew about a house you could rent on the Oregon coast—when Dad called to tell me he was coming to town.

"We're pretty busy, Dad," I said on the phone. "Christmas is practically right around the corner. I don't know how much I'll be able to get away."

"It's August, son," he said. "Don't be ridiculous. Christmas isn't for six months. I want to meet my granddaughter. Are you trying to tell me I can't meet my own granddaughter?" He laughed. It was a deep, happy laugh, one of those good laughs I'd known for years, and it fooled me.

My dad met his granddaughter in an IHOP off I-30. He told us he was on his way to Sedona. "To meet John Denver," he said. "I gave him the title for his new album." Uh-huh, I thought.

Wendy met me there half an hour before he arrived. Claire walked in with her, holding her hand. With the other arm she clutched a stuffed black poodle.

"Thanks for doing this," I said. I picked up Claire and held her in my lap.

"Daddy," Claire said. "Hi, Daddy." Suddenly she was shy. She placed her face against my neck. I took off one of my cufflinks for her to play with. I showed her how the back flipped on its platinum spring.

"I wanted to see your dad," Wendy said.

"You won't recognize him. What are you going to eat?" I asked her. "What should Claire have? What are you hungry for, honey? How about some pancakes? They have chocolate chip pancakes."

"She doesn't like chocolate chip pancakes. It's dinnertime. Why don't you have a hot dog, Claire? She should eat some protein," Wendy said. "Have you seen your dad yet? How is he?"

"I want pancakes, Daddy," Claire said. "I want chocolate pancakes. I do too like them. Yes, I do. I do not want a hot dog." She spoke precisely, emphasizing every sound, as if she had invented the word at the moment she used it.

"Yes, I saw him," I said to Wendy. Dad had come by the store earlier. I didn't want to talk about it. But Wendy always missed those cues or, more likely, ignored them. She used to tell me, "Don't make that face," and I would say, "You can't edit my facial expressions." But really she was in the right.

Jim and I had cleaned out his car that afternoon. It was full of clothing, books and tapes, old food, and cockroaches. There were other, smaller bugs. There was even a mouse. It jumped out of the car and ran away across the parking lot. Good for you, I thought. Better luck. Our dad had been sleeping in his car for weeks.

"Your poor dad."

"You are the only one who ever feels sorry for him," I said.

"You, too. You do, too. You feel sorry for him."

"Well, I'm still talking to him. Jim won't even talk to him now. But he helped me clean out his car."

My dad walked in the door. He had lost weight and there was more gray but he still had that aura around him, like his body was charged with a magnetic field that stimulated the nearby air molecules, atoms that were listless around the rest of us. His hazel eyes shone at me behind his heavy tortoiseshell glasses just as they always had. If things had been better in my own life I could have believed, maybe, looking at him and the easy way he walked, the same old Guccis and his gold rep tie, that he was not in this terrible state of degeneration. When he hugged me I smelled the cinnamon pipe smoke and the Yves Saint Laurent cologne in his beard.

"This is your grandfather, Claire."

"Yup, she's a girl, all right," he said, and sat down. "Did you order for me, son?"

Claire hid her face in my neck. I hugged her closer.

"Hello there, Claire. She has her mother's eyes," he said, and smiled at Wendy. You can't even see Claire's eyes, Dad, I

220

thought. But Wendy looked encouraged already. He was crazy, but he was sure the same good old Dad, too.

"Are you two doing all right? Are you better?" he asked my wife. She looked at her pancakes. She had ordered the chocolate chip pancakes and split them with Claire.

"Always take care of your family, son," he said. "A man takes care of his family."

I felt Wendy eyeing me, so I did not look over there.

"Let's talk about you, Dad," I said.

Over dinner he told us about his travels and his plans. He was going to open a church in Las Vegas or buy a motel in the mountains near Carmel. "I think Shirley is interested in investing, son," he said. "I'll ask her about jewelry if you like. But I think she prefers natural stuff. She's not into the material thing, you know. She's well beyond that."

"What's he like? John Denver. In person, I mean. You guys have been friends for years, right? Didn't you first meet at Ananda?"

I gave Wendy a look to say, Please don't encourage him. But that started him off. Claire and I sat back and played until he was done.

After Wendy and Claire left the pancake house my dad tried to extract the whole story from me.

"'Fess up, son. I can see what's going on here with my own two eyes. Your old man's not an ass."

I did not tell him about the separation. I explained that business was booming.

"Not the way your brother tells it. He says you guys are in serious shit with one of your big investors."

I was surprised that Jim had told him that. We had two one-year notes coming due for nearly a million bucks and our line of credit at our other bank was maxed out. And even Granddad was in no mood to float us. He said he wanted to see some green coming the other direction, for a change. But we had made it through the summer. Everybody was hurting in the summer.

"Dindy says you guys spend more time playing backgammon than you do balancing your books. He says you're three months behind on your P and Ls. That's no way to run a business, son."

"So where are you headed next, Dad? A new church, huh? That's the plan? What are you going to call it?"

"We are talking about your marriage, Robby. Your brother tells me things are on the rocks for you two. You can't afford a divorce, son. Emotionally, I mean. You can't do that to that beautiful little girl. That's what your mother did to me and look at the problems it's given you boys. Your mother's the reason you're in this mess right now."

Was Jim on drugs? Surely all of this wasn't coming from my big brother.

"This is not about Mom, Dad. And Wendy and I are fine. Jim doesn't know what he's talking about. Are you sure you got this from Jim?"

"How's your sex life, son? How are things in the sack with you two? Marriage can cool things down. You know the old saying. It's a great institution, if you want to live in an institution."

"It's fine, Dad."

"You can tell me, son. Does she have orgasms?"

"Dad, I do not want to talk about this."

"I understand. That can take time. That may be the heart of the problem. It can take years to learn how to make a woman come. But it's important, son. I can give you a book. If you need a little help, I mean." He gave me that sideways glance.

Why did you get married at all?"

Lisa came up with that question from nowhere I could see. We were lying in the sun with our eyes closed and our sunglasses on, side by side, holding hands between the deck chairs. I had thought she was asleep. Even with my new Persols on, the sun was as red as grapefruit through my eyelids. We were drinking those fresh-squeezed lime juice margaritas they have at the Four Seasons that are the best in Texas. The best north of the Rio Grande Valley.

I didn't mind telling her the truth.

"It was after you left me. Dumped me, I mean."

"Hey," she said. I lifted my glasses and saw that she was smiling. She wasn't looking at me, she was just lying there smiling. She looks so nice, I thought.

I should have gone ahead and said that to her.

"Anyway. I went back to Calgary. I got a job selling encyclopedias. Then my dad offered me eight grand to fly down to Florida and drive across the country with him. Even if he hadn't offered me the money I couldn't really say no. I had turned down a trip to India and a monastery in the Himalayas so I could hang out with Wendy. I still felt guilty about it. He called the Himalayas the Himahooleeyas. 'This summer me and my son here are going to the Himahooleeyas,' he would tell the checkout girl at the drugstore, 'want to come along?' So I flew down to Florida. We spent a few days in New Orleans and then we came across on I-10 to visit Jim and see his new store."

I took her hand and put it on my stomach. I was getting fatter, lately. I was sweating in the sun. We should get in the water, I thought. Cold water sounds nice right about now.

"If we would start doing drugs again I could lose this weight," I said.

"That is not funny, Bobby," she said.

"There was this cocktail waitress. I told my dad, 'That's the kind of girl I would ask out on a date if I had the balls to ask any girl out on a date.'

" 'So ask her out,' he said, and I said, 'That girl is way out of my league.' "

"You really do not get women at all," Lisa said.

"That's what my dad said. He was always telling me when I was a teenager, 'If you want to get laid, son, you have to learn to think like a woman.' And I would ask him if we could talk about something else. Anyway, when our waitress came back to the table my dad said, 'My son here thinks you are out of his league but I am betting you would go out with him. What do you think?' "

"That's a dad for you," Lisa said. She smiled. My dad and Lisa could have been friends, I bet, if I weren't in the middle of them. But because she was my lover my dad would not think of her with his usual generosity. He would treat her like I imagine he treated his own lovers, when he was married to my mother. He would treat her like she was only invited to join our civil company because she was providing a married man with his necessary recreational sex. For him she'd be one step up from a porno magazine on a newspaper stand. Or maybe even one step down.

"So what did she say? She didn't say okay."

"No. She said, 'I like both of you. I think you're both nice. Either one of you might ask me out and I might go.' "

"Well, that was honest of her. She was a friendly girl, wasn't she?"

"So he asked her," I said. "He asked me if it was okay when she left the table."

"I do not even believe you," she said.

"I know. That's how charming he is. He does it without even trying. It's like some old nurse who was a witch taught him the secret smile to use when he was born. I bet he got even more girls when he was drinking."

"I meant, for you," Lisa said. She sipped her margarita. I could tell her eyes were frowning behind her sunglasses and I felt like I was telling the story wrong. It wasn't anything against my dad, I wanted to tell her.

"It wasn't hurtful. It was just one of those things. He was teaching me something. Like hitting me on the head with a stick." Like a Zen master. He was helping me. To get free of him, maybe. Of trying to be like him.

"Okay," Lisa said. "It doesn't hurt to get hit with a stick?"

"I'm not explaining it right. Really it was a good thing. But anyway, that made me see things differently. Wendy, I mean. It made me see the value of Wendy. More clearly than I did, I mean." Was that what he wanted? "I mean, she loved me. She believed in me. I understood that I wasn't one of those guys I always wanted to be. With women, I mean."

Telling the story was making it less clear in my own mind.

"I need another margarita," I said. "Do you need another margarita?"

She was quiet. Her straw made a sucking sound at the bottom of her drink.

"Hey, not to change the subject, but when is Jim's baby coming?" she asked me. "Isn't their baby due any day?"

One of our salesmen had gotten a girl pregnant and Jim and

225

his latest wife were adopting the little baby boy, who would be born in a week or two. They were going to call him Tanner.

"Plus, you know, honestly, nobody will ever love me the way Wendy does," I said. "I mean, except for Jim, I guess. But he's my brother. That's reason enough to get married right there."

She reached out and took my sunglasses off. It was bright as a lightbulb out there by the surface of the pool.

"Let's have another drink," she said.

She sounded odd. But it may have been me. With the sun and not having eaten breakfast I was feeling a bit drunk.

"There was something I wanted to ask you, too," I said. Since you already said his name. Since you introduced him into the conversation. Better to get it out now, Bobby. In the open.

The thing was, a few days before, Jim had answered the phone and started having a conversation with someone who could only have been Lisa.

She didn't respond.

"Okay, I'm hot. I'm getting in the water," she said. She stood up. The sun was on her back and shoulders. She put her sunglasses on the table. Her movements were abrupt but had that fluidity beneath them like a tree branch shaking in the wind.

She was so slender that her belly curved in behind her hip bones.

"Can we talk for a minute, Lisa?" I said. But she dove in.

Later in the bungalow I questioned her about it directly.

"Did you call the store the other day? Did you talk to Jim on the phone?"

She said, "Don't be ridiculous."

Ridiculous was not a word she would use unless she was lying.

•

Monday morning when I was back at the store, I asked Jim. It was not really a question we were allowed to ask each other, but I didn't care.

"Yeah, she's called a couple of times. I picked up the phone when she was calling for you, I guess, and recognized her voice. She said you guys are dating a little."

I admitted to myself that I was not as surprised as I should have been. He was lying, too. The conversation I heard only a second of before he hung up had nothing to do with Lisa and me. He had been telling her about his last trip to Vegas. The return of Lisa to our lives should have been electrifying news. They didn't even have their stories straight. As developments go, it was oddly reassuring. By the way he said it I didn't think they were having sex or anything. Maybe they were just worried about me. They knew how bad things were with Wendy and they were hoping to protect me, trying not to add new worries and complications into my life. It could be that innocent, I thought. It was better if I left it alone. Also, that way, if I was wrong, if they were up to something together, I could keep an eye on them. By playing dumb, I mean.

So I understood immediately that it was Lisa he was hiding behind his idea of the trip.

"Get on a plane. You can use the store's AmEx. That's what it's there for," he said. "Relax with Kizakov in Tel Aviv. The way he splashed the green around on that place of his you wouldn't even think he's Jewish. Of course, they are different in Israel than they are over here."

"Okay," I said. I had always wanted to see Jerusalem. "That sounds good. Why not? I could use a little break. You're right. Good idea," I said.

"Buy us some diamonds. We can run a promotion when you get back."

I didn't think they were having sex. He wasn't trying to get me out of town so they could have a weekend together. They wouldn't do that to me. Jim wouldn't look at the sex as a betrayal. He would view that part recreationally. But Lisa would.

That was an advantage I had over them. Each understood what would count as a betrayal of me differently. I had double indemnity.

Then I thought: But what would Jim count as a betrayal?

"Keep it light. Don't go crazy. Spend a few hundred grand. I need a D Flawless six-carat marquise. A fine make. Ideal make if you can find one. It doesn't need to be certified. See what you can conjure up. Let Elie hold your hand."

So I left them both behind and flew to Israel. I stayed with Kizakov at his mansion in Netanya. I regretted this because I could not drink as much as I wanted or call a hooker. But the hookers seemed scarce in Israel. Hong Kong had been the same unfortunate way.

I tried calling Lisa several times while I was gone. I knew better than that. But I was up at all hours anyway. I crept down Kizakov's cool, breezy hallway in the dark and used a phone I had found on a hall table. There was no phone in my guest room, and my phone didn't work in Israel. One time her phone went straight to voice mail so, quickly, I called Jim's cell phone. His went straight to voice mail, too.

After we settled on the diamond buy we went to the coast and had dinner. Israel is an ugly, sandy country under construction, with more bulldozers than trees, but the food was excellent. We had roasted duck and many small plates of delicious pastes and hot flatbread. Kizakov did not drink, so I had a bottle of white Israeli wine to myself. It tasted like copper.

"Now you want to buy a piece of turquoise," Kizakov said.

"For my daughter Claire," I said. "She was born in December. Two years ago. It's her birthstone. You know how it is with your children. When you are traveling."

"Please, what's to apologize?" Kizakov said. "I admire turquoise. The true turquoise."

Not the next day but the following day, the day before I had to leave, he flew me in his little leather-seated jet to Cairo and we met with the turquoise sellers.

"This is turquoise *de la vieille roche*," the wrinkled Egyptian explained. It was like in a book you read when you were a boy. We sat on a red rug together in our bare feet and he poured the blue stones from leather pouches. The high-ceilinged room was quiet and decorated with many brass and silver ornaments. There was a large Koran on an ornate stand. He explained the quality of different turquoises to me and I learned. His turban was black. There was something in this Bedouin's ancient face that made me certain I could believe what he told me. But perhaps he merely came from an older, cleverer culture of sales. With Kizakov there, learning, too, serious and deliberate, I felt like a child among these men.

The Egyptian had finished pieces also, set in orange twenty-two-karat gold, but I selected a stone about the size of the top half of my thumb. It was a color of blue that you have not seen. After the long, patient discussion of price, while they drank tea and he graciously served me a beer, we settled at seventeen thousand. I still have the stone today. That is, my ex-wife has it, in one of that Muslim's simple leather pouches, in a safety deposit box at her bank, waiting for Claire to turn twenty-one.

•

Back in Fort Worth Jim was supposed to pick me up at the airport. I hung around the baggage check for half an hour or so, until the crowd cleared and I was there alone, watching the metal plates roll past, and then I called the store. At first there was no answer. I counted the rings. When I got to fifteen and the voice mail answered, I hung up in disgust and called again. Around ring eleven he answered. Of course, I thought. After eleven rings the owner answers the goddamn phone. I wished we could fire every salesperson we had and start fresh.

"Where are you?" I said.

"I'm just chatting with my dear friend Shelley," he said. I recognized his salesman voice. "You bring our big packages of diamonds, buddy? You find a bunch of bargains?"

"I thought you were picking me up," I said.

"Oh, good, good," he said. "Well, I better run, buddy. See you soon. See you as soon as you get those stones cleared through customs."

The diamonds were shipped under separate cover, of course, with insurance, and went through our customs broker.

I took a cab. But the way things were, since he was supposed to pick me up and left me here, I thought I would go home first and take an hour or two before getting back in to work. Maybe Lisa would have time for an early lunch. But I called and she didn't answer the phone.

Where is she all of a sudden? Just since I've been away, she disappears, I thought. I wondered if she knew when my plane got back. She didn't really work during the day. Obviously she wasn't with Jim. He was at the store.

•

"It's for Wendy," I told Jim.

A few days after I was back I bought Lisa an eighteen-karat gold and natural pearl bracelet that an antique dealer from Houston brought in. Normally I would not pay for natural pearls from a dealer because it was all bullshit, no one had a reliable way of confirming whether or not pearls were natural, you could use badly formed pearls from a farm and they would look like old naturals. But Jim had known this dealer for years and he never misrepresented his merchandise. The bracelet had been made by Cartier in the fifties and it had little knotted bars of gold wound all the way around. It was stamped, and not just on the clasp, which could have been added later. In between the bars were the pearls. Eight millimeters each. Eleven of them.

"Why would you divorce her and give her a bracelet?" Jim said.

"We go into arbitration in a few weeks."

"Mediation."

"That's what I meant," I said. "Mediation."

"Lord knows I have given my wives enough jewelry," he said. "But I never picked something out for my ex-wife."

It was only Lily he ever referred to when he referred to his ex-wife. The other two were like photocopies of Lily and with each new copy the image was inkier and more blurred. In the most recent divorce, which was only a few months old, Jim had relocated—on paper only, of course—to Nevada, for legal residence, and hired an actress to represent his wife in court. She never even knew they were divorced. She still thought they were merely separated. Tanner, their new little baby, lived with his mother, but Jim gave himself custody in the papers. "Because it was the right thing to do. I love my son. Also for leverage," he said, "in case she ever acts up."

"On the other hand, maybe it's smart thinking," Jim said, changing his mind. "She'll be generous, thinking she might still get you back if she isn't too greedy. But that brace- let's a find."

"This way it stays in the family," I said. "It'll be like a dowry for Claire." I felt guilty when I said that. I didn't like to use my daughter for material.

We were in the car talking when I gave Lisa the bracelet.

She said, "But Bobby. I don't wear jewelry."

It was true. I had considered that. But that was why she might wear one piece. For me. For us, even.

"You could try one bracelet," I said.

She knew jewelry and could see well enough for herself what kind of a bracelet it was. But I wished I could tell her they were natural pearls.

"It's very pretty," she said. "It's nice. But I'm so busy. I'm not one of these women who lives in a showcase, Bobby. I would just break it."

"It's old," I said. "It's stronger than it looks."

"You know how much I love to swim. I would forget it by the pool or I would break it swimming." She laughed. "I guess they are pearls, though."

"You are right," I said. "You might not want to wear those pearls in a swimming pool." I could not think about those pearls in water with chemicals.

"Anyway, the point is I can't wear jewelry in my business," she said. "It's asking for trouble. I would just have to take it off. And if I forget about it and leave it somewhere . . ."

"You wouldn't forget it," I said.

"I might," she said. "Sometimes I'm in a hurry to get out."

233

•

Lisa's boyfriend drove a blue Toyota pickup. They knew my car, so I stayed back. They went to an apartment complex off Eastchase. It was not too far from the temporary furnished apartment I had rented when I first left the house. It was a gated complex, like most of them over there, so I parked around the corner, on the street. You could not park there but I didn't think I would be long. I looked for a place to climb the fence. They would be on the second or third floor and the truck would be near the apartment. Most of the fence was metal and there was nothing to grip on but I found a section of old wooden fencing near the pool and used a plastic garbage can that was there to climb over. It was rainy and no one was at the pool. I walked into the laundry room to make myself inconspicuous. Often the manager's office was near the pool and I didn't know if I had been seen climbing the fence. It would have been better if I were not in a suit. I got a Diet Coke out of the machine. A man was there in a jogging outfit doing his laundry and he nodded at me.

"Cold for October," he said.

I tried to look as though I belonged. I opened the top of a washing machine.

"They work fine," he said. "New machines. But a buck-fifty a load is steep." He eyed me like he knew something was up.

"That is steep," I agreed. "I guess because they're new."

"Uh-huh," he said. He looked like the kind of person who would go to the office to report a suspicious person.

"My name is Plater," I said. "Adam Plater." We shook hands. He had a limp handshake like he didn't want to shake my hand.

"I've seen you on TV. You are that jeweler. Are you thinking of moving here?"

"That's right," I said. "But I'm not that jeweler. I get that all the time, though."

"No, you're him, all right. You got a girlfriend here or something? Don't worry, I won't say anything."

"It's nice to meet you," I said. He was baring his teeth. "If you ever need anything," I said, and hurried out of the laundry room.

I almost climbed back over the fence. Then I realized I could walk out the front. But I didn't want Lisa and her boyfriend to see me if they were leaving. Or if he was still in the truck, waiting. I knew that the man from the laundry room was watching me. But I could not look back over my shoulder to check. I walked into the manager's office. It was right there next to the pool. I came in a back door and sat down at the rental desk in front. I ate a candy from the dish on the desk. A vase on the desk held fake birds-of-paradise. There was dust on the orange and blue blossoms. In a minute an attractive young woman in a cheap nylon suit came around a corner with half a sandwich in her hand.

"You caught me," she said. "Can I help you?"

"I want to rent an apartment," I said.

"Good!" she said. She looked like a pleasant person. She was wearing a silver charm bracelet and CZ earrings.

"What sort of an apartment are you looking for?" she said. She looked past me into the parking lot for my car. She wanted to see what sort of apartment I could afford.

"My car's around the corner," I said. "I had some difficulty finding the office."

"I'm sorry," she said. "Are you looking for a one-bedroom or something larger?"

•

By the time I left the apartment complex with my copy of the application form in my hand my car had been towed. I sat on the curb for a few minutes. I took off my shoes and socks and rubbed my feet in the sand and pebbles in the gutter. The cold gravel felt good on my feet. But the rain was picking up and I was getting wet. I called Jim.

"Where have you been?" he said. "I've been calling you for an hour. Morgan was here. He waited and then gave up. I finally showed him the opal myself."

"Did he like it?"

"No," he said.

"That opal was perfect for him," I said.

"Is it a doublet? It looks like a doublet."

"No, it's not a doublet. It's eight grand a carat, Jim."

"I told him I thought it was a doublet. It looked too good. There was no price on the paper."

"I don't believe you told him it was a doublet. He'll think I was lying to him."

"Just tell him you screwed up. Where are you?"

It had taken me a month to find that opal. It was the perfect opal for Morgan. I was competing with a new dealer on Preston for the sale. I did not know how Morgan had found this independent dealer. He had been my best customer for three years. Now Jim had told him it was a doublet.

"My car was towed. I need you to come get me."

"We're stacked up over here. I can't come get you. Where the hell are you? Are you drunk? Are you at a titty bar?"

"I'm over on Eastchase. I parked illegally. I'm sitting in the rain. Send a salesman, then. Send Sosa."

"I'll send the Polack. Where are you? On Eastchase? What the hell are you doing on Eastchase?"

"No, don't send the Polack. Don't say anything to the Polack. If the Polack asks, I went to lunch. I'll explain when I get there."

I am going to catch a cold, I thought. That would be okay. I could use a few days off.

It started to rain more heavily. I pulled my blazer off and held it over my head. I held my phone with my chin.

"Bobby! Are you there? I can barely hear you. I thought you were going to lunch. What the fuck are you up to? You had better get your act together. You are fucking up. We needed that Morgan deal. You had better get your shit together."

We made the swap outside, at the curb.

"Thanks for coming to the store," I said.

It had been my day with Claire. I had taken her to the new meerkat show at the Fort Worth Zoo.

We could have met at the house but I avoided our house now, because she tried so hard to get me to come by the house. For a few months I carried a beeper she bought for me and it went off constantly. I kept my cell phone turned off. One night at three in the morning she beeped and then the cell phone rang because I had forgotten to turn it off. When I answered she told me she could hear a burglar outside. "He's out there right now," she said. This was my wife. I had married this woman. That comes with certain obligations.

My girlfriend was there in bed with me.

"I'll be right there," I said. "She lies to you," the Polack said. "You do not leave me in bed to go to her house in the middle of the night." "She doesn't lie," I said. "Say what you like about Wendy but she doesn't lie." "Maybe she does not know it. That she is lying. But, you trust me, she lies," she said. "And one more thing. Do not say her name like that when you are lying in bed with me. I do not want to hear that name," she said. "I told her I would go," I said. "I have to go. What if there is a burglar there? It's not just her. It's Claire, too. It's my daughter, too. My daughter, Polack."

Then I thought, Bobby, this woman is in bed with you, with her arms around you, and now you are going to drive across town on the cold road in the middle of the night to your wife. She may be the Polack, but she's a woman, too. Can you not have a little patience and sympathy? I reached to touch her cheek in the dark with my fingertips. But she turned her head away. "You do not bother coming back, then," she said. "You do not return here." "It's my apartment, Polack," I said. "Tonight, I am saying. Spend the night there. In your old bed with your old wife. You do not drive back here to hope to fuck me." "I'm not going to spend the night there," I said. "I'll be right back." "No, you will not," she said. Another night on the way back from Dallas the beeper went off and the Polack took it from the coin well and threw it out of the car. That's what you get for driving a convertible, I thought.

Wendy and I stood outside the store and I handed her our daughter. Claire did not want to go to her mother. She grabbed at my neck and my arms. She wrapped her little legs against my diaphragm and rib bones.

"No, you put her in her car seat," she said.

"Okay," I said. I did not know what else to say. There was nothing else to do except to put Claire in the car seat. I wondered if the Polack was watching us from inside the store. I wondered if it might be practical to kidnap Claire, drive to

Lisa's, and then the three of us could drive to Mexico. My new, improved family. We would have to wait until night so I could rifle the store's safes before we left.

"I want you to do it," Wendy said. "I want her to see who's doing it."

Because Jim wasn't taking his calls, Dad kept phoning me for money. I had relented and started up with the cocaine again. It was the buildup to the season and Jim and I were working fifteen- and sixteen-hour days. Black Friday was only a week away. I used one of those little brown bottles that Jim used to carry. I always offered it to Lisa. Out of politeness. Not because I thought she should have some. She said no for months and then she said, "Fine."

We were back at the Mansion on Turtle Creek. But not in the big suite I had moved us to for our last couple of visits. "I want to stay in our old room," Lisa said when we checked in. "Our regular room." It was one of the smaller rooms, on the third floor.

"Don't do it if you don't want it," I said. "But it is very good cocaine. I get it from the biggest importer in San Antonio. She is a little Mexican woman who weighs about three hundred pounds. Maria Garza is her name. She is the cocaine queen of Texas."

"I bet she has nice jewelry," Lisa said. She was being sarcastic but she knew it was true. It was sarcasm directed at me, not at the cocaine dealer.

I did not want to talk about that. You hated to think about putting your own diamonds and Rolexes up your nose.

"I don't know, Bobby," she said. "I like to feel clean when I take a bath."

"I'm used to doing it without you," I said. "But it is an awfully nice thing to do together."

Then, unexpectedly, and gracefully, not violently like I would have expected, she sniffed several small lines.

"Okay," she said. "We've done it now. We may as well go ahead and do it. Let's smoke some," she said after we had sex. There was something different about her. I did not like it, whatever it was, but it was spiritually stimulating. Suddenly she reminded me of Jim. Her face looked so independent. Like she had made a decision, and she was not going to tell me what it was. For my protection, maybe, or just because she didn't need to tell me, and I didn't need to know.

I wondered about that. Where precisely that change in her originated, I mean.

"Do you know how to do that?" Then I thought that was the wrong thing to say. "Can we even do that in here?"

"It's really easy. We'll smoke it in the bathroom. You know how it is, you don't let the smoke out of your lungs anyway. It tastes too good. We'll smoke a few grams and then go to the pool. It's dark, I bet we'll have it all to ourselves."

"It's ice-cold out there," I said.

"We'll have sex in the hot tub. We'll wear robes. It will be fun."

In the bathroom I sat on the edge of the tub and she sat on the floor with her back against my legs.

"I honestly can't sniff cocaine anymore, Bobby," Lisa added, as she started her cooking. "I quit sniffing it years ago. Sniffing it is too fake."

Jim was on the phone. I kept the pocket door between our offices open so that I could watch him when he grabbed the phone. This was not easy because we were very busy and the phones rang constantly. I always answered the phone now. With customers at my desk, too. I would smile and apologize and roll my eyes at the sales floor to express my frustration with my lazy salespeople and then get it on the second ring. "Clark's Precious Jewels." If it wasn't her I stuck them on hold. Even the Polack told me, "You are the boss. Let those salespeople answer your phone." But she didn't answer it any faster herself. It was never Lisa when I answered. But I knew that sometimes when Jim picked up it was her. I could see it on his face. He would stand, sometimes, too, and slide the door closed. He might do that just because the customer in his office wanted privacy. But he would do it when he was on the phone, too. I knew he could call out if he wanted. But when you called her she never answered, you always had to leave a message, and then she would call back. So I watched for that behavior especially closely. Call, leave a short message, watch the phones. When I could see him doing that I grabbed every call. I thought about cutting the line to his phone. If it was practical I would have done it. It would give me a few easy days. A few days before we got it fixed. He shouldn't be answering the phone anyway. The Polack was right about that. We were too busy to be answering the phone.

My boyfriend doesn't like you anymore," Lisa said.

"I don't blame him," I said.

It was late Saturday night and we were driving across I-10 to spend the night in a cabin on Caddo Lake in East Texas, in the Piney Woods. It was too far a drive for just one night and the next day. There was an oversized limestone fireplace in the cabin and I would make a real fire. In the morning there was a place on the lake we could have pancakes. This was our first trip there but I had read about it in a guidebook. I hoped the pancake place would be open with the cold snap. Maybe there will be ice on the edges of the lake, I thought. That will look nice against the dark water. In the guidebook it said it was the only natural lake in the state of Texas. And Texas was covered with lakes. All of those other lakes were made by human hands. That was upsetting to think about. Or bulldozers, more likely.

"He always liked you before. He always said you were a good one."

She tapped out two little polka dots of crank onto the plastic makeup mirror she carried with her. Then she sniffed them quickly up. She blinked.

"Do you want some of this?"

"I'm okay," I said. I wasn't in the mood. "If I were him I wouldn't like me, either."

"He's not like you. He's not jealous. He knows I love him."

"He still doesn't have to like me."

"I swear sometimes you act like I should be grateful to him. It's like you think most guys wouldn't want me for a girlfriend."

"That's a stupid thing to say. Hey, do you want some of this?"

I had brought a bottle of champagne for us to drink on the drive. It was a Louis Roederer I had not tried before. But when Lisa climbed in the car and saw it she was immediately irritated. "We're not celebrating anything, Bobby," she had said.

I tried to hand her the bottle. She ignored me. I thought she could use a drink.

"It's okay. I like it. I like how you think about me. You think something is wrong with me."

She is trying to let me in by faking a little bit of vulnerability, I thought. Or even not faking it.

"You don't know how I feel," I said. "Or if you do, you don't let me know."

I hadn't meant to be vulnerable back at her. But when I saw her face in the lights of the dashboard like that, with the cold champagne bottle between my legs, and the lights of my car on the highway, the truth just snuck up inside me and jumped out of my mouth.

"I'm sorry to be the one to give you the news, but you're not all that mysterious, Bobby."

I thought that through. I seemed plenty mysterious to myself.

I hated moments like this, but I noticed they were getting more common, in more than one of my relationships. It was like we were having two entirely different conversations, and each of us was talking only with ourselves. Yet along the way we managed to say enough to screw things up between each other.

"You should want me to break up with him. You should be afraid if I don't."

"Come on, Lisa. You know I would like it if you broke up with him. But I'm not going to ask you to."

"You should, though. You would if you knew."

I pulled the foil off the champagne bottle. Then I held the steering wheel with my knees and opened it. It was very good champagne and it did not bubble over. I took the steering wheel back and tried again to hand the bottle to Lisa. She waved it away.

"Maybe he's angry with me," I said. I took a swallow of the champagne. It was already much warmer than it should have been. I couldn't really tell what it tasted like anymore. "It's not like he hasn't always known what was going on with us. Anyway, I think he would be angrier if he knew I asked you to break up with him."

She was quiet.

Then it occurred to me that she was worried about herself.

I noticed what a small person she was, physically I mean, curled up in the car seat. Not much more than a kid, really.

"Afraid of what, Lisa?"

I looked at her but she wouldn't look over at me. She was staring down the road.

I took the last swallow of the champagne.

The highway was dark and seemed to be getting smaller and smaller in the night, as the tall black trees gathered closer to its sides.

At the lake the fireplace in the cabin started easily. That was a good sign. The flue was not stuck and I could see which way was open and which way was closed. The smoke went straight up the chimney.

We drove into the little town and looked for a bar. "I need a beer," she said. There were three of them, but two were al-

245

ready closing, because they were attached to restaurants. The third was a pool hall.

"Do we want to go in there?" I said. The men coming out of it looked like the men you see in small towns in Texas. Big men. I thought I noticed one looking at my car and laughing. He was drunk and was probably laughing about something else. But my car didn't look much like a truck. It was the contrary of a truck, in fact.

"Come on, let's play a game of pool. We need something fun right about now."

I thought my success with building the fire in the fireplace had already done that work for both of us.

When we parked she said, "Wait one second," and tapped out some more crank on that mirror of hers. I reached for it and did a couple of bumps myself. I figured it was about that time.

Inside, people were noisy and excited—it was Saturday night—and there were more men than women. I noticed the men looking at Lisa, first, and then the women, too.

I should have changed before we came over. I was still in my suit and tie from the store. I always made the salesmen wear a jacket and tie. Jim was the only man in the store who would wear a shirt and tie, or a jacket with an unbuttoned shirt collar.

"You want to play pool, little lady?"

A man about my own age in black jeans with a red bandanna tied around his hair was talking to Lisa. He had large dangerous lips. I was a few steps away, at the bar buying our beer.

"No, thank you. I am here with my boyfriend," she said.

It was nice to hear her describe me as her boyfriend. Even if it was a lie. But maybe she truly thought of herself as having two boyfriends. I could be her second boyfriend, I thought. That's one step away from being her first boyfriend.

"Hell, I bet he wouldn't mind if you play a game of pool. Hey, buddy, you mind if this pretty gal of yours plays a game of pool with me?"

I turned around. I tried to smile naturally. Naturally but confidently. Or naturally but faintly aggressively. Cockily, maybe.

"That's up to her."

"I already said no, thank you."

He took her by the arm. He had a pool cue in his other hand. She pulled her arm away. She looked at me for a second. There was something hopeful in the expression.

"One game." He pulled at her arm. I was unsure what to do. I was still waiting for the beers. But I had to do something. Then the bartender put down our beers next to me. I picked them up, one in each hand, and started for Lisa. I thought I might even say, Here, have a beer, buddy. We're not in the mood for pool right now, and give him one of them. That would settle him down, I bet. But as I elbowed my way out from the bar I saw Lisa struggle with the man—he was really tugging her arm—and when he turned to her with that same sloppy face she kneed him, as hard as she could, in the balls. If it had been any woman other than the woman I was with I would have admired it. She looked like she had done it many times before, like she was the blade of a jackknife folding up. He bent over and she pushed him to one side so that he collapsed, on his side and then on his back, onto the pool table. Then she took the pool cue he had dropped and poked it into his nose. She shoved the felt tip of the pool cue into his nostril and pushed. He was shouting. The ease with which she did it was almost comical. It looked like a kung fu move. She said, "You aren't much of a listener, are you?" Then she gave the pool cue

247

another push, but not as hard as she might have, and turned to me. The guy was still scrambling on his back on the pool table. I thought, Where do I find these violent, capable women? First the Polack and now this one. She stepped quickly over to me and took me by the arm—just like he had held her, I thought—and said, "Let's go. We're getting out of here."

People stepped out of our way and no one tried to stop us. When we got to the car I realized I still had the bottles of beer in my hands. I didn't know where to put them to get my keys. You couldn't balance them on the roof of the car because it was a convertible with a cloth top and they would just fall over. I was trying to hurry because I imagined the guy and his friends rushing upon us outside the bar. I was not drunk enough to want that to happen. I put one of the beers between my knees and got the keys from my suit pocket. We climbed into the car and drove back to the cabin. Lisa drank her beer. That was good. But the whole drive back we did not say one word to each other.

Inside, the fire had already gone out and the cabin was cold. I knelt to start it again but Lisa said, "I'm going to bed," and I thought, Why bother? I knew she couldn't sleep, not after the fight in the bar and the crank, but I couldn't bear the idea of sitting up there with her on the bed in the silence and the dark. If we still didn't have anything to say to each other, I mean. I sat in the living room, under the Navajo blanket that was across the back of the leather sofa, and drank a glass of water. There was no minibar in the cabin. Then I went to the car, opened the trunk, and found the Burgundy that I had brought for us to have with lunch tomorrow. I had planned for us to take the boat out and have a picnic on the lake.

In the morning we drove to the pancake place, but we weren't hungry.

*F*or weeks we had been building things. We drew designs and swapped them back and forth, we got out the stencils, the French curve set, and the Staedtler compass, we critiqued each other, we sent Sosa to the SMU art supply store for fresh 9000 pencils, we arranged tiny stones in black and purple sticky wax to evaluate sizes and patterns. We filled the holes in our inventory with pieces created by Jim and Bobby. The cocaine was helpful in this process—Jim was doing it with me now, too, or maybe he had never stopped and had just been hiding it from me—and we usually worked at Jim's desk, and late into the night. We drew sketches and checked diamonds for size against the open-pronged holes in yellow gold blanks. Christmas was rearing its fierce, beautiful head, and there was no time to dawdle or sleep.

"So she's a hooker now. Wonderful. Good for her. She's really moving up in the world. And you are paying her? I know you're not paying her. Why do you need a hooker for a girl-friend? In a way it's not fair to her. It's like you are making her into a liar. She's a hooker, so let her be a hooker. That's probably what she was meant to be all along."

"I pay her by the month now. She's not doing it for the money. I mean, she needs the money, of course. But that's not why we do it that way."

"Well, Lisa was always smart. Now she's a smart hooker. I'll give her that. What got her hooking anyway?" He paused for a minute. His eyes softened at the corners. "I guess it was the crystal. That's what does it to all of them. I told her not to smoke it. I told her and told her."

"She's not really doing drugs anymore. She doesn't do drugs at all, in fact."

She had done drugs once or twice with me, now, but I didn't know if she was doing them on her own. I didn't think she was. Not that I wouldn't have lied about it.

Except he might know better than I did what drugs she was doing. If they were doing them together.

"And I wouldn't say she's exactly a prostitute, Jim," I continued. If they were seeing each other he wouldn't say that. Unless he was paying her, too. "That's not fair. Or even accurate. It's more like a networking thing. That's what I'm saying. I was thinking we should hire her as a gift wrapper."

If I brought Lisa into the store I could understand whatever was going on between Jim and her. Then it would all be transparent, and my relationship would have the moral authority because I wasn't hiding anything from either of them. Plus, that would force me to end it with the Polack, which I needed to do regardless. I doubted I had the strength to remove the Polack from my life without outside help.

"Good idea. Hire the hooker. Free blow jobs with every Rolex."

"Like they don't get them already."

"Maybe I should call her."

Here it is, I thought. He's warming me up for it. The truth.

"You called her? She said something like that. I thought you had called her."

"I didn't call her. But maybe I should."

"Sylvia said something. She said she had given you her number."

"Don't you think I would tell you if I called her? Why don't you ask her? Do you think I would lie to you about a hooker?"

He had lied to me thousands of times. He lied to me almost as much as he lied to his customers. But that was beside the point. And if you told him he lied he would deny it with a sincere heart. He was extraordinarily healthy. Psychologically, I mean.

"She's not your type. I mean, not now, not anymore. She said something about it."

"I wasn't talking about having sex with her, Bobby. Jesus. Lisa and I used to be pretty good friends, you know. But maybe I should call her for sex. She would do it. Maybe that would show you. The point is you don't know anything about that girl. That hooker, I mean. I think she was fucking Popper, too. Did you know that? Did I ever tell you that? I bet she didn't tell you, did she? She's attracted to men like us. I bet she would like this new belly of mine." He patted his stomach. "The king muscle. Smart hooker."

I took the tweezers I had been playing with and put them back on his desk pad where I had found them. I folded the three carats back into their papers.

"The package looks fine to me," I said. "I like your bracelet idea. I bet Fadeen will go for it. But you better get terms," I said. "I have a few deals closing this week. But not enough to pay cash for these. You have anything working?"

I could not say anything directly about our numbers. But he had been behind me for months.

"Where are you going? I was kidding," Jim said. "Are you going to get your feelings hurt over a hooker?"

"Call her," I said. "It makes no difference to me."

I almost wanted him to. Or rather, I almost wanted him to believe that I wanted him to. If he already had.

"I was joking. Ha ha, a joke. I'm not going to call her. Hell, let's make her a gift wrapper if you want," he said. "I don't care. I remember she's good with her hands. That's a joke, too. Joking."

"Here. Here's her number." I wrote it in big, awkward numbers on his desk pad. The number he already had.

Bobby, I said to myself. Stop this now. Control yourself. If you let them know that you know it's real, then they can let you know it's real. And then it will be real.

I felt sick to my stomach. Like I'd been climbing the rubber-matted walls of one of those centrifuges we used to ride at the Calgary Stampede when we were kids. Jim was the only one who could ever get all the way up on his knees, or who dared to go to the top of the wall. The rest of us stayed on our backs about three-quarters of the way up.

"I'm not going to call her. I should, though. Remember those hookers in Vegas?"

In Vegas one time, at the Jewelers Circular Keystone Vegas show, we had been robbed by three black hookers of four hundred and twenty thousand dollars' worth of loose uncertified diamonds and thirty grand in cash. These women knew what they were doing. They demanded more money when we were in the middle of sex—I had two of them in bed with me, and Jim and the third one were already asleep, wrapped together in the next bed—and when I punched in the code to get a few extra hundreds, they must have watched me from behind. The next morning Jim woke me and said, "Did you move the diamonds? Because the safe is empty. Bobby, where are the diamonds?" I understood immediately what had happened, though it took a few hours before I could admit it to Jim. I remember rising from that bed, walking to the huge wall of glass that was one end of our enormous suite, and resting my forehead against it. There was Vegas, many floors beneath us, stretching out flat for brown and yellow miles, and farther out the line of the mountains.

Then I caught them. It was after midnight, and I had left my coke up at the store so that I wouldn't go through it all, but once I was home I changed my mind and drove back to the store. There they were, the Polack shouting in Russian or Polish on top of a jeweler's bench with her hands on the back of Jim's head. I watched them for a few minutes. She looked better with him than I imagined she did with me. I had never seen her naked from a distance like this. Naked, across the room like that, she didn't look like she thought about money as much as I knew she did. She looked so trustworthy. I thought, If you sold naked, no one could outsell you. In my desk I saw they'd found my cocaine and it was all gone. Naturally Jim's was gone, too. So I rifled the cash box to let him know I'd been there, and before he got the same idea.

I skipped work the next day and when Jim called at a quarter after ten I didn't answer the phone.

I wanted to kill her then. When I came in, after the weekend, I sat behind my desk with my diamond tweezers pinched around my pinkie finger or on the lobe of one ear and imagined her with that tiny red laser-targeting dot following the back of her slender skull.

First it was Jim and Lisa. Now it was Jim and the Polack. Or maybe it went in the opposite order.

When she finally came into my office I had a customer at my desk. Janie Krantz, one of my favorites, who was a publicist and on the side wrote books about child therapy. She was looking for a medium-sized cabochon-cut pink tourmaline. I loved these stones myself, so we were having a good time together shuffling gently with our rubber-tipped tweezers through the large cotton-wrapped parcels. She looked up and frowned impatiently at the Polack.

"We speak," the Polack said. "I explain something to you now."

"I am with Janie, Polack," I said.

"I'm on the run today anyway, Bobby," Janie said. "I should let you get home to your family." She gave the Polack a stare. Okay, Janie, I thought. "Put these three aside for me."

"Thank you, Janie," I said. We gave each other our private smile—I tell my salespeople, cultivate as many of those private smiles as you can—and she left.

"You said you wanted to talk to me," I said. "I really don't have anything to say to you at the moment."

"It is over. I leave the business, too! Time for me to go. Not the business. But this store. You and Jim. I have enough of this, now. I stay for the season. Then, I go!"

"Wait a second. What are you saying? I catch you screwing around with Jim and you dump me?"

"You are making me nauseated, Clark! I look at you and I want to vomit! I cannot watch this ugliness anymore. Fresh air. You need it. This place smells bad. And it is you! You are the cause! Why do I fuck your brother? He, at least, is a man!"

I rubbed my fingers against my thumbs, like you might if you were rolling a bit of earwax between them. My eyebrows were itchy.

"You're fired, Polack," I said. "Get the hell out of here."

"Fired?" she said. "You are joking me? I quit."

She walked out the front door of my office, and then out the front door of the store.

We were in the car, fighting. I was drunk and I shouldn't have been driving. At one point I thought I had somehow drifted over the line of the road and into oncoming traffic. I swerved back to the right, and then I realized that the lights I thought were headlights bearing down on us were just construction beacons.

"Let's tell the truth, Lisa," I plunged ahead. "You don't want me to leave my wife. And you won't be honest with me about why. I think it's because you are ready to leave your boyfriend. That's all I can guess it could be. And you don't want me to think that now it's going to be the two of us when you do. And Jim is in this somehow. I am just going to say it. I don't know how, but I know Jim is in this, Lisa."

I looked over at her. She looked back at me like I had thrown an object at her.

"You say you don't want to fight but you give me that. Nice."

She was shivering. I could have turned up the heat in the car but I knew I needed to keep both hands on the wheel.

"Why don't you just tell me what you want, Lisa?"

You are not selling her anything, Bobby, I told myself. Therefore you do not have to try to read her mind and repeat her thoughts. She is your girlfriend. Or your hooker. Your girlfriend-hooker. Calm down, I told myself. For that matter, come to think of it, I am the customer here, I told myself. Or at least I should be. That is how the natural order of this is and ought to be structured.

We better get home, I thought. We need to get in bed.

"Bobby. Bobby. Don't you get it? Did you even listen to a word I said to you? I'm pregnant, Bobby," she said. "That's what I have been telling you. If you would fucking listen. I'm pregnant."

The air took a kind of slide to the left, as though someone had divided the world's atmosphere into two halves, and then bumped the bottom to one side with her hip. I tried to steady the car. Someone blared their horn, and then again.

"I'm sorry," she said. "I don't know what I expect you to say now. Oh, fuck," she said. "I knew I wasn't supposed to see you tonight."

"Let's go back to my apartment," I said. One step at a time. "You've never seen the whole apartment. Do you want to see Claire's room?" Why did I say that? It was just a baby thing. It said itself.

"What a thing to say. Jesus. I need to get the hell out of here, Bobby," she said. She looked like she might start to cry. "Pull over. Pull over right now." I had never seen that expression on her face before.

"I am trying to talk to you. Give me a second, okay?" I said. "You just told me that we are having a baby. Can I catch up for a second? Can we talk for a minute?"

"Let me out of here. Get away from me, Bobby. Get your hands off me. Drive the fucking car, Bobby!"

I slammed on the brakes. There was a long, frightening noise, and I thought, that's it. But we missed the telephone pole. We were up on the curb. The lights didn't look right. I felt my face with my hands. Lisa pushed open her door and took off walking. I hurried out my door but I knew better than to try to grab her arm again. She needed her coat. All she had on was a skirt and a blue tank top. I had bought that tank top for her at Barneys one day, when I was in a hurry. I thought it was the wrong thing and almost didn't give it to her, but then she loved it. Occasionally she would let me buy her clothes. But it was loose, you could see her whole body beneath the holes under the arms, she couldn't wear it like that, walking down the street at two o'clock in the morning. Plus it was freezing. She would get sick. Who knew who might try to pick her up from the side of the road? She didn't even have any shoes on.

"Lisa!" I shouted after her. "Lisa, you don't even have your purse!"

She kept on going.

I turned around and looked at the car. I don't even know if the damn thing is going to drive, I thought. I climbed back in and tried to start it but I couldn't find my keys. When had I taken the keys from the ignition? I have to be at the store in six hours. I have a nine a.m. diamond appointment. My hangover was already starting.

•

When I arrived in the cab the two customers were outside our front door already, their hands in their coat pockets, waiting for me. I opened the door with my keys and let them in. Everyone smiled falsely up at them from their positions bent over the open showcases. Thousands of pieces of jewelry, our inventory twice as heavy as normal with the coming Christmas season, sat on the showcase tops in the white and blue plastic tubs. My salespeople were thinking: one less on the cases.

I had planned to switch these two to Sosa. They were referrals of mine but a young couple and easy to switch. I was exhausted. But I looked around for him and he wasn't in yet, naturally. So the hell with it. I would sell them myself.

I took a deep breath when I sat them down at my desk. Okay, I thought. Maybe this is what you need right now, Bobby. A clean sale. A bit of sanity to start the day.

How do you sell a diamond to a young couple? It is very, very easy to do. Find out who's in charge. Usually it is the woman. Then focus your attention on the other one: explain everything to the weak one, act as though the power's over on that half of your desk. He's grateful, he trusts you, he thinks you understand him, he thinks you like and respect him. Now, when you are getting down to selecting a diamond, subtly betray him. Let her know that you understand that she is the decision maker. How? Push on one stone that he likes. She won't like it, for the obvious reasons. When she insists that *that* diamond, some other diamond, is really the prettiest one, agree with her: You know, I think she's right. On your hand (ask her to extend the fingers of her left hand and hold them tightly together, and then with diamond tweezers lay the stone carefully in the groove between her ring and her index finger), there is something about that one, you are exactly right, I didn't see it myself until now, but that one is just right. You picked it. That's the one.

Sold.

It works just as well the other way, if the man is in charge. Maybe better, because they need it more. The belief you can give him. The belief you can sell him, sell them both. That way it's not just jewelry they are buying. You can sell her belief in him.

They purchased the stone. It was a carat and a quarter radiant, I VS2, pleasant. A faked GIA certificate. Sosa had made it for me a few days before on our copier.

She loves it. It will appraise for twice that price! Sosa arrived and walked casually through my office. I asked him to take the job envelope to Old John: I was going to set it while they waited, so she could try it on before she left. He might give it to her then. They often did. Propose right in front of the jeweler. Well, the diamond would last.

I introduced them to Sosa. "One of our best salespeople." I said it sincerely, but he laughed sarcastically to make them think I was mocking him. Why did he do that? I wondered.

The young woman, her hand oddly out as though the diamond were still balanced on her woven fingers, gave me an inquisitive, unhappy look. She did not want to believe I could be tricking them about anything, or that I was the kind of person who would ever do that. The particular sales technique I had used on them depended, like all lazy lying, upon unimpeachable sincerity. But he just kept on going, right through the office, and closed the rear door abruptly behind himself I smiled at them and said something funny, "He's late, and I get in trouble," to put us on the same side, and they were fine again.

I rang up the card (you never really expect it to go through, and then like a locked door opening it does, and everyone feels reassured, both about themselves and one another), walked them to their car, opened her door for her, and told them I'd see them tomorrow. Old John was behind and couldn't mount the diamond before closing, plus the platinum mounting took time to size.

Then I went into Jim's office.

"Do you have time for lunch today?" I asked him. "We need to talk about the Polack." He gave me a look. He was on the phone. It sounded like it was a customer he was talking to, at least.

He shook his head at me. While he was talking he wrote on his desk pad, "Let her go." Then he tapped his pen on it. He smiled at me.

Okay, I thought. That's how we were going to handle this. I went back to my office and sat in my chair. I tried to call Lisa. She was on the other line and she didn't pick up. Or her phone was turned off. Or she didn't have her phone because it was in her purse and her purse was still in my car, in the tow yard. I looked in my desk drawer for my coke. I was out. I picked up the phone and called Maria, my connection. One thing at a time, I thought. Another appointment had come in and was waiting for me there on the showroom floor. It was a custom order. He was coming to preview the diamonds for a necklace. I still had not picked the stones. I tried to decide on the best lie to tell him. Maria didn't answer the phone. I used the beeper option, and then stood up to go greet my customer.

•

The ceiling of the room was partially lit, through my curtains, by someone's headlights outside my bedroom window, a floor below. I could hear one voice and then another voice. Go back to sleep, Bobby, I thought. This is no time of the night to think about things. I closed my eyes. But just then there was a tiny movement on my pillow. I opened my eyes and there was a movement, again, in the dark. It could have been my body pulling at a sheet that tugged the fabric of the pillowcase. I reached and turned on the light. There was a very small brown bug on the pillow. I put on my glasses. It was a baby cockroach. About the size of the ash on a cigarette, but a cockroach. I crushed it between my thumb and forefinger. I would have let it live if it had been some other kind of bug, I thought. But, even in my present circumstances, I could not let a cockroach run around in my bed at night.

That made me think of another time, visiting my father in West Palm, in the summertime, when I was eight or nine. I had finished my eggs and I started to put my dishes in the dishwasher like we did at home. "Nope, not in there, son," my dad said. He opened the dishwasher so that I could see, but not too widely. Dozens of cockroaches scampered around the plastic walls. "There's a whole family of them living there," he said. "I just wash the dishes by hand."

Larry's bench was now behind Old John's: Jim had moved Larry up in the jeweler's line after he had successfully hand-fabricated a gold breastplate modeled after the breastplate of Aaron for a Jewish cardiologist in Houston. Except for Old John, who was working on a pink gold and chalcedony necklace for a client of mine, one of my Highland Park ladies, everyone had gone home. I sat at Larry's bench and watched Old John's deft, pretty torch-work. He had sections of the clouded, grayish blue stone masked off with tiny pieces of balsa wood to protect it from the heat.

Old John had his snake coiled over his shoulders. It knew to keep its head away from the invisible flame of the torch. It was moving, though, looking around with its neck and head, as it liked to do while he worked.

"When are you going to go to college, Bobby?" He said it

without turning his head. I was startled. I almost stood up. Then I tried to make it look as though I were only inspecting a tool on Larry's bench. But Old John hadn't noticed. He was focused on his work. "When are you going to start making a real life for yourself?"

"I'm a businessman, Old John," I said. "This is my life. This is the life I want. "

"Bobby, you are my friend. You are also my boss. But let's be frank, you aren't a businessman. You know it and I know it. Maybe everybody doesn't know it. Not for me to say. But you won't be able to hide it forever."

That hurt my feelings. It was something the Polack would say.

"I'm the best salesman in this store, Old John," I said. "For that matter, people say I'm the best salesman in the whole metroplex. Even Granddad says so."

"I didn't say you weren't a salesman. That's the chief problem, I'd say. I've never seen one better. But a salesman is the opposite of a businessman, Bobby. A businessman cares about the practical details of life. A salesman is an artist. He can't tie his own shoelaces. He lives on tomorrow. He's a cloud-and-sky guy, a rainbow man. He can't hold money. He can't make a goddamn dollar out of four quarters and a can of glue, if you want to hear the truth of it. That's you, Bobby."

I thought there was something I ought to reply. Because I was his employer.

"You can't snap your fingers and become American, Bobby. It has to come naturally. You didn't even watch the right commercials growing up."

I rubbed my hands together and looked down at my legs. Then I plucked up the creases in my pants. I was wearing my dark gray Zegna, my favorite winter suit.

"If you want the truth, you should just grab that girlfriend of yours and go. If I were your father, that's what I would tell you to do. Pack up everything you love and get on the road."

It was getting late, so these phrases imprinted on me. My father had told me a similar thing once, and Granddad and Kizakov had both dropped hints.

He couldn't mean the same girlfriend I meant. But that didn't matter.

The snake turned and looked deeply at me then. It seemed to freeze, and curl its dimpled lips.

The security gate to Lisa's apartment complex stayed open for a few minutes after a car went through. That is, it stayed open behind a car coming out. For the cars coming in, the gate was prompt and effective. So I waited to one side until a car left the complex and then swung around it—the driver honked the horn, but we weren't even close to hitting each other—and made it through the gate. The gate scraped the back corner of the car as I came in. I was irritated at myself because I had just picked up the repaired car from the paint-and-body shop a few days before. If I had to scrape the car I should have scraped the rental.

I knew she was home. I had been watching the apartment from a place where she couldn't see me. I saw a man drive up, walk up the stairs, and then leave again less than an hour later. He was in a new black Porsche. It still had the dealer tags on it. He was older than me but handsome and in a good suit. A client. I didn't get a very good look at him. But I could tell by the way he walked that he was a doctor. In my business we can spot doctors immediately.

I was surprised and angry that she worked out of her home. She is even breaking the hooker rules, I thought.

Maybe she had more than one apartment.

After another hour had passed I decided she was probably done for the evening. It was quarter after eleven. That was too early. Maybe it was a lag time.

I knew she was still in there. It wasn't like she had a back door. But she wasn't answering the phone.

I went up the stairs and rang her bell. I knocked on the door. I yelled through it. Nothing.

I stayed out there until two or three in the morning. I figured she had to come out eventually. I could stay all night if I had to. At one point a car pulled up and another man got out, a different man than the last one. He started up the stairs, with his keys in his hand, jingling, and then lifted his eyes when he was almost at the top and saw me sitting there against her door. He stopped. Then he turned around, jogged down the stairs two at a time, got back in his car, and drove off.

Do you know where Lisa is?" I asked her.

"No," she said.

"You're lying, Sylvia," I said.

"You do not call me a liar. No."

"She wanted me to call her, Sylvia. She told me to call. Her phone isn't working. She didn't leave a number."

"Uh-huh."

"No, really."

"Then I guess she'll call back."

Sylvia was not someone you could reason with. But I did not have any way to threaten her.

"What if she's in trouble? What if she needs money?"

"She's fine. She doesn't need your money."

"So you know where she is? You know how to get in touch with her?"

"I have to go, Bobby," Sylvia said.

"No. No, don't go," I said. "When's the last time you talked to her?"

"When's the last time you talked to her?" Sylvia asked me.

I didn't want to say.

"I don't think she wants to talk to you, Bobby," she said. "Go home to your wife, Bobby."

"Please help me, Sylvia," I said.

"Why don't you ask your brother," she said, and hung up.

I told him everything. I had wanted to be strong but then I gave up. Just tell him the truth, Bobby, I allowed myself. It was a great relief. He was my big brother. I needed his help.

But he didn't talk about Lisa. He only talked about the baby.

"Tell her she can't have it. It's your baby, too. Tell her she has to get an abortion. How far along is she? I can talk to Watkins for you. Watkins does them all the time. Only for friends, of course. It can be totally private, like a regular doctor's appointment at his office. He would probably even do it on trade. His girlfriend wants a Cartier tank."

"I can't very well tell her it's my baby, too, and use that

premise to argue her into having an abortion. Plus she won't return my calls."

"Don't argue with her. Sell her. You are a salesman, for crying out loud."

"She won't talk to me, Jim. I don't even know where she is. You don't know, do you? Do you know where she is, Jim?"

"Good. That's better. Problem solved. In the worst-case scenario it's a paternity suit. That wouldn't be the end of the world. Plenty of dads have paternity-suit babies. Hell, that one ob-gyn client of mine has five or six paternity-suit kids. He even hangs out with some of them. I'm astonished I don't have one myself."

I cut us both a line. I made his twice as fat as mine. I didn't want the cocaine. But I wanted to keep him talking. I handed him the mirror.

"Anyway, it's not a baby," Jim said. He sniffed the cocaine up. "Stop calling it a baby. It's one of those things at this stage. A dot of cells. What's its name? A bathysphere."

"A blastocyst."

"Whatever. The way I see it you need an argument for not having an abortion, not the other way around. I never get these idiots who think you should have a right to life. A right not to live is what we need. Don't bring me there unless you really have no choice! If you're gonna do this thing I hope you've got everything arranged! The way it's supposed to be! That's what I would have said to Mom and Dad if I could have. Why did you do this to me! That's what I feel like most of the time. Here, have another drink. Let me fill you up. Drink up, Robby. You can use it."

He poured me another glass of wine. He used a new glass. I already had a first glass half empty there next to it. It was a bottle from a case of Pomerol he was giving me for Christmas. He said,

"I hate to spoil the surprise, but under the circumstances." I was glad he did, because I hadn't bought him anything yet, and hadn't even thought about it. It didn't seem like a year we would buy each other gifts. But we bought presents for each other every year.

Dad had once told me that two babies were easier than one. That made me happy because, after all, I had been his second baby. Of course, my two babies couldn't really be in the same house. I did not think I would ever have custody of my other baby. But that was another reason for wanting this one. A baby to live with me in my home. To dress in the morning and bathe at night. We could even name the baby Robby, maybe. That name works for a boy or a girl.

"Anyway, what makes you think this blasto—this blasto—what makes you think this baby is yours? I mean, considering. It doesn't seem statistically likely."

"Don't be ridiculous. Of course it's mine. Who else's could it be?"

My question was supposed to be rhetorical, but I didn't like the way it came out. Nevertheless, I was sure it was the fact of the matter. That the baby was my baby, I mean. Our baby.

"Listen. Maybe there's something I better tell you. Maybe there's something you need to know, Bobby."

He sniffed the other line, my line. He looked up at me with his cheeks and his chin bright red from the cocaine. It was cut with something hard that made your nose hurt.

"Let me tell you the story," he said.

I took a swallow of my wine. It was too late for confessions now. Even I could see that.

"No, Jim."

I don't believe I had ever said those words before.

•

*I*t was after midnight when Lisa came to the store and knocked on the glass. Her eyes were circular. They looked like they might roll out of her head. She was chewing gum. Those are not cocaine signals but crank signals.

I had turned off the CLARK'S PRECIOUS JEWELS sign before she came but the yellow overhead lights were on in the parking lot. She must have parked on the other side, because my car was all alone out there. I said, "Hi." I didn't know what to say. When I called her on the number Jim finally gave me she said, "How did you get this number?" I said, "Lisa. Please. I have to see you," and she said, "Fine. Tonight. At the store."

So I said, "Welcome to the store."

I didn't know what to do, either. I didn't know where to put my hands. So I showed her around. I took her to the back.

She said, "Where do you want to do it? Here in the back?"

I said, "I don't know. I don't care, Lisa. That's a weird thing to say. Why do you say that?"

That's the crank talking, I told myself.

Suddenly I felt shy. Shy like you are with prostitutes the first few times. Like masturbating in front of your lover.

This was the first time she had ever reminded me of a prostitute. Like a hooker, I mean.

We walked through the safe room and into my office.

She picked up the tweezers off my desk. "Nice desk," she said, and patted it with her hand. I realized, How strange, that she's never been in the store before.

I started to tell her the story we always told about the desks. We had bought them from a friend of ours who was one of the top guys in the Russian underworld diamond cartel. They were stolen. It was a good story. They were too big for the offices. They were three hundred years old. They matched. They were from the old Fabergé offices in St. Petersburg. But I stopped myself before I started the story.

She abruptly walked back into the back-of-the-house. That made me upset. I didn't need her roaming around. Our hidden cameras were back there and they were on a twenty-four-hour tape. They never turned off. They could keep an eye on her. Because I could not very well tell her not to go back there.

She walked into the wrapping room, where the fridge was. I tried not to follow her too closely. She spun the wrapping paper on the big rolls in the wrapping room. I took a beer from the refrigerator.

"Do you want a beer?" I said. "Maybe we should have a drink? I think that's a good idea." One or two drinks would not hurt anything or anybody. The baby, I mean.

"Do you have Crown?" she said.

Crown? I thought. Since when did she drink Crown Royal?

"Okay," I said. "It's in the other room."

"I am going to light a pipe," she said. "Do you want to smoke?"

"Okay," I said. That was an awful idea. I did not want to know what we would be smoking. But it did not matter.

That could not be good for the baby, though, I wanted to say. Of course, I couldn't say it. It was crystal we would be smoking, I bet. I did not even know if there was still a baby living in there.

We reserved the hard liquor under the cappuccino machine with the mixer and the nuts and cocktail napkins. I went to the other room and thought, Why isn't she following me? The safes were closed but there was the mailroom, and the phone sales people always left things out that they were looking at while they were selling them. In a busy jewelry store you never manage to get everything into the safe. Not to mention the cash box. You couldn't get that cash box open. But she could hide the whole cash box somewhere while I was mixing her drink. I wasn't worried about the money. It was the explaining. It was easy to know who had been the last in and the last out. If you had a key you had a unique alarm code. There were only three keys. And then Jim would look at the cameras.

It was like she knew the Crown was in the other room.

"Lisa. Are you okay?" I wanted to hear where she was in the store. By her voice I could know if she was doing anything.

"I'm here," she said.

When I brought her the drink she had taken her shirt and her bra off. She was sitting with her legs open on Jim's brass elephant we had brought back from one of the Thailand trips. She had the lapis lazuli ball of Jim's desk globe in her hands. It was about the size of a volleyball and very heavy. It was inlaid with gold, silver, and various semiprecious gems: topaz, citrine, amethyst, that sort of thing. Cheap stuff. He thought those globes would sell like wildfire. I knew they were too expensive.

"Let's go somewhere," I said. "Let's have this drink and go somewhere fun. Are you hungry? We could go to Dallas. It's been almost a month since we've been to Dallas. We could stay in a hotel."

"Let's do it here," she said. She put the globe on Jim's desk. If it rolls off it will chip, crack, or even break, I thought. "I said we were going to do it in your office."

I held her drink in my hand. "Here," I said. I motioned her into my office. "Why don't we have a drink?" I said.

"Where do you want to do it?" she said. I wondered if she

was already drunk. I could not ask her that, either. "What about on your desk?"

"Let's look," I said. I put her drink on my desk. "Here's your drink," I said. "It's kind of messy in here."

"We'll clear it off. I don't mind." She got off the elephant. She walked into my office. She picked up Jim's stapler before she left his office.

"We'll clear off anything sharp," she said. She took her drink. "This is strong," she said. She swallowed the whole drink quickly.

"I hate all this Christmas crap," she said. "Why do you guys fuck up this nice store with hanging all this Santa Claus shit?"

"I don't know," I said.

She was moving things on my desk.

"The mess is kind of organized," I said.

"I want to do it on your desk. We don't have to do it on your desk. Could I have another one?" She clicked the stapler. Folded staples fell out of it.

"Diamond scales are funny. I would have to recalibrate my diamond scale. You know how sensitive they are. You can weigh a human hair on a diamond scale."

"Move the damn scale, Bobby. I want to fuck. Like we used to fuck. Let's really fuck like we're fucking fucking."

"That's what I'm saying. That's the problem. They are like tropical fish. Like saltwater fish. You know you can't really move them."

"What about under the desk? Are you going to make me another drink?"

She might be in a hurry for another drink because she wants another drink, I thought. But she might want me out of the room again. She never took her shirt off like that. But she wasn't encouraging me to drink.

"You won't fit under there. Not with my legs."

"I meant both of us, Bobby. Why are you nervous now? What's wrong, little Bobby?" Suddenly she was sarcastic. I was afraid of that. "Don't you want to say it? Just say it, Bobby. Say what I know you want to fucking say."

Now I suppose I understand what she wanted me to say. I'm pretty sure I do. But I did not know that night. And it might have helped me if I had. At least, I don't believe I knew.

"Seriously. You are not in a position to be nervous, Bobby." She gave me an unexpectedly cogent look. "I am the one who should be acting nervous, here."

"I'm not nervous."

"You are acting weird."

"I am the same me. I promise." I didn't know what to say. So I said, "I'm sorry."

"Nice." She laughed. "That's real nice. Good, Bobby, I'm real glad. I'm real happy for you. Fuck it. I give up. Let's do it, then. Let's do it right here. But I want another drink."

Maybe that could help us out of this, I thought. Sex, I mean, not another drink. It couldn't make this situation any sadder or more dangerous. Worth a try.

Another drink was a good idea, too.

"Maybe in back. Anyone could walk up here."

"No." She clicked the stapler some more. "You said. You said in your office."

"The whole thing is the office. The whole store. It's all my office. I own the whole thing."

"I thought Jim owns it. Jim owns it."

"What are you talking about? We both own it. Is this some bullshit Sylvia told you? We own it together."

"But Jim started it. Sorry," she said, and laughed. "I mean, I'm sorry but it's true."

I did not have anything to say. She stumbled and caught herself on the desk. When she looked up at me her mouth curled like she wanted to bite me.

"You coward. You fucking coward."

Don't disagree with her, Bobby. She's drunk, and worse. Let her say whatever she wants you to say. None of this matters.

"And Sylvia knows more than you think."

"About the store, I mean. That's all I was saying, Lisa. I wasn't trying to say anything big. Can we just—" Don't tell her to calm down, Bobby, you know what that will do. "Sylvia doesn't know about the store."

"I don't know," she said. She laughed. "It's none of your business." She laughed harder. "I like this office," she said, and went back into Jim's office. "This office is comfortable," she said. She sat in his chair and crossed her legs. She put her empty drink down on the desk. "Another drink, please," she said.

"We are not having sex in this office," I said.

"I think I should say where we're having sex. I'm the whore. It's my rules."

"Let's go to my apartment. You were right," I said. "Put your shirt back on, Lisa."

"No. We're doing it right here," she said. "Right here where you promised. Right here in this chair. But first I want another drink." She laughed again. I tried to laugh along with her. "What the fuck do you think I'm doing here, Bobby?"

Right, I wanted to say. That's the question.

"I want to fuck you and then I want you to pay me for it," she said. "That is how this is supposed to work. Works. That's how I work, Bobby."

"I know what kind of work you do, Lisa. You don't have to remind me." Cool it, Bobby. That is not helping. Slow down.

"Are you going to fuck me or not? I need some money. I need some fucking money, Bobby. Will you listen to what somebody is saying for once in your life? Get it? Give me some fucking money."

"Lisa, if you need some money I'll give you some money. Why didn't you just say you needed some money?"

"Oh that's real nice. Thanks a lot."

She was rubbing her hands on her hips, quickly, over and over. She had lost some weight and she looked like she might rub her jeans right down her legs. Suddenly she grabbed her T-shirt off Jim's desk and pulled it over her head. That was something. It was inside out, but I wasn't saying anything.

"I'm not your fucking charity case, Bobby."

I gave her three thousand dollars, which was what we had in the cash box, and she left in a hurry. I knew I shouldn't have let her drive but I couldn't imagine trying to put her in my car. We both had plenty of practice driving drunk. The crank would help her see. If Jim asked me any questions I would be pleased to tell him the truth.

The winter morning was very cold and the parking lot was still dark. I pulled in, running late, looking for Lisa's car, hoping, maybe, that she had slept in it. Slept in it but not frozen to death.

When I came in Sosa was sitting at my desk, with his jacket off and his elbows jutting out. I worried that there might be some evidence on my desk from the night before. But we hadn't done anything. In the end we hadn't even done any drugs.

He was gaining weight in his arms, I noticed. I sat down and ignored him for a minute while I looked through my messages. I had a stack of them, pink papers like playing cards, spilled all over my desk pad.

"Boss, I'm going to tell you the truth," he said. Bad news, I thought. He had not called me boss in months. "I've found another job."

"It's nearly Christmas, Sosa," I said. "You cannot quit at Christmas."

"It's not my fault. I didn't have a choice," he said. "It's with Waltham's. A real Rolex dealer."

Even my employees do it to me now, I thought. Real Rolexes. As opposed to the other kind? I was past explaining this to people.

"Can you tell Jim for me? I'm afraid to."

"Give us the season, Sosa. Start on the twenty-seventh. That's not too much to ask."

"I want to, boss. I would love to. But it was the only way they would hire me. If I start immediately. They need me for Christmas is the thing. They have to make money, too. Plus it's when I'll make my best commissions. I owe it to them. Since they offered me the job, after all. I mean, ethically speaking. Fair is fair."

•

She's having a party. She wants you to come. Don't ask me why."

"She asked you to tell me that she wants me to come to her party," I said. "She doesn't want to ask me herself."

"I don't know. She just said to tell you she was having a party and she said you could come if you want."

"That I could come if I want," I said. "Not that she wants me to come."

"I didn't have a fucking tape recorder with me, Bobby," Sylvia said. "I don't know. The facts are she is having a party and you are invited."

*T*here had been snow. I drove carefully because these Texans did not know how to drive in the weather. But I was in a hurry. I did a few bumps from the bottle. I did not even want the coke. But it was best if I did some. I wanted to be charming and robust. Convincing. Also I wanted to be able to drink a lot, securely, if I needed to.

When I got to the party her apartment was empty. Someone had lied to me or I had the date wrong, or I had assumed it was at her apartment but it was at a restaurant or a hotel, and Sylvia had told me and I had not heard her or she had forgotten to tell me, or she had failed to tell me deliberately. Sylvia. With her crabs. I never liked her.

I saw there were open bottles around the apartment like from a party.

Then I heard a noise. It came from the hallway.

In the bathroom on the floor was her boyfriend. He had an arm resting on the bowl of the toilet. Or rather he was sitting next to the toilet and using it to prop himself up. He had his elbow oddly over the top of the bowl. He had a Dallas Cowboys baseball cap on. In his other hand he had a wad of bills. He looked up.

"Here," he said. "This belongs to you."

He threw the money at me. But it fluttered up into the air, like tossed tissue paper or moths, and drifted down around us.

"Are you hurt?" I said. "Should I call an ambulance? Where's Lisa?"

He had blood on his sleeves and the front of his shirt. But his hands were clean.

"She's downstairs," he said.

He was drunk.

"Downstairs. Waiting on you." He laughed. "Them Indians," he said. "Fucking cowboys and Indians."

When I went downstairs I saw blood on the graveled steps. I had not noticed it coming up. He must have been drunk and fallen down the iced stairs. And climbed back up again. Or maybe they had carried him up and that was what cleared out the party. The two of them had a fight. Over drugs, and therefore the money in his hands. He was her connection, too, and she was always owing him money.

Lisa was not in the parking lot and her car was not there, so I supposed she had left. I checked around back. Then I saw her. She was folded into the Dumpster like she had been climbing into it and then, when she got to her middle, her hips, became discouraged and decided to lie there, bent over in half. I pulled her out. She did not look dead to me. I knew I should perform mouth-to-mouth resuscitation on her but the bottom parts of her face were not available. Her right eye, no, not her right eye, her left eye was out of its socket. Under her hair I could see a large part of her bruised brain. I tried to fold her arms around my shoulders. To lift her up, to carry her. But the whole thing was limp and heavy. We fell, and then we were sitting on the concrete and she was in my lap. Across my legs. I managed to rest her face on myself, by my chin and the knot of my tie. "She is pregnant," I said. You better hurry. Come on, Lisa, let's get going. Time to go, now. Up. She was always quick about getting ready. She was considerate that way. She was even quick in the bathroom. I was sitting there like that with my back against the cold metal of the blue and yellow Dumpster and my suited legs out in front of me when the prowlers arrived.

*T*o look out on that sales floor of ours, customers like a sea, my salespeople's heads bobbing among them, credit cards in the air, wrapped packages, Wayne Newton's Christmas album on the CD player, a row of ten clients, fifteen clients, more, standing to see me, lined up outside my office door, one always at my desk, one leaves and as he opens the door the next rushes in, all men, all with their wallets in their hands, their wives' presents already waiting like children in toy boats in my safe, beaming, steamed and shining, the preprinted receipts sitting beneath the little silk boxes. Seventeen thousand, twenty thousand, forty-five thousand, seventy thousand. Due. Receivable.

With that many people in the store I often looked up and saw Lisa among them. You know how that works, when you look up and you see someone you know, because the environment is familiar and you might expect them, there.

•

*J*im leaned in my office door.

"Bobby, it's time to lock up."

"You go ahead," I said. "I'll close it down."

I didn't lift my eyes to see how he might be looking at me. I didn't want to see his expression.

When he left I watched him walk out the door. Then I stood and looked around at my office. On the wall next to my desk was a picture of our father. Beside it was a framed-and-glass-protected carpet we bought in Tibet, from a man with no fingers: a carpet covered with semiprecious and several precious jewels, depicting a white elephant with a ruby-crowned prince on her back. I remembered when Dad's picture was resting there, on the floor, where I was going to hang it. That was when we expanded the store, opened the new side, and put in our own private offices. I made sure the offices were separated only by a sliding pocket door. In the picture my dad is fifteen and crouching in the blocks before a sprint. His hair is brushed back, waxed, and he wears a loose-fitting sweat suit, blue or dark green (it is a black-and-white picture). The sleeves are pushed up the wrists. You can almost see the word SHATTUCK, his military school, printed across his chest, and the school logo beneath it. The number 5 something, his number, is on one arm. He had that same school logo tattooed in green ink on his left forearm. Sometimes a tan arm, sometimes white, on a white sheet.

The look in his eye, ready to sprint. Those eyes, triangular at the corners, eyebrows peaked over them, light shading half his face, a small frown for the camera, handsome, but soft in his chin.

Customers would ask me, "Why do you have a picture of

your brother on the wall?" Or they said, "I did not know Jim was a runner." The two of them are that much alike. Then they might say, "How much is that carpet? Is that for sale? That is really a beautiful rug. Is that real gold? Are those real rubies and sapphires?"

"Yes, it's all real," I would tell them.

I sat back down at my desk and looked at that photo of our father. This was not Jim's fault, I knew.

But if it was Jim's fault it was my fault, too.

I used to tell Lisa, sometimes, like if we were at Chuy's on McKinney, where they have one of those black-and-white photo booths, "Why don't we take our picture?" I knew better than to write her letters or manufacture documents of any kind but I thought I would like one strip of pictures and I worried that I knew why she did not want one. There was always a place you could secrete something like that and I was starting to feel like we might not have to be in secrecy all that much longer, and then we might want an image of this hidden time. But she would always say, "What's wrong with your memory? Isn't it nicer to remember it? That way you have to remember it." I had no response to that. Well, I had one now, naturally.

When Jim had come to get me at the police station he had put his arm around my shoulders and said, "I'm sorry, Robby." I had looked at him because of the tone in his voice. For a moment I had thought he sounded relieved.

But I had seen in his face that no, he was as lost as I was.

*T*here are two cops waiting for you at your desk," Jim said.

Granddad and I were walking in the door from the cold and everyone else was putting out the cases. He wanted to talk business, he had said on the phone, but he didn't want Jim joining us.

We had breakfast together across the street. How's your old man? I kept expecting him to say, to introduce a line of questioning. You know a father's advice can be helpful at a time like this. But he was only asking for simple, specific stories about big deals I had made, about who was selling best among the sales staff, and other ordinary details of the season. He wasn't even talking about the bank balances, or what we would have left over after we squared up with our vendors, like he should have been.

285

Am I being coherent? I asked myself as I replied to him. Can he understand what I am saying?

I see now that it was essential for him to hide what he must, of course, have known about my situation. In order to help me he had to communicate indirectly.

"Cops, Grandson?" Granddad said to Jim. "What the hell are you fellas up to over here?"

He wasn't dismayed. He seemed unconcerned about everything. It was like he had the Christmas spirit. That didn't happen to those of us in the business, though. He must have been faking it.

"It's nothing, Granddad," Jim said. "It's just the Lisa thing."

Just the Lisa thing.

Granddad Windexed the cases to help us out and to flirt with the saleswomen, and I sat down at my desk with the pair of police. Lisa's boyfriend had explained the case to them in detail. He had bludgeoned her with a baseball bat. I did not know where the bat had come from. Why would she have a baseball bat in her apartment? Had he brought it with him? There were more questions I would never ask.

"He blames it on you, you should know," they told me. "Not that you did it or anything. But that you made him do it."

"Fucked up," the younger cop said.

"Sorry," the older cop said. "We are professionals. Even if we don't always act that way. We only need you to confirm the facts he's given us. We might need you to come downtown."

"I'm pretty busy," I said, and gestured with both my hands at the buzzing confusion of my opening store. "It's Christmas, gentlemen," I said.

I did not want to take a chance that I might see him. I had

shaken that man's hand, and when Lisa had complained about him I would defend him, often, in the way one man will fraternally defend another, as part of the code of manliness. Once at a bar I had bought him a drink. If I saw him I was afraid of the look we might exchange.

I was afraid, too, that I was too cowardly to want to kill him myself. Even after the murder he kept on seeming like the same old Lisa's boyfriend to me.

Was I trying to tell myself that Lisa had wanted to be murdered?

"It's homicide, sir," the older cop said. "We are doing our best not to make this difficult for you. But if this guy hadn't confessed you would be the main suspect."

"Yeah," the younger one said. "Jeez. Hey, is this Baileys? Do you guys pour your customers Baileys? That's a good idea. You got any good deals? What's this pearl bracelet cost? That looks expensive. How expensive is expensive, anyway? In the jewelry business?"

"Gray!" the older cop said. "Please excuse Officer Gray, sir," he said. "He's still learning. He's pretty new."

"He can have it," I said. "I buy them by the hundreds." It was a silver charm bracelet with Christmas trees and a Santa Claus and a reindeer on it that cost us forty bucks. They had rice pearls between the charms that I guess were supposed to look like snow. I ran a promo ad on them for forty-nine dollars as a loss leader. We were going to be stuck with about five hundred of them after the season was over. You can't sell Santa Claus bracelets on Valentine's Day, I thought. Not on Mother's Day, either. I'd still be selling those fucking bracelets for forty-nine bucks three years from now.

"It's a gift," I said. "Take it."

"No, he really can't, sir," the older one said. "Let's get

287

moving." He stood and walked out of my office. He left his card on my desk. The younger one lingered behind for a second, winked at me, and stuck the bracelet in his pocket.

"Thanks!" he whispered, and winked again. "Merry Christmas! Sorry about your girlfriend. We'll be in touch." He did not leave a card. Granddad opened the door for them.

"You fellows have a safe Christmas season, now," he said. "Stay warm."

"Fucking pigs," Granddad added after the door had closed behind them.

I did not hear from them again until after the season was over.

I did not want this specter in my jewelry store. He wasn't a customer. He wasn't a salesman or a vendor, either. He was like Santa Claus, he came with a gift, a delivery. Or just the opposite, to take something away. Santa Claus in reverse, Santa Claus inside out, Santa Claus upside down. Like those satanic rituals when they hang Jesus with his head down on the cross. Maybe if Santa Claus accidentally caught sight of himself in a mirror that's what looked back at him from the reversed world of the reflection. Father Death.

After work I bought a six-pack of beer and drove around. I drank two of the beers and then I gave up driving and headed for my apartment. I couldn't go home but there was nowhere to go. At my exit I saw a homeless guy with his sign and I handed him the rest of the six-pack. Someone honked at me from behind. I wanted to park right there at the bottom of the ramp and get out of the car and sit with the black bum and drink the beer. To teach them a lesson. But then the car pulled around me, still honking, so I followed it for a while, with my brights on. When they finally lost me I was in north Dallas. I searched for a familiar highway. I thought I might just sleep in my car. But there was no safe place to park. A cop would come and knock on the window and wake me up. I would want a shower in the morning.

Son. I need to tell you something."

Our dad was calling from a pay phone in Coral Springs, Florida. He had just told me they had repossessed his car, which was a serious problem because he was still living in it. He had checked himself into a hospital but they kicked him out after a few days. He had no plans to go anywhere next. That worried me more than the rest of his situation.

"I have to go, Dad," I said. "I'll send the money. I'll have one of my salespeople go and wire it as soon as I get off the phone. The sooner I get off the phone, the sooner I can send the money, Dad," I said.

"Listen to me, son," he said. "This is important."

I could hear the murmur and rattle of the road traffic behind him.

A customer was sitting at my desk draping three different diamond tennis bracelets over the back of his hairy, pale hand. I smiled at him in apology for being on the phone.

Hang up, Dad, I thought. I promised I will Western Union you the fifteen hundred bucks, and I will Western Union you your goddamn, undeserved, one more time, always "this is the last time, son," one thousand and five hundred. Measly. Fucking. Dollars.

"Son. Pay attention. What are you doing? Are you waiting on a customer? Listen to what I am telling you, Bobby."

I sat there.

"Son, it is as easy for the dead to talk to the living as it is for the living to talk to the dead."

I looked at the tennis bracelet dangling off the reddish-green skin of my customer's knuckles. With those wiry hairs.

"Wait. What? What did you say, Dad?"

I had not spoken a word to my father about Lisa. What had Jim told him? But Jim wasn't speaking to him.

"Dad? Dad, are you there?"

He had hung up.

Years later, if I was at a restaurant with Claire, or if we were just riding around in the car, she might be looking the other way and then I would search her features for that other child of mine, that second child who disappeared back into Lisa.

Was that what Dad meant? I wondered. Was that how he might have reincarnated in a new life to speak with me?

To hear her voice for a minute I thought I might try to call her old cell phone number to see if it was still on. She didn't say who she was on the voice mail. Because of her work. When it beeped I started a message. I couldn't really say what I needed to, and I was afraid her phone was going to disconnect me, so I started to tell her a story about my mother and father, a story about one time when they were having a party and the song "Mr. Bojangles" was playing and my father picked me up to dance with me, in that crowd of dark and tall adults. It was after my bedtime. I didn't understand why I hadn't told her this story before. I was starting to say that and then the cell phone stopped. "If you want to hear the message you have recorded, press one." Et cetera.

I pulled over to the side of the highway and sat there, with the car running, and watched my headlights stare off into the night.

*J*oe Morgan was in my office picking up his wife's Christmas present when the call came in from Florida. While resetting Joe's diamond one of my jewelers—in fact, surprisingly, it was Old John—had overheated an invisible seam in the six-carat radiant I had sold Joe a few weeks before and turned it into a frightening long inclusion that looked like an internal crack. When I saw the diamond I knew I could not show it to Morgan. He would think either that we had cracked it or that the crack had always been there and somehow he had failed to notice it. Either way we lost. I thought about drilling and filling it, but that would take two months, and I did not have more than twenty-four hours. And it might be a crack and not fill at all but just drain out in another place. So I was trying to up-sell Morgan to a much larger diamond that I did not yet possess but had invented in my imagination. The way the crack was placed I could have the six-carat radiant recut to a terrific-looking two-and-a-half- or maybe even nearly three-carat marquise, and the cutter might even salvage a couple little third-carat rounds to use as accent stones. So as long as I could sell Morgan this fictional nine-carat oval it would all work out for everyone concerned.

Saving this deal represented something to me in my mind.

But it is awkward to sell a man a very expensive diamond he cannot even see because you cannot return to him his now-damaged diamond that he also is not permitted to see. Even when he is one of your best regulars it is real exercise. Morgan was going for it.

I had an advantage. It was December 22 and the new mounting was Margaret's big Christmas present. But a nine-carat oval was much more impressive than a new mounting. Morgan thought his wife did not like ovals, which was true, but I had confided in him that she had oohed and aahed over a seven-carat oval that I had in my office the other day (false) that unfortunately was unavailable (true), perhaps because, carat for carat, ovals look about fifty percent larger than most radiants (true). So this nine-carat was perfect. This is how to sell. A golden lie in a nest of truths. I had chosen an oval despite the fact that Morgan's wife, Margaret, did not like ovals, because the day before Christmas a big oval would be all I would be able to find, and even that only if I got lucky, and because big ovals are cheaper than any cut other than heart shapes and I knew I could never get Morgan to go for a heart shape, and even if I did, Margaret would return it, which would be still worse than the present mess, because then I would own it. But as I poured Morgan a fourth bourbon-and-champagne—that was what I had him drinking now, Pappy Van Winkle twenty-three-year-old mixed half-and-half with Veuve Clicquot—and began to walk him gracefully toward closing, Jim half opened the pocket door that separated our offices. I waved him away without looking. Morgan was telling me one of his cowboy stories. Never interrupt a customer's story. My father used to tell us, "No one will pay you to hear you talk, but everyone will pay you to listen."

Jim said, "Bobby," and the way he said it I looked at him. He was crying. Morgan stopped his story. You just killed the deal, Jim, I thought. The whole room changed because of his red face and tears.

I said, "Sorry, Joe," and took Jim into the back-of-the-house. There, with the phone girls around us, with their headsets on and the phones ringing, with their hands on us, like women in the Middle East mourning in a movie, with the wires from their headsets tangling in a circle, Jim cried in my arms. "He's dead," he said. "He's dead, he's dead."

I had Dad's ashes in a box in my lap, along with the paperwork so that I could take it on the plane.

"Do you want to get some coffee?" Jim said.

I looked at my wrist and then remembered I didn't have a watch. I had left all of my jewelry on my desk. Lisa's pearl bracelet, too.

"I guess we better get moving," I said.

"If you're in a hurry," he said.

We got on the highway.

"It's supposed to snow," Jim said. "Look at that. Look how low the sky is."

I-30 was clear. We would be at the airport in half an hour.

"One of us has to take care of the store. But I'm still sorry I'm not going with you," he said.

Outside the windows, dry yellow grass lined the sides of the highway.

"I don't want to ask," he said. "I don't want to be pushy. But could you tell me when you think you'll come back? I mean, so I know what to say to your customers."

But he didn't say it like a question.

"No, Jim," I said. "Tell them you don't know when he'll be back."

Acknowledgments

The author would like to thank the following people for their help with this book:

Deb Olin Unferth; Laura Kirk; Jim Hankinson; Karen Vorst and UMKC; Deborah Wilkes; Olivier Deparis; Lary Wallace; Jordan Bass; Hank, Wayne, George, Jim, and Bruce; Simon Gatsby; Paul, Megan, and Jimmy; Robert C. Solomon and Kathleen Higgins; Blair Moody, Lisa Moody, and my mother, Vickie Moody; my Links: Joe, Margaret, Matt, and Emily; Pat, Adrianna, Gabrielle, and Carter; my father, Bill Martin; Alicia; Darren and Tanner; my teacher Diane Williams; my editor, Lorin Stein; my agent, Susan Golomb; my daughters, Zelly, Margaret, and Portia; and above all my dear, dear wife, Rebecca.